The Master Blaster

The Master Blaster

A NOVEL

P.F. Kluge

THE OVERLOOK PRESS
NEW YORK, NY

This edition published in the United States in 2012 by
The Overlook Press, Peter Mayer Publishers, Inc.

141 Wooster Street
New York, NY 10012
www.overlookpress.com

For bulk and special sales, please contact sales@overlookny.com

Cataloguing-in-Publication Data is available from the Library of Congress.

Book design and typeformatting by Bernard Schlelifer

Printed in the United States of America

1 3 5 7 9 10 8 6 4 2

ISBN 978-1-59020-322-4

This is for old friends on some
Pacific islands I keep returning to,
and continue to wonder about,
wherever I am

I

The Master Blaster

❦

Welcome to Saipan:

Where America's Nightmares Begin
Warning! Turn Back Now
We Apologize in Advance
The Other West Virginia
Spit Happens

Every night, The Master Blaster checked his web site for new entries in his slogan contest. By now there were hundreds. Some bitter: "The Ultimate Kleptocracy." Some vulgar: "Where All Things Suck." So far, he liked his own contribution most: "It's Not the Heat, It's the Cupidity." The contest was free-for-all fun, unlike the home page. That was no fun at all: sleazy politics, bankruptcy, waste, nepotism, self-dealing in the far Pacific, the Northern Marianas, under the American flag. The Master Blaster meant every word he'd written there. But something pleaded to him the way islands always pleaded: hey, lighten up, it's a small place, it's far away, almost nobody knows or cares. Besides, moralists faded and died young in the tropics, jesters laughed and lasted. Didn't Magellan consider Saipan one of the Islas de Ladrones, "islands of thieves"? And look what happened to him! Lighten up, he told himself. After all, the dream of islands, the same dream that had brought The Master Blaster here forty years ago, was still working. Amazing! Shrewd men and women, shark-eyed businessmen, accomplished professionals, they all still fell for it: a simple, deep life in a small, far place. Romantics and predators, they kept showing up, trying their luck. Out of the future, they came to Saipan. And sometimes, just yesterday, they came from out of the past. *Just yesterday*. Interesting phrase. Haunting. Could be about the day before today. Or something that had happened a lifetime ago and—time-warped and twilight-zoned—reached out from darkness to daylight. *Just yesterday*. Just yesterday was the sixtieth anniversary of the World War II capture of Saipan and Tinian. And just yesterday, sixty years after the *Enola Gay* had lifted off for Hiroshima, Paul Tibbets, its pilot, had arisen to speak at the American War Memorial. Nearly ninety, nearly deaf, but a bright star on Saipan. The audience applauded heartily, despite the rain that pounded onto the tents, soaked the grass, kicked up a chill breeze that you wouldn't expect in the tropics. They were there for Tibbets, they wanted him to know they were on his side, they were all Americans. After warm-ups from U.S. Navy officers and Commonwealth officials, Tibbets at last began and it didn't take more than a minute for The Master Blaster to realize that the old pilot was winging it. He began at the beginning, the assembly of the *Enola Gay*'s crew, their training in Nebraska, the quirks and properties of the B-29. Tibbets was excruciatingly . . . and deliberately . . . slow. Half an hour later, the Pacific was nowhere in sight. No way, would they come close to the famous flight, the sight of the Japanese coastline, the target city down below, the mushroom cloud. There was no choice. At last, someone caught Tibbets' attention, signaled that it was time to close and, though there were objections from the audience, Tibbets readily obliged. Well, he said, you know what we did, and you can read about it in my book. With that, he sat down. He was gone. He was Saipan's second most famous historical figure after Ferdinand Magellan. But it wasn't much of a good-bye. The Master Blaster walked across soggy grass and drove home. Maybe Tibbets was on to something, ending with the famous flight still in front of him. *Just yesterday*.

He thought of Tibbets. Headed back to—was it Columbus, Ohio?—probably over the Pacific now, carried away from the place that made him famous. No way would he ever return; it was amazing he'd come at all, after sixty years. What high school class, military outfit, famous team reunited after so long? Yet he'd come back, just yesterday. And now he was flying back to wherever he'd spend the time he had left. It couldn't be long.

Night was The Master Blaster's favorite time. After he checked his site, he stepped out into his yard with a beer or cognac—sometimes both—and, always, a cigar. He sat in a chair, sipped his drink, lit his cigar and considered himself a happy man. He loved the night air—liquid, warm, velvety stuff—and the rugged shoreline down below, the lights white and red, of the international airport, the shadowy shape of Tibbets' island, Tinian, three miles offshore. On moonlit nights he could see things, on dark nights he sensed them.

Once he lit his cigar, the game was on, his nightly ritual, seeing whether he could finish his smoke before the mosquitoes found him. Sometimes the mosquitoes won, sometimes the cigar. It depended, he guessed, on the strength of the breeze, the length of the cigar, on heat and rain as well. All kinds of variables. Even the mosquitoes. They had their good and bad nights, too.

Past midnight, a plane made its way along the invasion beach, over the tourist hotels, garment factories, barracks and offices that began at one end of the island and extended a dozen miles to the north. There were fewer planes these days: major airlines had cut back their schedules or pulled out altogether. Tourism was down, garment factories were in trouble, gas and electricity rates were rocketing, investigations, indictments, litigation were the currency of the realm. Interesting times for The Master Blaster, no lack of material.

His web site was secure, he was sure of that. But that didn't stop hate-filled messages from coming in, threats of all kinds. This was no surprise. He'd sat at tables where people pictured the things that ought to happen to him, locals and state-siders, all outraged. Smashed car, burned house, that was easy to picture. And more. The Master Blaster needed anonymity, no getting around it; what he had done in the name of free speech was unforgivable, an act of betrayal and treason.

The first mosquito found him, scout for a squadron to come, strafing his earlobe. He blew a smoke ring in its direction, crossed and recrossed his legs. Score one for the mosquitoes. It would be hard to explain—he knew he'd never try, nobody would ever listen—how much he loved his life on Saipan, all the daily pleasures that never failed to delight. He wondered what had brought him here, courage or cowardice? Running from something or towards it? In the same way, he wondered what had made him stay. The pendulum swung back and forth, whenever he interrogated himself. Strength or weakness, loyalty or lethargy? But in between these moments, a life he liked resided, a life on a handsome, rogue-run island that he missed almost instantly, whenever he left. When people in the world's major places, in its great cities, dreamed of islands, they pictured serenely beautiful, tranquil places, empty beaches, swaying palms and suntans. A recipe for relaxation, so they thought. A recipe for boredom! Except for a walk at dawn or dusk, beaches were tedious and torturous. Lying on them, jogging on them, making love on them: an overrated trio. The sweat, the grit, the itch, the skin cancer! Sans conflict, sans history, sans hurly-burly, islands were for shipwreck cartoons. Who wouldn't stuff a note in a bottle and hope for rescue? That was why he fell for Saipan, a scarred battleground, a piece of America, Bedlam and Babylon. Where shit happened on an island that was the tag end of that tide of Manifest Destiny that had rolled across America, inhaled Alaska and Hawaii, Guam and Samoa and finally . . . wearily . . . embraced Saipan, Tinian and the rest of the U.S. Commonwealth of the Northern Marianas.

He stepped back to the "tool shed," the air-conditioned cubicle where he kept his computer. A message must have arrived within the last few minutes. Someone else was awake past midnight. Odd. There were always a handful of hate notes, but they came during the daylight hours, office hours, from Internet cafés or, he suspected, government offices. Late night traffic was rarer. More intimate. When he glanced at the screen and saw just one line, he assumed it was another slogan: someone had a bright idea in a bar and didn't want to wait until morning. But the message was measured, calm and—for that very reason—ominous. "Be very careful," it said.

George Griffin

Time zones, datelines, who cares? Is that the Atlantic or the Pacific, the Med or the Carib, the Red or the Yellow? Doesn't matter. Where the hell am I and what the hell am I doing? Doesn't matter. I find myself in an airport waiting room at one in the morning, sitting in one of those molded plastic chairs that's designed to deny comfort, to prevent sleep. A poster behind an empty ticket counter says: WELCOME TO GUAM—WHERE AMERICA'S DAY BEGINS. JFK to LAX to Honolulu to—would you believe?—Guam! I've been on and off planes for twenty-four hours and I'm not done yet. How many movies have I watched but not listened to—a return to silent film—and how many empty mini-bottles of scotch and wine lie behind me?

I pace around the airport lounge. So far I'm the only waiting passenger, my next and last flight is ninety minutes from now. There are no clerks in view, no passengers or crew, just me walking down a sterile corridor past one empty gate after another, flights to Nagoya, Seoul, Palau, Yap, Manila, Taipei. I can't help wondering about such an empty airport. Is that the future I'm looking at? The Super Sonic Transport disappears, maybe that was the beginning of the end. Airlines shrink, degrade, and eventually the whole world stays at home. And who would miss airports? What would they be good for? Still groggy, I find the men's room, slap some cold water on my face and avoid eye contact with the man in the mirror. I fill the sink with cold water, baptize myself, turning my head from one side of the sink to the other, and when I surface I notice what I should have checked before: no paper towels, only one of those hot-air blowers that brags about what a break they're giving the environment. So I go to the toilet and yank off about half a roll which I rub into my face, my unshaven face. In no time, the wet paper is a soggy pulp, and my stubble is covered with stubborn white flecks. So it's back to the sink. I submerge all over again, then dry myself on the past-ripe shirt I've worn since New York. As soon as I smell it, I laugh. And then it ends: that tiny armistice between waking and thinking, about what I am and where I am, and the fact that back across the international date-line, I've just had the worst day of my life.

For more than twenty years, I've been the proprietor of a popular travel column, *Faraway Places, Backyard Adventures*. It's travel for the masses, tips for tourists who go out picturing the moment they drive back up the driveway, pronouncing that there's no place like home. My column took them away from home and returned them happy. My readers were the terminal stage of travel, the lowest and by far the largest group. The flakes came first, the chance takers, the people who collected hard countries. Along with them came travelers-of-conscience, drawing down on the national guilt: the Lonely Planet crowd, backpacking soli-taires, ex–Peace Corps types, living on the level of the locals. After that, when the five-star hotels came on line, there were elite tourists, happy to fight through night markets and entangle themselves in rain forests, but insisting on air-con comfort at night. Last to come were readers of *Faraway Places, Backyard Adventures,* syndicated in the Sunday supple-ments of one hundred newspapers, tucked right in between the funnies and the sports pages. My people. They traveled scared, which somehow made them braver than the cocky adventurers who preceded them. They wrote postcards, not journals. They worried about what they ate. They tipped too much or too little because they never figured out the monkey bucks. Not a word of language, not a scrap of history, no more guid-ance than what I provided. God love them! It took guts to go out into the world without a clue.

Back in the departure lounge, there's nobody behind the ticket counter, but there are some other passengers, four black men with straight hair and cheap clothing, knockoff running shoes, jeans and T-shirts, sitting together in a tight group while someone else—a Filipino, I guess—works a cell phone. Away from them, a fortyish American woman concentrates on a Rough Guide, as though cramming for an exam. She knows more about where I'm going than I do. I walk over to the window, touch the glass and feel the heat, even in the hours before dawn. When it comes to Saipan, I am, it just occurs to me, like my read-ers, clueless. I guess where I'm headed is another would-be paradise that's about fifteen degrees too hot. It could be that I'm going to a party—not my first—that no one's coming to. That's okay with me.

I never planned on writing *Faraway Places* forever. I kept telling myself it was transient, trivial stuff, an apprenticeship that would lead to better things. In time, I hoped to join the literati, the club of travel writers who explored places no one went—Patagonia, Borneo, Siberia. Armchair travel, à la Chatwin and Theroux. And I wanted to be known as a better writer, not just a look-ma-no-hands hack. If you believed, and I guess I did, that you were judged by your work—the degree of difficulty, the quality of execution, like divers in the Olympics—I wanted to do better. I wanted to be known as a humorist and an ironist, a combiner of outward travel and inward journey. I had a lot of ideas, damn good ideas, and my latest was a winner, that I'd sent Hubb Bartley, my agent.

Resorts Out of Season felt like a service ace. The idea was straightforward and elegant. In an age of tourism, I contended, the best—possibly the last—way a visitor could discover the essence of a place was to arrive after the mobs had gone and the hotels were half empty, when the yearly show was over. That was when places most resembled what they once had been, when locals relaxed and reclaimed ownership: Venice in the winter, when cold fogs drifted in off the Adriatic; New England when the leaves were down, raked and burned; Paris in August, when the French took their attitude on the road; Norway—make that northern Norway, above the Arctic Circle—in winter, when the midday sun was reduced to a green smudge at the end of a long, black tunnel. Combine moody photographs—this was a coffee table book, but of the highest order—with thoughtful prose, that was the idea. This was a quality project, I'd told Hubb, so it wouldn't necessarily go to the highest bidder: he'd better get comfortable with that. And, after a while, my agent called me.

♪

"George!" Hubb came around from behind his desk and hugged me. He was heavier now, and more important, but I could still see the kid he used to be, the junior agent, shagging phone calls for the heavy-hitters and trying to place a few books of his own. We'd been together forever, but lately things had changed. Nobody's fault, but once we were two outsiders conspiring over hamburgers to assault the publishing world.

Now, it seemed, Hubb didn't assault much. He represented. Like most agents, he'd become the publishers' first line of defense, their co-proprietor. It was like seeing your bodyguard turn into someone else's bouncer.

"So," he said. This was after five minutes on my travels, his vacations, that stuff. He took a deep breath. Now business, which was never exactly good. Crazy times all over publishing. Bad books that prospered, awesome works that tanked. We were on familiar ground, Hubb's heartfelt complaints about the way things were, his scathing attacks on package deals, talk-show pseudo celebrities, MBA bean counters, predatory conglomerates, and yet nothing would slow him down, if the White House astrologer showed up outside his door. In a way, he was signaling that he was still a good guy, a lover of quality. But, let's face it, he'd remind me, the bad books that sell carried the good books that don't. Okay, I had done my share of bad work and now I was ready to do good. Fair enough? Hubb sensed that I was tired of waiting.

"Now "—he looked at me, brightening—"for some good news."

My eyes met his. This was the moment I'd been working toward for years, when my writing would move from newspapers stacked in cellars to a hardcover book displayed on coffee tables. After this, *Faraway Places* wouldn't much matter; I could take it or leave it. My heart and my best work would be somewhere else.

"*Resorts Out of Season*," Hubb announced. Then he stopped, whether to organize his thoughts or to tease me, I couldn't tell.

"Let's have it, Hubb," I urged.

"A splendid idea," he said. "That's the important thing. Congratulations. I had my doubts. But the concept—your concept—seems to have caught fire."

"That's . . ." I was overcome. I was blessed. I was grateful. "You've made my day—my year—my . . ."

"Well." Hubb stopped me, short of "decade," short of "whole life." He reached for a manila folder and scanned responses. How odd it was, I thought, that important decisions came from the strangers and got recorded on telephone pads—"We'll pass" and "Not right for us"—or in half-page notes—"I like it but can't get anyone else to like it" and "We're sure this will find a home someplace else."

"Of the six places I tried, four showed interest," Hubb said. "Lively interest. The other two . . ."

"To hell with them," I snapped.

"Right," Hubb agreed. "To hell with them," he said it as though he were quoting me, not speaking for himself.

"We only need one," I said.

"Right." And then he read the names of four publishers, top notch, the kind that took in memoriam ads on the book pages when one of their writers died. We were talking quality. If the *Faraway Places* guy croaked, what would happen? A moment of silence at Club Med?

"My God," I said. "I've got goose bumps. What do we do now?"

"Calm down is what we do. You've got an important decision here."

"I'll take your advice," I replied. "I'd be pleased to go with any one of the houses you mentioned. Have they talked money yet? It's not that I care that much . . . I know I'm not supposed to say this, but just so you know . . . and there are expenses. There's the photographer. The photographer might not come cheap. And I don't want someone who's just adequate. . ."

"George!" Hubb interrupted me and I didn't blame him. I admit, I was babbling. He leaned forward, put his hands together, fingertips meeting, like people who want to look judicious. "There's a lot of enthusiasm, as I say, for the *concept*."

The *concept*. I pictured an idea out there, floating, like a balloon of words over a cartoon character's head. I was the cartoon character. And the balloon was starting to drift away.

"They love your idea," Hubb said. "All four of them. But the enthusiasm for your involvement on the . . . uh . . . writing side of things . . . is sparse."

"Sparse? We only need one!"

"Well, sparse might be on the high side. What I mean is . . ." Now Hubb was uncomfortable. I'd put him on the spot. It was like what Carl Bernstein's agent must have felt when he told them he thought he had a novel in him, or what Red Skelton's nearest and dearest once endured when invited to a viewing of the comedian's latest paintings.

"Take this," Hubb said, picking up a letter. " 'Much as we like the idea, George Griffin is an impediment. His readership, track record, and reputation, though substantial, is not the sort that will garner the attention we need. One does not send Colonel Sanders on a trip to France, appraising five-star restaurants. If Griffin's involvement is mandatory, we pass. If he'll yield to someone more suitable, we can talk. Sorry if this puts you in an awkward position, but there you have it.' "

Halfway through, I turned away, stared out of Hubb's window, out west, out at New Jersey, the docks and condos, shores and highways of my home state. Out there, when I was a kid, New York was my Oz. It was the magic city, where I'd make my way—what a dream!—as a journalist and climb the ladder. *Faraway Places* was only a step along the way to the serious writing I wanted. And now, my ultimate goal was denied. My record, a record of success and accomplishment, followed me around like a rap sheet, a record of facile writing as long as my arm. As I gazed out east, I wondered what New Jersey would think of me.

"I called her up," Hubb asked. "Just to talk."

"Called who?"

"The woman who signed this letter," Hubb said. I noticed he didn't mention her name. I didn't press him. "I was wondering who she had in mind to write this thing. It's your idea. We're all on the same page. You're the man. What you say goes. I told her not to even think about developing it on her own . . . ."

I raised my hands. When Hubb told me tough things he'd told a publisher—his warnings, his conditions, his fighting stances—we both knew it was for the record. My money came from the publishers. So did Hubb's. Going up against editors, he was like a kid on the edge of a fight: "Hold me back! I'll kill the guy. . . Hold me back!"

"I wondered who she had in mind. For the writer. And I knew that you'd be wondering too. After you got done feeling sorry for yourself."

"So?"

"Guess. Go for it. Dream big."

"Don't make a game out of this, Hubb. I'm in pain here."

"It's a compliment. Look at it that way. It shows how good an idea you had."

"Okay," I said. I pictured them around a table, members of the club that had just blackballed me. I decided to get my worst nightmare out of the way first. "V. S. Naipaul."

"Too obvious."

"Paul Theroux."

"Ditto."

"Jonathan Raban."

"I love the way your mind works. No."

"Oh my God!" It came to me and I knew it had to be right. Recall that bit in *1984*: everyone has their own idea of the worst thing in the world. A cage of rats placed over your face. This was Orwell's definition. Mine was worse.

"William Least Heat Moon."

"No."

"Joan Didion?"

"No again . . . but getting warm."

"A woman?"

"So they tell me."

"Oh my God!" I had it then. And picturing a cruel God wasn't enough. This was a cruel God with a sense of humor. "Amelia Bligh."

Hubb nodded and smiled. "Another idea of *yours*! Another winner! See how things come together?" Hubb thought the worst was over. We were out of the tunnel. The deal was on: Amelia Bligh, "Woman Wanderer," would write *Resorts Out of Season*. I would write it, under another name, that is, I would write the work that meant the most to me, my salvation, my redemption, under the name of a character I'd offered as a lark, a joke, a little something on the side. So watch out Walt Disney! Mickey—no, Minnie—was taking over the park.

"I know you've been wanting to move to higher ground," Hubb said. "The column's getting tired. Or you're getting tired of it. You've lasted a long time. Who lasted longer? Buchwald? Landers? But now . . . time to move on."

"In a skirt?"

"Take it as a compliment," he said. He started stirring and I sensed our audience was almost over. He looked like he believed everything was wonderful. But it didn't feel that way to me.

"Do you remember when I came up with Amelia Bligh?" I asked.

"Sure do." I could almost picture him on camera, recalling the birth of the idea, when *Entertainment Tonight* came visiting.

"It was a gambit. A shtick," I said.

"That's how these things start sometimes. In any case, you've created a strong, quirky female character. Someone people care about. Tough-minded but sensitive. Adventurous, frisky. They want more of her, George."

"And of me? They've had enough of me . . . that's what you're saying."

Hubb raised his hands. "When you get to feeling sorry for yourself," he said, "just think of all the writers who would kill to be in your shoes right this minute."

"Okay," I said. I got up. "Remember we said we'd keep this a secret?"

"Which we have. And will."

"Remember *why*? I was worried if word got out that George Griffin was Amelia Bligh, then George Griffin would get hurt. It could be embarrassing to me. But now if people hear that I'm writing Amelia, it embarrasses *her*! I would say that something's changed. Amelia's my Frankenstein!"

"Things change, George. This started as a joke . . ."

"Yeah. Now it's on me."

Another glance at New Jersey. Twenty years ago I'd moved back to Jersey, into the same house I'd grown up in. My father gave it to me. I'd lived there for three years. I cobbled my column together but most of the time I worked on a novel. I learned my lesson back then. Stay in my zone, as they say, which was the tourist zone, the travel column. But now I heard laughter from across the Hudson. Know how it is when you do something on the spur of the moment—a whim, an improvisation, a tossed-off line—that gets taken way more seriously than you intended? That takes on a life of its own? And then takes over your life? Amelia Bligh! A column written from the point of view of a female traveler, a one-off caprice that led to maybe two dozen more columns. A little something on the side, that's all, not a new career.

"Think about it," Hubb said. "Take your time."

"I will," I said. "It might take awhile."

"I understand, George," Hubb said. "Something like this . . . you've got to be comfortable." Time was on his side, he thought. I'd come around eventually. I'd figure it out. We meet the world on its terms, not ours.

◊

At home, at the side of my desk, I kept a wire basket piled high with invitations. They came from PR guys who specialized in "press trips," junkets for travel writers to places that aspired to be tourist destinations. Mostly they attracted hacks. "Surprising Burma," "Three Days in Guthrie, Oklahoma." I turned them down. Until now. I wanted to go someplace and decide what to do with *Resorts Out of Season*, with Amelia Bligh, and how long should I stick with *Faraway Places, Backyard Adventures*. So I sifted through the pile. In some ultimate way, I didn't even care where I went. That, after all, was the point: not caring. Still, I couldn't help being a little choosy. So I decided on an island. The invitation came not from a typical PR man, but from someone who was evidently a lobbyist on behalf of a place I'd never heard of, the U.S. Commonwealth of the Northern Marianas, a potential tourist mecca, a little bit of America nestled in the lap of Asia. It sounded like a nonstarter. Hawaii was about as far west as my readers ever went. But anyway, I called. They were tickled to death. When did I want to travel to Saipan? they asked. Why not the day after tomorrow? I asked. Why not? they replied.

Stephanie Warner

From Guam, Saipan is a half-hour flight. The island I've never seen, the life I've never led, is so close I can taste it. And quite a gamble, at my age. I don't mean I'm old. Or young. I'm in between, in my forties, the age when you have to get things right. You make a change, you take chances, when you're in your twenties it doesn't matter what happens. You've got time. Misadventures are par for the course; you laugh about them later. And if you gamble when you're old, like some vigorous golden agers going into the Peace Corps or Teach for America, it doesn't matter much either. The returns are in, the performance is over, except for the closing notes. But at my age the stakes are huge. Make or break.

I'm traveling alone, still married, but only nominally. "A trial separation" is what we agreed upon. To a point, our talk was amiable because Eddie Covington was all for trial, improvisation, et cetera. That had been part of his charm, back in the day. He made things up as he went along—plans and schemes and stories at first, apologies and excuses later. He joked and danced and, better than anyone else, he remembered the words of popular songs, not just the words but the squeaks, the grunts, the ejaculations. He did a wonderful James Brown. There were whole days he declined to speak in anything but song lyrics, from "Get On Up" and "It's a Beautiful Morning" to "Goodnight My Love," "Midnight Hour" and "It's Almost Tomorrow." In between, given his employment record, "Take This Job and Shove It" would have fit nicely. I'm not one of those women who, in breaking up with her husband, revises their history to the point of insisting on misery from day one. We'd been happy for a while but now it was time to say, "We have to talk." I hoped for an amiable separation; the greater the distance between us, the better.

"Never heard of the place," he said. This was after I told him I had taken a job halfway around the world. "How big is Saipan? It's an island, right?"

"Part of a chain of islands." I said. "The Marianas."

"Chain, chain, chain . . ." he sang. "Chain of Fools. Is it bigger than a bread box?"

"A little larger than Manhattan," I said. I'd been studying assiduously, as soon as I saw the advertisement in the *Chronicle of Higher Education*. By now I had a plethora of facts at my fingertips. And no sense at all of what I was getting into at the College of the Islands, Saipan, Commonwealth of the Northern Marianas. It was a wild card, an unwritten page. Terra incognita, tabula rasa. That applied to me. It also scared me. I told myself that I wanted a change in my work, in my life. And yet when it came to make a choice, I'd gambled. It was as if I'd spun a globe and decided to go where my finger landed.

"What's the lingo out there?" Eddie asked.

"English. It's a U.S. Commonwealth."

"I get it. Like Puerto Rico."

"Maybe."

"But a hell of a lot further offshore. Was that the point? Getting as far away as possible from me?"

I didn't respond. If I'd said yes, he'd take it hard. I didn't want to hurt him. If I said no, it wasn't about him, then it was about me. I'd come off as selfish. If I said it's about *us* that would be the worst of all. We didn't exist anymore, as a couple. All my life I have trusted my instincts: if I could not picture Eddie traveling to Saipan, my future didn't include him.

❧

I glance out the porthole, if that's what you called the smudged, scratched circle that perforates the side of an airplane. I'm in luck. There's a full moon and silvery white clouds and it's bright enough so you can see the very texture of the sea, currents and patterns and dark spots, shadows on the ocean, that might be islands but are not. It's middle of the night, magic, haunting. It reminds me of the opening scenes of the Victory at Sea series I watched with my father, that gleaming ocean, menacing and beautiful, that swelling music. Then, down below, there's a patch of lights. That means Rota and, a while later, there'll be Tinian. Saipan is at the middle of a chain of islands, not a chain so much as a convoy, more like ships at sea than pieces of land. The smaller islands are empty rocks and volcanic piles, and Saipan was—that's right, Eddie—a little bigger than Manhattan.

"What do they do out there for work?" he had asked me. But when Eddie asked about work, it wasn't about performing it, it was about avoiding it. He asked about work the way a burglar asks about police in the neighborhood.

"Tourism, government," I said. "Golf, gambling. Garment factories. It was a battleground during World War II."

"What side were they on . . . those people?"

"Neither one," I said. "They were caught in between. That's the story: first the Spanish, then the Germans, the Japanese, the Americans. But they're very pro-American, I gather."

"Sounds interesting," Eddie mused. "My kind of place. Could be I'll look in on you, one of these days."

"Eddie . . ."

"Might be, I could operate in a place like that. Government, golf, gambling—I could hack it. Warm weather, nobody kills themselves. Small islands . . . American money . . . piece of cake."

"You say you can operate in a place like that? Fine. But, Eddie . . . please . . . not in that place."

"You never know. American flag. It's a free country."

❦

Now I could feel the small plane locking onto a bank of lights. We were nearing Saipan. It was just as well that I hadn't gone into the details of my hiring with Eddie. I'd attended an academic convention in Honolulu and had met my future at the Ala Moana shopping center in Honolulu, in the food court on the ground floor, a United Nations of fast food, a vast trough of dim sum, kalbi, empanadas, noodles, rice, pad thai, pizza, tacos and the like, everyone in aloha shirts, shorts and sandals. And there I was, soberly dressed, carrying a valise with my résumé, my transcript, my handful of publications. I'd been told to find my way to Paddy's Kitchen. "Look for the hanging ducks." I found the ducks, barbecued red and dripping grease. Now I waited to be recognized, I stood there, a rock in a river of piled-high cafeteria trays.

There were problems with the College of the Islands, I already knew.

It was small, remote, politically supported, at the mercy of an annual appropriation from local politicians. Its accreditation was in question. Its campus consisted of nondescript buildings, many of them inherited from an island hospital. Moreover, its representatives were late. I glanced at my watch, debating how long I should wait. Twenty minutes was my rule, for a beautician or a dentist, half an hour for a doctor. How long for a potential employer? Were they testing me? Were they determining whether I could adapt to "island time"?

"Are you Dr. Warner?" I confronted someone who appeared to be another tourist, a middle-aged woman in island wear, slacks and a flowered blouse.

"Yes. And you're from the College of the Islands?"

"Bernadette Diaz," she said. I offered my hand before I realized she was loaded with shopping bags from Ala Moana stores, Sears, Long's Drugs, Old Navy.

"Shopping?" I asked, needlessly. I was startled that she would come to a business appointment that way. Still, I cheerfully hefted two shopping bags and followed her to an open table. Bernadette was a sweating, jovial woman, overweight and unconcerned: the unsinkable kind. I watched over the packages and waited until she came back with a tray of fried rice, roast duck, barbecued pork and a pile of noodles. I told her I'd had breakfast.

"Shopping for my kids," she said, gesturing at the loot under the table. "They all want something. So much shopping, so little time. How many children do you have?"

"None, actually," I responded, deciding not to add "thank God." Saipan was a Catholic island. A look of concern crossed her face. "My students are my children," I countered, wincing at the banality of it. It was something I used to believe. Maybe I still did, a little bit. But what appealed to me now, at this improbable little college, was that there'd be room to move up. I'd checked out the current staff, from president on down, and the competition was, shall we say, unprepossessing. I'd be quiet about it at the start. I'd profess my love of classroom teaching, the molding of young lives. I'd be Albert Schweitzer, Father Damien, Mother Teresa, if that's what it took. But when the time came, when I found an opening, I'd reluctantly agree to be wrenched away from lecture notes, pop quizzes, student papers and the like. I'd consent to have greatness thrust upon me.

"So many children!" someone said. I knew that voice, turned to face Henry Rosales, head of the college's Board of Trustees, who turned out to be a fiftyish man, well dressed, with a gorgeous head of snow-white hair. Just the way he waved off the idea of lunch, I guessed that here was a man at ease with himself and in love with his appearance. A smoothie. He and my ex-husband could duel until dawn in a karaoke bar.

I expected we'd talk about the job, the problems and opportunities of teaching in a community college. But it was all about their travels in the United States. Bernadette Diaz had relatives in Reading, California. Henry Rosales actually owned a small place near Seattle. They told me about themselves, I offered something of my vita, but it was all no deeper than a conversation you might have on an airplane, before you managed to pick up your book.

"Well then," Rosales said. "I'm sure you have researched our college. And our island. Small place, lots of problems. Many things you are used to, you will not have."

"I'm ready."

"Yes, yes, I'm sure you've prepared yourself. Still, you may be in for a shock . . . a series of shocks." He smiled. "Shock treatment. But you need to know that as small and poor as the place is now, the college has ways in which to grow. But you will need to be patient and flexible. Do you think you would like to be part of our struggle?"

"Yes," I said. "I don't know about your other candidates. But I want you to know that if you offer me this position, I will accept it . . ."

"Well then . . ." Rosales and Bernadette looked at each other. My heart sank. They'd say they enjoyed our little chat, they found my résumé very impressive, they esteemed my references—none of which, according to my best information, they'd called. They'd promise to give me their most serious consideration, but surely I understood that in attempting to find the perfect fit for such an unusual position, they would have to review a number of other candidates. Bernadette bustled off and I confronted Henry Rosales, one on one.

"So," I said. "How should we leave things?"

"You want to know now?"

"Yes."

"Tell me, did you mean what you said to Bernadette? How the students were all your children?"

"Not all of them," I corrected. "Some. Some is plenty."

"But you've worked most recently in administration. No children there."

"I taught for years. I was tenured. I chaired the department and then one thing led to another. I was an interim provost. And I liked a job that lots of people hate. But that's not the job you advertised."

"Yes, but you strike me . . . I know we've just met . . . as the kind of woman who likes to run things."

I didn't respond. But I nodded.

"Well then," he asked. "When can you come?"

"For what?" I was baffled. Had this perfunctory chat been the prelude to another series of interviews across the Pacific? "Are there more interviews?"

"No more interviews," he said, extending his hand. "The job is yours. Welcome to Saipan."

A minute later, I was alone. The pay was low—forty thousands dollars—but exempt from taxes. Housing allowance was included. They'd put me in a hotel until I found a place. And they looked forward to seeing me in a month; that would give me time to wind up my "affairs on the mainland." (I spent that month in Hawaii.) The job was mine! The island was mine! And yet . . . something stirred in me. They hardly know you, an inner voice protested. Not a single hard question. Doesn't that matter to you? Maybe not. Maybe it was island style; maybe it was Henry Rosales' style, a sense that we'd be getting to know each other soon enough.

❦

The plane hits the tarmac, bounces and taxis towards the terminal. All places look alike, at least when you arrive at an airport at night. That's the disappointment of arrival, the sense that there aren't so many differences in the world. The same ritual, standing up, wrestling hand luggage out of the overhead bin, waiting for the door to open and a new place to declare itself. Out of the front seat arises a disheveled fellow I'd seen in Guam; he'd managed to spend the short flight snoring. Now he stands, stretches, runs a hand through his hair, over his eyes.

"What are you doing here?" he asks me. "Witness protection program?"

I laugh, it sounds flippant, even rude, but it comes at me in a friendly way. And anyone who flies into a small hot island at three in the morning is cause for wonder. Not a bad-looking fellow, six feet tall, hair more black than gray, and a kind of edge in his voice. Just now, though, he was bleary, red eyed, rumpled and downcast. Jet lag, maybe. Or something more.

"I've got a job here," I say. "Heading to the College of the Islands. How about you?"

"I'm a travel writer," he says. "George Griffin. *Faraway Places, Backyard Adventures*. Seen it? It's hard to not see it."

"I think I have seen it somewhere. I can't say I read it regularly."

"Regular reading isn't recommended," he says. "Without a prescription."

"Isn't your column the one that switches around? I mean, if you live in New Jersey, the Delaware Water Gap is a Backyard Adventure and if you live in Arizona it's a Faraway Place . . ."

"You figured it out. Not everybody does."

"Well, who decides? I've always wondered. If it's more than a certain number of miles away it's a *Faraway* . . . How many miles . . ."

"It's up to the editors at the newspapers that take the column. It's their call. It gets them involved, that's the idea. At least they have to read the thing. I used to think that was a good idea, their reading it."

"So there's no inherent difference in a Faraway Place and a Backyard Adventure. It's all about . . ."

"Location, location, location," he interrupts. "Like the realtors say. It's about the distance you travel . . . Not the place you arrive. It's about the traveler. It's all in the head."

I think about it a moment and grant that he might be right. We see things as we are, not as they are. Still, it didn't quite make sense.

"So what you're telling me is . . . a Faraway Place and a Backyard Adventure are the same."

"Sad, huh?"

"Are you writing about Saipan?"

"Probably not. I'm on a junket. A free gander at America's bouncing baby Commonwealth."

"Will you be here for a while?"

"I haven't decided. A week? A month?"

"That's not much," I say, comparing it to my stay, which might go on for years.

"Long run for a short slide," he responds. There is sadness and burnout in him, no doubt about it. Travel without purpose, voyage turned into drift. On a ship, not an airplane, we might become friends. Now we head down the steps to the tarmac, onto the island where my future is waiting for me. And the air, the night air, is like nothing I've ever breathed! It's moist, heavy, warm. It invites, seduces, smothers. Even now, close to midnight. This, I suppose, is my first discovery. And that's remarkable. Back in the U.S., get off a small plane in the middle of the night, you'd feel you were in the middle of nowhere. Here, landing on an island, it feels like a beginning.

Mel Brodie

◗

"Saipan," says Lou Maxim, "is a place that's dying to meet you. You've got to go. You have what they need."

"What's that?" I ask. We're standing outside a synagogue in Bethesda, Maryland, talking after services. To Lou, I'm sort of an uncle. After my father got killed in the war, after my mother fell apart, his parents took an interest in me. Mel and Sarah, old-line Jewish liberals, generous and opinionated, died believing in the complete innocence of the Rosenbergs. If it happened today, their son would flip the switch on Julius and Ethel at no charge and write it down as pro bono work.

"Entrepreneurship. Energy. Ideas."

"On Saipan?"

"U.S. Commonwealth . . . with tax breaks you won't believe. Forty years they were a U.N. Trusteeship. They were in a museum. Then they decided to join us . . . and play catch up ball."

"So why's there a Commonwealth way over there?"

"Military interest. Thousands of our boys died fighting over there . . ."

"We're still fighting the last war?"

"Or the next one. Okinawa is gonna be history. We need a place we can count on. So we made 'em citizens."

"Wait a minute, Lou," I say. "I'm thinking these people are your clients." Lou's a lobbyist specializing in the kind of people his parents detested. Go figure. Neoconservative is putting it mildly. He's the only person I know who still calls people "commies." I know about Maximum Lou's clients. Misunderstood foreign governments, cruelly vilified industries, gambling casinos on riverboats and reservations.

"I'd do what I'm doing for nothing," he says. "Just for the asking."

"That's a yes answer."

"Okay. Yes. Clients. Just listen. Part of my job is sending the right kind of people to the island. On me."

"On them, you mean."

"Fair enough. On them. You get a round-trip ticket, a hotel for as long as you like and a few names you can call. After that it's all up to you, Uncle Mel. I think you'll come up with something interesting. You want, I can brief you, I can brief you for hours. They've had booms and busts already that you wouldn't believe. Headlines, exposés, the works. But I like the idea of your going over there and sorting it out for your-self. You come back, say thank you for the lovely trip but I'm not inter-ested, we'll leave it at that. Believe me, I wouldn't send you if I didn't believe you and Saipan go together like . . ." He tried to think of some-thing that didn't come. Me, I had a million of 'em, like, Bonnie and Clyde, pigs and shit, Ferrante and Teicher. "You belong there. A piece of America, way out beyond the dateline and nobody knows about it. It's Florida all over again. Better than Florida. It's like we're creating a piece of America out there, creating it from scratch. It may never happen again, I hate to say."

So here I am, taking my first steps on Saipan, waiting at a luggage carousel in an empty airport. Across the hall, customs and immigration works the graveyard shift. There's a couple of Americans; no need pay-ing attention to Americans, I see enough of them every day. And a cou-ple of cute Filipinos who look at me, smiling back while I check them out. "Older Jewish gent with a few bucks to spend, girls." Not a bad line, it's worked before. And there's a bunch of workers, wetbacks, what-ever. I wonder what they think about when they think about home.

So we're standing around waiting for luggage, checked luggage. The passengers with hand luggage are long gone, like they knew something we didn't. So it's the dark guys and their Filipino minder, the two Filip-ina hotties and three Americans, myself included.

"How long," I say to the blonde, "do they need to unload a plane like that?"

"Didn't you hear?" Is she saying I'm deaf, I wonder, or just oblivi-ous? "The announcement?"

"Passed me by. I never pay attention to those things."

"A problem with the door."

"On that plane? Get a can opener." That draws a smile from one of the guys, who looks like he needs to sleep really bad. And sober up: I smell booze on him. Silence resumes, but I'm a guy who has a hard time with that. You're standing around, you talk, you schmooze, you make a connection.

"I'm Mel Brodie, out of Miami and Washington, and I'm in real estate," I announce. "And I'm here . . . well, Willie Loman said it . . . You got to know the territory."

"I'm Stephanie Warner," says the blonde, in a way that says she wants to cut through my banter. "I have an appointment at the College of the Islands."

"Appointment? You gonna be late?"

"Not that kind. Appointment as in job. I'm a professor."

"Okay! And you, sir?"

"George Griffin," he manages to say. "Travel writer."

"What a life! A regular Marco Polo! Who wouldn't want to be you?" Actually, when you take a gander at the guy, you don't envy Griffin so much. He looks punch-drunk.

"Christ!" he bursts out. "You fly halfway around the frigging world and at the end . . ." The conveyor belt didn't move, the rubber drapes that the bags came through were motionless. "I thought that those five minutes after a plane lands and before they open the door, when the passengers start moving, yanking their damn loser suitcases and loser shopping bags out of the overheads, are the longest five minutes . . . Until now."

"I can't wait to see this island," I say, aiming to cheer things up. "How long you here for?"

"No idea." Marco Polo shrugs.

"And you, professor . . ."

"It's an open-ended appointment," she says. "Might be years."

"And . . ." I had spotted one of our dark-skinned travelers nearby and, merry old me, I didn't want to exclude the poor guy. And there was something that told me he'd been listening in. Well, I don't like leaving people out. And this was a humdinger of a left-out guy. Not one of life's heavy winners. "What brings you here, friend?"

"Work. I come from Bangladesh . . ."

"Well, aren't we something. Tell you what. Let's make a bet on who lasts longest here. I'll go first. And, old as I am, I'll bet on myself."

"I'll vote for myself, if that's permitted," says the professor.

"Just to stay in formation, I'll vote for myself," says Marco Polo. "Win-win situation. Okay if I leave, and a little bonus if I don't."

Now we all turned to the dark-skinned guy named Khan.

"I will win this bet," he said..Just like that, not boasting, just matter of fact. "I cannot leave, even if I want to. It's not up to me. You others, you come and go, it's up to you. Not us."

That kind of killed the spirit of the occasion: three tourists and a slave. Luckily, right then the luggage started arriving and mine came out first. "Must be clean living." I wave at the Filipinas. "See you later, ladies." I show my American passport and get waved right through, out of the air-con and into the night air that's like a steam room. In the parking lot I see a van with the name of the hotel I'm in. There's a driver sleeping inside. When I'm a few feet away, he snaps out of it, goes from asleep to obsequious in a nanosecond: how was my flight, is this my first trip to Saipan, has all my luggage arrived, where's my wife? That's in the first minute. When I'm tucked in back, he turns the key and, before shifting gears, switches on a radio and some woman—definitely not Celine Dion—is offering me the theme song from *Titanic*. Some people, some whole races, can't stand silence.

"Turn that damn thing off," I say.

"Yes, sir," he obliges. But I can tell he thinks I'm a prick.

"You from here? Saipan?"

"Oh, no sir," he answers. He can't help laughing, as if the idea of a Saipanese working at three a.m. is kind of a hoot. "I'm a Cebuano."

"I see."

"From Cebu. Many of the people from the hotel are from Philippines. And from China, Thailand . . ."

"I get it," I say, sitting back. My man drives to the end of the parking lot, pauses at a stop sign and turns to me.

"Please, sir," he says. "You are my passenger. But two of my friends are arriving from Manila and she is needing a ride . . ."

So we pull to the front of the terminal and, after a few words, the two hotties pop into the front seat next to the driver. Behind them, I see the laborers getting into the back of a pickup truck while, out on the sidewalk, their minder shouts into a cell phone. "This is actionable!" I hear him say. Meanwhile, the girls greet me. Lourdes and Cori. One of them reaches for the music. The driver stops them, just in the nick of time. And we drive out onto the highway in a puzzled silence.

Khan

❧

We are not like the other passengers, not like the blonde American woman with a leather bag, not like the old fellow with a gold star in a nest of white chest hair, not like the man who is sleepy and drunk. They exit the plane ahead of us; take their luggage, sail through immigration. They are passengers. We are freight.

Gregorio motions for us to stand, when all the others have left. He walks ahead of us, our passports and tickets in his hands. Anxious, he approaches customs and immigration. The way a waiter puts on charm when he leaves a kitchen to enter a dining room, Gregorio makes himself into a friendly, funny fellow.

"Is it America?" Qazi asks me. "This place?"

"You saw the flag, when we came in," I tell him.

I had known the Azis brothers—Abdullah and Qazi—growing up. We were playmates, the kind you leave behind. Born to farmers, destined to be farmers. My father was a rice merchant. He had plans for me. I was "scholarship material," he told me. He shipped me off to school and I did not disappoint him. I'd come back for his funeral. It was also mine. It turned out that my father's life and fortune expired together. There was no money for school and no question of remaining in the village with my confused mother, suddenly poor. So I joined the Azis brothers, joined my country's army of overseas workers. An army that fights a war it cannot win, a war that never ends. There were jobs in the Middle East in construction; in Malaysia, there were garment factories and computer plants. But we feared the Arabs and it was mainly women who went to Malaysia. If there was nothing else, we would have gone, we could have gone anywhere. But then: America! We were startled when the recruiter mentioned it. I had my doubts. Was it South America? The recruiting agent was surprised. Most of the people he rounded up went quietly, grateful for anything they could get. I was the only one in our village who could name a South American country. Brazil? No, no, United States of America, for sure. Saipan. It was like Hawaii, only newer. There were three of us, at first, the Azis brothers and I, all from the same place. And a fourth who would join us at the Dhaka airport. His name, the agent told us, was X. X, it turned out, was different. He was impatient, shrewd and lazy. A tall, strong fellow, he must have been an athlete once, a local hero. Now something was wrong. I couldn't say what, but it was something. I asked him about his one-letter name, why he chose it, what was his real name, his trade, his home. He shrugged, turned away. "X," he said, "is all you need to know."

❢

Gregorio went first and we followed a safe distance behind him. He was our contact on Saipan, our new boss. He'd boarded at Guam and, after collecting our passports and papers, he ignored us completely. The immigration official turned the other way as we went by: he could say he'd seen nothing of our arrival on Saipan. We were out on the sidewalk of a deserted airport. Everything was quiet. The rental car stations, the refreshment stand, the airline check in counters, all closed. Gregorio paced the sidewalk, as if we were pressing our luck to stay here too long. Yet no one came. Then he walked away from us, out into the parking lot, and took out his cell phone.

At last, a truck came, its headlights aiming at us. Gregorio motioned us into the back. There were fishnets and machetes and beer cans that started rolling from side to side as soon as we moved. But it felt good, being out of the airport. I liked the breeze, and the air was clean and smelled of trees and rain. Though it was dark, I tried my best to learn what I could of our new place. The others were doing the same. The way X looked back, I guessed he was memorizing the way from the airport to wherever they were taking us.

Soon we were on a main road that ran along a beach, close to the sea. On the ocean side, I saw there were hotels, one after the other. Inland, there were factories, apartments, houses, restaurants and stores, all mixed together, new places and old, active and abandoned. There were nightclubs with neon signs. I saw a shopping center and a sports field. The truck picked up speed; I closed my eyes and enjoyed the wind.

How long had it been since I felt this good?

Suddenly, a sharp turn threw the four of us to one side of the truck, and I heard laughter from inside the cab. We braced ourselves tightly as we went up a dirt road, away from the ocean. This was different: poor houses, laundromats, auto body shops. I kept waiting for the center of the town but it never came. We turned, more carefully this time, onto a very bad road. Trees leaned overhead, branches tangling. Our ride ended with a barbed wire fence and dogs barking, and a gate of hammered-together metal sheets. The driver got out and pulled open the gate; it wasn't locked. Inside, I saw metal fences, piles of wood, cars without wheels and a concrete house with no lights, no windows and oil barrels to the sides.

"Get out," Gregorio said, without leaving the truck. He motioned towards the house. No one lived there, I was sure. No one had lived there for a while. He motioned for us to enter, he signaled sleep. I pointed at my mouth. Food? He reached in back for a garbage bag. Rice and canned fish. I made washing motions with my hands. He pointed to the oil barrels; they caught the rain off the roof. And whatever else fell into them. Gregorio handed over a flashlight. I felt X's eyes on me. I reached into my pocket, pulled out a card with a name I already knew, and pretended to read it. "BVD Enterprise?" I asked, struggling with my pronunciation. It was an act. I spoke English well; my father believed it was the language of success. My pronunciation, vocabulary, my everything was better than Gregorio's. But I did not want him to know it. Not yet. "3D Enterprise," I repeated, after rereading the card I held in my hand. I glanced around, as if to ask, Is this our workplace? No, no, Gregorio waved me off and left.

The building was older than anything we'd seen on the way from the airport: tiles on the floor, a sink in one corner, a bathtub. There were no windows, no screens; the sink was rusted, the bathtub cracked and broken. The electric wires looked like the roots of a dead plant reaching for an overhead fan that would never turn again. There were wasp nests all over the ceiling and mosquitoes were everywhere. People had been here. There were some damp straw mats in the corner and a kerosene stove near the sink. People like us probably. It was too late, too dark to do anything but sit against the wall. Then we noticed bullet holes in the wall and a ragged hole in the back of the sink. A war had been fought here. We sat down against the wall, found extra T-shirts to pull over our heads. We tried and failed to sleep. The mosquitoes found our wrists, our ankles. And then, outside, there was movement, grunting, sounds I didn't know. We smelled animals.

"What's that?" X demanded. He had stolen the machete from the truck. Now he raised it.

"Animals," I supposed. "This is a farm."

"What kind of animals?" I think he knew the answer. So did I. Not the Azis brothers. They had no way of imagining what was just outside. "Give me your flashlight," X said.

"Please," I said. "Can we wait until the morning?"

"You can. I can't." He took the flashlight to the back wall, to the blasted open hall. We followed, the animal smell growing stronger at every step. The smell of shit. The flashlight was weak. X shook it up and down until it found a pool of mud, chopped and trampled. A fence of rusted metal. And then, coming towards us, slowly, steadily, curiously, the animal he feared, pink-eyed and expecting to be fed.

"Where are we?" asked one of the Azis brothers, almost in tears.

"We're living with pigs," X answered, shaking his head, as if this were just what he'd expected. "This is how it is, my friends. This is our home. Go anywhere, go to rich places, beautiful places, and you can always find a place like this, where they put the slaves. Go to Saudi Arabia, go to Singapore, it's all the same. Away from the wide streets, the beaches, the homes and stores and schools . . . Away from them . . . You have to look . . . No maps . . . no signs . . . but there's always a place they put us. Does a rich man have a toilet? Does a restaurant make garbage? That's us. That's where we live. That's how we live. With the pigs."

The Master Blaster

❧

The Master Blaster pushed his breakfast plate away, took a last swallow of coffee, and listened to himself be introduced, not for the first time, as a beloved teacher, a dedicated and innovative high school principal, a founder of the College of the Islands, a renowned poet and—of particular interest this morning at the Hyatt hotel—an American who'd arrived in the early 1960s, "the Kennedy years," and was now the American who'd lived longest in Saipan. The Master Blaster had done this sort of thing before, popping up in front of journalists, World War II veterans, potential investors. It used to be visitors found him at work, when he still worked. They sought him out in bars, they drove down his driveway, knocked on his door. Nobody, it was said, knew Saipan like he did. He was worth calling on for a bit of background, some anecdotes, a colorful quote.

"Fifty years on Saipan," he said when he reached the podium. "It's not what I was aiming for when I came here. It was supposed to be a tropical adventure, two years tops. But it grew, a year at a time. It's not my home, not yet, in the way a place is home in the United States. Let me make that clear. There's always a sense of being a stranger on this island. An outsider. But that's all right. If it isn't home. It's close enough . . ."

He talked, and he liked talking, about the early years. The battered, rugged, war-littered island, the Quonset huts and jeeps, the landing craft impaled on the reef, Japanese caves and bombs and . . . yes . . . skeletons out in the boondocks. A fateful, fated island that felt like it had been waiting for him to come; waiting, as well, for his wife to leave. Bit of a laugh there. He might have given them more. He and his wife had come to refresh, or repair, a marriage that had gotten strained. They thought they needed a second chance. They joined a long line of Americans looking for a new start, moving west. The island, he had learned, ate troubled marriages for breakfast. Never mind. Resuming his talk, he recalled the American community that was on Saipan. Ex-marines, Department of Interior bureaucrats, political appointees out of Hawaii and Alaska, all presided over by the so-called High Commissioner of the Trust Territory of the Pacific Islands, not just the Northern Marianas but also the Marshalls and the Carolines, two thousand islands aggregating half the landmass of Rhode Island, with a population that could be accommodated in the Pasadena Rose Bowl. A backwater, an afterthought, an accident. And, for him, a blessing. He described tin-roofed schoolrooms, rattle trap bars, lazy island picnics, the piece-by-piece discovery of the island itself, beaches, cliffs, caves. It was, he said, like coming to know a woman, intimately, intricately, her secrets, her charms, her moods. Her checkered history: near genocide under the Spanish, rigorous rule under the Germans, hectic labor under the Japanese, and then the Americans came, the naval administration, the CIA, the Department of Interior.

He moved quickly now, less comfortable with the present than the past, and anyway, visitors' curiosity wasn't infinite. The Trust Territory ended, the islands fractured: the Federated States of Micronesia, the Republic of the Marshall Islands, the Republic of Palau, all closely tied to the United States but none more closely than the Northern Marianas. When the Americans offered Commonwealth in exchange for military rights, the islanders accepted. Citizens overnight, citizenship delivered from halfway around the world. "The Spanish came for God, the Germans came for glory, the Japanese came for gold and the Americans came for good." The oldest line in the book, but The Master Blaster still used it.

"Now I've been told there's a few minutes for questions," The Master Blaster said. "I hope to see some hands. Or we could skip that." He pulled a thin volume out of his back pocket, "I could read some of my poems. I could read a lot of them. There's a sestina I wrote about geckos . . ."

Like that, and with the uniform crispness of a military salute, hands sprang up.

"It never fails," The Master Blaster said, sliding his poetry back into his pocket. Question one was about his favorite spots on the island. Number two was about Saipan's use and abuse of outside labor in the garment factories, on farms, in bars/brothels and in private homes. The third wondered how the Saipanese liked being American. What did it mean to them? The Master Blaster dodged that one. There was no shortage of Saipanese to ask. They had voted, three quarters of them, to marry America.

"Anyway," The Master Blaster concluded, "welcome to Saipan. It can be beautiful. And it can be interesting. Know why? Americans dream of islands. Islanders dream of America. This is where the dreams converge. This is what they come to."

A polite round of applause started, only to be quickly interrupted. "Excuse me," said a tall, round-shouldered, red-eyed American in an aloha shirt. "I'm just wondering about you and this island. You said it was a love story, right?"

"Yes?"

"And you talked about the old days, laid back, low key, free and easy in the islands. A jungle full of war relics, a comic opera government, and a load of country Western shit-kicker bars . . ."

"I wouldn't . . . didn't . . . quite put it that way," he said. He sensed he was facing someone who used language skillfully, cynically. And he wanted that man to know that he knew. "But I'll take it. Your question?"

"The island you described is not the island I saw on the way from the airport. I saw factories, barracks, shopping centers and poker parlors . . ."

"And your question? Are we there yet?"

"We're there, thanks. You're Saipan's number one stayer-on. Local historian and poet. Mr. Memory. You traveled far away from America. Right to the very edge. And you loved where you were. But now America's come closer. Swallowed this place in one gulp, like an hors d'oeuvre, a piggy in a blanket. And so, let me ask, in the nicest possible way, if you came here now, young again, and this were your first day, would you fall in love with this island again, the way you did, you surely did, back then?"

He has me, The Master Blaster thought. Whoever he is. The rest of the audience didn't care for him or his long-winded question. They were from Washington, a couple of congressmen, a gaggle of aides and wonks. They wanted to go on a tour. This fellow was different.

"Good question," I said. And that was it. The applause resumed and ended, the room emptied quickly. I followed my audience out, towards the front of the Hyatt, past a cluster of Japanese with bagged golf clubs. I headed across the parking lot, only to confront my questioner, who offered me his hand.

"Good question," I repeated.

"Good answer," he said. He handed me his card, nodded, and trotted over to the tour bus. The name on the card was George Griffin. *Faraway Places, Backyard Adventures*, it said. A travel agent, I assumed.

George Griffin

❦

Old habits die hard, bad habits die harder. I didn't come here to work. And yet, like an ex-prostitute turning a trick for old time's sake—vintage lines, familiar tickle, the old snap, crackle and pop—I found myself playing around with a column about Saipan. This was after three days on the island. Not much time, I grant, but more than enough for the kind of work I used to do.

FARAWAY PLACES
By George Griffin

It's America's best-kept secret: a rugged, raggedly beautiful Pacific island, a crucial World War II battlefield, a beehive of international industry, a blossoming tourist destination—are you ready for this?—America's newest neighborhood, a U.S. Commonwealth, Stars and Stripes flying, English spoken, and dollars—plenty of them—in circulation. Not many Americans know about this place, but some who do pronounce it "Hawaii like it used to be."

Let's face it: some places have more history than others. It's not a matter of how many years you have. It's what you do with time . . . and what times does to you. History, after all, is not an equal opportunity employer. . .

Okay, a highly charged opening—hyperbolic, I guess—but you've got to grab the reader by the short and curlies and not let go. You have to convince people that there's something new under the sun, places worth visiting, and now and then avoiding.

. . . Saipan is a page that's been written, erased, ripped, crumpled, shredded and recycled. Magellan was the first: he found the place en route to his death in the Philippines. The Spaniards who followed depopulated the island. Totally. After war and disease took their toll, they moved the remaining islanders—Chamorros—to Guam. For a century the island was empty, and when the locals came back, they carried Catholic Bibles and Spanish names. The Germans came next, the Japanese and then, in 1944, the Americans. Three thousand Americans died. Kilroy was here, dozens of Kilroys, and Colonel Paul Tibbets, whose B-29 took off for Hiroshima from Saipan's neighboring island of Tinian.

After that, under U.S. Naval administration, the island quieted down. As in hush-hush. The CIA ran a training camp for spies and saboteurs, the locals fished, worked for the government and wondered what next. In the 1970s the place voted to become a U.S. Commonwealth and the islanders were U.S. citizens. Saipan was invaded a second time. Tourist hotels captured the old beaches, garment factories and barracks captured the interior. Property prices escalated as paradise was leased. Foreign workers flooded into the newborn America that visiting Congressman Tom DeLay called a "Petri dish of American capitalism."

Hello out there! Anybody awake? Is everybody fascinated? I knew the travel writer's slogan: Always Think of the Reader as Someone Who Is Looking for an Excuse to Stop Reading. And I was feeling like a frigging bore. So much history, brutally oversimplified, and not a line about where to eat and shop. No gnarly locals commenting comically on island ways, no tourists exclaiming, Eureka, I've found it! No best-kept secrets, no tips from insiders, no advice on how someone who arrived that morning could find "the real" Saipan. Enough! Saipan wasn't Bali Hai. The hotels were generic resort hotels, the food was resort food, okay, maybe better than okay, not great. The tourists who showed up might be staying anywhere—Aruba, Puerto Rico, Fiji—any of those places that erect an air-con high-rise, put in a kidney-shaped swimming pool, play a Don Ho tape and wait for the visitors to come rolling in. As for shopping: my hosts took me to a duty-free shopping center, a cavernous, marble-floored, frostily air-conditioned place with rooftop parking. All the names were there, Boss, de la Renta, Hilfiger, Mont Blanc, and neatly packaged multilingual women were standing in the doorways, waiting for company. But traffic was sparse and the place had a sense of desperation behind its smiles. In high-end shops, I could imagine days between sales. I made my way to the tourist shop at the far end of the mall, down from the Hard Rock Cafe. This was where you could buy low-end items that had Saipan's name on them: T-shirts, golf shirts, tote bags, ballpoint pens, boxes of chocolates, wooden plates and carved wooden warriors. But I couldn't find a single item made on the island. That said it all, that and the piano down the hall, among the boutiques, playing "Somewhere Out There," as I passed, played perfectly because there was no pianist involved, no fingers on the keys or feet on the pedals. And yet, there was something about the place that drew me in, even though it was nothing I'd use in *Faraway Places, Backyard Adventures*. Maybe, come to think of it, that was its appeal.

◊

On my first day, I found a schedule under my door from the tourist people. After breakfast, my group—the other junketeers—were departing for a tour of the island, which I was welcome to join. Or not. I was a special guest and my VIP status included an exclusive tour, whenever I wanted it. Five minutes later I stepped out into the lobby. You need to be a tourist before you become a traveler, like it or not. And you have to sit through a place's self-presentation before you write your own account. It's a kind of courtesy.

Something was up, I could tell, as I approached the buffet table in the Hyatt dining room. It had been years since I'd gone on a junket but I know the types: free-wheeling, hard-drinking, heavy-eating hacks. Some promoter had a budget to spend on publicity and a certain kind of person was willing to oblige. Brasilia by Night, Chernobyl Bounces Back, Taipei for Lovers, it was all the same. By their comp tote bags, by their thirst and hunger, you knew them, also by their self-protective jadedness and cynicism. I saw none of this now, and what clinched it was that there was no stir at my arrival. There's a (fairly) recent picture of me accompanying every article I write. I'd been in the public eye a long time, and my being on a Saipan press trip was like Steven Spielberg showing up as a contestant on *America's Funniest Home Videos*. But these peoples' glances passed right over me. What's more, they were well dressed, creased, scrubbed, they carried attaché cases and cell phones, consulted papers.

"Mr. Griffin," said a pretty girl identified as Donna from the local tourist bureau. She had a name tag for me, a schedule and—it took a while to notice—a manner which asked, *pleaded*, that I please not turn out to be an asshole, at least not today. "These people are the other members of your party," she said.

"Yes. The odd thing is I don't seem to know them. Do you have a list?"

"Yes. But that is what I wanted to discuss." She had a list in her hand. I took it before she quite presented it and found names and offices, all in D.C., many in the U.S. Congress. Two congressmen and lots of aides, plus a scattering of people from think tanks with furniture store names: Design for America and Family Values Foundation.

"What is this? Not a travel writer in the bunch."

"Yes sir, this is not a press tour. These people are from Washington who want to find out for themselves what is happening here."

"I see."

"Might it not be better . . . if we took you out tomorrow. Something more in tune with your interests as a travel writer . . ."

"No thanks," I snapped. I was willing to play ball until she referred to my now nonexistent interest in travel writing. "I'll just tag along with this bunch."

"You wouldn't prefer. . . " There was alarm on her face. I was making her job harder. A writer, even a harmless travel hack, could always do harm.

"If there's something I need that I don't get today, I'll contact you," I said. "And thanks for your help . . ."

"It's all right, Donna. Mr. Griffin is welcome."

I turned around and saw—how to put it—a sumo wrestler, a weight lifter, a jolly brown giant in an aloha shirt with tropical flowers and hula dancers.

"My name is Ben, Mr. Griffin. I'll be your guide." Guide! There's a word that makes me wince. Numbed out panhandlers, cracking jokes and angling to take the tourists shopping. What a job, what a life! But there was something in this fellow that was sharp, something in his eyes that warned me to watch myself. This wasn't just another colorful local character.

"Well thanks," I said. "That's nice of you."

"You're a VIP. Anything you need, you let me know."

The star of the breakfast show they put on for us was a local old-timer who talked about Saipan once upon a time. The local poet, whatever that meant. I couldn't imagine much competition. I've met them before, these expat experts. Big fish in a small and often stagnant pond. Local characters. But I couldn't help wondering what it was like to spend the one life you have on Saipan and I threw him a question. Don't know why I did it, felt a little shitty afterwards, gave my card. My guess is I'm becoming a connoisseur of failure.

I climbed on to the tour bus and took a seat right behind the driver, watching Saipan's Washington friends come up the steps and reading their name tags as they passed. I spotted the two congressmen, one laboring mightily in the heat, the other fit and earnest. The aides were kids, serious kids, student council superachievers that Washington is full of. Ambitious and opinionated, they were on official business, a mission to Saipan. But—they couldn't help it—they were silly and giddy, tickled to be knocking around for nothing and living for the moment.

"Hafa Adai!" Ben shouted, explaining that this was a Saipanese aloha. He was our escort today, not his ordinary line of work, he said, but he knew and loved Saipan and was eager to show it to important visitors. A bit of housekeeping first, though. He had a list of names and needed to check if we were all on board. Also, he asked us to introduce ourselves and say where we were from. Starting with the front of the bus. Starting with me.

"I'm George Griffin," I said. "Out of New York City." He didn't let me get away with that.

"Something more," he said, as if offering an extra trust or warning. "Mr. Griffin is a prominent writer—a travel writer."

Immediately, I sensed a ripple of dismay. Fingered before I got out the gate. *What's a writer doing on this bus?* I saw shrugs exchanged. But then, as they introduced themselves, names and offices and inside jokes, they began to relax. I was still a leper, but a burnt out case. Infected but not infectious. They could handle it.

The real Saipan, Ben resumed, might be different from things we had read in newspapers and seen on television. This was "the newest part of America . . . and the most misunderstood." Today they'd see the Saipan of the past and present, of peace and war, an island that worked hard and played hard, died gallantly and believed in God and loved America. He hadn't gotten far past Magellan's arrival and the guests were ignoring him, chatting away. Maybe he didn't care, maybe he did, maybe he knew better than to show it, but it was rude. I was the passenger closest to him and while others gabbed and laughed, I listened to his narrative of conquest, conversion, near genocide, colonization and a couple of world wars, climaxed by the American flag getting raised over a new Commonwealth.

Our first stop was to be one of Saipan's "notorious" garment factories. Big Ben earned his pay, just then. When the island became a U.S. Commonwealth, the agreement with the U.S., the "Covenant," gave the islanders control of immigration and an exemption from minimum age laws. It was recognized, Big Ben said, that a small island in a faraway neighborhood couldn't always be held to mainland standards. So the Commonwealth was granted "exemptions" and "protections." And Saipan boomed. Newcomers flooded the island, hired help, alien labor, guest workers, whatever: Bangladeshi farmers, Filipino maids, clerks, cooks, beauticians, Korean grocers, Nepali security guards and, most of all, garment workers from Thailand and China. In no time, dozens of factories were turning out clothing stamped "Made in the U.S.A.," exempt from tariffs and quotas. Were there problems? Big Ben asked. A rhetorical question. Of course there were problems, in the early days, and certain reporters found and dramatized and magnified those woes: sweatshop Saipan, long hours, barbed wire fences, low wages, high charges for food and lodging, forced abortions. Sensational stories, hurtful stories that resonated long after the few abuses had been corrected. No way of exaggerating the harm that had been done back then! Now, thank God, we were here—this he said just as we were waved through a gate—to find out the truth for ourselves and carry it home. A line of workers representatives was waiting to greet us as we came off the bus.

"I guess they knew we were coming," I said to no one in particular. Big Ben heard me. I could see him consider saying something, then turn away without response. When I . . . and I alone . . . had attended to his history of the island, he'd nodded appreciatively at the end. Maybe that was the credit I earned. Now I'd spent it. I didn't want to be the first to get off the bus. And neither did Big Ben. At the end it was just Ben, the driver and me. He nodded, even smiled.

"Okay, so it's not a raid," he said, "You want to stay on the bus? In protest?"

"No . . . I'll go . . ."

"If it doesn't insult you," he said, in the tone of someone who'd taken his fair share of flack.

"Not me," I said. "Forget about it." We sat in silence after that, oddly relaxed. "You do this all the time?"

"God, no!"

"What else do you do?"

"Help out my friends. They help me . . ."

"Not much of a job description," I said.

"You'd be surprised," he said. "Oh, I used to do tours when I came back from school. Lots of tours. You know what the roughest part was?"

"Giving the same old lecture to a bunch of jet-lagged junketeers on a tour bus?"

"No. It was airport greetings. And airport good-byes. Seeing them in and seeing them off."

"Why?"

"Because I didn't like pretending that I was happy to see them come. Or a little bit sad to see them go."

"More like the other way around?" I asked. But he gestured me towards the door of the bus and I complied, joining the tour.

What happened at that garment factory reminded me of an elementary school visit to a factory where a bunch of fourth graders could see how ice cream was made, with a free scoop or two at the end. We visited high-ceilinged, well-lit air-conditioned places. Nothing to complain about, no one to complain, the day we visited. The burly congressman—Tex Von Schmidt—pressed flesh with some workers who were happy to be on Saipan, and the congressman said that any country could learn a lot about handling foreign workers by visiting here, and that included some of his colleagues back home. The aliens entered legally, they worked, they saved, they left. Why couldn't we manage to do this with Mexicans? I kept my mouth shut. Walking down long rows of women at sewing machines, I wondered what it would take to enter the lives of these women. To talk honestly. It wasn't just that this was a controlled visit or that there were barriers of language and nationality. There was no way of getting from here to there, at least none that came to me. So I kept quiet. I heard Congressman Von Schmidt telling one of the women that he very much hoped she liked her bit of time under the American flag and that she'd speak well of the system, when she went back home. The woman waited for a translation that didn't come, nodded and said thanks.

"We could learn something on this island," Von Schmidt repeated as he headed out. "Learn a lot."

"Yes," a trailing aide acknowledged. Then he made the most of his chance to shine. "But . . . in particular . . . what?"

By now I'd divided the kids into two teams: the ones who, propelled by ambition, would work for anyone left or right, and the others who were about ideology, which on this bus meant conservative or neoconservative. I put this one in the first group.

"You bring 'em in, you control 'em, you ship 'em back. Everybody wins . . . and no entanglements. No illegals, no amnesty . . . no protests. Jobs aren't bad here . . . working conditions . . . I've seen worse in my own district. Worked in worse, summers, when I was a kid . . ."

" 'Give me your tired, your poor, your huddled masses yearning to be free. . .' " What an ass I was! What an ass I had to be, quoting a poem I only half-remembered and only half-believed. I found the last line, all right. " 'I lift my lamp beside the golden door.' "

"It's from the Statue of Liberty, sir," the aide volunteered.

"Okay, so who's the turd in the punch bowl?" Congressman Tex Von Schmidt asked, looking my way.

Just then Big Ben announced that, next to the garment factory offices, visitors could find a boutique with a selection of items just off the line, generously discounted. "These are not factory seconds," he said. "These are factory firsts."

That killed the argument. The kids, especially, had oohed and aahed at the designer names in the factory, Italian names, Veni Vidi Vici, whatever. "Twenty minutes," Big Ben shouted after them. I headed back for the bus. I couldn't picture myself among those others, not after the Statue of Liberty poem. If I joined them, I'd be contaminated; if I stayed away,

I'd be stigmatized. I voted for stigma. And I had plenty of shirts already.

"So," Big Ben said, "here we are, together again." He plopped into a seat across the aisle.

"No need for shirts?" I asked.

"I'm not supposed to buy," he said.

"You want, I'll buy for you."

"My size . . ." He gestured at his girth. "But maybe you should buy something. These factories will not be around forever."

"Why?"

"The laws are changing. Quotas and tariffs. Some factories have already closed. We might lose them all."

"That would be a blow," I said.

"Well, you live on an island, this island, you get used to seeing things come and go." He shrugged and paused and I guessed he was on the edge of telling me more. But he thought of something else.

"I have a question for you," Ben said. "What is your relation to Mr. Maxim?"

I groped. Mr. Maxim? Sounded like a hair stylist. Then, a little something worked its way to the surface. "The guy who sent me?" I wondered how to answer. Truthfully, I decided, not because it was better. Only easier. And besides, Ben was smart. "I've never met the man. Never talked to him."

"Really? That's not like him."

"Listen, I get invitations all the time. Free trips. I keep a pile by my desk, kill a few minutes with them now and then. Toilet reading. Makes me feel loved. So one day I finally reached into the pile and, out of all the places dying to host the man from *Faraway Places, Backyard Adventures*, Saipan was the lucky winner."

"Do you know anything about Lou Maxim?"

"Nope. Does it matter?"

He sat there, as if at a loss for words. Maybe he was just choosing them carefully.

"Lou Maxim is the most powerful lobbyist in Washington. He befriends congressmen and staffers, collects and channels donations, trades in contracts and contacts, promotes people and projects. All on the Republican side of things. You would not want him for an enemy."

"So what is it you do?"

"I'm an advisor to the governor," he said. "I evaluate projects that outsiders propose."

"You evaluate the projects?"

"And the people who propose them."

"I see," I said. I didn't really see but I'd heard enough to sense a behind-the-scenes expediter and bagman. "And that's what connects you to this bunch today?"

"New friends," he said. The Commonwealth was courting friends in Washington, I gathered, and he was part of it. These days they dealt with Republicans. But I had to wonder if that was enough.

"Okay," I said. "I'm just asking. If the Republicans are in charge, you're a bastion of free enterprise. Like the congressman said, if we could only get those wetbacks behind fences and into barracks . . . But what about . . ."

"Democrats?"

"Shit happens."

"No problem," he said. "We're a racial minority, a remote island, an endangered culture. Spare us the fate of the American Indians—save us from the fate of Indian reservations."

"I see."

"Excepting, of course, a well-placed casino here and there."

"Very good."

"Actually, you can combine the two approaches. There's all sorts of—what do we call it?—wiggle room? The arrangement with the United States included certain protections. We retain the exclusive right to own land. Outsiders cannot own land here. Your Native Americans kept a tiny fraction of their land. Same for the Hawaiians. We have it all. And we have the right to control immigration. We're exempt from U.S. taxes. And minimum wage laws."

"What a deal!" I said. "How'd you get it?"

"Friends in Washington," Big Ben replied. "Lou Maxim among them. Listen, Griffin, outsiders are crazy about islands. Not just crazy-in-love with them. There's that. But there's more. They want us to remain placid, charming, pristine, primitive paradises. Fishing, farming, sailing, with lots of time left for handicrafts. Wood huts, thatched roofs. Quaint. Others picture a little America, a transplanted California, solid houses, automobiles, air-conditioning, televisions, steak and beer. If we remain primitive, we're patronized. If we become Americans, prosperous and fat, they laugh at us, revile at us for being corrupt, for selling out. At the end, they don't know what they want."

I wondered why he was being so straight with me. I'd been marked out as one, a writer; and two, a wise guy. Maybe that was the charm. Somebody different included in the tour. I wanted to know what he wanted for the island. But before I could ask, Big Ben lifted himself out of his seat—it was a project—and went down to greet the shoppers advancing across the parking lot, tickled to death with their purchases. Duty-free shops were an airport commonplace, this was a duty-free island, a gift that kept on giving.

I followed him out—I liked his company—and stood beside him. God, it was hot. I wondered what took the place of weather in conversation in Saipan. In the States, the nuances were endless, spring, summer, autumn, winter, late or early, hard or mild, rushing off or lingering a while. What took the place of that on Saipan? I asked Big Ben. "Nothing," he said, laughing a little, kind of friendly, though there was no pretending that we were playing for the same team.

"Did you hear the congressman say that this island was 'Hawaii like it used to be?' " Big Ben asked.

"Sure."

"I hear a lot of that," he said. "Almost all the groups that come here say that. I'm wondering how you think that sounds to me. To any local. The Hawaiians had their islands. Their monarchy was overthrown, they lost their land and power, their islands were flooded by outsiders. Now they live on the edges, in their own place. 'Hawaii like it used to be.' I'm amazed that they say it in front of us. That we listen and smile and take it as a compliment."

Now I had him, at least I thought I did. Another one of those clownish fat men, joking and hospitable, but with shrewd eyes and an angry inner life and, probably, a few radical years, way behind him now. Trapped in a role, trapped in a body, trapped on an island.

"What I say to you . . . you don't write."

"No worries," I responded. Amazing how quickly I forfeited any professional purpose, how ready I was to discount myself. None of the do-si-do about confidentiality, anonymity, off-the-record, deep background. Glad to be rid of it, I was.

"I'm here to help, if I can be of any assistance," he said. "How long are you staying?"

"That sounds like, When are you leaving? Answer is, I don't know yet."

"Well, the longer you stay, the greater the chance that you'll need something."

❧

"Now, I have a surprise," Ben said when we were all back in the bus. "We are going to a place that is not—never has been—on the tour." He nodded at the bus driver and we headed away from the garment factory, uphill, towards the back side of the island. "Congressman Von Schmidt is a veteran of the Battle of Saipan. A marine. And here on Saipan, the slogan we use is: A Grateful Island Remembers. So, from his and other accounts, we have located the site of some of the war's most difficult fighting, a place that was called 'Death Valley.' We will be there in ten minutes."

"Well, I'll be damned," the congressman said. "Didn't see this coming. Feels like that old TV show, *This Is Your Life*!" He said that loud enough for everyone to hear. Then he leaned over to his aide. "Got a camera crew?"

"I'm sorry, Tex. They just sprang this thing on us."

"See if we can do it again tomorrow, okay?"

The bus left the main road and climbed up a rutted dirt track that went from bad to worse, climbing past funny little farms, with goats and cattle, chickens, dogs, and shacks with water catchment barrels, a tarp or a piece of plywood shading a picnic table. Small time, part time, and kind of pleasing.

"Well then," Ben said. "We're almost there, Congressman. Anything you want to say? Before we walk? It's just ten minutes, by the way, but it's not easy."

"Not easy puts it mildly," Von Schmidt answered. He made a point of appraising Ben, up and down. "Think you can make it?"

"Yes, sir," Ben said, after the laughter quieted. "In the line of duty."

"Okay then. If you can walk, I can talk."

Big Ben handed him the microphone.

"Listen up," Von Schmidt said. "We're taking a little side trip to a place I saw a long time ago. The summer of 1944. A bunch of us came over. There was a line of caves up here. Armed to the teeth. It was the worst fighting I saw which, in a way, was the best fighting. It brought out the best of me. I wasn't an Audie Murphy. But I wish I could be as good a congressman as I was a soldier. And if I had to choose between the two . . . Well, don't ask. That's all. This little field trip won't mean much to you. You weren't here. I was. And right now . . . I've got goose bumps."

◊

Somebody had come up a day or two before and cut a passage through saw grass and brush thickets, but the trail, most of it, was a dried out creek bed, filled with stones and branches, all of it uphill, and there wasn't a hint of a breeze.

"Hey, Tex!" someone shouted from the back of the line. "Is this worth the trip?"

"Sure as hell was, back then," the congressman rejoindered. It sounded like he was rehearsing lines for cameras tomorrow. At last we came up against the base of the ridge, a mass of trees and boulders, elements of a sawmill and a quarry jumbled together. A couple of Saipanese men stood beside a table covered with water bottles, beers, sandwiches and fruit, that the hikers fell upon.

"Is this the place?" someone asked after a while. He might have been asking, Is this all there is? Von Schmidt was a war hero but, hey, he wasn't Kennedy and this wasn't PT-109.

"Yeah, this is it all right."

"What are we supposed to . . . uh . . . notice?"

"You don't even see them, do you?" Von Schmidt asked. "You'd've been dead." He pointed to the side of the cliff, blocked by rock piles, screened by trees and vines. "You don't even see them," he repeated. He pointed to something that might have been a dark spot, a patch of shadow. Like a dark spot on an X-ray, a cavity in a tooth.

"Let's go look," he said. "I'm feeling young. Pay for it later, but I don't mind it now, this hiking."

"Just a moment," Ben said. He gestured to two Saipanese men, a pair of oldsters who'd been standing at the picnic table, beaming. They came forward and Ben gave their names, had them shake hands with the congressman who wondered—as did I—whether he was supposed to thank them for the catered lunch.

"These men were also here," Ben said, "then."

"Well, damn! Extra glad to meet you." Von Schmidt maneuvered between the two while Ben explained that one man had been a scout for the marines, the other lived nearby and hid out in a cave during the fighting. Then, after the pictures were taken, we marched to the bottom of the cliff.

❧

They were like mouths. Dark, gaping holes that swallowed lives, surrounded by a cliff that was pockmarked and discolored by shell fire. In front of the caves we found rusted cooking pots and plates, rotted rubber sandals, sake bottles. Souvenirs. There were three caves, it turned out, or maybe three entrances into one cave. Anyway, we divided and clambered up and in. These were natural limestone caverns but the Japanese had improved on nature: there were doorways, firing holes, electric wires and, at the back, a hole—whether for ventilation or escape—that put you on the side of the cliff, just above the cave. Inside, it was cool, mortuary cool, dank and wet-feeling. You looked out front, it was sunny and green—hot colors—and in here, brown of soil, gray of stone. This was a tomb in waiting.

We came out dirty, sweating, ready to leave. Some of us had found sake bottles. Banzai, they shouted. Someone conjectured that there had to be bones left, no way they'd all be found, not on this island.

"Listen up," Tex Von Schmidt shouted. He was pumped up, it was easy to see. Way overweight, an athlete gone to seed on beer and barbecue, golf course buffets and lobbyists' lunches, but Saipan made him young again. "You all can stay here. Have a drink. There's a place down here means a little something to me. Just want to see it." He glanced at his aide, a fellow named Jared. "Maybe get a snapshot. Come if you like, or stay here and relax."

If he were a senator, more of us would have followed, more than Big Ben, Von Schmidt's aide, the two Saipanese. And me. The turd in the punch bowl. But I was curious what it was he wanted to see, after all these years.

It was another cave, this one wholly natural, no signs of fortification, no debris outside, and the mouth still clogged with dirt and boulders, with only a little gap at the top where the pile had subsided.

"Sometimes the caves were blasted shut when the Japanese didn't surrender," Ben said. "Sealed alive . . ."

"Nobody left alive in that cave, I can guarantee you that," Von Schmidt said. "I killed a lot of Japs in that cave. We took no prisoners that day."

He stepped over to the bottom of the rock pile, clambered halfway up, posing for photos. Then I heard the two Saipanese guys talking among themselves, one of them insistent, the other laughing, and Ben listening, whispering, telling them to keep it down.

"What's that about?" Von Schmidt asked. "What's so funny?"

"It's nothing, sir," Ben said. "Some local . . . kidding."

"Well, let's hear it. We're all family here." he said. "And I'm hoping we'll be here tomorrow, take some film. Great stuff . . . so why the chuckles?"

"That cave . . ." one of the Saipanese began, quietly, in decent English. He was polite but there was something firm about him: I'm old and I'll say what I want.

"I think we should go," Big Ben interrupted.

But the congressman held up his hand for silence. "What about the cave?"

"That is where they put the Koreans," the old man said. "Koreans stayed there. We called it the Korean cave."

"Koreans?"

"Yes, sir. Workers. Unarmed"

Von Schmidt froze. The color drained from his face. He shuddered. Everything changed. He started walking, stunned, back towards the bus, like a man given a death sentence by a doctor. He didn't look back. Ben and the two others talked in Chamorro and it sounded like one was protesting, What did I do?, it wasn't my fault, and the other said, Yes, I understand, and then Ben offered a Don't worry about it. That's what it sounded like, and when you travel you get good at guessing the thrust of things, even if you don't know a single word.

❧

Back on the bus, the word was out. No chatter about tonight's barbecue, tomorrow's golf trip to Tinian. Congressman Von Schmidt sat among us, sulking, brooding, unapproachable, inconsolable. Whatever else I felt about him, I felt some pity too. He'd just discovered that he wasn't quite what he thought he was. And lately I'd learned the same about myself. In silence, we headed north.

"The best is yet to come," Ben announced. But the bus was gloomy; Von Schmidt set the tone.

Ten minutes later we stepped out onto a high ridge at the end of the island; a lofty, windswept place that was the primal Saipan. Below us, straight down, was a canopy of green, rolling down to the coastline, to the pounding sea. The picture-taking began, posing against the railing, feigning a leap over the rail.

"This is our Suicide Cliff," Ben told them. He gave us the story of the invasion, onto the beaches, off the beaches, up Mount Tapochau through places named Death Valley and Purple Heart Ridge, driving northward to the place where we were standing. The last Japanese attack came a few miles south, when a couple of thousand Japanese swarmed out of a place later called Hara Kiri Gulch. Armed with guns, swords, rocks, sticks and stones, they broke through American lines in some places, got down to the beach, even out to the fringing reef. Then they were annihilated. At the same time, after a last meal of sake and canned crab, Japanese Commander Yoshisugu Saito knelt in his command post and cut himself with his sword just before an adjutant shot him in the head. That was the end of the battle but not the dying. Hundreds of Japanese soldiers and civilians fled ahead of the advancing Americans. And this cliff was where they ran out of room to run. This place—where we'd been taking snapshots—was the scene of a mass suicide.

The timing—Big Ben's timing—was perfect. Now it was afternoon. You could see white sea birds floating on air currents, warm breezes that we shared with them, and the blues and greens we noticed all day long now deepened and mellowed as the sun descended and there was a kind of agreement that we'd stay here until the sun met the sea. Meanwhile people talked about the green flash, what it was or was supposed to be, had anybody seen it, this split second pulse of green color at the very moment the sun plunged beneath the sea. I'd done research, learned and forgotten and relearned the science of the green flash, mirages, prisms, refraction, dispersion. The explanation was like one of those elusive words—everybody has at least a couple of them—that you can't be sure about the spelling of. As often as you look it up, you forget it.

I settled for watching the sunset. Such clichés. What drum solos were for rock concerts, what dream sequences were for movies, sunsets were in nature. But on this day, the sunset proved me wrong. It sank into the sea when we were still on Suicide Cliff but that wasn't the end, that was the beginning, and I kept gawking all the way back to the hotel, yellow and bright orange yielding to red and purple. Saipan had the long horizon and the big sky you needed to take it all in. And you needed time: a sunset, well watched, lasts as long as a feature movie. When we got back to the hotel, it was still happening.

"Dinner tonight at the Pacific Island Club," Big Ben said. "Are you coming?"

"I have another appointment," I said. With the sunset, what was left of it.

"It's just as well," Ben replied. A burden was lifting, along with a twinge of regret that we couldn't talk any more. "How about tomorrow? We have a boat to Tinian, a tour of the famous airfields. And a gala buffet at the casino."

"I'll save it for another time."

"Another trip?"

"No. This trip, another time," I answered. "I think I'll stick around a while. I find Saipan . . ." I vapor-locked just then. None of my *Faraway Places* adjectives fit: pristine, romantic, off-the-beaten-track exotic. ". . . interesting. So . . . I guess you're good for the hotel tonight and tomorrow night. Okay. After that I'm on my own."

He nodded. But, whatever he was thinking, he didn't say it, not at first. But then he changed his mind. Curiosity got the better of him.

"Why?" he asked.

"Why what?"

"Why stay here? You're not a tourist. Or an investor or a fugitive. You weren't in the war. And you can go to a thousand other places. You can go anywhere. So, why here?"

"I honestly don't know," I answered. "I really don't. Things came together. Or fell apart. Anyway, this is where I landed. Is that good enough?"

"No," he said. "Not really. But you're not the first."

"The first what?"

"The first person to come without a good reason. And stay. Then again, good reasons aren't required."

◊

Past the lily ponds, the swimming pool, the thatch-roofed nightclub where some Filipinos covered the Bee Gees, past cabanas and out onto the sand, a beach chair awaited me. I had the place to myself then and I sat there, watching the end of it, not just what was out over the reef, but what was overhead, and in the sky behind me, the remnants of the sunset, and I was captured by the oldest cliché in the business. Oh, I'd produced my share: powdery beaches, tempting night markets, hole-in-the-wall restaurants, the smells of flowers and spices, sea air, mountain air. I was the Johnny Appleseed of clichés, I was a cliché myself, the burnt-out (cliché) hack (cliché) writer (cliché) in search of (cliché) he knew not what (cliché). How long had it been since I'd enjoyed a sunset?

I walked back to the hotel. The beachside bar was into Credence Clearwater Revival's "Proud Mary." I stepped onto the elevator. "Hold the door," someone said, and I pushed the button that kept the door open. My beneficiary didn't thank me, though.

"It's you," Congressman Von Schmidt said. He was with an aide who followed him inside. "It's okay, Jared. I can make it upstairs on my own. And I want to talk to this guy."

"What about your dinner?"

"They have room service, son," he said. "Anyway, I'm not so hungry. And it's been a helluva long day."

The aide backed off, done for the night, and the congressman pushed—make it punched—the elevator button. We were on the same floor, it turned out.

"Got a question for you," he said.

"Shoot."

"Who the hell do you think you are? And what the hell do you think you're doing here? A smart ass like you, sniping, negative little pissant."

"Whoa. I quoted a few lines from a poem. Is that a hanging crime, where you come from?"

"You guys never get it. We've got these islands that got bought with American blood . . ."

"And American dollars . . ."

"That too, and money well spent. For military bases that we can have when we want. We got our bases, we got ships off shore, we got the beaches. Ain't much around here that isn't for sale, if the price is right. And . . . believe it or not . . . they like us. They like business. They're not afraid of turning a profit. And there you are. You don't know shit about how the world works. You try and make everybody look bad. You ought to check out what you see in the mirror, boy."

"This is our floor," I said. We walked down the hall. He was in 610, I was in 614. There was a single room between us.

"That's my cave," I said, gesturing at the door of my room "And that's your cave. Don't mix them up."

"God damn you!" he said, and right then I had no doubt he was going to jump me. Congressman Attacks Travel Writer. Hard to know who readers would root for. But I've got to admit, he was impressive, admirable. He walked away from me, pulled out his key, went to his room. "Well that's what I call room service," he said, before he closed the door.

I barely gave my room a glance. I have three things I always check though. The closet clothes hangers: are they real hangers or the attached we-don't-trust-you-not-to-steal kind? The ballpoint pen on the table: is it capless to avoid pilferage? And—the crucial test—is there a good reading lamp by the bed? This place went 0-for-3. I slid open the window, stepped out onto the terrace which, good news here, I didn't share with an air-conditioning unit. I sat on the terrace, air-con behind me, tropics in front, on the border between the two, enjoying the early evening. I was tired; I could feel the flight catching up with me, heaviness in my legs and in my eyelids. They were always the first to go.

I've never in my life spent more than a minute in a shower, and that first night on Saipan was no exception. A minute, tops. But as soon as I turned off the faucet, I knew something had happened: I heard shouts and screams from down below. I grabbed a terrycloth robe (the kind that hotels invite you to buy) and stepped back out onto the terrace, only to see another bathrobe down in the pool and someone inside it, floating right at the edge, where he must have cracked his head, because blood was leaking into the pool, the way a maraschino cherry slowly stains a cocktail. It was Congressman Tex Von Schmidt and people were running to the pool and—you couldn't blame them—running away from it. They were talking on cell phones, they were vomiting on ferns and lilies. Security people were there right away and then some cops. In the distance I could hear a wailing of sirens, getting louder.

I stepped back in the room, leaving the door to the terrace open. And then I opened the door. No one was in the hall, but that would be changing fast. I walked down to Room 614. What—if anything—was in there? Someone alive or dead? I reached for the door, knowing it would be locked from within, just giving it a try, and it swung open and I was eye to eye with a blonde-haired blue-eyed woman in a black dress, flowered silk shawl, black shoes.

"Mister," she said. "Please. I didn't do something."

"I'm not a policeman," I said. She had a Russian accent, part of a legion of high-priced Natashas in diaspora around the world. I heard an elevator heading upwards, bells ringing as it ascended, so there was no thinking about what I did. I grabbed her hand, rushed to my room, pulled her inside and closed the door the instant before the elevator opened. I could hear people moving down the hall. Fingers on my lips, I gestured for Natasha to be quiet and then I pointed her towards the bathroom, though not before wondering if I'd left anything in there that she might steal. Razor, sun block and a tube of herbal toothpaste were the only things at risk. My wallet was in my pants, which were on the no-steal-um hanger in the closet. I stepped back out onto the terrace where anyone would expect me to be, because no one would have slept through the commotion down below. I watched them haul the congressman out of the pool, onto a stretcher, and quickly cover him with a sheet. The security guards had something to do now: they diligently chased away photographers. All the time, I expected a knock on the door. I guessed they were working their way down the hall, once they got done with the congressman's room. But I was wrong. They knocked on my door right away. I opened and there was Big Ben with Jared, the congressman's aide, and a couple of uniformed cops.

"Hey," I said. "What a thing. How did it happen?"

"Quick," Big Ben said. "Have you seen anyone up here? Heard anyone?"

"The congressman. He's the only one. We came up the elevator together. He went into his place. I went into mine."

"You had a beef on the bus," said Jared. "Any problems on the elevator?"

"Yes."

"Did it continue?"

"All the way up. Six floors."

"And then?"

"We went to our rooms. Look, we didn't hit it off. But that was the end of it. When I heard the noise I went outside . . . onto the terrace . . . and saw what I saw. It didn't look good."

"No one else up here?" the aide persisted.

"I wasn't watching the hall. I was watching the pool. Some mess. Do you think they'll have to change the water?"

Now was the moment. I stood there. They looked past me, into the room. They could see the edge of my bed, the opening to the terrace. Not the television, the minibar, the dresser or the bathroom. Now was the moment.

"When are you leaving the island?" asked the aide.

"Don't know yet," I said. "I'm staying on a bit."

"We may want to talk to you some more." He was a hard-charging guy, shirt sleeves up and no nonsense. But his moment had passed.

"Keep in touch with Ben here," he said. "If you move. If you leave."

"A pleasure. Keep in touch yourself." I turned to Big Ben. He hadn't liked the kid, maybe five years out of Student Council, delegating work to him. I couldn't see it but I sensed it. "No trip to Tinian tomorrow, I guess."

"Maybe not," he said.

❧

Now I studied her. Blonde hair, quite a lot of it, but then she was in a part of the world where men with money prized blondes. Being Russian was a thrown-in. Her face wasn't a blonde's face: high cheekbones, pouty lips, dark eyes, a little narrow. The wind blew off the steppes. And all around the world.

"Do you speak English?"

"Sure do," she said. A Russian who spoke like a Valley Girl.

"What happened with that man?"

"Accident," she said, automatically, grudgingly, like it was a run in her stocking.

"What kind of accident?"

She waved me off. "Never mind." She was tough. She sounded dismissive. But then she turned away with her eyes closed, coming to terms with something. She was tough and she was scared.

"My name is George," I said. "Griffin."

"Larissa," she said. No last name. If pressed, she might have said "Zhivago."

"Are you in trouble?"

"For sure."

"Do you want to talk about it?"

"No," she said.

"They'll be looking for you."

"Yes," she said. "For sure."

"Stop saying 'for sure,' " I said. But I had to admit she could make it sound jaunty or panicky, upbeat or way down. Even if she hadn't killed him, they'd be after her. Suicide, accidental fall, no matter how they said it, there couldn't be a Russian prostitute in the room.

"So," I asked. "What do you want?

"I'm wanting to say thank you."

"You're welcome," I hesitated. "It's okay."

"I stay here a while until maybe . . ." She looked at her watch. I'd bet it glowed in the dark, measuring the minutes on the job, more like a meter than a watch. "Until. . ." She held up three fingers.

"And then, where to?" I asked. "If they found you before, if they found you to hire you, they can find you again. It's an island and it's not your island, either."

"I have friend," she said. Was she being cocky? Was she kidding herself? Counting on some hooker sisterhood? Or on one of those Russian thugs I'd seen in Eastern European hotels, leather jacketed, shavenheaded bruisers, talking on cell phones, while their cold-eyed girls sat around listlessly, like idle taxi drivers, waiting to flip the meter and take someone for a ride.

"Okay," I said. I turned out the light and walked to the terrace. The place was empty now. They hadn't changed the water: it had a pink flamingo tinge. Maybe if you didn't know someone had died there, you'd think it was something tropical. I stretched out on the bed—there were twins—and gestured for her to take the other. I kept my bathrobe on and lay down on top of the bedspread. She stood over me—a tall girl who, in California, might show up playing beach volleyball. She sat down at the edge and reached out for my bathrobe, as if to brush off a breadcrumb, then found an opening above where I'd tied the terry cloth cord. She played with my chest hairs, and then began contending with the knot.

"Mister," she said, "you've been so nice to me."

I could feel something stirring and from quite a long sleep. I hadn't felt much like it, for reasons that weren't hard to figure out. Low self-esteem, loss of purpose, blah blah blah. But I felt it now. Did I mind turning my disinterested act of kindness into something else? Or was this just her disinterested act of kindness, matching mine? Anyway, something stopped me. The thought of her hooking up with the late congressman. A Russian hooker and a Texas politician, a last, little Cold War skirmish in a Saipan hotel room. Was that it? Rivalry? Jealousy? A remnant of self-respect?

"You want to be nice?"

"Oh yes," she said. "For sure."

"Okay," I said, pointing to a sofa that was against the wall. "Be nice enough to sleep over there."

❦

When I awoke in the hour before dawn, she was gone. So I went back to my closet, reached for my wallet, felt relieved to feel it, then to open it. My money and cards were still there. Then I reproached myself for not trusting her. Nice girl. I worried what would become of her, where she would go and who would protect her. In the bathroom, a lip-sticked smiling face was on the mirror, with THANKX!! written below. And then: P.S. COME SEE ABOUT ME! An old song. So I wondered about her in something like the way I wondered about myself. We were connected to this extent: two strangers on Saipan, trying our luck.

Stephanie Warner

❦

Towards late afternoon, the campus of the College of the Islands empties out. Oh, there's always someone around, sitting on a bench beneath the breezeways that cover the sidewalks connecting one building to another. They're waiting for a ride home or studying or maybe they've got a night class; the place revs up again at seven, neon lights humming, moths against the screens, geckos up and down the walls. Still, around five, things settle down nicely, and there's a bench up from the campus where you can look down towards the hotels and the sea and if you've got to feel lonely, it's a great view. There are always ships out there, four of them, and they never seem to go anywhere. It's as if they've been put there just for me, a place where I can think. And there's plenty to think about.

Last week, the day after I arrived, we had a start-of-the-year meeting, faculty and staff and our president, Ken Simpson, in his third year, an edge-of-retirement type who felt, he announced, like he had "something left to give." He's a polite, bland little man who tries not to offend: he was like a lot of older male educators I'd come across. Call him a president, a dean, a provost, he always looked, dressed, talked like a high school principal, polite and serviceable and by no means indispensable. After ten minutes on the importance of our work, he asked newcomers to stand while he introduced us and, in no time, there I was, Dr. Stephanie Warner coming "on board" from Elroy College, North Carolina, Department of Literature. *Doctor* Warner, he emphasized. "A PhD," he stressed, as if a pearl had shown up in a can of smoked oysters. After me came a custodian from Chuuk, once known as Truk. All this was happening in an open auditorium, heat seeping in from outside, overhead fans sluggishly slapping the humidity. After the introductions, I was tempted to flee, but decided against it: no need to be cast as a snob.

What followed was like one of those mixers that happens on the evening of the day you move into a dorm. You have to be careful, not to confide too quickly, bond too closely. So I watched folks move down a buffet table loaded with fried chicken and fish, piles of yellow rice, bananas, cut up green papayas, donuts and cakes, lemonade and ice tea. I got tired just looking at the table. Savvy diners took three paper plates so that they could carry extra weight.

Since then, I've opened up just a little to the faculty. Some Filipinos and one Indian excepted, they're stateside Americans, mostly kids, master's degrees or A.B.D., making the most of a bad job market to have an overseas adventure. The middle-aged people are spouses of businessmen, food and beverage managers at the hotels and—oh my God!—lawyers. The place must go through them like Kleenex. And then there are stragglers, old ones, semiretired government employees, Peace Corps volunteers who never quite made it home. And a lot of secretaries, office managers: the Saipanese. They were the ones, I sensed, who had been here before us and would be here when we were long gone. And it would be suicide, I'm sure, to get on the wrong side of them. On the wrong side, especially, of Bernadette Diaz. In Hawaii, she'd appeared to be a cheerful, chatty secretary. Here, behind her desk outside the president's office, she was different. Proprietary, fussy. Sitting in judgment. This was her place. Not mine. Not yet.

◊

"Hello?" I was sitting on a bench and hadn't heard anyone come up from behind me. I'd met a couple of dozen people up and down rows of faculty offices, one air-conditioned trailer after another, and I didn't know him. It must have showed.

"How soon they forget . . . *Faraway Places, Backyard Adventures.*"

"Of course," I said. "George Griffin . . . right?"

He nodded. He appeared livelier, more cheerful than on the plane but still, there was something hangdog about him, as if his life hadn't quite lived up to expectations.

"I was wondering how you were doing . . . in the witness protection program . . ."

"I thought you'd be gone by now. Isn't a junket just a matter of days?"

"In and out for a quick feel," he said. "I'm staying a while on my own."

"To write?"

"No," he answered firmly. "To think."

"You make it sound like either-or." I mimed a shopper, hefting fruit.

"You'd be surprised," he said. "I was on automatic pilot."

"Was?"

"The column's got three months of material ready to go. After then, I don't know. It isn't going as well as it used to. Financially and artistically. That's if art comes into it at all. That's another discussion."

"Well, if you're sorry . . . I'm sorry, too."

"I had a good run. Record breaking, for a travel writer. Not that anyone keeps track . . ."

His voice trailed off. He needed reviving. I imitated a voice from a movie.

"So, of all the little islands in all the oceans of the world . . ."

"I landed on the island you were coming to," he answered. "On the same small plane. At three in the morning. How about that?"

The question hung in the air. I had nothing to say about coincidences.

"Those ships out there," he asked, pointing to the fleet that never moved. "Are they for tourists? Are they in storage?"

"Nope," I answered. "I wondered too. Those are chartered by the military. Freighters, 'pre-positioned.' Weapons, vehicles, ammunition, food, medicine, in case trouble breaks out somewhere. 'Saipan's Navy,' The Master Blaster calls it."

"Who?"

"Didn't you do any research before you came?"

"No," he said. "I was . . . preoccupied."

"Well then." I told Griffin about the web site, about the way people reacted when I mentioned it. Some hated The Master Blaster, absolutely. He was demeaning and, since it was assumed he was an American, a racist. Other reviewers were mixed, cautiously affirmative. It was delicious, naughty. Someone operated a web site that offered the dark side of Saipan, politics, crime, scandal. It wasn't all true, of course, they dutifully said; it was one-sided, racist, neocolonial, fueled by a grudge. But everybody read it. Griffin, I could see, was hooked.

"Now that," he said, "is something. Somebody is putting his ass on the line."

"Or her . . . ass," I added.

"I'd like to meet that guy," he said.

"Or gal," I said. "Lots of luck. Many have tried, I gather. Not with the nicest of intentions."

"There must be a way."

"Well, you can send an e-mail. But for the sake of whoever's behind it, I hope the site is safe."

"There's a way," he insisted. He was fascinated, I could see. Some sort of connection had been made, I guess, between a writer whose work mattered and a writer whose work didn't matter.

"I'll bet they hate him," he said.

"The problem is, whenever you Google Saipan, The Master Blaster site is one of the first things that pops up. Can't miss it. And there's no way of telling how many trips have been canceled. Or, for that matter, how many offers of employment have been declined. And it probably scares off investors too. It must be very annoying."

"A turd in a punch bowl," he mused.

"What?"

"That's what the late congressman called me. Now I discover I've got company. I'd really like to meet him." It took him a bit to shake loose of The Master Blaster. After a while, he arose and so did I. We walked back to the campus together. "I guess you're all set up here. Got a place to stay?"

"Yes. You?"

"I'm moving into one tomorrow. Actually, it's a hotel that's down on its luck. A ghost hotel. How about your place. Furnished? Nice?"

"Sort of. It's like lots of things here. At first glance it looks like America. The grounds, the exterior, the layout—bedroom, bathroom, galley-size kitchen, tiny verandah, cottage cheese ceiling, tile floor. Then, after you move in, you learn it's not America, not quite, and it may never be. Those patches of mold on the side of the building. Those stalks of metal coming out of the roof, in case they decide to go from two floors to three. The taste of the water that comes out of the tap. The air conditioners, the way they clank, bang, drip, leak, rust. And what happens to food when you leave it out at night . . . Cockroaches, geckos, long lines of ants. No rats yet, though I see them on the road and even up in palm trees, jumping around like monkeys. And stray dogs everywhere. They're supposed to be descendants of the dogs, the mascots, that came ashore with the marines. And, oh my God, when the power goes out, and it does go out, you're sitting in the dark. And when it's on, you're impoverishing yourself."

I hadn't meant to give a speech, but something in him—a sense that he was smart and depressed and needed to talk—had combined with a loneliness that I'd contended with myself.

"You'll never make it as a travel writer," he said.

"That wasn't in my plans," I snapped. But then I heard my husband's voice, coming at me from a long distance, from the kind of, Yeah, but how about making it *with* a travel writer? one-liner. Looking at Griffin though, it was hard to picture.

"Hey," he said. "I meant what I said as a compliment."

"Well, thanks. I guess." We were back at the college now. I glanced inside my classroom. It was full but it had none of the noisy disorder I was accustomed to. The students sat quietly and in groups, because that's how they came. They were Filipino, Saipanese, stateside American, a daunting Russian woman who was usually late. I wanted to get her into my office so we could chat. I supposed she was, or had been, a prostitute. I'd noticed a bar near the tourist hotels called Russian Roulette: apt metaphor for the game they played. All of this was diversity, admirable in theory and a problem in fact: God knows what I would have to do to induce class discussion, get them to talk to me and to each other.

"Could I just say this?" George Griffin asked. "I know you've got to go. I don't know what you think of me. How I look to you . . ."

It was sweet, and pathetic. I was back in high school, in a car parked in my driveway, the lights on my front porch were bright, and inside, my parents were not asleep. Or I was in college, outside a dorm, or later, in front of every apartment I'd ever had. No matter how old and wise, or wised up, you were, it always came down to this. Maybe it always would. In some tidy retirement community, would a man with a cane be confronting a woman with a walker? But now there was a class behind me and I could play this scene no longer.

"The fact is," he said, "I don't much like myself right now."

"I see," I said, clinically. "But I've got to get into that classroom."

Night classes play hell with sleep. Whether you flounder or soar, it makes no difference, you come home wired. You want to sleep, you ought to sleep, but that wave of weariness, the one that enfolds you, stays way offshore. You're not up to reading something, you shrug off television, you sit out on the balcony. And you think, not in an organized way but randomly. The faces in class, the body language, the silence that followed my questions. Back home I let the silence hang in the air. Time was on my side. Someone would speak, eventually. I didn't feel that way tonight. It took forever before the Russian girl, Galina, came to my rescue. Unless I guess wrong, she's a bar girl, sex worker, whatever. Maybe I could pay her to lead class discussions. Then, in my lonesome mood, I think of Eddie Covington. I've traveled a world away from him, to a place he couldn't imagine. And yet Saipan seems to be full of Eddies—regular guys, good old boys, people who wouldn't get to first base in Japan or China but camp out happily here. Eddie would fit right in. But will I? That's a harder call.

Khan

Our first morning on Saipan, a Filipino drove up on a motorbike, unlocked the gate, entered the compound where he fed and watered the pigs. He never glanced at us, though we were impossible to miss. We were nothing. "Go talk to him," X told me.

"Hello," I said. The Filipino was emptying buckets of old food—fruit peels, wilted vegetables, sour rice, stale bread—to the pigs, crowded and grunting at the fence. He did not answer me.

"Hello," I said a little louder.

He kept feeding the pigs. Was he stupid or under instructions?

"Hello!" This time I shouted. Another failure. He was tense, ready to run, but he kept at the pigs. Was there a Filipino who could not say hello? By now X had enough. He rushed from behind me, kicked the pail out of the man's hands. Garbage covered the Filipino's pants and X's shoes. The Filipino looked up now. He was an older man. His hair was black—too black to go with the wrinkles on his face and hands, the few teeth that remained in his mouth.

"Hello!" X shouted. And when the Filipino shrugged again, and I realized it took some courage to shrug like that, X put his hand in front of the Filipino's face, moving his thumb and first finger, together and apart: talk. He pointed my way. Talk to me. And now he showed the man the machete he'd taken from Gregorio's truck.

"What are you wanting?" the Filipino finally asked. He was frightened, but not just of X or his machete. Talking to us scared him as well. It was forbidden, unhealthy, shameful even. More comfortable to whisper to the pigs.

"You know Gregorio?" I asked.

He nodded. If he could manage to use signs, not words, he might not catch whatever disease we carried.

"Is he your boss? You work for him?"

Another nod.

"Where is he?"

A shrug

"On Saipan?"

"Maybe . . ."

"Everything is maybe," X said in our language. "Maybe somebody is going to get cut."

"Not him," I said. "He's an old man feeding pigs. He's no better than we are."

With that, X shrugged and backed away. It later came to me, there were other things I might have asked. Where did the man stay? Where did Gregorio live? Work? Those were things we needed to know. But I backed away too, for I feared that with one more shrug, just one, X would kill the old man. I could see it in X. Somebody was going to be cut. It was not if, it was when.

§

We stayed with the pigs for a month. Sometimes a truck picked us up for a day's work, cutting down trees, sorting scrap metal. A day here, a day there. It was not the work that was in our contract. And though the truck driver brought rice and canned fish and bottled water, we were never paid. At last, X had had enough. All of us had had enough, but X was the one who confronted the driver in the pickup truck.

"Where is Gregorio?"

"I don't know."

"No money, no work," X said.

"No work, no food," the driver answered. And drove away.

That morning we made a plan. We couldn't just leave the Azis brothers behind. They needed to believe they could do something more than sit and wait. So we made a plan that included them. X and I would go out into the island, looking for information, work, help, whatever offered. After we left, they would wait, but only for a short time. If the old man came to feed the pigs, he would come in the morning. And this time he might not come alone. No matter. They would stay where they were until the pigs were fed. Then they were to walk in circles, wider and wider circles, avoiding people and seeing what they could find.

"Find?" asked Qazi. "What . . . to find?" Their mission sounded point-less. Until I told them they were to look for food, wherever they found it. We were spies, I said, and they were hunters. I made it into a game that they could play.

As I arose that morning, slapped water on my face, I sensed the pigs behind the broken wall. We had shared this place with them, come to know them—their eating and shitting, their grunts, their movement in mud, their play, their lazy sleep. I knew the males and females, the young and old. And the day before, the Filipino who fed the pigs had come back with three others. We thought they were coming after us. But they wanted a pig.

The death of a fish or chicken is accomplished quickly. A goat takes a little longer. But those squeals of fear and pain were new to us, and awful. And the way they did it, laughing, joking. We stayed inside. We'd threatened one of them; now there were more of them and they all had knives. I had thought of pigs as very far from human, an animal not to eat and touch, an unclean beast. Now I wondered not if the pig was too far below us, but too close. On this island, were we any better off? The pig's life was measured in pounds, ours in working days. What difference was that?

❧

At first it was cool, an early morning cool that would not last. We were on the dirt road that led away from the pig farm. This close to where Gregorio had left us, we did not want to be seen walking. We would run off the road at the sound of an approaching car. If a car came, we would hear it. The road was terrible, lots of holes, boulders, washouts; you'd have to go slowly, driving up such a road. And just off the road, the trees and brush were thick. No one would find us if we ran in there, no one would follow.

On the next road there was traffic, cars and yellow school buses, trucks with workers in back, still half asleep. There were gas stations and shops and houses. After an hour, we crossed another road, a high-way, and all I could see were stores, left and right—restaurants, auto repair, groceries, barbers, nightclubs, law offices—and signs in Chinese and in something else, Japanese or Korean, maybe both. Whose island was this?

"Look!" X suddenly said. He put his hand on my shoulder, turning me to the left. I saw a factory, China Star Garments, a long metal building surrounded by smaller structures with laundry hanging outside windows and off railings. A tall fence ran around the property, and at the entrance was a guardhouse. This was what X wanted me to see, for the women coming in and out were Chinese but the guard had skin and hair like ours. Now he had seen us: his eyes were on us. Then he nodded, but when I took a step in his direction, he signaled for us to halt, then to move on. Keep walking, get out of here, be gone.

"He's one of us," X said. "We're not the only ones."

"I never thought we were," I said.

"I wish we could talk to him. It could save us this walk."

"We could come back later. Maybe when he is about to finish work, off duty. We stand outside and he sees us . . ."

"You think they let him out? Because he keeps workers in, they let him out? You think he steps in his car and drives home . . ."

He made me feel foolish. X had a way of seeing the worst of things. Too bad, he was often right. He knew more than I did. Four years he'd been in Saudi Arabia, on a construction site, later as a driver. Hating it, hating the way the people there—though having the same religion as us—treated him. He'd learned about the limits of faith and the power of money. The Americans on this island, if that's what the Saipanese were, might be bad to us. But not worse than the people X had worked for in Saudi Arabia. The Saipanese were amateur rich people, little beginners.

When we were almost past the factory, I turned for a last look. The guard—our countryman, our brother—was still staring at us. Was it to remember us later? Or make sure we were gone?

We came to a beach. A thin patch of soft grass separated the sea from the highway and there were trees that made for shady places, picnic tables. An old Japanese tank sat on a pedestal that had a marker, and nearby there was a public bathroom which was locked. We sat in the grass for a moment, and neither of us spoke. This was a moment I was grateful for, studying the colors of the water from clear to pale blue to deep blue to golden, where it crashed off the reef and exploded into sunlight. There was wind too, our sweat cooled. For a moment we were part of—we shared—the life around us, the idea of being on a beach with nothing to do.

"What now?" X finally asked. "What do we do now?" It did not come as a challenge, in his usual manner. He sounded tired, out of hope, out of anger, beyond all that. There was nothing to do and nowhere to go. No point in staying here, no point in returning to that camp where the poor Azis brothers waited to hear of our discoveries. Why not stay here? I could hear that in X's voice. Giving up. And what happened to him was happening to me. A creeping feeling of laziness, indifference, a willingness to let things happen. What now? I asked myself. We had our walk. We had gone as far as it was possible to go, at least this way. Coming off the sea, I would have found an island. But coming to the sea, I had discovered nothing.

There were hotels up and down the beach and though we would not have dreamed of entering, we walked past, at the edge of gardens, outdoor restaurants, swimming pools, past docks that offered boat rides, fishing, snorkeling. We had dressed in our best clothing, the jeans and T-shirts we had worn on the plane, but I worried that two dark-skinned men might attract notice. No problem. It was a world of outsiders.

"Look at that!" X said. Suddenly he was excited. Thrilled. He pointed at a hotel swimming pool where a man was testing the water with his toes. He was covered, from his shoulders to his stomach, with tattoos, dragons. "Yakuza!" X said, full of wonder. He walked towards the pool, as close as he could come to all the splashing, the noise, the umbrellas. He stood and waited. Finally the Japanese saw him. He stared back, on guard, expecting trouble. But X just waved to him, a friendly wave, until you noticed that he concealed three fingers of the hand he was waving. The yakuza turned away and X rejoined me, laughing. Then he explained to me what he knew from movies, about tattoos and missing fingers. A Japanese gangster was on vacation here. That impressed him.

Between the hotels, when the road came too close to the sea to allow construction, there were many picnics, families, fishermen, even a motorcycle gang. These, I guessed, were local people. Everywhere we passed there was alcohol: trays of cocktails behind the hotels, glasses full of fruit and flowers, beer and soda along the beach, bought by the case. We heard music too, guitars among the local people, strolling musicians at the hotels. And food! After days of rice and canned fish, the smell of it made us crazy. The smell, the smoke! We were starving! And how these people piled the food on plates, more than a plate could hold, more than anyone could eat. What was hardest of all was the food that remained after the eating was done; plates filled with rice, chicken legs with one bite gone, thrown into garbage cans, left behind on tables and chairs, fallen to the ground for ants and dogs to find. But not for us.

We left the beach and headed back. It was early afternoon and we were hungry, maddened by the smell of food. We had not eaten since before we started walking. Being poor in your own poor country was one thing, being poor with drinking and feasting all around you was another.

"Khan," X said and stopped. That was unusual. He rarely thought before he spoke. "I'm hungry," X said. It came out like a confession, a sign of weakness. From X, it was sad.

"So am I," I admitted.

"Do you have any money?"

"Do you?" I asked. That was something else we never talked about: the little money of our own we might be carrying. Whatever it was, it was no one else's business. That was why I answered his question to me with the same question to him. I expected a shrug or a lie. Not an answer.

"A little," he said.

And if he had given me time to answer, I'd have said, A little. But he didn't give me a chance.

"Come with me," he said, taking charge. He led the way to a store called Winchell's Donuts, with lots of sweet things, baked goods, on display. I wondered if we might come food-gathering here. Surely, they did not sell all they baked. There was something left at the end of every day. Would it come to that? Ninja garbage collectors creeping in the dark, poking into Dumpsters?

❧

We step inside and the air-conditioning surprises us. It is something we'd almost forgotten. We order two donuts each. Mine are banana and chocolate, X's are pink and green, but that is all I can tell. Canned soda is expensive so we order hot coffee. X takes a five-dollar bill out of his pocket, a bill which had been folded to the size of a postage stamp. The woman behind the counter laughs at him. Of all the people we've passed all day, she is the only one who sees us. And she laughs when she does. Bit by bit, as in a ceremony, X opens his bill in front of the cashier, turns it over to her, receives a few coins in change. Incredibly, he leaves them on the counter.

"It's simpler like this," he says to me when we sit down. "When you have no money, you have no choice."

◊

What could I tell the brothers? What had we learned? That we'd eaten donuts and had coffee in an air-conditioned restaurant? That we'd noticed a Bangladeshi guard outside a garment factory? That we had to do something, but I had no idea what?

We walked back along a road that was littered with beer cans, diapers, rusted appliances that might have been discarded last week or forty years ago. Then we came to the compound gate, doorway to pigs and slaves, creatures with little or no hope, and just as we entered, we confronted something unbelievable! The smell of meat cooking. Impossible! But there were the Azis brothers, holding sticks over a fire, and there were chickens on the end of the sticks.

"What happened?" X asked at the same second I put the question another way: "Where did you get those?"

They beamed at us, as if they'd planned to surprise us with a party and we had walked in at the perfect time. Instantly, I forgot my guilt at not having brought donuts.

"See . . ." Abdul says, gesturing at a piece of cardboard, spread with papayas, pineapples, coconuts.

"What did you do?" I asked, and, as with children, a story they couldn't wait to tell came tumbling out, silly and disorganized. They did as we told them. They stepped behind the pigpen and made a circle which brought them to where they started. Another circle followed and an even wider circle after that. How many circles in all? They weren't sure, they argued and corrected each other. The first one took five minutes and the last one almost two hours. As for the ones in between. . .

"Enough," X interrupted. "Many circles. But when did these circles include chickens?"

Was it the third circle or the fourth? Not the last, that was papayas, not the second, that was pineapples. Was it the circle that included the old Japanese house, like ours, only no roof? Or the one in which they climbed up into a cave, left behind from the war, because there were rusted canteens and cooking pots, sake bottles and rusted shells. Back and forth, around and around they went, having fun. Were they teasing us or amusing themselves? When we sat down to eat—the first meal we'd enjoyed in a week—the story started to make sense.

The island was like no place else, they said, you never knew what you would find. A wild jungle, a little stream, ridges, caves. Places to fall, to hide, traps and hideouts. Abandoned buildings. Farms that they'd avoided, not farms really, no one was living there, but part-time places, shacks with water barrels and scraps of gardens. Chickens wandered around where they wanted. These two were beyond a fence, away from any building. Wild chickens, they were sure, or at least almost wild. Now they choreographed the hunt, the pursuit, the near misses, even as we sat on the ground, tearing flesh from bone. The papaya and mango were stringy, not like what we knew, but we ate them. The pineapple were tiny but sweet. These, the brothers had come across. You never knew what you would find. That was their point. There were cattle nearby, goats. How did all these things come to be here? Wild pigs, wasps and crabs! What a crazy place, they said.

We'd eaten too quickly. Now we lay back, contented. Our luck had changed. We would not stay here, we would not go back to fish and rice. That was what I said to them. And I added one more thing. "We will not keep waiting for Gregorio." I saw X smile at that.

For the first time, we had garbage after a meal. Some cold rice, some bones and peels. Qazi Azis pushed it all to the center of the flattened cardboard box we'd been sitting around. Then he picked it up and headed for the fence.

"Stop it," I said. Come here.

"What?" he asked, glancing down at the mess he was carrying. "You are still hungry?"

I took the cardboard from him and walked into the house, to the hole in the wall that looked over the pigs' place. The others were watching me. They would not have done this. It surprised me, even, as I watched the pigs approach, grunting, splashing, pink eyes upon me. A large male—he was the largest now, largest since yesterday—and two females and three or four little ones. All doomed. I had gotten used to watching them, their feeding, their sleep, their play. I wondered how they reacted to the subtraction of one of their family. Sadness? Thoughts of escape? Now they crowded in towards me, snout on snout. I did not loathe them. Now, more than ever, I would not eat the meat of a pig. I threw them the food and watched the contest that followed, pushing, shoving, eating fast, before another pig could take their dinner.

When I turned, I saw the others talking about me, laughing about the new friend of pigs. I didn't respond. I wondered about tomorrow. Pigs, I thought, did not wonder. But what was the difference between something that did not think about the future and something else that attempted to think . . . but nothing came? Why think at all, then? I looked at the other three and guessed what was on their minds. Where would the next meal come from? Where would we go? The pigs were ahead of us in that. They knew their place and they could count on food. That was when Abdul turned to Qazi and, receiving a nod, spoke.

"On the fifth circle," he said, "we found a place."

"What place?"

"For us to stay."

Mel Brodie

❔

So I arrive at the hotel and there's a letter waiting for me at the front desk and my heart sinks. Just lately, mail scares me, phone calls too. Can I give it back? Then I take a closer look. False alarm. It's only from my uncle, my father's kid brother, Norm. No kid anymore, Norm, a dentist retired outside of Palm Springs. We keep in touch. I called him before leaving, got an answering machine—"Leave me a message if you think there's a chance I'll call you back"—told him where I was bound and how he could reach me.

I ask them to take my luggage up to my room. It's a few hours before dawn and I need a drink. Late as it is, long as it's been, that sense of being in a new place stirs me up. You don't fly halfway around the world, arrive in the hours before dawn and go straight to bed. You don't. The clerk tells me to call room service. I do that, get it billed to my room and delivered to the lobby: a double gin and tonic with lime. The room service guy, heavy lidded, carries it out to the pool. The moment of panic about the letter has passed. But not completely. There's a part of me, down deep, that worries 24-7. It's about a deal Lou got me with one of his Indian tribes in Florida. "RESERVATION: A Destination Resort . . ." I was the front man, the spokesman, the on-site glad-hand canoodling the customers inside the tent. Our slogan: Spend Forever in the Everglades. You got it: a senior citizen place. Maximum Lou persuaded the tribal council to announce a plush yet daring leisure village, the kind of place that begins with a tidy apartment, moves you into assisted living and when you're way past ripe, deposits you in a hospice/hostel/hospital, aka God's Waiting Room. It wasn't a bad idea on paper, and we had some spectacular brochures and a lot of pre-construction deposits, getting in on the ground floor, which probably isn't the right phrase to describe a building in a swamp. It might have worked, most certainly. Take it from me, there was something appealing about the Everglades. It was the idea of living on an Indian reservation, in the middle of wild nature. And throw in a casino that had gambling and ginch, prize fights and beauty contests, bars with happy hours that never ended, all-you-can-eat buffet tables the length of an Olympic swimming pool. What's not to like, in your senior years?

I can't say for sure where you're supposed to go when you get old. You do get old: you're in your forties and all of a sudden there's not a single baseball player who's not younger than you are. Along comes Bill Clinton, who was in grammar school when I was in high. And here's the coup de grace, a Supreme Court justice who's some punk kid, compared to me. So I dealt with old timers, I got to be one myself but in Florida. For the first time, I really *liked* what I was selling. It just didn't make sense for customers; it appealed to me. Those adult communities that got carved into the woody Poconos, into potato fields in Long Island, into pine barrens in South Jersey were okay. But they were sad places, all those oldsters puttering and playing, waiting for their damn kids to visit, waiting for bad news from their doctor, checking which neighbor "didn't look so good today." Sure, they all had benches and walks and an artificial lake, a community center for card games and "functions." But Florida was an adventure. The damn swamps gave me a buzz. I liked spending time in our sales office, never resented a minute I spent there, out on the porch—like I owned the place—sitting in a rocker that looked out onto the palmettos, which led to a swamp, which led to the Gulf of Mexico, though it's up for grabs down there, where land ends and water begins.

The land they promised us title to was swamp. So what else is new? This is Florida. The clever part was that the federal government, wanting to protect wetlands, would trade us for other, better land in the area and, with the money we made, we'd be way ahead. But the feds decided they couldn't or shouldn't trade in Native American lands. And Maximum Lou's tribal Tontos lost an election. Then there were some questions about the deposits we'd received which, in Maximum Lou's words, "had failed to perform up to expectations." Anyway, I made the newspapers, left and right, a "shadowy promoter," "a serial con man," and so forth. There were calls from reporters, there was talk of subpoenas. This would rev up anybody's interest in small, faraway but English-speaking islands.

It's fine just sitting here by my lonesome, taking in the night, not bothering anybody, nobody bothering me. Okay by me. Get away from it all. That's what islands are for, isn't it? I drink some gin and set the glass back on the table, I feel Norm's letter. So okay, I open the letter, moving my chair within range of an outdoor lamp.

Dear Mel:

This is about your father. I know you never knew him, never heard much about him either. Let me just say, when I look at you, I see him, to this day even, though you're way older than he ever got to be. You have his eyes, sharp and smart, his lips and, goes without saying, that beak. You have his voice too, the voice of one of those old newscasters, could make a bathtub fart-lighting contest sound like a world-historical event. Have you ever wondered—I have— what would happen if they made those stentorian news-readers do the weather, and gave wars and elections to the weather people like Willard Scott? What an attitude adjustment that would be.

Anyway, about your dad. How many people are left alive who remember him? I guess you knew that he died in the war and that he was a flyer. I doubt you know more. He was a navigator, actually, on a B-29 that took off for Japan in June 1945 and didn't come back. The island he flew out of was Tinian, which I believe is a neighbor of Saipan. I guess it's the last piece of earth he walked on. So do me a favor and yourself one too. Go over there, why don't you . . . and pay your respects. Just do it.

Love,

Uncle Norm

I folded the letter, tucked it into my shirt pocket and walked to the beach. I slipped off my shoes and socks and waded into the water, piss-warm and shallow. God knows how far you'd have to walk to be able to swim. Out to the reef, probably. On the other side of the reef it was another story. I looked south, down along the Saipan shoreline, past a row of beach hotels. Then I turned to face the sea, towards where Tinian might be. A blast from the past, all right. Son of a bitch, I said to myself. My father!

When I got up to my room, I hung a Do Not Disturb sign on the door and went straight to sleep. It didn't matter to me or anyone else how long I slept. And when I awoke, I had that scary vapor lock that ambushes travelers: waking up in a room not sure where you are. Panic. You lie there wondering and getting no answer and you ask yourself if this is what death is like or if this is what happens *after* death. Then it comes back to me: I'm on Saipan.

The day had pretty much passed me by, no loss on an island where one day was pretty much like another. Saipan or Florida, you lived the morning, you loved the night and the rest of it was something you got through. The sun had set by the time I came down in the elevator, but there was color on the horizon and color in the tourist zone in back of the hotel: neon white inside beachy convenience stores, pink and blue and yellow in front of stores that sold jewelry, in front of restaurants and massage parlors, all of this in one neighborhood, shopping, eating, massage and more. While the sun died, the neon blossomed; when the sky turned black, it buzzed, like fireworks.

I started out in a noisy bar, Western-themed, with two leggy Miss Kitty–types out of Manila, busy pool tables, joking around the bar. There were deal makers in booths, outsiders and locals was my guess. The locals were Cuban-looking guys with a trace of something else, Japanese or Malay. Who knew? After two San Miguel drafts I was ready to order a burger, but a band started tuning up and I was out of there and into an Indian restaurant I instantly felt sorry for; a couple of depressed waiters presiding over a buffet left over from lunch, in fact it was barely dented, and so I sat and ate while they hovered, anxious to chat me up. There wasn't much I could say to them.

When I left, the neon ruled, gaudy stripes of blue and green and pink. Music came out of doorways and women stood in entrances, some masseuses, some bar girls. What was odd was the way they dressed, not like hookers, at least not always, but like schoolgirls, cheerleaders maybe, like they'd come off a school bus with Julie Andrews in the lead. What a world. Russian women! Filipinos, Chinese and who knows what else? Not me. With nationalities I'm like I am with colors. I recognize the primary colors, red and white, black and blue, green and brown and yellow, but the in-betweeners—puce, mauve, taupe—get away from me. So do the people in between. Anyway, they were loitering outside, waiting for business, a party that might or might not happen. "Good evening, sir." "Massage, sir?" "Come inside, please." I'm in my sixties and I'm not handsome, no way, but I'm not a codger. Back in Washington, I attracted more than my share of widows. Some looking for friendship, company, et cetera, but sex was "out of the question." Some still wanted it, said they did anyway. But I didn't want them. Sex or company. Sorry, ladies, I'll grow old alone. But out here, these were girls. I kept walking, but not fast; in fact, maybe a little slower than before. Suddenly there were footsteps behind me, and giggles, and on either side someone had their arm around me.

"You did not forget us?" a girl asked. Dressed like prom night. "I am Lourdes. From the plane."

"I am Cori."

"Hey. Sure. How's it going?"

"Please, what is your name, sir?" Lourdes asked.

We're still walking, but very slowly. My hotel-ward walk is losing momentum. It's like an awards ceremony, where a couple of starlets escort a duffer who just got a lifetime achievement award on stage.

"I'm Mel."

"Mr. Mel? You like a massage?" They made it sound so innocent, as if it were a charity fundraiser, a carwash or something.

"From both of you?" I said.

"Yes . . . you're so big!" Cori said.

"And we have no business," Lourdes confided, a little forlornly. No customers. "You will be our first. You will bring us luck."

"What kind of massage? Thai? Swedish? Acupressure?"

Then, as if on cue, they both raised up on their toes and whispered in my ears, not-so-schoolgirlish things, speaking at the same time, words and tongues tickling me in stereo. Together they steered me off the sidewalk, through a doorway with a couple of neon flamingos entangled in ways that you don't see on the Nature Channel. Then it was upstairs with some Filipino crooner on tape, a knockoff Julio Iglesias. This time I didn't tell them to turn it off. But I had another request to make.

"Listen, girls. I like you fine and I want you to get off to a good start here. But there's something particular I want you to do."

"Special service?" Lourdes asked.

"I guess you could call it that." Now they were scared. It was easy to see. They had no way of telling what might be in store for them.

"What are you wanting, Uncle Mel?"

"I want a massage. Just that. No more. Can do?"

Amazing. They still had their doubts. The idea of a massage without an extra sounded bizarre.

"But we must charge you for special service," Lourdes said. "Or Mama Ruffa thinks we are taking money for ourselves."

"Okay. No service is special service."

They nodded at that. I took off my clothes while they waited outside the cubicle. They'd decorated it with a crucifix and some plastic flowers and a cutout picture of what looked like Tahiti. I lay down on my stomach and awaited what I was willing to bet would be a mediocre massage.

◊

There were small planes that went to Tinian a couple of times a day—the flight took all of twelve minutes—and there was a ship that took gamblers across to a Chinese-operated casino. It sounded like a *Twilight Zone* episode: shooting craps on the A-bomb island. I wasn't sure about joining some Chinese high rollers. Then the clerk nodded across the lobby to where a group of men were gathered around a table marked MILITARY HISTORICAL TOURS. They were oldsters, veterans, some with canes, one in a wheelchair and a few that made a special point of being spry and healthy. It was like the American Legion on Memorial Day. Was I a veteran? the group leader asked. No, I told him, just a tourist. But I was the son of a man who served on Tinian. He told me I'd have to pay for my way on the boat but he'd be delighted to have me tag along. He even made me a name tag right on the spot: MEL BRODIE JR.

Ninety percent of the Tinian passengers were Chinese, the video that played on the cabin TV was Chinese, the crew was Filipino. The Americans sat by themselves at the front of the top deck, watching Tinian come closer, Saipan back off a little. I'd expected the veterans to be jabbering excitedly, coming back at eighty to where they could have been killed, sixty years ago. I expected memories, insights, arguments. It was as if they were sailing through time, after all, going back to war and youth. Boy, was I wrong! They were sleeping, every last one of them. The cabin was stuffy, the windows sealed shut, and the TV was part karate, part karaoke, chopping and humping. So they snoozed. And snored. There was such a thing as waiting too long. I'd seen it again and again, selling to seniors, to couples who'd waited to realize their dreams, to take those trips they'd planned for years, only to have one slip away, right on the edge of the golden years. "He told me that I would have to do the living for both of us," more than one teary widow told me, before ordering a second portion of *zuppa inglese*. Well, I'd waited a while myself.

"Excuse me . . ." A tapping of the microphone jarred me. I must have dozed off myself. We were a stone's throw off the coast—do islands have coasts, or only beaches?—of Tinian. The shore was limestone, pocked and pitted, all spray and blowholes; coming ashore would be like rubbing against a giant cheese grater. Now and then there was a sandy patch.

Tinian, the guide said, was the perfect amphibious operation. The Americans had feinted to one side of the island, then landed on this lightly defended beach and moved north, losing a tenth of the men they'd lost on Saipan. It sounded like a quail hunt, moving across the island in a line, flushing out and killing Japanese. And there was never any doubt about the outcome.

We turned in towards the tiny port of San Jose, past rusted break-waters, to a dock where schoolchildren waited to greet the veterans as they, hobbled, limped and, in one case, were wheeled ashore. I was the last one off, on purpose, but there was a lei for me, a necklace of shells and a "Welcome back, sir" for Mel Brodie Jr. We piled obediently on to a waiting bus and headed to the far end of Tinian, where the battle ended and the Japanese had made this little Peace Park. All the monuments, so far as I could tell, were Japanese. They were like tombstones and tablets at the edge of the sea, no beach, just rocks. But it didn't feel like a cemetery, didn't have that mood, because there was no particular sadness, and it was so damn hot now, the monuments were glaring at you, pissed off, you felt like you'd burn if you touched them. I sensed anger that I kind of understood, dying in a no-hope battle, a sideshow after Saipan, like a boxing match so one-sided that it didn't have to be fixed. Christ, they watched Saipan getting taken, maybe could trace the progress of the battle from day to day. Then it was their turn. They were termites, we were the exterminator.

It was midday now, brutal, and the veterans were happy to climb in the bus, happier still to step into an air-conditioned Chinese casino and hunt for food they could recognize on the buffet tables. I'd figured out that most of them were marines who'd been on Saipan. They'd moved on by the time Tinian was attacked. No point in even asking about my father. I sat by myself, ate fast. The others were in no rush to go back outside, while Memory Lane was broiling. Most of the casino shops were closed but I found a Tinian postcard and a U.S. stamp and addressed it to Uncle Norm. "Mission accomplished," I wrote. The next line escaped me. There was an embarrassing amount of white space left. Couldn't I fill a postcard? Was I going to draw a smiley face?

Then they took us to the A-bomb strips, the main attraction. We sped down unexpected highways, left over from the war. The Americans noticed Tinian was shaped like Manhattan and the thoroughfares they built were named after similarly located Manhattan streets. So we were on Broadway, cutting through cattle fields, past Japanese buildings and temples, bullet pocked. Then we turned and we were bouncing along a dirt track, tunneling through thickets of brushy saplings that covered the sky and slapped at the windows; it smelled green but it was a hot green, like everything was being cooked as it grew. You were fried in the sun, poached in the shade. But at last we felt a hard final bump and we drove out onto North Field, which the guide told us had once been the largest air base in the world, four 8,500-foot runways. We were on one of them now, riding where B-29s had taxied and taken off. The place was deserted. It was like one of those end-of-the-world movies: planes and tents, Quonset huts and hangars and fuel tanks all gone, only the airstrips remained, like footprints of another time, another race even. The airstrips were hanging tough, too, weeds and brush encroaching at the edges. A weed whacker could restore the strips. What a commercial that would make.

The place had me, that long, straight runway that launched you—my father—off the earth, into the sky, over the sea and out of life. It got me then, it just ambushed me, and I guessed it was possible, after all, to miss what I never had. It got me. My unknown old man. They say that when you mourn, even at a funeral, you mourn for yourself. There's something to that, I guess. But it was him I thought about. Wondered.

When I came out of it, we had parked in a cul-de-sac just off the runway. These were the A-bomb pits, the high point of the tour, and we walked over to where some Plexiglas tent-shaped shelters covered these holes in the ground. Other places you'd expected broken pottery or the relics of some saints, here it was just a hole with some plumbing and pipes. A manhole. For the place that ended the war and ushered in the nuclear age, it was kind of a flop. And, oh my God, was it hot: the sun slammed down and bounced back up, hitting you from all directions, like a turkey in a convection oven, roasted on all sides. Look away and there were shimmering heat mirages down the runway. I searched for shade and saw it, near a Japanese pillbox at the edge of the runway. One of the veterans, the one in the wheelchair, had found it before me. Now he watched me approach.

"God," I said when I joined him. "How did you do it? I know you were young and there was a war going on . . . but still. This heat isn't fair."

"I didn't do it," he answered, nodding his head and smiling. The nametag dangling on a string around his neck identified him as Harold Strauss. Some military unit stuff, numbers and letters, followed.

"You weren't here?" I asked.

"No, I wasn't," Strauss replied. "Some younger version of me. Nice kid. Distant relative. He wouldn't know me now."

"I get you."

"No way," he mused. "A distant relative."

"Why'd you come back? It can't be easy for you."

Strauss was a heavy man; like a lot of people in wheelchairs, he'd put on weight. It wasn't fair, all the meals and moods he couldn't walk off.

"Same reason people go to college reunions," he said. And then he changed his mind. "No, wait. I take that back. It's not about these guys."

He lifted an arm off the edge of his wheelchair and gestured towards the other veterans who were taking pictures in front of the *Enola Gay*'s bomb pit. Actually, they were getting their pictures taken, rushing out of ranks to hand a camera to a guide, then joining the group. In this kind of sun, it was only a matter of minutes before one of those old boys went down for the count.

"They're not classmates. I came when they were gone. I was Air Force." He showed me his name tag. This time, I attended to it: 313TH WING, 504TH BOMB GROUP. "Sound familiar?"

"Not to me."

"I thought it might . . ." He sounded like he'd decided to drop a subject. "Anyway, it's a reunion with the place. This place. That's what it is. Seeing it one last time. Letting it see me. Sound corny?"

"Not at all," I said, wishing, but not saying, there was no place in my life I had to go back to, that I owed a visit or that wanted to see my mug again.

"Think about it," Strauss said. "Where we're standing . . . the A-bomb pits . . . It's the Bethlehem, it's the very manger of American power. Were we ever a bigger deal than when those planes took off from here?"

"I guess not." And it was all downhill from there. Korea, Vietnam and Iraq. These little islands were the top of the world for us, back then. Maybe that was why we'd held on to them. I couldn't think of any other reason.

"So what's your story?" Strauss asked. "Tourist? War buff?"

"No." I turned away and faked an interest in the pillbox, those thick concrete walls, tiny firing apertures. So formidable, so doomed. What a place to wait for the Americans. You'd sit there knowing that you would kill someone at the start, when you opened fire, sure as shooting, but then the distance would narrow and they'd get to you, through the firing holes, the ventilator, around the back, get to you with tanks, bazookas, demolition charges, grenades, flamethrowers.

"Why don't you say it?" Strauss said from behind me.

"Beg your pardon?" I said as I turned to face him.

"Say who you are."

"It's on my name tag," I said. And, for a second, I wondered if he made me out: fugitive financier, on-the-run realtor, et cetera.

"Yeah, I know," he said. "I can read. Mel Brodie the second. Come over here a second."

I walked over to him.

"Down to my level," he said. So I hunkered down in front of him, like I was changing a tire.

"I knew your father," he said. "I knew him well."

And I just stayed there. Then I sat—my legs couldn't take the crouch—and I gazed up at him. He had me and he knew it, a little boy in front of a storyteller.

"I didn't know him at all," I said. "They married right before he left. In a rush. Bad move, maybe."

"I'd call it a good move," Strauss said. "You want me to talk about him?"

"Yes," I said. "A lot."

"Know something? I can say, with absolute certainty, I'll never be back here. An island like this . . . This was my last outing. From now on my world shrinks. A town, a neighborhood. A house. A room. A bed. A box. No getting away from it. That'll be the trend, all right."

I just nodded. No point in jolly-talking him, the best is yet to come, take each day as it arrives. As we sat there, I wondered if life were a day, what time of day was it for me? Ten p.m.? For him? Five minutes before midnight? And then I realized there were all these men who died in the mid-morning, like my father.

"So tell me about him."

"Okay. I was in camp administration. And your father was a navigator. A couple of Jewish guys who'd missed our shot at Hitler. We talked. I was quiet . . . not exactly unpopular . . . but not a regular guy, not the life of the party. Your father was the joker, the card player, a character. Remember Phil Silvers as Sergeant Bilko? He had a lot of that in him."

He stopped and I couldn't tell whether he was deciding to say, or not say, something. When he spoke, it's like the needle jumped out of the groove. My father wasn't in it.

"God, it's hot. These guys today, they're saying to each other, they forgot how hot it was. I never did."

He stopped again and gestured for me to wheel him towards the bus. The vets were getting on board. I helped him, a couple of others did too, and we settled down for the ten-minute ride to the dock and got back on the boat. Was there anyone on board who'd ever be back? No way, I guessed.

The vets watched the island disappear. It fit, I guessed, sailing away into the evening and into what was left of their lives, the darkness ahead. It was one of those situations—like the long plane ride that brought me here—when no one tried resisting sleep. Why bother? It was the best use of your time. The slightest yawn, you closed your eyes and hope you'd fall asleep. What would you be missing? Strauss slept too, like everyone else, with no apologies for keeping me waiting.

So I sat there, just wondering. I wondered, for instance, how my father died. Was it a ball of fire in the air, a second's incineration?

Or a sickening six-mile belly-whopping dive into the sea? Or onto land, maybe. He could have come down over Japan, might even have parachuted and been slaughtered by angry peasants before he untangled himself. Clubs and pitchforks. And maybe—what did I know— he was the kind of old-fashioned Jewish guy who figured that along with his pain and a load of bad luck, there was a measure of justice in it all. Then again, maybe they tied him up and took him to a camp where they worked him to death. It was late, so late, the war was about over and everybody knew it. Was my father the last man to die, August 1945? How long did he hang on? Coughing his lungs out on the eve of V-J Day? Or, oh my God, what about those mad scientist medical experiments on POWs I saw on the History Channel? Human guinea pigs!

I gave up. There were so many ways he could have died. Did it matter, after he'd been dead so long? The distance between the living and the dead—this boatload of survivors and their long-lost buddies—seemed so wide. I took off my name tag and held it. When would I need it again?

"Wear it with pride," Strauss said. He was awake and watching me. I had a feeling he'd been watching me a while.

I nodded but couldn't manage to pin the name card back on. So I tucked it in my pocket.

"A bright, funny guy," he resumed. "Alive. Always up to something. A bet, a proposition. Anyone who knew him would tell you that. But there's stuff they didn't know. He was always wondering. I saw that. Not that we had big conversations about the meaning of it all, or what we'd do after the war, like they have in the movies. I could tell though . . . that wise guy act, Jew-boy joker, was only part of it. I've thought about him more than you would think, over the years. And you know what else?"

He held up for a minute, collecting himself, clearing something that caught in his throat. Then he was back.

"The older I get, the more I think of him, that's all," he said. "More not less. It's not supposed to be that way, is it?"

"I'm not sure 'supposed to' comes into it," I said.

"Any of him in you?"

"Wish I could say," I answered.

"Well, you can't shake his hand," Strauss said. "But you can shake mine." He held it out and I took it. Whatever was wrong with his legs, he had a good grip. And he held on to me for a while. "There you go, young Mel. One degree of separation." He let go of my hand and snapped his fingers. "That's like no separation at all."

Just then I felt the casino boat cut speed as we neared the Saipan dock. I could see a bus in the parking lot and my hotel, farther down the beach. The old-timers started to stir, as anxious as passengers elbowing their way down the aisle of an airplane. It didn't make sense, rushing off into the unknown, the little time they had left. I didn't have much time left to ask Strauss the question I couldn't escape.

"Do you know . . ." I began. "Maybe you don't . . ."

"What's that?" he asked. He sensed something coming. I was sure.

"How far he got?

"Got?" He was making me spell it out.

"That last flight."

"Oh," he said, sighing. "That. Sorry. I guess I can't blame you for wondering."

"Saying somewhere out there," I said, with a vague wave of my hand, "leaves me wondering. Where? How? Was he on the way out or on the way back?"

"Does it matter? Really?"

"Enough for me to ask. Who else is there, can tell me?"

"Okay." He glanced around. The last passengers were crossing in front of us, nodding good-bye as they went. Tomorrow they'd all be on a fifteen-hour plane ride together. But this was it for them.

"I really want to talk," I begged.

Now the driver was standing in the doorway, waving his hands. Strauss gestured for him to leave, gesturing twice, go ahead get out of here, it's okay. Then he asked me where I was staying.

"Down the beach, in the Ginza. Small hotel, apartment style. You?"

"The big deal place. Where that congressman fell. You can push me there. You push, I'll talk. Think you can do it?"

"Not in sand."

"Along the road. It's not so far. Hell, I can see it from here." So I started pushing towards the port gates.

"It's not like I was watching the planes go in and out," Strauss said, "standing on the tarmac counting how many of our birds came back to nest. Sometimes the traffic was almost constant. A plane a minute. So I didn't see. But I heard later . . . about your father . . ."

The evening was a warm, wet blanket. Sit and do nothing, you could enjoy life, which lots of people did. Do something, push a wheelchair say, and you were going to sweat. This was an event in the handicapped Olympics.

"Those B-29s were monsters, right?" Strauss said. "Had to be. Everybody knows that. And of course we lost some, lost them to fighters and antiaircraft guns and weather and all. People know that, too. What's less well-known was that these planes that took off were overloaded and underpowered. Any little glitch, any burp or hiccup in a single engine . . . down they went. Some of them crashed on takeoff . . . a mechanical problem . . . or pilot error. Could be the pilot pulled back too early, before the plane had enough speed for liftoff. I saw them, sometimes they lifted up, bounced down two or three times before they finally made it."

"And my father?" How long, how many times in my life had I asked about him. Thought about him, even?

"He went down right off Tinian. In the water we just went over."

So I had it wrong, for all my imagining. It wasn't a long fall to earth. It was twenty feet or forty. And then, whatever was left of him had miles to sink before landing on the bottom of the Mariana Trench.

"When they hit, skimming the water, the waves peeled off the fuselage . . . like the skin off a banana. Plane usually broke in two, right near the middle. There wasn't a lot of time. The water came in fast. You had to be quick. Lucky, too."

I kept pushing the wheelchair, grateful for something to do while hearing all this. We passed warehouses, a junkyard. We were on an old road, paralleling the main highway, potholed and bordered by weeds. I was working hard, sweating.

"That what you wanted to know?" Strauss asked.

"Pathetic," I said.

"What?"

"He barely got off the ground."

"Jesus Christ on a cross! You know how many missions he was on over Japan? Back and forth? No, you don't. You don't know anything. Do you think he didn't know those planes were overloaded? And he went anyway!"

The way a father shames a son, he shamed me. In a way, my father shamed me, speaking through Strauss.

"I'm sorry," I said. "I'm an asshole." He sat there and didn't contradict me. "I'm the pathetic one." I didn't know if it was true before I said it, but when it came out it was right on the money.

"Well," Strauss relented. "You made it here." He thought I'd come here for my father's sake. I didn't correct him. "You got as close as you can get. That's something."

We passed mountains of empty shipping containers. Saipan was using more than it produced, from the looks of things. Shipping containers were supposed to be an economic indicator: the more empties around, the worse off you were. Only here they'd probably argue it was good news, taking more than you were making.

My sweat felt good, there was a breeze, and a little color in the night sky. Now we were close to the ocean, I could feel it, smell it, broad-leafed swampy plants and thickets of brush and that sewer smell you get at low tide, when the water recedes and the lagoon shows you its ugly bottom. We came to a marina, lots of boats with dumb, cute names. Three things you should never buy: a boat, a swimming pool and a second home. Then we were in the Memorial Park, among grassy lawns, sunburned, on a winding sidewalk meant for joggers and bicyclists during the day, and for a wheelchair solo in the dark. The amphitheater was empty, the museum was closed, the wall of names—fallen soldiers, unlucky locals—was unattended. But the invasion beach was there, long-needled pine trees that reminded me of weeping willows and soft, powdery sand on a user-friendly beach. Out beyond the reef were the waters that swallowed my father. A tiny island, a tropical beach, a warm lagoon; it felt like the wrong place for a battle.

As we neared the lobby, a bellboy rushed out to help us. I motioned for him to stop.

"Mr. Strauss . . ."

"Yes?"

"Thanks."

"I feel good about this," he said. "We made a connection . . . a real long shot, if you think about it. Good luck, Mel."

"Same to you," I said.

"Yeah," he said, not kidding himself about the kind of luck that he'd be having.

◊

Next morning I got to work. I stepped out to the hotel parking lot, the taxi drivers' hangout, a couple of benches where they sat and slept. You didn't hustle fares in this place, you waited for work to show up, and waiting for work was the same as working. There they were, chatting, reading newspapers, snoozing. Okay, I asked if any one of them was from Saipan. No such luck, they were all Manila's finest. Then I asked who had been on the island the longest. Now it got interesting, a jump ball leading to a prolonged scramble. Did a stay on Saipan that was interrupted by two years back in the Philippines count? Or was it continuous service I was looking for? They were terrific, in a hang-around-the-barbershop-and-bullshit kind of way. Would I define my terms? Did *jeepney* driving back home count? And if someone were married to a local woman, did that make him "from Saipan"? I finally pointed to a guy who said he'd been on Saipan for fifteen years.

"Okay," I said, "you know this island, right?"

"Very well, sir. Many years."

"Every road?"

"Yes, sir. Not so hard."

"That's what I want."

"You are wanting what?"

"Every road."

"To drive?"

"If I wanted to walk it, I wouldn't be over here."

"Okay," he said, a provisional agreement, shaded by misgiving and depending on money.

"We'll take our time," I said. "I want you to tell me what you know about what I see. The names of things. The story behind them. Got that? I'm not looking for a driver. I'm looking for a guide."

"Driver and guide," he repeated. He liked the sound of that.

"Don't care how long it takes. If we run late, there's always tomorrow." Just then, I could feel our average miles per hour sharply dropping.

"Okay," he said.

"What's your price for this? Off the meter, of course."

"Off the meter, certainly," he agreed. "It breaks all the time, my meter. Sometimes she goes slow, sometimes she goes fast." The beginnings of a dirty joke in there someplace, I sensed.

"So . . . how much?"

"You pay me what you wish, sir," he answered, gambling that I'd overpay him.

"All right then," I said. "I wish to pay you one hundred dollars . . . per day."

"But, sir." An automatic protest, for the record.

"That's for the driving. Another hundred for what you tell me about this island, along the way. And if that's not enough, I'll talk to your friends."

"Not necessary." he answered. "Please, sir, come this way." As he led me away he shouted something to his buddies. This was one of those times I wished I knew the language, not that Filipino-speak appealed to me. Cori and Lourdes did just fine in English. Had he told his buddies what he was getting? Understated it, so they wouldn't hit him up? Overstated it?

"Please, sir," he said, opening the back door.

I opened the front. On a seat where you'd expect to find newspapers and fast food containers, there sat a black leather valise, like a businessman would carry into negotiations. He reached over and slipped it under his seat.

"Not what I'd expect from a taxi driver."

"I do many business, sir," he said. "All kinds. What is your name, sir?"

"Mel Brodie."

"And yours?"

"Call me Gregorio," he answered, offering me his hands and a friends-forever smile.

The Master Blaster

❡

The island was in trouble, more every day. Half-empty hotels, shuttered apartment buildings, tenant-free shopping centers, closed restaurants, gas through the roof, car sales declining, government cutbacks and lay-offs, garment factories in trouble, power outages at random and, just lately, thefts of copper wire from buildings, building sites, power stations. The copper wire thing—that was telling. It was as if termites had taken over the building, animals crept out of a forest to pick over the remains of an abandoned city.

The Master Blaster was sitting in his chair, at night, cognac and cigar in hand, trying to sort out his own feelings about hard times. His web site audience might picture him gloating, all filled with schadenfreude. But his feelings were mixed. You didn't like to see people broke, jobless, clueless. That went for puzzled locals and it went double for the thousands of foreigners who'd come here, and paid heavily, for the chance to work on American soil, to save and send money home. He felt for them, all right. But there was something else in him, more righteous, less generous: they had it coming. What goes up must come down. That was physics. What goes up *should* come back down. That was justice.

It started in the mid seventies, when Saipan and the other Northern Marianas pulled out of the old Micronesian Trust Territory and cut a deal with the United States to become a U.S. Commonwealth. With the stroke of a pen, this small far place became as American as California or Virginia, its people U.S. citizens, with no waiting in line, no sojourn to Ellis Island, no voyage or flight anywhere. U.S. citizenship, home delivered, halfway around the world. No civics classes, no language or history tests, no hand-raising oaths. It was as if the cable TV guy had delivered one hundred channels at no charge.

The Americans did it for military reasons, the islanders did it because it was the easy thing, possibly the only thing. Who else to connect with but the wealthiest nation on the planet? Until then, the island was a quiet, left-behind place; fifteen thousand people working for the government, fishing a little, farming on weekends. Then the money rolled in. The war claims—$16 million from the U.S.—were the first bonanzas. They were for losses, a palm tree or a parent, during the battle. Later there was $16 million for "post secure losses," private property turned into airfields and highways. Suddenly there were wealthy people on the island. And more arriving all the time. With Commonwealth status came a land boom, hotels along the beach, garment factories inland, and the soon outnumbered Saipanese were left clinging to their government as their sole source of employment, a life raft. What a raft, what a life!

Bangladeshi farmers working for eighty dollars a month. People on food stamps hiring Filipino maids. Politicians on fact-finding trips to Manila's red-light district, hungover government entourages all over the world. The old military highways, already the best in the Pacific, widened and repaved. Stoplights blossomed, traffic thickened. An old World War II airstrip, Isely Field, mutated into an international airport with an air-conditioned terminal and duty-free shops. There were franchise foods— Subway, McDonald's, Hard Rock Cafe—franchise stores—Costco, Athlete's Foot—and a new multiplex theater edged out the old rattletrap that could be counted on for X-rated films, nicknamed Mickey Mouse, on Saturday night. A casino on Tinian, a nest of massage parlors and girlie bars in the Ginza, lawyers, speculators, tax evaders and suddenly rich land-leasing locals. Palaces claimed high ground, hilltops and ridges all over the island, Southern mansions, Japanese pagodas, Tuscan villages, Rhineland castles, vitality, variety and vulgarity without limit. What a spectacular place! A version of America, created overnight, a kingdom of golf, gambling, garments and government. So when had it happened, the turning point, the tipping point, when good times gave in to the bad. Whose fault was it? Arab oil sheikhs? Fickle tourists? Opportunistic airlines? Predatory investors? Was it everyone in general and no one in particular? Did failure come from outside, or arise within? It wasn't murder, what had happened here. It was suicide. And suicides rarely had a single cause. Things came together, all sorts of big and little things. Death was overdetermined. Was it true that the Japanese were pulling out because when the Emperor visited this solemn battleground, the governor showed up late, wearing an aloha shirt and sandals?

It was cigar time now. Traffic on his web site was slow, plenty of hits but not many messages. And not much for him to say. It was less fun being scathing, now that times were bad. To combat his view of Saipan, a group was proposing an iluvsaipan.com He planned to attend their first meeting. Life was complicated, island life doubly so, and he was sure he wanted to be counted among Saipan's lovers. And it had been love at first sight, back in the sixties. Oh, how he remembered those tin-roofed schools, suffocatingly hot, full of big-eyed kids with a million lessons to learn. Some lessons they'd learned, some they hadn't. When the Trust Territory stumbled towards closure, The Master Blaster had hoped that this late in the game, the islanders would learn from history—Hawaii, Guam, Tahiti. He'd hoped that old mistakes would not be repeated.

He stared towards the airport, at the tip of the islands. These nights there was something about the red and white lights, blinking hopefully, distress signals, pleading for help. Where from? Now it came to him. An idea that appalled and then seduced him. At first he rejected it, as if the very notion had come from someone else, not from him. It wouldn't go away, though. He had thought of Saipan as a place that trailed American history, an afterthought. What came now felt truer. Saipan was an omen, a harbinger, a sign of things to come in America itself. When he sorted it out, it came to this. Long after the United States had been completed, its character set, its frontiers confirmed, this one little straggling exception had been admitted: the invited guest who had traveled farthest to the feast. A mosquito buzzed his ears—time to go to bed now, it whispered, or else—but he swiped it away impatiently. He was on to something. Saipan was America in extremis and in miniature, an America at the end of the world. And—could it be?—Saipan's history repeated America's, but in a speeded-up way. Saipan had been an undiscovered land, a colony, three times, like the U.S., then an outlying territory and now an outright, permanent part of America. They'd had conquests, slavery, near genocide and mass conversion, then a war. Not a civil war, not quite, but they'd been civilians, caught in the crossfire. In the eighties, they'd had their gilded age, fat cat robber barons, mass immigration, corrupt politics. Now they were in their depression, praying to Washington politicians, praying to Las Vegas and Macao gamblers, praying to the Pentagon. Now what? Depression and then what? Would they re-peat the Eisenhower fifties, the tumult of the sixties and seventies? He doubted it. At first Saipan recapitulated the course of U.S. history. Now, in its downward trajectory, it was leading. A cutting edge of failure, a precedent-setting flop. What came here was headed back across to the U.S. Here's looking at you! It might be here, right here, that America's future arrived just as, the local paper said, America's day began here. And afternoon. And night.

Night. He'd meant to work on the web page. A halfhearted prom-ise. But it was hard to keep up with the bad news in the newspapers. He stepped into the tool shed one last time. It was a quirk, his last peek. His life was full of quirks. The cigar and the mosquitoes, standing in a trop-ical rain as if in a shower, soaping and rinsing outside, and the way he drove around the north end of the island on moonlit nights, with his headlights off. Now . . . how like underground fighters in occupied France . . . he stepped into his office for that last look at his computer.

Master Blaster—My name is George Griffin and I'm a writer—a travel columnist, pretty well known—and I've been on Saipan for a while. The place fascinates me, in a way that has nothing to do with my column. The fascination is about you, about the kind of writing you do, the chance that you are the kind of writer I am not, and I want to meet you. I've heard people speculate about who you are. Lots of suggestions and, because I'm new here, I have no way of knowing whether they are on the money or way off base. It's not even clear whether you are on the island now or way out of range, safe and far away. That would not sur-prise me. But I suspect you are here. And I want very much to meet you, in any way, and at any place or time that you feel com-fortable. All the best—George Griffin

So the travel agent he'd crossed paths with at the Hyatt was a word-smith, "pretty well known." It wasn't the first time someone had asked to meet him. Behind compliments, vehement enthusiasm, he sensed an ef-fort to unmask him. But this George Griffin message felt different. It wasn't so much an effort to learn his name as a desire to know him, maybe be like him. It was interesting, flattering, tantalizing.

The Master Blaster sat at his keyboard, realizing that he'd been waiting for someone like this Griffin to come along eventually. Part of him, only a part, wanted to take a chance. The other part knew he might regret it. What to do? He was tired of his master blasting. So many bad things had come true. What more was there to say: I told you so? Meanwhile, what about this Griffin? He leaned forward. This, he told himself, is a mistake I have to make: "I'll think about it," he wrote.

George Griffin

❦

Drive north from the main tourist district and the clutter thins out. Sure, you were never out of range of gasoline, cold beer or a place to gamble on poker machines. But there were some not-yet-built-upon stretches along the shoreline, grassy meadows and clumps of palm that hadn't given birth to a Korean or Chinese or Japanese joint venture, and you hoped it stayed that way, that the world's appetite for resorts and golf courses isn't, like the appetite for pornography, infinite. Three weeks on Saipan and somehow I was feeling proprietary. And I was looking for a place to stay.

Cruising along with the windows open and the air-conditioning on—the best of all possible worlds—I had noticed a startling tangle of vines and blossoms crawling over a lava rock wall, a blitz of red and orange and pink which reconfirmed the old rule that, in nature, unlike in clothing, colors don't clash. This was the Pacific Holiday Resort and we turned in the driveway, into a parking lot that was empty, except for a crew of gardeners installing some palms and orchids outside the main entrance.

Nothing was happening in the lobby. No one at the front desk. The souvenir shop was closed and the dining room was empty. Music was coming out of the kitchen, but not the smell of food.

I walked out the back and it wasn't bad at all. There was a conventionally irregular swimming pool, like a pancreas or a kidney. My theory was that they avoided rectangular pools to keep guests from feeling that they ought to swim laps. They were on vacation! Behind the pool, not more than twenty sandy feet away, was the Philippine Sea, empty, too.

Back at the desk, I pushed a bell. I shouted. No one came. I stepped out into the parking lot and leaned on my horn, first in beep-beep pattern, the way you do when you're stuck in traffic. Then I tried one long blast, like you might hear from a ship in a fogbank. Just as I gave up, I saw someone come into the lobby.

"Is there something the matter?" he asked. The guy had on a jacket with a badge that identified him as Wilfredo, but that was where the uniform ended. He wore shorts and sandals.

"No, nothing wrong," I said. Did he think my car was acting up? "Actually, I was interested in the hotel."

"Yes?"

"In staying here."

"Oh."

I could see his confusion.

"Why?" he asked.

"May I have a look? See a room, maybe?"

"Maybe so," he allowed. He led me into the lobby and stepped behind the desk. Installed there, he asked if I had a reservation. This meant he was part of that brotherhood of waiters and maître d's who survey an empty dining room, no one in sight, a neutron bomb might have been dropped, yet they ask about a reservation.

"No reservation," I confessed. "Does it matter?" I saw Wilfredo make a show of riffling through a pile of papers, faxes, forms, flowcharts.

"Ocean view? Or mountain?" They never quite know what to call the cheap side of a hotel, the one that overlooks the parking lots.

"Ocean view. Top floor."

"Oh, sir, the elevator is not working."

"Are the stairs working?"

"Yes." The stairs were working. Not Wilfredo. He had business at the front desk, he said. He handed me a room key and pointed me to a door that said EMERGENCY and I began my climb.

The room, when I got to it, suited me fine. Musty but comfortable, and the more I considered it, the more I liked living like a castaway in a derelict hotel, like Miss Havisham in *Great Expectations* or Jack Nicholson in *The Shining* or maybe one of those people in *On the Beach*, watching post-nuclear radiation take the population of Australia from many to some to none. Just then, I found the place appealing.

"It's perfect!" I exclaimed when I came back downstairs.

Wilfredo was startled. "Sir, our restaurant is closed."

"For the day?"

"For the . . . longer."

"Okay by me. I saw you had a coffee maker upstairs and a little refrigerator. That'll come in handy. I like to eat out, anyway."

"We have no lifeguard at the swimming pool."

"No problem. I'll swim at my own risk. Sign something, too . . . release you from all responsibility." At that moment, unbidden, the memory of a Texas congressman bleeding into a swimming pool came back to me.

"No room service, sir . . . those steps."

"Great exercise. No room service . . . no matter."

"Well." Wilfredo looked over what appeared to be a list of room rates that, I was sure, dated from happier times. It was something he hadn't studied lately. I saw his finger tracing columns of numbers, like some girlfriends of mine, reading menus from right to left, first the price and then the food. Wilfredo, like my flames, settled on the highest number he could find, which was $270 per night. When he quoted it, he seemed sure I'd be back in my car in no time.

"The thing is," I persisted, "I am planning a long-term stay. At least a month. Do you have a rate for long-term stays? Surely . . ."

"Wait," Wilfredo said, addressing himself to a pocket calculator. He came up with a startling figure.

"Did you say $8,100?" I asked. "All you did was take 270 and multiply it by 30. What kind of rate is that? The hotel's half shut down. I have to walk up five floors, and there's no food."

"I do not have authority for discounts."

"We're not authorized to shit, my friend. Still, we do." Now I knew for sure that the place was dead or dying. That made it more appealing. Appealing, appalling, they came together nicely.

"Is there a supervisor in this hotel? A manager?" This was when I expected him to shrug and report that someone, somewhere, was not available and maybe if I came back later.

"Yes, supervisor." From out of a back office, through a curtain, an old Japanese man emerged, wearing shirt, shoes and sandals, with dirt on his hands. "Why do you want to stay here?"

"It's simple. I'm a writer. I like a quiet place to work. And this place is plenty quiet."

"Ah . . ." He nodded.

"And I liked your gardening. The flowers in front . . . they made me come inside."

"Bougainvillea," he said, carefully. The word didn't come easy to him. Then he turned to Wilfredo. "This man can stay for fifty dollars." Then he nodded my way. "Enjoy your stay."

"Excuse me," I called out. "What is your name?"

"Saito," he responded.

"From Japan?"

"Yes," he said. "And no. Japanese father, Saipan mother. Born here, 1942."

"So you came home?"

"Yes," he said. "Home."

"No place like it," I said. Not true, I told myself. And, if true, not good.

Saito didn't respond. He nodded a little.

❦

I moved in that afternoon and the first thing I did, once I unpacked, was to walk out onto the terrace, from which I saw Saito step through a gate in a fence that surrounded a grove of trees, just in from the beach. He was in the same shorts he'd worn earlier. He had that wiry, muscular, bowlegged look you see in Japanese old men. If they'd had milk on this island when he was a youngster, he may have stood six feet tall. He noticed me—hard to miss the only paying guest. He gestured at me with a hoe he was carrying. Come on down.

This trip better be worth it, I told myself, wondering how many round-trips I'd be making every day. I counted on the way down: 124 steps. When I stepped out into the late afternoon, I found him in the garden.

"Take look." He opened the gate and, as soon as I stepped through, I sensed all kinds of changes. There were crushed coral paths winding through flower beds, lots of orchids, and behind a hedge of croton and hibiscus was a grove of trees and shrubs. He had roses growing between rows of strawberries, underneath mangoes. The soil was dark, like humus, that had nothing to do with the sand and clay outside.

"I love fruit," Saito said. "I try to have many fruit." It was Noah's

Ark, two of each kind, coconuts, mangoes, mangosteens, soursops, papaya, mountain apple, lychees, loquats, rambutan, oranges, lemons (sour and sweet) and half a dozen kinds of bananas. It was a shaded, orderly, sweet-smelling place with benches under some of the trees. Apart from gesturing for me to look this way and that, Saito said nothing. The place spoke for itself.

"You like?"

"A lot," I said. "Do you lock it at night?"

"Must. Boys come. Take what they want. They see me coming, they laugh. They take one bite, throw on the ground. Leave cigarettes and beer cans. I come out, they say, Go to hell old man, this our island. Now I lock." He pointed to some thin wires running from just above the ground to eight feet. Electric. It made the place look like a kennel.

"Why did you make this garden? Why do you keep at it when . . ." I motioned at the hotel where just one room on the fifth floor, mine, showed signs of life, a towel hung out to dry and a pair of shorts. On every other terrace, the curtains were closed, the place was empty. It was like a post office where only one box holder had gotten mail that day, or week, or month.

"I do it for me," he said. He paused, not quite done. "Some people come small island, they build boat. I plant garden." It sounded, just then, like a profound distinction.

He locked the gate and we walked back to the hotel. How had he landed here in a hotel like this? Was it punishment, a Siberia where they sent you when you screwed up someplace else? Had the place succeeded before it failed, or flat lined from day one? How long before they called it quits?

❦

Hardly anybody knew me on Saipan. There was Mr. Saito, Big Ben and Stephanie Warner, out at the College of the Islands. In my first weeks, I was in no rush to announce my presence, to make new friends. Take it slow, I told myself. Don't come at the island, let the island come at you. Then I remembered one more person. That Russian girl. I had a hunch we'd meet again. I didn't have to look for her. Our paths would cross. And I looked forward to it. I wondered what it would be like, whoop of recognition and a hug? I had done her a favor, no reward attached. Or would it be a cold-eyed appraisal. What did I want, what could she get? That would disappoint me: she seemed nicer than that. Much nicer, the little adventuress. For sure. I knew better, of course I did, but I felt a kind of connection with the Russian Valley Girl. I had a name, a reputation, a clutch of credit cards and an expense account. She had none of those. And I couldn't help wondering what it took for her to test fortune on an indifferent, half-American island.

I woke up at first light, something new for me, and walked along the beach, drove around, shopped, drank coffee here and there. I learned fast not to mess with the middle of the day. From ten to four you needed to be indoors, air-conditioned, or at least in the shade. So there were siestas, reading from a shelf of hotel left-behinds, most were in Japanese, but *Salem's Lot* was waiting for me. I read both local newspapers, beginning to end. There was a crisis, not just in the hotel but on the whole island. That interested me. After the heat subsided, I walked, later jogged, and when I came home at dusk, I used my key into Saito's garden, turned on the hose and showered and watered at the same time. In that moment, in that place I was happy. But I wondered how long it would last.

"Excuse me. Hey, anybody home?" A voice from outside interrupted us, Saito and me, watching the sunset out in back of the hotel.

"Hello? Company's here . . ."

I wondered if I'd sounded like that the first time I visited. For sure, the voice outside belonged to an American.

Saito nodded at me as if to say, sorry, over now, thank you.

"How you doin', sir?" I heard the visitor say. "My name's Mel Brodie."

"Yes, sir. Saito."

"I hear there's a hotel for sale around here. Could this be it?"

"A moment," Saito said. He turned to me. "You do not want to hear this."

"No, I don't," I said. "Thanks." On my way back to my room, I passed a short American guy, the hair receding on his head but growing robustly on his forearms, rioting out of his eyebrows and fighting its way out from under the top of the undershirt he wore beneath his aloha wear. He had the kind of old-fashioned Jewish nose you don't see as much as you used to: was that gene receding or was cosmetic surgery winning out?

"Mel Brodie," he said, offering a hand. "How's it going?"

"Going good," I answered. "George Griffin. I just moved here."

"Remember me? From the plane?"

"Sure do," I said, walking away rudely. Sometimes, it's as if the obligation to be nice to fellow Americans is suspended as soon as you leave the country. That can be a good thing.

One night I went looking for the Russian girl. Business or pleasure? Maybe both. Moscow Nights was a good place to begin. Neon lights, droning air conditioner and a sign advertising happy hours that went past midnight. A lot of tourist district places had women standing in doorways. Glance up at the second story and you saw the A-team looking down. And though it was all about money, you sensed that the old dream still flickered, for Madame Butterfly, World of Suzie Wong, Miss Saigon. Mr. Right coming to the rescue. Moscow Nights had no such enticement. It felt, from the outside, like a members-only club.

First I sensed the air-conditioning. It was like I'd jumped into a swimming pool. It was crisp, it was sweater weather. The place was darkly lit, with couches and sofas scattered in semi-darkness, cozy and confidential. In back of the room a woman languorously wrapping herself around a pole, to the sound of "Do It to Me One More Time." She didn't acknowledge me. Behind the bar sat an older woman, an emeritus hostess. After she served me a drink, she walked away towards the end of the bar, where three other women were sitting quietly. I guessed they were checking me out. Around the room, every now and then, I heard low voices, scraps of laughter. I sensed motion. But I couldn't see much. Most places, they swarmed you, hello, what's your name, buy me a drink. Here they let me alone. I just sat there, taking a not more than offhand interest in the pole dancer, which exceeded her interest in me.

"Would you like to talk to someone?" the boss lady finally asked.

"That would be nice."

"You know who you like?"

"My first time here."

"You want to look?" She turned towards the end of the bar. The girls were stirring. "You decide. Up to you."

"I'm sure they're all fine," I said, and it wasn't politeness. I could see them. Blonde amazons, ice-skaters, ballerinas with handsome, cold faces. "Tell you what," I said. "Give me the one who speaks the best English."

"Galina!" she called out. "You will like Galina," she told me. "She is college lady." Galina approached, tall, blonde and—how to put it?—capable. Of all sorts of things, I was sure.

"You want good English?" Galina said. "Try my English?"

We repaired to a little alcove, drinks in front of us, mine a scotch and hers . . . well, I didn't know what. Expensive. That was okay. No more than fair. I saw her appraising me, the way I appraised any place I wrote about. What did I need, what would it take, how much time and effort. The same calculations.

"So, okay," she said. "We talk. What is your choice of subject?"

"Saipan. What are you doing here?"

"You must clarify," she corrected me. "Do you mean what I am doing, working, performing et cetera, et cetera? Or how did I come to Saipan?"

"Both," I said. Sex was in the neighborhood, no doubt about it. The way she folded her legs underneath her as she curled up on the couch, the way she leaned towards me when she spoke, the way her fingers touched my arm. Artful, subtle, and if I'd named an act and a price, it would have happened without delay. But that wasn't the whole story. She had a wised-up smile, just like Larissa, a leisurely pace; slow dance or fast, it was my call. So she told me about a university degree in literature, an escape from a place I'd never heard of, training as a pianist, no way of telling if it was true or she changed her autobiography nightly. Saipan wasn't so bad, she said, she liked the weather and the beaches. Then she got curious about me and I told her I was a writer, a sort of reporter, a world-traveler, and at some point she must have guessed that I wasn't interested, at least not right away, in sex. Did that mean I was more than the other men who came in? Or much less.

"Is there a girl who works here who calls herself Larissa?" I asked.

"You know Larissa?" She was surprised and not in a nice way. Professional jealousy? Or something else? "Where you know her?"

"I met her around the Hyatt a while ago."

"You do business?"

"Like I do business with you," I countered. "We talked."

"Excuse," she said. She stood up, without waiting for acknowledgment, and walked off, without a backward glance. I hoped she'd come back arm and arm with Larissa, the Russian Valley Girl. I decided to throw "for sure" into my greeting. But what came out of a door behind the bar was a guy you've seen in any film involving the Russian mob: black leather jacket, tight denim trousers, shaved head.

"You come," he said. We went out the door. The air was warm and full of night smells, gasoline and barbecue smoke and sea air, and some kind of perfume, whether it came off tropical flowers or exotic hookers, I couldn't say. But I was glad to be outside. There was a limit to what could happen to me in public, I thought.

"Look in my eyes," said the Russian. "What do you see?"

Hostility? Bestiality? Evolution in reverse? Oh, he was a cliché and writers have fun with them. But not tonight. "Seriousness," I said.

"Yes. Now tell me how you know Larissa."

"We met at the Hyatt. She stayed in my room awhile. I guess there was a problem with a customer. So I let her in. And we talked. I liked her. I wondered how she was doing."

"This night at the Hyatt. That night, did anything else happen? Anything?"

"I know what you mean. The congressman in the swimming pool."

He nodded. Right answer, I guessed. "And you're a writer. And you want to find Larissa. To talk some more." He moved towards me. We were face to face, his hands were on my shoulder. "You don't come to this place again."

"Okay." What a tiny voice I had. I was that close to a seven-year-old kid whose next line would be, Can I go now?

"You don't look for Larissa. No questions."

"She isn't here?"

"That's a question," he said with a sigh, like a patient teacher confronting a student who'd given a wrong answer. He stepped back. I didn't see it coming, a knee that caught me right where it hurt the most, the kind of shot that causes instant astonishing pain, but you know that's only the beginning because it's going to get worse, much worse, before it's over. I folded onto the ground, paralyzed, and all I could do was curl up on the sidewalk and wait, and wait. Wait to inhale. I couldn't. For at least a minute. Then I managed a shallow breath. I rolled over onto my hands and knees. I got to my feet and started walking towards the Hyatt parking lot, where I'd left my car. I was a hundred years old. A ten-minute walk took half an hour, past girly bars, convenience stores, late-night restaurants. Lots of bright lights, but there were patches of darkness, too, shut-down night clubs, boarded up buildings, some out of business, others walked away from in mid-construction, with piles of sand and broken rubble and rusted rebar all around, tangles of weeds and brush. This was the other side of the paradise. And here I was. Mr. *Faraway Places, Backyard Adventures*. With every step my Moscow Nights adventure got a little sad. Or funny. Was I a sucker for punishment? Was it punishment for a sucker? I wondered what was happening to me here. And, go figure, I wondered about the Russian girl. About comparing notes on Saipan. And comparing pains.

Stephanie Warner

❡

"Let's talk about discovery," I propose. "What does the word *discovery* mean to you?"

They sit before me, some who can answer, some who can't. They have one thing in common: their silence.

"It's not such a hard question," I say in mild reproof. "The discovery of a new species? A new planet? A new singer? The discovery of America? Of Saipan?"

The Russian girl, Galina, she could speak, if she wanted. She drops by my office. She tells me I am a candidate for a makeover. I can feel her checking me out, my hair, makeup, dress and shoes. And there are some stylish Chinese women who work in high-end tourist shops, they could give me a makeover, too. I see intelligence on their faces. But such shyness! Cultural restraint? A couple of American kids, acting like laid-back islanders, a German and a Filipino, a half dozen Saipanese, two of them nuns, a woman from Nepal, an Italian whose husband is a hotel chef, a scattering of kids from far-off islands, Palau, Chuuk, Pohnpei. Was America like this once? Is it now?

"All right then," I say. "You have all made discoveries. Today I make a discovery myself. I discover that you don't want to talk. And now I have a discovery in mind for you. It is called a pop quiz . . . in which you take the things that you don't feel like saying aloud and you convert them to writing on a piece of paper which I will collect and grade. It's your choice. Talk to me or write to me. Now I'm going to look out the window for a moment."

Nonchalant, I walk over to the side of the classroom and glance out at the parking lot. The morning cool has been blasted away, and we are crossing through a desert that lasts until four in the afternoon. I see my red Nissan out there, windows down, but I know the steering wheel and gear shift are a pair of branding irons this time of day.

I turn. Almost half the class has hands up and all of them are smiling. The Russian, Galina, actually winks at me as if to say, "You go, girl!" And we begin to talk about what it means to discover something, and what it means to be discovered.

❧

I love it mostly but when I don't love it, I hate it. I'll be specific. I like the idea of teaching students who are passionate about education, in a way that was way out of style at the costly liberal arts college that employed me. And I like the idea of running such a place. Gifted and talented as my students were back home, they were entitled. Entitled to be challenged, to accept that challenge, or not, to work hard or hardly.

I like my students. They can't read or write half as well as the ones I left behind, they don't raise their hands much, and when I call on them, they giggle, flush, panic. They're new to a college classroom and strangers to each other. A mini America here, a class attendance list full of tongue-twisting names.

So we discuss discovery and the discovered, in the United States, in the Pacific, from Hawaii to Tahiti to Saipan. Thank God for xerox places that ask no awkward questions about copyright. I've excerpted explorers' narratives, histories, historical novels and anthropological testimony, a couple of hundred dollars out of my own pocket. That's for one course. There's another course on minorities in the U.S., from melting pot to salad bowl, European immigration, slave narratives, more recent Asian and Hispanic stories, from Cahan to Puzo to Amy Tan, with time out for viewings of *America, America, The Joy Luck Club* and *El Norte*.

It interests me. Will it interest them? I can't say. Does that Russian girl need to know all this? That Chuukese youth? Would a course in basic English composition and conversation serve them better? Is that what it comes down to? Perfecting their English so they can lead a tour group, or chat up customers, or sit comfortably in an air-conditioned office? Well, like it or not, they'll be getting more. And so, I hope, will I.

❧

It's the oddest friendship I've ever had, this business with George Griffin. What began with a random comment—"What are you doing here? Witness protection program?"—led to his dropping by the campus. First he found me on my bench, between classes, later he sat in back of my classroom. He's substitute teaching and some colleagues in English are talking about having him do a writing workshop.

If he left tomorrow, which he won't, I'd remember him as a companion to my discovery—there's that arrogant, inevitable word—of Saipan. We both realized that Saipan wasn't the kind of place that you mastered in a day: been there, seen it, done it. It was too big, but it was more than a matter of size. It was the character of the place, its variety and density and mystery. Everywhere you went, there were side roads, dead ends, turns and loops, tracks that became trails. We had maps of the island, and on weekends we explored. Around the international airport, within earshot of takeoffs and landings, swallowed in thickets of brush and woods, we found a Japanese headquarters, with office buildings, hospitals, bunkers and revetments. Just below the peak of Mount Tapochau were the remnants of a coffee plantation. On the north end there were caves, natural and military, and mysterious foundations left behind from CIA days. And here and there, along an otherwise rocky and forbidden coastline, were tiny beaches which, so it felt, we were the first to . . . damn it all . . . *discover.*

It was good natured, amiable, relaxed, all of it, yet after a few weeks I wondered when he would make a move on me. Or I on him. We'd spent so much time together, hiking, climbing, sweating. We'd slogged through fields of mud, swatted our way through a maze of branches, hoisted each other around rocks and yet, after any number of entangled, complicated, potentially intimate situations, nothing had happened. We both surely knew that a remote location invited flings, carefree and closed-ended. But in our case, the opposite was true. The past made us more careful; we did not want to repeat old mistakes. I understood that. And regretted it a little, too. I have seldom been without a man for very long.

Then, one afternoon, we went for a run down to Lau Lau Beach, a place we'd only heard of. Waiting until late afternoon, we parked off the main road, next to a bus shelter, and began a slow downhill jog to a place neither of us had ever been. That discovery thing again. Dense brush and trees leaned in from both sides of the road, pressing towards the center, growing, it seemed, out of walls of broken rocks. The island never let you forget that it had been bombed and burned. We passed an old Quonset hut, unpainted wood, badly weathered metal, warped doors, rusted, torn screens—not everyone was wealthy here—and, after that, a pistachio-colored apartment building where Filipinos drank bottles of beer and probed under the hood of a pickup truck. That was the last house. The way downhill got steeper, the road was washed out, more like a streambed that flooded and dried, season to season. Saipan closed in on us, ferns and breadfruit, tangan-tangan brush, so that it was as though we were running through a tunnel where we had to place every foot carefully, lest we go, as the columnist put it, ass over elbows. We passed a driveway that led to an abandoned building—a restaurant, we later learned. A yellow jeep was parked near the bottom of the driveway, and someone had climbed up the broken driveway, maybe a realtor or investor, maybe an insurance man. Now he stood in front of the restaurant photographing the place. He quickly turned away from us, as if he was embarrassed to be discovered there, and stepped into a yellow Volkswagon. Was he a former owner? Potential buyer? Grieving customer?

Suddenly, the downhill turned gentle and we came out of the shade, into a zone of afternoon sunlight. We could see the ocean down below, the line of white caps on the reef, turning gold now. We picked up speed; the wind, the road, everything was on our side. We stopped when we came to the beach. Not a word said, we left the road and went down to the water's edge. Above the waterline, flowering vines that looked like morning glory shared the sand with pine trees, picnic tables and barbecue pits. Way down the beach, a couple of men were casting nets. It was a magic time and place; every now and then the island matched the hopes you had for it, the dream you had. That's when I felt Griffin's arm around my shoulder.

"Thanks," he said.

"What for?"

"All these outings," he said. "I wouldn't have done them on my own. Getting lost and found, all over Saipan. Suddenly, I like it here. I liked it from the start but I never thought I'd . . . hang around."

"I like it, too," I said. With so much to complain about, and I heard lots of complaints, it came out like a confession. Was it Lau Lau or Saipan? Was it a feeling that might last or was it connected to a lucky afternoon? We both knew better. We had no illusions about island paradises, Bali-Hai style, least of all on beat-up Saipan. But there was still part of us, the kid that never grows up, that felt drawn to tropical islands.

❦

"Mr. Rosales needs to see you," Bernadette Diaz said, standing in, all but blocking, the entrance to a classroom where my students waited, waited noisily. It pleased me, they were kidding around, even if at my expense. In this group, a cheat sheet passed from hand to hand would be a giant step. Caring enough to cheat.

"Well, I'd be happy to meet him." I couldn't help wondering what mistake I'd made, who had complained. "What about?"

"I can't say. Very important."

"I'll come right after class," I said. I was already late.

"He . . . is . . . waiting . . . now . . . for . . . you," she said.

I gestured inside to a gang of students who'd been struggling with Melville's *Typee* all week—how many zones, how many light years were we from *Moby-Dick*? "They have been waiting also."

❦

I'd been in the president's office just once, because Ken was committed to chat with newcomers. It was important that we get together, stay on the same page, remember that the door was always open. Now the door was open, the desk was clean, and he was gone.

"Ken Simpson has resigned," Henry Rosales said.

"That was sudden," I said.

"Sudden to you," he answered. "It was . . . to others . . . easy to see coming."

"When's he leaving? I'm sure people would like to say good-bye." It sounded vacuous.

"He's already left," Rosales said. "On the way back to, was it Arizona? New Mexico?"

"Why did he leave?"

"Nothing unpleasant. It was more a difference of opinion, about what the college is, and needs to be."

"Oh, I see." But one of the things I didn't see was why I needed to be told this. Surely there'd be a faculty assembly, before the day was out. I wondered, too, how Ken Simpson would have managed to say no to anyone. He was an affable, malleable fellow, a Mr. Rogers who must have wandered out of his neighborhood. Did he have any idea what he was getting into?

"You're the first person, outside of the regents and Bernadette, who knows."

"Do I need to know . . . first?"

"Perhaps. Dr. Warner, I saw this conflict coming. It was easy to see. No hard feelings, I wish my friend Ken all the best. And I am sure he has the same wish for the College of the Islands."

What platitudes. I pictured poor Simpson, somewhere on the long flight across the Pacific, his wife beside him. Arriving home early, saying hello to people who had just gotten accustomed to not having him around. Pacific adventure, canceled out. Just another person who used to live on Saipan. If going there had not cast him as a loser, returning early certainly did.

"When I saw your résumé, I was impressed by your teaching credentials. You are a rare commodity at a community college like this, leaving a tenured chair at a high-ranking college. Twenty-ninth, was it, in the *USA Today* poll?"

"Tied for twenty-ninth. Yes." The ratings had crossed the Pacific, reached a college that didn't even appear on the poll! So much for my hunch that Rosales had done no research on me. A canard. He'd read the newspapers. And, I soon learned, had gone a little further.

"When I studied your vita, I thought you were overqualified. You probably wouldn't come and you certainly wouldn't stay."

"I like my classes so far," I pitched in gamely.

"So I gather," he replied, smiling as he forgave me for keeping him waiting. "But what intrigued me in your *administrative* experience . . . You were acting dean of the Elroy faculty, no? And a senior advisor to the president. Am I right?"

"Yes."

"Did you enjoy that work? The administrative side of things? In Honolulu, I asked if you were the sort of woman"—he looked at me closely, appraising me in a way I couldn't mistake—"who likes to run things. Remember?"

"Yes," I said. "It was challenging."

"Challenging." He mulled it over. Let it pass. "What I gather is that the jobs you had . . . are not the kind of jobs one hopes to keep forever. I may be wrong, but I am told that one has such jobs because they may lead to something else. Something better. At someplace better. Am I right about this?"

"I suppose you are," I said. I wasn't smart enough to lie to him. At least not that kind of smart.

"You tried to move out? And up? How many times?" Now the unfinished part of the sentence hung in the air, the air-conditioned air, the clanking, dripping air-conditioner outside leaking onto a rust-stained sidewalk. "Tried and failed, how many times?"

"I don't know if I need to tell you that." His familiarity bothered me. When we met in Hawaii, he'd barely attended to me. I'd felt snubbed. Now I felt invaded. Was I that transparent? Was he guessing? Or had he made some phone calls?

"Never mind," he said, waving away the question. "Your time has come."

"My time?"

"The faculty and staff will meet at noon. We will have a moment for nice things about Mr. Simpson . . ."

I heard it in his voice, lighthearted as it was. Saipan and foreigners, if things didn't work out, you were gone. Island rules.

"And then, Dr. Warner, I propose to announce your nomination as acting president of the college . . . subject to board approval. I would not lose sleep on that point, however."

"Do I have time to think this over?" I asked.

"Of course." He glanced at his watch. "Almost an hour."

"It won't take that long," I said. Here it was, what I always wanted, offered as nonchalantly as a ride home from work. I would take it, period. No time for teasing coyness, when you're getting what you want. And so quickly! Maybe this was the land—the island—of opportunity, after all. Informal, hands on, straight ahead. A last frontier, about as far out west as an American could go.

"It might help if I told you that there'll be an adjustment of about thirty percent in your salary. And a nice house on Capitol Hill. You can move in tomorrow. The view in the morning . . . you can see all the way to the northern islands from there, Anatahan."

"Move in tomorrow?"

"The house awaits you."

"It was Simpson's?"

"Yes."

"Why did he leave?" One last stab at a question I had every right to ask.

"We have a plan for the college to grow. He opposed it completely."

"Why?"

"Laziness. Some of the Americans who have come have already retired. And they have a habit . . . They talk, they don't listen."

"I work," I said. "And I listen."

"Is that a yes?"

"Yes. On one condition. If my acting presidency is satisfactory . . ."

"I like the way your mind works!" Rosales exclaimed, slapping the table, laughing. "Yes. Of course. Why search if we have already found?"

❧

That night, I waited for the campus to empty. The announcement had been made. Tomorrow was the first day of my presidency, but for a little while I lingered in my office, a cramped place in the past-ripe building, yet I'd been happy there. Not as happy as I wanted to be, but happy enough. So I wanted to sit there, turn off the lights, play some music and think things over. God knows when I'd have the chance again.

"Knock, knock. Anybody is home?"

"Galina." The Russian girl. She worked at a bar in the Ginza and was probably my best student. But when we talked, it was woman to woman.

"You are having office hours?"

"I forgot. Sorry. Was there something you needed?"

"Maybe you slip mind. I am confirming, we go shopping Saturday. Remember?"

"You're right. I forgot."

"You promise." Galina wanted to make me over. My body was good, my wardrobe was junk, I was wasting myself, the whole package—her phrase—was "just not happening."

"Okay then," I said. "Let's do it. Not this week, or next. Two weeks."

"Good. We have fun. I bring some other girls."

I winced. A newly named president modeling clothes with a gaggle of Russian bar girls?

"Only two or three?"

"Okay."

"And, please, nice girls."

"Everyone is nice."

"You know what I mean?"

"For sure," she replied.

◊

Capitol Hill! Or as the locals once called it, Mount Olympus. Not so Olympian, really, a few hundred feet above the beach, a few hundred feet below the top of Mount Tapochau. But still, another world. It must have been something, back in the CIA days, its tennis court and movie theater, social club, a little America, manicured lawns and paved roads with curbs and—Rosales was right—a view of the world.

The house I got was a college president's house, suitable for entertaining, ready to accommodate a visit from stateside relatives. An exception. I had arrived late on Capitol Hill. The CIA had been gone since the early 1960s. The Trust Territory government, a U.S. Department of Interior operation, inherited the place. But in the last twenty years, Commonwealth years, the place declined. Some houses had been awkwardly converted into government offices. Others had been abandoned altogether, the roofs cracked, the walls mold covered, the screens in tatters, saplings growing on the roofs, wasps nesting in the ceiling, rats scurrying down the halls, the driveway covered by weeds and fallen palm fronds. Here and there a few residents were hanging on, painting and puttering, gardening a little. Mostly, though, the place was a wreck.

In early evening I jogged a lot. Anything was better than rattling around that empty, underfurnished house. I was too preoccupied by the college to decorate or even unpack, too nervous to read, or sleep. It felt like a senior-citizen town that had somehow stopped admitting newcomers; instead, the original population died out, household by household, until only a few remained, and would the last one please turn off the lights, assuming there wasn't a power outage at the time. How many left-behind places like this were there already? China Beach and Cam Ranh Bay? Subic and Clark? The Panama Canal zone? Guantanamo and Okinawa, sooner or later? All those cozy communities, surrounded by guards and fences. What did the world make of them, after we were gone?

I jogged uphill to the highest building on Capitol Hill, the CIA's community club. After the spy-trainers left, it had been an office building, later a nursing school. Now it was a tear down, broken glass and tangled wire and water damage everywhere. I got a new respect for the world's great ruins, Angkor Wat to Athens, the ones that rode out time. How many other American places would look like this as they, and the country that built them, grew older? I thought about things like this, when I ran through the neighborhood. A *Twilight Zone* episode, twilight on Saipan, twilight of empire. From Spain to Germany to Japan, from U.S. Navy to CIA to Department of Interior to Commonwealth. I had it down.

No matter how long you waited to jog, or how slowly, you always broke a sweat on Saipan. And you sweated for a while, long after you stopped moving. I'd learned that lesson the hard way, running, then rushing into a shower, jumping into clothes and hurrying to campus for a meeting. I arrived dripping, and the air-conditioning made me feel sick half an hour later. And I couldn't turn it down. This was the realm of Bernadette Diaz, who kept the air-conditioning on full, for as long as it lasted. "It can rest during power outages," she told me. We had lots of those on Saipan. Like a golfer out on the course, felled by a heart attack in mid-swing, an air-conditioner shuddered and crumped out. Minutes, sometimes hours, later, it revived with a hammering cardiac jolt.

The headlights of a car found me from behind. That surprised me, because there wasn't much traffic after four-thirty. What bothered me was that the car didn't pass me. I was ready for that, any woman runner is a nonchalant obscenity, an indecent proposal, an empty beer can rolling towards the curb. Around here, in addition, you get a list of lip-smacking, sucking noises, "the Filipino national anthem," it was called, in acknowledgment of its most adept practitioners. Now the car caught up with me, came right alongside. It didn't pass me, though.

"You haven't lost a step," said a voice from inside. George Griffin. "And you're running at altitude besides."

"Hello, George," I said. "Still getting into Saipan?"

"Maybe Saipan is getting into me. That's an interesting question, by the way. Hey, I heard about the coup d'état at the college. Congratulations!"

"Acting president . . . with a chance of permanent appointment if I do the right thing. It isn't clear what the right thing is."

"The guy before you, did he jump or was he pushed?"

"Another interesting question."

"All these questions—we should have dinner ASAP." Something in him had grown, or healed, since I'd seen him. It pleased me. Griffin was intelligent, likeable, decent looking. I'd done better but—oh, yes!—I'd done worse. He wasn't a local; there'd be talk, but not the inflamed kind that an island partner would generate. And, clearly, he was transient. Another plus. Yes, Griffin might do, for a while.

"Fine," I said. "When?"

"Tonight," he said. "Don't tell me you've got something in the oven."

"I'm so busy," I said. An autopilot response, it was true enough. But so what? "Okay, if you can wait for me to stop sweating. And shower."

"Sure."

I gestured down the street, to my house. "Go ahead. It's the one with the light on."

He drove off and parked behind my car, stepped out to the curb, gazing up and down the street of ruined houses.

"Jesus, this is creepy," he said. "Vacancies on Mount Olympus."

"The gods don't live here anymore."

We went inside, down the hall, out onto the screened porch. I brought him a beer, poured myself some bottled water, and we sat awhile, looking out at the remnants of somebody's garden, a tangle of trunks, weeds and vines, parasites, epiphytes, invaders and originals; you couldn't tell what was meant to be there and what just wandered in.

"A good bar is hard to find," Griffin announced as he finished his beer.

"Is that so?" I asked, wondering where we were headed.

"The nights are long here," he continued. "Maybe you've noticed."

Actually, I'd kept busy at night, in my office, trying to understand the college I now led. Nonetheless, the very fact that I was grateful for the work I had to do suggested that what he said wasn't wrong.

"I've tried," he said. "Russian places, Chinese, Filipino. Sad when they're empty, annoying when busy. There's no place you can sit, stay quiet if you want, talk if you feel like it."

"So where are you taking me?"

"Well, I was in this one place down in Garapan that attracts a lot of merchant marine guys, the ones assigned to those four ships out beyond the reef. They have apartments in towns and girlfriends. They talk, they talk a lot if you show a little interest. Story usually involves early wedding to a high school flame, a hellish nut-cutting marriage, divorce and escape overseas and a late discovery that Oriental women know how to treat a man right. It's funny, the women are sitting there and you can't tell if they've stopped listening or caring. Well, one of these guys tells me about an old-fashioned American bar. Way out of the way. And he draws me a map. Okay?"

"Okay," I answered. "But if . . ."

"I know. If it's a nest of assholes, we'll leave. And dinner's on me at the elite hotel dining room of your choice."

"Thanks. I don't mean to come off as a snob, but Americans overseas are a problem. I remember this piece I read, a travel piece actually, about the world's most annoying human being."

"Go on."

"It's the long-term American resident—'expatriate,' they would call themselves—of any place you happen to visit. Tuscany, Mexico, the Philippines, you name it. The men bend your ears, in a wised-up way, knocking the locals. 'These people' this . . . 'These people' that . . . And the women are worse. If you've just bought something local, a shirt or a belt or a basket, and you bargained the way you're supposed to, good)naturedly, then this woman asks where you bought it and what was the price and it's, 'Oh, you paid too much!' You've corrupted the natives, you've subverted the woman's lifestyle, you've triggered inflation. I remember one phrase, I can even quote it: 'Self-centered characters who make a career of having gotten to some place before you.' Does any of this ring a bell?"

"No," he answered. "Who wrote it?"

"Sorry," I said. "I forgot, some woman."

❧

The place called Hamilton's was inland and uphill and you had to turn into a broken-up driveway, drive past a cluster of rental units, walk to an open air patio—the Saipan trivial pursuit club was there—and inside, a bar that was a shrine to booze and talk, an American place, a roadhouse, part restaurant, part jukebox and pool hall, mostly, the biggest part, a tavern. You could eat, you could drink and maybe dance, you could shoot pool, you could talk. It was one of those edge-of-town places where locals meet people who come in off the road.

The place made no concession to its Pacific island location, no tropical plants or hanging fishnets, no bamboo, rattan, or thatch. Here they had pictures of naval stuff, sailors in their youth and ships photographed and framed like old girlfriends. Behind the bar there were three or four reference volumes, almanacs, sports records, well thumbed and out of date but, come to think of it, the people who argue in bars aren't arguing about what happened lately.

We sat at the bar and ordered food—blackened tuna sashimi for me, fried chicken for George—because we were hungry and also because, by quietly dining, it wouldn't look like we were being standoffish. Or eavesdropping. But there was certainly a lot to listen to. Hamilton's was a free-fire zone, conversations ranging from Jeb Stuart's absence from Gettysburg, the death of Sonny Liston in Las Vegas, the search for Amelia Earhart, the local governor's marital history, the character and motives of a recently formed group of "indigenous entrepreneurs" who wanted to bring casino gambling on Saipan. It whirled around me willy-nilly and "dickhead" was among the milder epithets.

The main topic was war crimes, Serbian, Japanese, German and— could it be?—American. These were men who had read some history and had opinions about whether Albert Speer had gotten lucky, Alfred Jodl unlucky, at Nuremberg. Victor's justice, someone said. Military trials were to justice what military marches were to music. Better imperfect justice than none, in the wake of a holocaust, someone countered. The drinks kept coming. They moved to war crimes trials in Manila. Tomoyuki Yamashita, the Tiger of Malaya, hanged for late-war atrocities in Manila, crimes he didn't plan, had no knowledge or control of, since he was holed up in the mountainous interior of Luzon.

"The Kiangen pocket," George said during a lull in the talk. They looked over at us, four or five of them.

"Kiangen?" asked one of them, the lead arguer.

"It's where Yamashita went," George answered. "Some of the meanest, slowest fighting of the war, up in those rainy mountains. No telling how long he could have held out. But he knew he was doomed after the Americans took Aparri—that was the last port—and there'd be no help from Japan. So out he walked, in August. Doubt if he knew he'd be hanged. I'm sure that came as a surprise."

"He was guilty of war crimes."

"He was guilty of defeating MacArthur," George responded.

A moment's pause. Then he remembered something else.

"You can see the rope that went around his neck," he said. "It's in a museum on Bataan. At Mount . . . Mariveles, I think." Next, he asked the bartender what the men at the bar were drinking. Tequila, with beer. He ordered a round, sat back and listened to them get back on war crimes. They were trying to recall the other Japanese general who'd been tried and hanged in Manila.

"Homma," George said. "Masaharu Homma. Only he wasn't hanged. He was shot. Kind of ironic. Spoke English, liked American movies. A liberal . . . the 'poet-general,' they called him."

"Hey, buddy," one guy, an argumentative bantam, said. "Who are you anyway? I've seen you in here but, you know, first-timers, one-timers, who cares."

"George Griffin."

"No, no, I know your name. I mean, what are you? How do you come up with that stuff?"

"I read."

"Reading got you to Yamashita's noose?"

"I travel, too."

"You a salesman?"

"Kind of. I'm a travel writer."

"Nine o'clock!" the bartender shouted. I was puzzled. It was way too early for last call. He bought a round of drinks and I raised mine as the others raised theirs. "To the chief," said the bartender. "To the chief," the drinkers responded.

"Who's the chief?" I asked.

"Hamilton." The man who answered was Davey, the bantam, who, as much as he drank, stayed smart. Wherever it went, to his legs or hands, the alcohol didn't reach his head. He pointed to half a dozen photos, a young sailor newlywed to, I guessed, a Saipanese woman, a pot-bellied rogue pouring drinks, arguing, gesturing, playing the harmonica, wrapping his arms around some partying, pink-eyed women. That was Hamilton.

"Where is he?"

"Outside," Davey said. "This is the time of night he died. He had a hard-on towards local politicians, feminists, Peace Corps volunteers . . . He shot from the hip."

"I see," George said. "Like The Master Blaster." I suppose he thought it was worth taking a shot, trying to find out about a mystery man he'd been told about. The idea of an unknown writer taking chances on a small island intrigued him. Nonchalantly, so he thought, he floated a question. Nobody was fooled. He got no response.

"What's wrong?"

"You want to know about The Master Blaster?" Davey asked. "You buy us another round of drinks."

He bought another round. By now he'd had too much. Not that George slurred or mumbled. He just took a conversational chance.

"Okay," said a bearded guy, a heavyweight named Herb. "You'll have gathered that this isn't the first time the question's been asked. So let me tell you, I'm The Master Blaster." Soon as he said it, he downed his shot.

"I'm The Master Blaster," said Davey. He drank the tequila.

"I'm The Master Blaster." This from an accountant. Then an empty glass.

"I'm The Master Blaster." From a taciturn lawyer at the end of the bar. Another empty glass.

"I'm The Master Blaster." The bartender was last. It was straight out of *Spartacus,* after the Romans have crushed the slave revolt and are interrogating their captives, determined to crucify the leader. The real Spartacus confesses. "I'm Spartacus," he shouts. Only to be drowned out by dozens of voices, an army of them, equally vehement, shouting the same thing and condemning themselves to die with him.

Then, the evening started winding down. One man left with his wife, a local woman. A pair of Chinese women showed up to drive their sixty-year-old partners home. I suspected that all these men had come to Saipan with American wives. But in the heat of the day, the stillness of the night, on beaches and in bars, in typhoons and power outages, their marriages died, their women left, embittered. And the men stayed, newly single, but not for long, because the island had a plan for them, a kind of regimen that was like one of those cardio-fitness trails with periodic stops along the way, where you did stretches and chin-ups and knee-bends before moving on. The American wife was the first step. The local wife—Saipanese or Palauan, usually—came next. The third stop was often Filipina. The fourth was upscale Chinese, two of them tonight, very nicely dressed, sitting next to their men, a glass of white wine in one hand and car keys in the other. One of them smiled at me. They waited while their men finished their arguments and settled their bill, escorted by beauties, those men stepped out of the bar with grins on their faces, like baseball players who'd hit an inside the park homerun.

Mel Brodie

❧

"I know what you're thinking," I tell my audience. "Here's another out-sider with a bright idea for Saipan. You've had your share of those al-ready. Carpetbaggers, right?"

I gaze out across the Hyatt dining room at the Saipan Rotary Club, locals and Americans, about half and half. The lunch is over, the coffee's being poured and I've just been asked to introduce myself and say a lit-tle about my mission here. My new best friend, Jaime Lopez, he made it happen, spur of the moment, a few words to the chairwoman, who read-ily introduced me as a well-experienced businessman from Washington, D.C., so everybody applauded and sat back, waiting to be amused. I was dessert.

"Thanks for the hospitality," I said. "You're wondering who I am and what I'm doing here. And the answer is . . . Why dance around it? I needed a break, a get-away-from-it-all kind of thing, and a good friend of mine, Lou Maxim, mentioned Saipan, and instead of asking Why? I decided on, Why not?" Wow! I had no idea what Lou Maxim meant out here. It was like a charge passed through every seat in the room. Heads turned, butts shifted weight, legs crossed and recrossed and they looked at each other as if to ask, Do you hear what I hear? I stopped and took it in. Maybe they thought I was milking the moment. No way. I was giv-ing them time to recover.

"So let's skip the part where I tell you that I've studied your history, your culture, your economy and politics, that I'm connected with a list of internationally recognized experts and deep-pocketed investors. All I've got right now is a hunch. Not a cinch. A hunch. And a friend back in D.C. who thought I might like it here."

❧

The hunch had come to me on Tinian, but Tinian wasn't in the picture. For one thing, there was a casino on Tinian, a Chinese casino, about as sexy as a methadone clinic. No boxing, no babes, no bullshit, no oldies-but-goodies lounge act. No fun. But the land problem was what really tore it. Most of Tinian was controlled by the military—the harbors, the beaches, those long yawning airstrips, they might be needed, once we pulled out of Okinawa. What I had in mind required land. And Saipan had a lot of that, so I spent three days with my taxi driver, Gregorio, my not-quite-local guide, my not-quite-faithful companion.

About half the island was a mess of cheap buildings, nothing classy about the place. More failure than success around, I guessed, but my driver corrected me. When land was sold, money was made, when buildings were built, or half built, abandoned or never occupied, money was made, and when money was lost, it didn't disappear, it just got transferred, almost always from an outsider to local. And outsiders, including, most recently, Mel Brodie Jr., kept on coming. That old dream of islands died hard.

I needed land that was at a distance from everything that had happened on Saipan lately, this boneyard of big ideas. I needed land that wasn't developed. Something with a cliff in back and the ocean in front. So we spent a lot of time on the back side of the island, on the slopes of Mount Tapochau and, most of all, on the north end, called Marpi, where the war ended on Banzai and Suicide Cliffs, and I saw half a dozen places that might work. I hid my reactions from Gregorio, shrugged and yawned when my heart thumped, when I wanted to shout, This must be the place! at a rocky promontory that looked across at Tinian, at a kind of Alpine meadow above Lau Lau Beach, at three or four sites in Marpi, chunks of green on the edge of geysering blowholes, jagged rocks, bullet-pocked cliffs behind. Any of these places would do, I told myself, and I was in no rush to choose. It tickled me, just thinking about them.

"So I came here because I felt like taking a trip," I went on, and I knew I had them because I've always had the gift of gab, chatting with folks, maybe not the big shots, the lawyers and the MBAs of the world, but ordinary people. "Since then I've been learning a lot, not that I don't have a lot left to learn." It was bullshit but it was a likeable bullshit, funny and good-natured and unpretentious. I didn't come on as too smart for my own good. Or too rich. I told them about my background in real estate, most recently outside of Miami. I liked Saipan's recent connection with the United States; amazing how few people knew about this little America, just open for business, and I guessed there'd been some early goof ups but it was only a matter of time before they hit their stride. There was nothing that had happened in Florida that couldn't not happen here, but Saipan was small and it had to pick its shots. At this point, I sensed a certain amount of restlessness, this long line of whereas clauses that hadn't yet come to be resolved.

"Cut to the chase. I toured Tinian with a bunch of World War II veterans. One of them knew a guy I'd never met. He knew my father, who died out here a few weeks before the end of the war. And . . ."

I choked up. Right where I thought it might happen, it did. I'd worried about it. But worrying didn't help, when it came. I turned away. A minute later I was okay, I faced them again, this audience of island hotshots who didn't know me but who, I saw, had concern and pity on their faces.

"Sorry, folks," I resumed. "Stuff happens. I never knew my father. And neither, hardly, did my mother. They got married a week after they met. A week before the war pointed him in this direction. Here."

Now I was back and they were listening, maybe more closely than before.

"I've been in real estate. It's what I do. And after I got back to Saipan, I thought of all the old-timers I've sold retirement homes to, thousands of them, it must be, and I thought of how much I liked Saipan and how appealing others would find it. Other Americans. I thought they would do well here, and do good too, spending their last years in some beautiful place, so exotic yet so American. This was a good place for them . . . and for me. You don't know me yet and I don't know you. But I hope the day will come, sooner rather than later, that we greet each other as neighbors."

❧

About a dozen people came over to shake my hand, introduce themselves, pass me a business card, invite me to get in touch with them, "when you're ready." Three or four were lawyers, two were in the construction business. Some of those and some others knew of property, including some preexisting or used or partially completed hotels. And there was the guy whose name Lou Maxim had given me. Benjamin Romero. Big Ben. It had to be him. I'd noticed him watching me while I was shaking hands and exchanging business cards, listening to people assure me any friend of Lou's had a friend in them. Lou was a great man, he'd fought and won in Washington, kept the feds off the new Commonwealth's back. He deserved a statue. When that was over, Big Ben was still watching me, from the same way-in-the-back table where he'd sat through lunch. Now our eyes met and he nodded me over.

"Uncle Mel," he said.

"Big Ben?"

"I thought you'd come to see me."

"I wanted to wait until I had something to say."

"Well, you said it today. Have you spoken to Lou about your plan?"

"Not yet. But when I do, I bet he calls you to ask if I've lost my mind. What'll you tell him?"

"I like your project, Uncle Mel. It could work."

"Oh, come on, you say that to all the girls."

"No, really. It has a nice feeling about it. But can I take a risk with you? Can I tell you a thing or two that I do *not* say to all the girls?"

"I'd be grateful."

"We're part of the U.S. now and fellow citizens. It's sinking in a little bit at a time. But there's another, older way of doing things. It's not all aloha here. There's another tradition, and you did not hear this from me."

"Okay. What?"

"Anyone who comes to an island is an outsider."

"I know that."

"And any outsider is fair game." He let that sink in, then shook my hand and used it to draw me into a hug and whisper something in my ear. "Be careful," he said.

❧

"Wonderful presentation," Jaime Lopez, aka J. Lo, said, when I walked out into the parking lot. "I could see it on their faces, Mel, the way they looked at you, the way they looked at each other. They respected you. Your age. Your hero father. Your business experience. Your race."

"My what?"

"They asked, were you Jewish? And I told them, yes, I think so, you bet. Okay?"

"Why not?" I met Jaime Lopez on the third day of my tour with Gregorio. There he was in the front seat. Call me J. Lo, he suggested. I guessed Gregorio meant to give him a lift to an office somewhere; he dressed like someone who sat behind a desk, loved air-con, took lunch at a hotel buffet and wasn't worth spit after two in the afternoon. He had a line of gab, right from the first, comparisons of Guam and Hawaii, of San Francisco and LA and later on, when it was clear he was going to be with us for the day, he and Gregorio entertained each other with war stories—whore stories—from Manila. Dwarf hookers, mother-and-daughter acts, lots of laughs between the boys, and when I didn't join in, they guessed it was because I was hearing all this for the first time and had to be loving it and them, these fun-loving regular guys.

"Who's your friend?" I asked Gregorio as soon as I could. We'd bribed our way past a security guard and were on the grounds of a half-finished Korean hotel near the airport that Gregorio thought might be of interest. That, it turned out, was the theme of the day, checking out hotels, mansions, subdivisions, restaurants that had been built by investors who lacked the shrewdness and tenacity of a Mel Brodie. J. Lo was relieving himself against a fence and Gregorio was standing on wooden planking next to piles of cement blocks and plastic piping, crates of toilets still waiting for their first flush. Against the chain-link fence that ran around the site, there were raw-wood shacks and wash lines. People got up to work one morning and everything all of a sudden stopped. Someone lost money here, someone made money, and the result was what you saw, a place that went from ripening to ruined, overnight. And there was J. Lo, pissing against the fence.

"Sir, I'm sorry," said Gregorio, "but he is my boss and a very big businessman. We do some small things together. Only small. I am his right hand, he says, but I am just a little, tiny finger. He does construction and real estate and many others. And when I tell him about you . . ."

"What did you tell him?"

"Only good! That you are a wise man who is wanting to learn about Saipan. And he says, 'I want to friend that man.' "

"He wants to *friend* me?"

"Yes."

"Do I need a friend like him?"

"Maybe so," Gregorio said, which meant absolutely yes. "You have me as a friend, too. I am your *first* friend. If I cannot do your wish, I can find someone who will. Someone local, you will need. And Mr. Lopez has great experience with outside projects."

And that was the last I saw of Gregorio. He just stopped showing up. J. Lo kind of took over and when I asked about our friend, he guessed he might have gone to Manila. It wasn't as though he really knew, or cared. More like I'd been passed on to him. That was okay. I guessed I was going to need a local assistant. I said as much and added I needed a lawyer, too. Bingo, it turned out J. Lo was a lawyer. News to me, a lucky break, things coming together nicely. But I kind of missed knocking around Saipan with Gregorio, those early days when I knew nothing and everything I saw was new.

❦

Talking points re. Saipan project, by Lou Maxim

1. Under the U.S. flag, U.S. law, U.S. dollars, English spoken mostly, and they drive on the right side of the road. A tropical island, but American.
2. Exotic location . . . tropical climate, clean air, open land, beaches, boondocks and big sunsets!
3. Diverse mix of cultures, islanders and mainlanders, Filipinos, Chinese, Koreans, Thai, Japanese. Cheap help—maids, gardeners, nurses, drivers, watchmen, masseuses . . .
4. History Channel . . . World War II and all that. Colonists—Spain, Germany, Japan, America. We win. The war *and* the peace! They vote to join us. We agree (military interest). Hands across the water. And handouts. A win-win deal. A feel-good kind of place.
5. Exemption from federal taxes. Ninety percent rebate. What more can a gentleman say?
6. Half an hour from air hub on Guam, flights to Asia—Taipei, Japan, mainland China, Hawaii, Australia, Bali.
7. U.S. products in stores. U.S. cars, U.S. names. Costco, Winchells, Ace Hardware, Subway, Hard Rock Cafe, Athlete's Foot. Japanese baseball teams come down for spring training.

8. Medical care. IMPORTANT. Not great. But will improve. Staff doctor at retirement facility? Helicopter life flight to Guam?
9. Pioneer/frontier angle. Place is a new America. Now private sector is foreign dominated. Spend your last years building and contributing to an American community. Discounts for former servicemen . . .

❧

In the days after my Rotary Club show, people started to call me. There were invitations to lunch, lots of them, to weddings and baptisms. Hospitality, curiosity, they came together, along with barbecue smoke and beer, and a murderer's row of liquor. People were careful about talking with me—shyness, politeness, whatever—but they enjoyed talking to each other in front of me, old stories, island politics, family feuds, big deals and dealers. It went on for hours, after they'd eaten, while kids were napping and women moved to other tables. Before you knew it, afternoon turned into evening and someone was maybe playing a guitar and singing vintage country and Western songs, "Your Cheating Heart" and "Please Release Me." I listened, laughed, nodded. That was all they needed from me. Spirit of aloha, I guess. I couldn't picture this happening back home.

Every day I took notes, worked on a proposal. I read the local newspapers, visited museums, got used to seeing people and being seen. And I found my way back, unescorted, to some of the potential sites I visited. I went at different times of day and night, matching my mood and the way the place felt. It sounds touchy-feely which, believe me, isn't my style. I'd never acted this way before, anywhere I sold things. But I did it here. And after three weeks, I was about ready to call Maximum Lou to tell him what I found and what I needed. But before then, something else happened. I became a local hero. By accident.

❧

Believe me, I'm not the kind of man who needs two women at a time. These days one is plenty, more than enough. But I'd met Lourdes and Cori at the same time and they both needed money, that was for sure, and so there I was, anticipating a crappy massage, stepping through the Magic Fingers entrance, under those copulating flamingos. As soon as I was inside and they took me upstairs, I realized it was the wrong night;

it was busy, a bunch of drunken Chinese singing karaoke songs, tumbling around, groping everything in sight. They got on my nerves and so did the music in the place, mindless thumping disco crap that accompanied slaps, grunts, and giggles, *ooh*s and *aah*s from up and down the halls, easy to hear because the walls between the rooms didn't go all the way up to the ceiling or down to the floor, so it was like a row of toilets. This one night, my girls are ashamed and so am I.

"You want to go someplace nice?" I ask. "My place?"

"Cannot, Uncle Mel," says Lourdes. "Miss Ruffa says no."

Miss Ruffa is a mama-san, but there's nothing motherly about her. A dominatrix—whips and spankings—with the mind of an accountant, and, likely, a knife in her purse.

"When do you get off duty?"

"Off duty?"

"You know, work over. End of shift. Free time."

"We are to remain here all the time," says Lourdes. "On call . . ."

"They pay you for twenty-four hours?" I ask. They shake their heads, no. I look at their suitcases in the corner, some dresses hanging along a metal rod behind a curtain.

"Get packed," I say. "I'll take care of this."

❧

When we head out towards the front, Miss Ruffa is sitting on the sidewalk with three other girls. I know trouble is coming but I can't help taking a good deep breath of Saipan's finest, that night air that you could bottle, much appreciated after you've been in a closet that smells of perfume and sweat.

"Where are you going?" Miss Ruffa asks me.

"Out."

She looks at the girls, these teenage kids, these orphans. "Cannot take."

"Can," I say. "Will." I'm on shaky ground now but I go for the trifecta. "Shall."

With that, Miss Ruffa turns on the girls, switching into Tagalog. Cori stays quiet but Lourdes doesn't give an inch. By now, the three girls who were on the sidewalk have come out from inside with suitcases, too. We're talking exodus here: these girls are mine, God gave these girls to me. Sing it. Miss Ruffa makes a phone call—for backup, I guess—and I decide not to wait around. I lead a parade over to the taxi stand and tell the driver to take us to this down-on-its-luck hotel I looked at, a 90 percent empty place. When we get there, the manager is leery at first—an older Japanese man who doesn't want any trouble—but I give him a couple of hundred dollars and promise more in the morning. The guy, Saito, has zero sense of humor but he doesn't take too long to cut a deal. And he smiles when we shake hands on it.

"Still on the island?" asks someone from behind me. I turn and it's the travel guy from the plane and with him is the blonde professor, with a just-slammed look on her face.

"Still here," I reply. "Keeping busy. And by the way, I'm pretty sure I saw that Bangladeshi guy along the road the other day. We're all present and accounted for. But, hey . . ." I throw them a look, like I know what they've been up to. "Hanging out with each other. That's cheating."

"And what," asks the professor, "do you call that?"

Behind me are a half dozen escapees from a massage parlor, white uniforms cut short, like X-rated nurses, and little suitcases and hang-up bags in their hands. Two of them were on the plane we came in on.

"This," I say, "is not what it looks like."

"No?" asks the professor. "Too bad. It looks like fun." Then she plants a kiss on my cheek. "Go get 'em, Mel." And the travel writer claps me on the shoulder. "You da man," he says. When I get back to my place, the cops are waiting for me, but they're easy to work with, amused that a sixtyish guy who looks like George Burns has hijacked a load of ginch. I get some respect, kind of like that last time Ted Williams showed up at an All Star game, way past his playing days but everyone wanted to know about how he held a bat.

The girls were being confined day and night, I tell the cops, and I sure doubt that their contracts say they can't leave the premises. And I doubt they're paid for round-the-clock confinement. What's more, I wonder whether the work they're doing at Magic Fingers is the work that was specified in the contracts that brought them to Saipan. The cops guess, and I agree, that this is something that the higher-ups would have to sort out. We shake hands and I head for the elevator up to my room. But someone follows me.

"Excuse me, sir." It's a fellow named Erwin, from a local newspaper.

He heard me talk, he says, but wonders if we could chat a bit longer. I did a very brave thing and he wants to write it up. I figure there's going to be a story, no matter what, so why say no?

WAR HERO'S SON BOMBS
GINZA MASSAGE PARLOR

"All I wanted was a massage," says Mel Brodie, junior, 65, of Washington, D.C., who escorted five "customer service" representatives at the Happy Fingers massage parlor in Garapan's Ginza district to freedom Friday night.

"I was shocked to discover that a lot more than massage was on offer," Mr. Brodie told this reporter. "The girls weren't happy. And what bothered me was that they were confined to premises when not working. If that's not slavery, it's a pretty good imitation of it."

Mrs. Ruffa Salvador, manager of the Happy Fingers declined to comment. "He stole our girls," she said. "We keep them here because the island is dangerous. It is for their own good."

"Uncle Mel"

The five girls, all Filipinas, met with this reporter at an undisclosed location. They had been recruited as "waitresses and hostesses," they claimed, and were coerced into acts of sex at Happy Fingers. Their contracts—made available to this reporter—make no mention of restriction to promises.

"Uncle Mel comes to our rescue," said one worker. "He is a kind, brave man and he is knowing how to protect a woman. We love Uncle Mel and thank him plenty."

A Labor of Love

Mr. Mel Brodie is a businessman with long experience in the "silver-hair market" which caters to older citizens.

"Here on Saipan you live and die in the place you were born," he explains. "Back on the U.S. mainland, it's not so easy. It's sad. Old folks living on Social Security and savings can't afford to keep the houses they raised their kids in. The property taxes kill them. So off they go, to New Jersey, Pennsylvania, Florida, Arizona. Even Mexico. So why not Saipan?"

Patriot's Rest is the project Mr. Brodie plans for Saipan, at a to-be-announced location. He is in contact with major financiers in the U.S. for this $25 to $35 million project. "There are a lot of good people, and groups of people, who want to play a part in this newest piece of America," he says. "Sure, they want to make money. But they also want to establish a major American presence in the Commonwealth's private sector. And I guarantee you that what we build will look a lot better and last a lot longer than these garment factories all over the place. So there's a lot more at stake here than my money."

More Than Money

In his first days here, Mr. Brodie learned, from a relative, that his father died in a B-29 that took off from Tinian Island in April 1945.

"I never knew my father," he says, brushing a tear from his eye. "And my mother married him just one week before he shipped overseas. Now, though, I feel connected to this place. And I'll do what I can here."

Help Wanted

Mr. Brodie has teamed with no less than Jaime "J. Lo" Lopez, local entrepreneur, in planning Patriot's Rest. "When the time comes, we'll be hiring locals, first priority, as much as we can," he says, "and qualified foreigners as necessary. I'm looking to put together a first-rate team."

The team already has its first members. Two of the Filipinas rescued from Happy Fingers are on Brodie's office staff, one as an executive secretary, the other an accountant. The other three, says Brodie, are working as waitresses at a local restaurant.

"Happy endings all around," he says. "And this is just the beginning. America is a land of opportunity. And Saipan is America, am I right?"

Khan

❦

"We're close," Abdul finally said. We'd stayed off roads and away from houses and we now hugged a shoreline that wanted nothing to do with us; the sea was angry, the rocks were sharp, the trees poked and scratched at us. At last we turned inland and things changed. There were trees, some with needles, others with leaves, both planted in orderly rows, and grass, waving in the wind, that had once been cared for and cut. Not lately, though, not for a long time. Suddenly we came onto a paved square, a net sagging in the middle, with benches for spectators. A tennis court. And then we found a swimming pool with curving tiled walls, a diving board. That was what it had been: easy to picture the women, the food, the alcohol, all the pleasures of the rich, better by far than anything X and I had seen at beach hotels. Those places were for anyone who could rent a room. This was for private pleasure. But what had happened? The water in the pool was black and septic. To drink it would be to die; to touch it, a finger or a toe, would be to scratch forever. The tiles were cracked and covered with slime, and the diving board itself had fallen into the pool.

So we sat and rested, the brothers chattering away, X sitting quietly, verbally replaying a movie he'd seen where a naked man and woman performed sex acts on a diving board while guests looked on applauding, judging the quality of performance, waiting for their own moment on the board. X closed his eyes, smiling. I sat there wondering what we would do and when, and what we would eat, where we would sleep. The rich man's party was over and there was nothing left for us here.

Behind, in a grove of trees, we found some small buildings: a garage with a jeep covered with bird shit and dust, a storage shed with a generator and fuel cans, tools and parts, and lastly, a place where the workers—the ones who poured the drinks and cut the grass and swept the courts—had lived. The brothers stood in the doorway, beaming, as if welcoming us to our new home. X and I, following, not leading, walked over to take a look.

The island was cruel to things people left behind. The richer the people, the harder the punishment. Or the revenge, for that is how I thought of it. That was the lesson of the tennis court, the swimming pool. The servants' place was no better. The door was off its hinges, the screens were rusted, there were puddles on the floor, mosquitoes in the air. On the wall, a picture of Jesus Christ hung lopsidedly, with some sort of electric wire dangling. The wire moved back and forth in a place that had no wind, and as I came nearer, it moved faster, the tail of a rat that jumped out from behind the picture, landing on the floor and rushing out the door, into daylight. The Jesus picture held on a moment, swaying, before it dropped.

"This is it?" I asked the brothers.

They nodded.

"This is all?"

Another nod.

"Nothing else?"

They shrugged.

"You went no farther?" Now I was the leader. "Well, then take a broom." I gestured at the toolshed. "Some rags. Some buckets. Use sea water if you have to." I pointed to some oil barrels that might catch the rain. "Clean those out." I nodded at the rice we'd brought. "Find some wood. But no fire. Not until we come back."

"Where are you going?" Abdul asked. His authority was gone.

"X will come with me. Around the property. Not far."

"Is there a road?"

I pointed to the garage, where the abandoned jeep shared its fate with an abandoned boat. "Is there a jeep?" I asked. "Then there is a road. Why is it you can follow and catch a chicken but you cannot follow a road?"

"We could look for a chicken," Abdul volunteered. That was a game the brothers loved.

"No. Not now. Not here."

X and I started at the garage. It was easy to find a track that led uphill, what was left of the driveway that people had come down, those tennis players and swimmers, drinkers and party goers. The driveway was overgrown and blocked by branches but there were stones neatly placed alongside and a line of trees and hibiscus guided us up to the edge of the property and to something that had escaped the Azis brothers entirely. A palace, three stories, set against a hill, painted white, with a view of the pool, the tennis court, the limestone cliffs, the sea. You might think, on a small island, people would measure their ambitions. Think small. This place had belonged to someone who thought big. "Your friends missed this," X told me. "They stopped at the servants' quarters."

We crawled over some coral, underneath the lowest deck—"Like ninja," X said—and pulled ourselves through a hole onto the lowest porch. We picked our steps carefully; in another year, this would be gone, the whole place was like a tree that was rotting limb by limb, root by root, withdrawing into its trunk before its final fall. The windows and doors were cracked and warped but they held tight. X wouldn't stop and wouldn't let me leave. But he was scared, too, when he saw a rusted-through stairway that curled upward in half circles. Half the steps were gone. There was a gap in the middle, between two rusty fingers that had lost touch forever. The railings were thicker and a little stronger. But not much.

X went first. Step where I step, he told me. If anybody fell, he would fall first. So up we went, climbing over a step that was gone to a step that was going, carefully spreading our legs on either side so that what was left of the step might, one last time, bear weight. Our hands were covered with flakes of rust, bleeding from small cuts, and our clothing was soaked with sweat, from heat and fear. The second floor was sealed as well, and that meant another flight of rusted stairs, worse than the first; the stairway was dying from the top. But on the third floor a window gave way when we pushed and we lifted our legs over the windowsill and climbed inside, landing head first on a marble floor that was covered with green slime. It felt like the building had swallowed us.

"Look at this," X said. He walked over the marble floor, sliding through mold, and stared out from a floor-to-ceiling window, cracked and grimy yet still giving whomever stood there command of the sun rising, storms blowing clouds, passing on parade. The house was a ruin but X saw it as it might have been, the way he'd pictured an X-rated film at a swimming pool that was now a sewer. The place filled him with the same sense of the power that whoever lived here must have had. We entered a room that was all wooden shelves, stained by rain, blistered by heat. It had been someone's library. And next to it a kitchen, a stove covered with bird shit. We then tiptoed down carpeted steps that had been soaked a hundred times. I gagged at it. But X was making a grand entrance, descending into a room of sexy guests, laughing, amused, impressed. And then, it happened, the way it always happened: the anger in him won.

"What happened here?" he asked.

"I don't know."

"Why did they leave it? Leave it empty? Leave it to fall apart?"

"Death, maybe. Illness. Business trouble. Family trouble. Something bad."

"Something good," he corrected.

"Good?"

"Bad things that happen to bad people are good, no?"

"Are you sure these people were bad?"

"How could they not be?"

From the house, we had a better sense of the property now. The rich man's home had its back against a cliff. Anyone who came, came from that direction, came to a gate which opened on to the driveway. Fences ran off in both directions down to the sea, the same sort of fence that protected the garment factory. And no one would come in off the sea. If trouble came, it would come off the road, through the fence.

"Not even a guard or caretaker," X said. But then we heard a car come to the gate. We stood quiet. Had someone called the police? In no time, I saw us held in a jail, waiting to be deported. On Saipan, I always pictured the worst for us.

I prayed the car had stopped on the other side of the gate, that I would hear it reverse, turn, leave. X waited for the same sounds. Then we heard car doors opening and shutting. We looked out through a broken window at the side of a door. The main gate was shut but we saw some men get out. One of them opened a valise, found a key and unlocked the gate.

"It's Gregorio," X said. He recognized him first, the white curtain of a shirt hanging over his belly and his belt, the creased pants and shined black shoes, which matched his polished black hair. And the valise that he carried like a diplomat.

There were two others, one local, well dressed but relaxed, the other short, white haired, his head turning in all directions, here and there, as if he couldn't quite remember where he was "He was on the plane with us," I whispered. "American." Now Gregorio searched his pocket and produced more keys as he walked towards the front door.

"Quick," X said. We rushed to the inside of the front door. It had a bolt that could bar the door from the inside. It was not in place. We tried to slide it over, we tapped it, teased it, but it would not move. X grabbed the door handle, held it tight with both hands.

"You're not going to believe what you see," we heard Gregorio say. "The owner lived like a king. An American like you, a wealthy businessman and a wonderful, wonderful man. A personal friend of mine."

"Why'd he come here?"

"The taxes."

"Absence of?"

"Of course. Also, he liked being a big man in a small place. He plunged into the life of the place. The politics. He was . . . how should I say . . . generous to his friends."

"And he died."

"Hard to believe. A small plane crash. Or should I say, small plane, big crash. At sea, coming back from Pagan Island. And now they fight over his estate. But this place . . . wait until you see it. Ah, here we are."

"You have more keys than a jailer."

"This is no prison, I promise you."

We heard the key, we heard—we felt—it attempt to turn. I prayed for the strength in X's hands. X's fingers were long and strong and the veins stood out.

"Sticks . . ." Gregorio tried harder, moved the key down and up, to one side and the other, a little further in a little father out, searching for the perfect spot. "This is embarrassing." He tried to force it; any harder and the key would break off. "It's just not . . ." He slapped the door with his hands. Then he stepped back and tackled the door. The thud of his shoulders sounded against it. The door held; X held the door. And smiled.

"Don't need to put yourself out this way for me," the American said. "It's rusted shut. Another day."

"Yes, of course," Gregorio chimed in. "I know a locksmith."

"But I insist," said the other man, the rich-looking Saipanese, "to see what is here. Walk a little bit . . . The possibilities are so clear. Please, come. Today you see the outside. The estate, the grounds. We save the inside—the marble floors, the tropical hardwood, the picture windows—for another day. It needs cleaning, I must tell you. But I was invited in the glory days and it was spectacular. Host and hostesses. Lots of hostesses. Nothing like it here, since then. I truly believe a building like this must be rescued. I feel a moral obligation to connect a man like you to a place like this."

"Moral obligation?" said the American. "Well, let's just walk around a little."

We heard them walk away, downhill, and hoped they would not surprise the brothers at the swimming pool. We stood at a window and watched the visitors make their way past the row of trees and hibiscus. At the bottom, they turned to consider the house we were in.

"They're coming back now," I said. But X wasn't there. He was at the front door, out of the front door, leaving it open, then through the gate, off the property, at the taxi, inside of it. He came out quickly, comparing what was written on his hand with what was on the door: a phone number to call for service. He saw the visitors coming up the hill and hurried back inside the house.

"We're going to get our passports back," he said.

❧

The next day X and I went back down to the beach, but this time we waited until late afternoon, so it was almost dark when we came to the tourist zone, a different place from what we'd seen before, lit up in many colors, restaurants and stores, massage parlors and nightclubs where women called out to men who might be customers. They fell silent, though, when we passed by. If we asked them, would they name a price? Very low for us? Or very high?

We found a little restaurant of the sort we needed, on the edge of things and just off the beach. Beef and Brew. I went to a tourist shop, broke a five-dollar bill and made a phone call.

"Yes?"

"Mr. Gregorio?"

"Yes?"

"Excuse me, sir, we have not met. But my name is Sandy. I just arrived from Guam. I work for a gentleman you showed a house to yesterday."

"Mel Brodie."

"I wish you had not said his name."

"Sorry."

"But yes . . . that gentleman wants to talk to you about the place he saw. In privacy and in confidence. And sir? Only you."

"We went with J. Lo."

"Only you."

"Ah . . . well, I appreciate this confidence in me. Your boss will not regret it."

"The man is finishing dinner at a restaurant called Beef and Brew."

"I'm five minutes away . . ."

"Take twenty," I said.

"Shall I join the gentleman inside?"

"No. Better you wait outside. Wait at the edge of the lot. You will see Mr. Brodie when he comes out. And please, remember this needs privacy and confidence."

I hung up the receiver. Somehow it had worked. I didn't know the American's name, or the Saipanese man's. Only Gregorio. How excited he got, when he heard that he, he alone, was asked for, that his friend was cut out of the deal.

Twenty minutes was a long time. We watched a tour group of Japanese step out of the restaurant and march off, a Chinese streetwalker strolling up the street, an overpowered jeep rocking on its tires with pounding music, that came and went like a small storm. Then it got quiet; only a dog moved across the parking lot, stopping to drink from a puddle.

Gregorio parked at the edge of the lot, near us, away from other cars. His headlights were off, his eyes on the restaurant. After a moment, he opened both front doors, to catch a breeze. He didn't mind waiting. And then something happened that we had not expected: an explosion just down the beach, two or three explosions, hollow, thumping sounds and then the sky over the tourist zone was painted with colors, bursts of color, blooming and dying. So Gregorio didn't hear us and he didn't see us until it was too late. I was in the seat next to him and X was in the backseat, just behind. Gregorio did not know X was there.

"Not for hire," he said to me. "Get out."

"I work for Mr. Brodie," I said. "I called."

"You?" He didn't know me. He should have but he didn't. No more than he would know a particular chicken or a specific pig.

"Sandy Kumar," I said, offering my hand. To his credit, he took it weakly.

"Now we wait."

"When does Brodie come?"

"Not long." I saw his valise on the floor of the taxi. My feet were on it. "I'm sorry, sir. I stepped on your valise. My footprint is on it." I brushed the dirt off the valise, spat on it, as if to polish it. The sight of my feet in cheap sneakers, wet and mud-covered must have told him I was not what I was supposed to be.

"You give that to me." He reached for the valise and this was when X came from behind, pinning him against the back of the seat, as planned, while I removed the car keys, as planned, and stepped out and around to the other side, as planned. Then X locked his arms around Gregorio's neck and held him tight, as if he could not bear to part with him, and Gregorio, pinned from behind, was choking, kicking, struggling as X held him fast. This was not planned and I just stood there, wishing that it was not happening, wishing for it to be over, annoyed that it took so long. I turned away. I looked back. I turned away again. And then it was finished.

"Give me the car keys," X said. "Quick!"

I gave him the keys.

"Now the valise."

I held on to that.

"All right," X said. He glanced around the lot. It was empty. The fireworks were climbing higher and higher in the sky, great beautiful flights of color. "Open it."

There were two zippers that met at the top, in the middle. I pulled each of them and the valise parted. Our passports were easy to find, and others, too.

"Take yours and the brothers'. I want mine." I helped X move Gregorio from behind the steering wheel to the other side of the front seat. X slipped behind the wheel. No license, of course, but he had driven before, in Saudi Arabia. "Get in back," he said.

What if we were stopped somewhere, in traffic, at a stoplight, at a police check point. What if a flashlight found Gregorio?

"Come on," X said. "You worry too much." In control of the taxi, X became a different man. He revved the engine, turned on music; he was a rich man, a king of the road, a yakuza gangster, a porn film outlaw. He rolled down the windows, sang along, enjoying himself, the shift of gears, the high beams and the low, the smooth roads. Next to him, Gregorio moved with the road, side to side, with the brakes, back and forth. He might have been sleeping.

"You cannot keep this car," I warned. "They will be looking for it, tomorrow at the latest. If they find you in it, you're finished. Keep this car and you might as well drive straight to the police. And that will be the end for all of us."

He nodded. He heard, but he did not heed. I knew what he was thinking: a paint job, a stolen license plate, and he could keep the car. I couldn't picture him stepping out at the edge of a cliff, putting the car in neutral, sending it into the Pacific. He'd be an alien worker all over again, walking along the side of the road, or with luck, packed in the back of a pickup truck for the drive to a construction site. He handed Gregorio's valise to me. There were papers, too, employment contracts. He let me keep them. There were personal items also, letters from the Philippines, family pictures: Gregorio with his wife and children. A family portrait. I showed that to X. He waved me off.

"There must be money," X said. "This man . . ." With that, he gestured at Gregorio. Sometimes, after someone dies, the spirit lingers, over the bed, around the house. So I've heard. But I felt nothing here. I searched the valise, compartment by compartment, and found a confetti of business cards, many with Gregorio's last name, Espinosa, and a variety of companies: Island Development, Pacific Manpower, Fil-Am Enterprises. At last, I found an envelope. Just touching it, I knew there was money inside: thirteen one-hundred-dollar bills, two fifties, half a dozen tens and twenties.

"Half for me," X said. "Is okay?"

I nodded. I would not have stopped him if he took it all. He'd killed for it.

"You have to throw out the valise," I warned. "Do that first. Put some stones in it, so it sinks. Can you promise me that much?"

"Promise," he said.

I didn't believe him. "Good luck, X," I said. He nodded and said nothing. I couldn't leave it at that. "I wonder what will happen to us." Was I talking to him or to myself? "I wonder when we will meet again."

"Always so many questions from you," Khan said. "All I can say is, tonight I am feeling lucky."

IV

The Master Blaster

❦

Nero fiddled while Rome burned, The Master Blaster learned in school, though he couldn't say which course it came from. Civics? Music? Latin? He also had no idea who set the fire. It was just an image, and lately—lately in his tenure in this little corner of the American empire—he'd been wondering, what was Nero's music? What was his taste, his ability? Did he saw away like a Nashville fiddler, a sprightly dance or reel? A plangent, mournful country Western loser song? Were his strokes more classical? A poignant adagio? What if he couldn't play at all, screeching unbearably, torturing the instrument, the air, his ears?

Nero could fiddle on Saipan. Not everyone grasped it yet, but a lesson was staring the island in the face. You could see it in the stunned puzzlement of locals, in newspapers and lawsuits, in the hangdog, hungover rhetoric of politicians, in the end-of-days cults that grew up around casino gambling and hopes for new American military bases.

As for his site, The Master Blaster couldn't escape a sense of endings for himself as well. The time for words had passed. The next phase, the last phase, was photos. Every week he'd offer a portrait of this or that human enterprise on Saipan: prehistoric pillars, decrepit government buildings, hospitals and jails, abandoned factories and apartment buildings, an American radar station—part of Reagan's Strategic Defense Initiative—that lay rusted and decrepit on a Marpi ridge. Some of his photos would show well-known places, along main roads; others would be of places buried deep in the boondocks, out of sight, off the map and on an island with a short memory, forgotten. He'd already taken photographs—important to do that before the series began. Later, it would be dangerous. And oh, would they be after him! Every week they'd confront another example of expedience and greed, of crimes committed against the island that they claimed to love. Not just the photo, but the caption below, a kind of tombstone, with date of birth, date of death, names of landowner, investor, manager, nature of business, cost of construction, cause of death, current value, if any. No telling where it would end, it might not end at all.

The Master Blaster arose from his computer and stepped outside. First the sip of cognac, then the first puff of a cigar. What a wonderful partnership. Hard for him to imagine the one without the other. His new project excited him, he had to admit. Better than the mix of investigation and opinion he'd offered for years. It was a kind of album, a series of postcards, an exhibition of what had become of the island, what confronted the people who claimed to love it. *We love this island, this small, precious place!* He'd heard it again and again out of the mouths of people who were born here, from wide-eyed school children to hardened politicians. He heard it from visitors, from people just off the plane. But somewhere along the line, what had started as a profession of love, pure love, mutated into a sales pitch. At the end of it all, there were no words, no arguments. Only photos of what people, locals and outsiders, had done to the island they claimed to love.

George Griffin

❦

After a couple of months, we were a couple and I needed to share. I told Stephanie about shutting down the column. She understood that, having made some pretty drastic changes in her own life. The difference was her sense of purpose, teaching at a small college where now, for reasons that weren't quite clear, she was Acting President Warner. She'd come with an ambition, something that I'd arrived without. And she wondered about the next move. I didn't, much.

"I don't need the money," I said. "Believe it or not, I could last for years out here, at these prices."

"I guess," she granted. "You can afford to do it. But . . ."

"Well, I like teaching,"

"And we like to have you teach," she answered. Interesting, how she switched from I to we, first person to third. The power of office. "But really . . ."

I'd caught on, at Peace Corps wages, up at the College of the Islands. In the English and History departments, whenever someone was sick or related to someone who was sick, or had a baptism or a weeklong funeral to attend to, they called me. They called me a couple of days a week. I was a substitute teacher and it challenged me—it was fun—to walk into somebody's classroom and see if I could light it up, sail into a class on Pacific Island Literature, say, that Acting President Warner had recently vacated, halfway through Melville's *Typee*.

"I know you saw *Faraway Places, Backyard Adventures*. I asked you on the plane."

"Not a faithful reader. It wasn't something I looked for . . . but yes."

"It wasn't something I looked for either. I traveled, I wrote, so I became a travel writer. But let me run another name past you. Amelia Bligh."

"Oh, yes," she said. And instantly she laughed. "Sorry. There was this column about menus . . . and waiters . . . and how they described specials . . . in a way that sounds like they're hitting on a customer. That kind of thing. Sort of Erma Bombeck, with attitude. Another piece, she was walking around Rome in a tight T-shirt that had 'Eat Me' written across the front. She's a hoot. Have you crossed paths with her?"

"Did you know it was a pen name?"

"No."

"Amelia, as in Earhart. And Bligh as in Captain Bligh."

"What's her real name? Something awkward, I suppose."

" 'Awkward' is putting it mildly," I replied. "George Griffin."

♪

So I finished the whole sad story of my brilliant idea that no publisher wanted under my real name, of my yearning to do the kind of writing that stayed around the house a while, and when all that was over, she snapped out two words and repeated them.

"George Eliot. Need I say more? George Eliot. Born Mary Anne Evans. Had to change her name in order to get published. That didn't stop her from writing *Middlemarch*. Which I'll bet you haven't read."

"No," I said. "But I thought times had changed."

"They have."

"For the better?"

"I didn't say that. The tide comes in, the tide flows out. Woman changes her name, man changes his. But writers write. That doesn't change. You've got a great idea, you can get a contract that other writers would die for. Take the deal." She snapped her fingers for emphasis. "And, George, there's one other thing. I might be out of line here. You're a writer, I'm not. But your Amelia Bligh stuff? It's so much better than that column of yours. Fresher, funnier, sharper. It surprises me, because I never thought you had that kind of snap, crackle and pop. And crossing gender lines, taking on a woman's voice . . ." She stopped and giggled. "I can't believe I've been sleeping with Amelia Bligh!"

She had a point. My stuff was wised-up, experienced, ironic but always user-friendly, with lots of cues and hints and tips. There were two underlying assumptions: first, the world was full of splendid places; and second, at the end of the day there was no place like home. Compared to me, Amelia Bligh was a loose cannon, surprised, surprising, humorous, sharp tongued and well sexed. More fun to be around.

That night I called Hubb Bartley, left a message from Amelia Bligh, his newest client. Hubb responded quickly. For a veteran agent, as overbooked as a Hollywood health club, that meant money was in the air. Mystery, too: a phantom writer. The deal was a sure thing, he said; he was already working on the campaign. What to reveal, how much and when. I told him to leave me out of that, all of it. Not even the editor would know Amelia. He balked, then yielded. I guess he thought I'd change my mind. All secrets are meant to be told eventually. I'm sure that's what he thought. It was all about timing.

The book started making demands that took me into the early afternoon. I rummaged through Amelia Bligh's columns. It was odd, introducing myself to the writer I would become. Or meeting a new boss. Where had this stuff come from?

WOMAN WANDERER
By Amelia Bligh

I love full-service gas stations. There's something mean-spirited about self-service. It smacks of penny-pinching introversion, sweaty palmed self-abuse, and unappetizing box lunches. But there's more, much more to this. There's not a woman who won't agree with me. Full-service is sexy. When you pull into full-service, you make a date with the horniest, hang-doggiest of high-school dropouts, the kind who are uncomfortable in bookstores, except the kind that stay open all night. It's too much like homework. But when a woman appears in a car, a passion play begins. Maybe it's because of the process itself, the empty tank in need of filling, the nozzle waiting to be whipped out of its socket and—after a bit of probing foreplay—jammed into the body by Fisher. Next come those leading, sexually loaded questions. "Check your oil?" "Wipe your windows?" "Look under the hood?" All the while, we are being pumped so full, filled to overflowing, and oh, those last few stubborn squirts before the still-dripping beast withdraws . . .

I pictured Amelia Bligh, not in a factual police-identi-kit way, but in bits and pieces. Muscular legs, from years of dancing. Long, musical fingers. Amused, pouting mouth. I liked seeing the world through her eyes.

WOMAN WANDERER
BY AMELIA BLIGH

Is there anything like the sinking feeling you get at the approach of a trio of strolling musicians across a crowded dining room? Short of a rude command—and a hurt retreat—is there anything that can dent their faith that all meals are better with a sound track? Women have even more to fear. When the musicians arrive, the steak gets cold, the stakes go up. If, like this traveler, you prefer to eat alone— you really, really don't mind—the jeopardy increases. Nature abhors that vacuum on the other side of the table. Never mind that you're enjoying an arugula salad, reading Joseph Brodsky, any woman dining alone is Eleanor Rigby.

There was no denying it. After I read her stuff, which I thought of as her stuff, not mine, I felt pleased. Trust your instincts, I told myself. If it came easily, if it was fun to write and a pleasure to read, how could it be a mistake? I finished early and went to Hamilton's. I found Herb and Davey at the bar, deep in conversation, which stopped when I came into range.

"Hey, boys," I said. "What's wrong? Three's a crowd?"

"You see what The Master Blaster did?"

"No. When?"

"Today. You weren't in your hotel room all day or you would have heard."

"What is it?"

"Take a look," he said, signaling for the bartender to escort me into a back room where he sat down at a computer. I wondered what was up. The web site had been around awhile and people on Saipan seemed to have a way of accustoming themselves to any kind of strangeness: Yakuza holidaymakers, Russian hookers, Spanish galleons, tax-dodging millionaires. The Master Blaster was old hat. But then he revealed his secret weapon, a new feature called "Monuments of Saipan."

The piece began with a photo of a boarded up restaurant called Magellan's Palace, born in 1986, closed in 1993. Died because of disputes about who owned the property. Proprietors, erstwhile partners, a Saipan local and a Filipino-Chinese. Business: food, hospitality, special services. Cause of death: litigation between management and investors; also a dispute over title to the land. Employees: fourteen. Pending actions in regard to unpaid wages, unpaid suppliers, unpaid utility bills.

In itself, the restaurant was a place of no importance; restaurants come and go all the time. So The Master Blaster started small. But, I suspected, it was the beginning of a pattern: foreign money, foreign labor, vagueness about land, dispute over money, stated purpose (food) commingling with side-dishes, red ink, probable litigation and abandoned workers at the end of it all. And a ruin at the side of the road. At the end, bottom of the page, there was a coming attraction about an abandoned Korean hotel near the airport.

"So what do you say?" Davey asked when I got back to the bar.

"Interesting stuff."

"Shit!" Davey said, exchanging a glance with Herb, as if they were reconsidering their decision to talk to me.

"Listen, George," Big Herb said. He was the calmer of the two. Davey bristled, Big Herb brooded. "This is going to shake people up," he said.

"What do you ever complain about in your column?" Davey asked. "Maybe take a chance on saying that a five-star hotel forgot to leave a Godiva chocolate on your pillow? This is like waking up with the cut-off head of a horse next to you. It's not about hiring relatives or junkets to Manila. It's not padded expense accounts, sinecure jobs, stolen elections. This is about dirty private dealings. Foreign investors, local fronts. Land fraud. Abuse of workers. It's not just about corruption. It's about stupidity. Failure . . ."

"Okay," I said. "I get it. A bridge too far."

"A death wish," Davey said. "He's in for it."

"Can they find him?"

"They've tried before. This time they'll try harder."

"Dare I ask?"

"What?"

"Do you know who he is?"

"Nope. Don't want to know either. I've guessed. Everybody's guessed. Now . . . I don't want to guess."

That night I couldn't stop wondering about The Master Blaster. We were connected. He was an anonymous writer. So was I, with Amelia Bligh. But he was taking chances that I wasn't and he was doing it for free. And now that I was on the edge of leaving—Amelia summoned me—I wanted to pay my respects. It was the least I could do.

The photo of the ruined restaurant stayed in my mind. There was something artful, almost baroque, about tropical decrepitude, a combination of time and weather, wind, rain, heat, mold and rust in partnership with rats, geckos, wasps, dogs, thieves and vandals. I kept the image in mind that night, and the next day, on a hunch, I drove to the place The Master Blaster had memorialized. As soon as I arrived, I knew that I was right: down a rock road, up an overgrown driveway, across what used to be a parking lot, I found what was left of Magellan's Palace. And then I remembered seeing someone outside, a photographer who quickly turned away when Stephanie and I came jogging by. His vehicle was a sturdy yellow jeep, a perky little thing that could handle the road down to the beach; it could take The Master Blaster anywhere he needed to go, I guessed. I might be wrong, but I doubted it. And there couldn't be that many yellow jeeps on the island. A process of elimination would lead me to the man I wondered about. It wouldn't take long. And it didn't. That night, as I was leaving the bar, I saw a yellow jeep parked nearby. The Master Blaster, whoever he was, drank at Hamilton's.

Stephanie Warner

❦

"You might be the best president the College of the Islands has ever had," Henry Rosales told me. "Also, the last."

You can't reply to a line so carefully prepared and delivered. So I responded in island style, smiling and arching my eyebrow, the way people did around here. It took me a while to master the gesture, standing in front of the mirror. I practiced it on George Griffin. It was like learning how to wink. Now I had it down. That arched eyebrow could signal mere acknowledgment. Or silent agreement. Or withheld demurral.

"You've been here long enough to have an opinion about this place," Rosales proceeded. "You've been working. And you've been thinking. I'm sure of it."

"A bit . . . a little while." For a month, I'd reviewed years of budgets, read legislative transcripts and newspaper stories, accreditation reports, enough to know that it was a miracle the college had been founded and another miracle that it had lasted so long. I'd studied applications, enrollments, attrition and completion, hiring searches, faculty performance reviews. And I sat in classes, vocational, remedial, liberal arts and science, horrid to heroic.

"There are people who believe that we do not need a college on Saipan," Rosales said. "Politicians, some of them. They say it's a luxury we cannot afford. There are off-island places, as near as Guam."

I nodded. I knew about these places, not just on Guam or in Hawaii, but in California, Montana, Texas, no-name institutions in obscure towns, but probably not that different from what was here, or that much better.

"These are bad times on Saipan. Cutbacks everywhere. Retired people worry about their pensions, working people worry about their jobs, businessmen worry about their profits, sick people don't trust the hospital and young people line up to join the military, Iraq, Afghanistan, no matter. They choose a future on a battlefield over a present life in"—he met my eyes—"paradise."

"All right," I said, raising my hand. "Give me a minute." I took a cup of coffee. We had met in an espresso place just across from the American Memorial Park. I scanned the museum, the amphitheater, the memorial wall. Someone told me the list had been expanded to include people who had died of natural causes during the war. Still, the wall made its point. Taking my time—everybody else did, why not me?—I shifted my attention to the beach, that grassy shoreline on the edge of the lagoon, a grove of shade trees and ironwood coming down to the lagoon. How full that horizon must have been in 1944, that vast armada, impressive in black-and-white film (I'd seen the newsreel at the museum), and that much more terrifying in full, fatal color. And, today, to the south were those four or five military-chartered freighters that never moved, awaiting the day that trouble broke out again, somewhere in the neighborhood.

"Okay," I said. "The college is a hodgepodge of buildings, students, faculty. Mixed up, messy, living from year to year, appropriation to appropriation. More often than not, there are accreditation issues. The college's offerings are mixed. That's putting it charitably. I can say with absolute confidence that what you have going here is part high school, part vocational school, part college."

Rosales nodded, agreeably. What'd I'd said had pleased him. He was feeling that he'd guessed right about me, that I was someone he could work with. But I wasn't done yet.

"So this place isn't even minor league. That doesn't mean you stop playing baseball. I have a lot to learn. But I've been one place you haven't been, in a classroom at the College of the Islands . . . in front, and in back, of a lot of classrooms. Where did you go to college, may I ask?"

"U.P.," he answered.

"Pennsylvania? Happy Valley?"

"U.P. Manila. Also happy."

"Well, at the College of the Islands I've seen people light up, come alive. All ages, races, men and women. It happens. A kid in the back row raises his hand, a woman in the first row stops taking notes and starts talking, talking seriously, maybe for the first time in her life, to an audience of strangers. They change in front of you. And you can talk all you want about bigger places, better places, other places. But something tells me that most of our people aren't going to show up in California or, forgive me, Quezon City. We can deal with them here, or not. But if we don't, we lose something . . . and it's more than a baseball team."

"Well said," Rosales said, clapping his hands.

Had I been too theatrical? I'd aimed on impressing, on surprising. He acted as if I'd done something precisely as expected; no surprise at all. It was discomfiting.

"But if the college is not to die," he said, "it has to grow. Can you accept that?"

"Grow or die? Yes."

"Good. Come with me."

❧

We were headed to the north end, a zone of caves, cliffs, war memorials, the handsomest part of Saipan and, it hardly needs to be added, the least developed. I drove there sometimes, parked and watched the waves, which was something I could do for hours. I liked the idea of running there, but you took your chances. George Griffin had locked his car but that didn't stop someone from running their keys all over it.

Rosales parked at an expensive Japanese hotel, and I wondered if he meant to steer me to drinks, maybe to a room where we could "grow or die" together. But we headed across the street, where we confronted a deserted complex of buildings, painted pink. A dead mall, it turned out.

"Be careful," he said, pointing to stagnant puddles that passed a gallery of empty shops. Here was a duty-free shop, he said, this was a boutique, a salon, an Italian restaurant, a place for ribs. "It was a lovely place," Rosales said, shaking his head. "They tried everything. They ran buses from all over the island and when you arrived, the shop girls stood in front, welcoming, inviting, pleading with people to come inside. Special promotions, strolling musicians, cultural dancers. You felt you had to buy something, you were so sorry for them."

He guided me to a bench that he had wiped off with a cloth he pulled out of his pocket. He signaled gallantly for me to sit beside him. He then evaluated the handkerchief and threw it on the ground behind us.

"It goes without saying that the place is for sale," he said. "I think we should buy it." Then it began, his grand plan for the College of the Islands. One of the great advantages that Saipan had was that it was part of America, an American island close, so close, to Asia. And since the local, not the federal, government controlled immigration, they could admit whom they pleased, with none of the post 9/11 fussiness that foreign students coming to the U.S. mainland encountered. So far, Saipan had brought in used and abused farmers, hostesses, night watchmen and Chinese garment makers.

"Stupid," Rosales said. "We can do much better. The whole world wants American education, American diplomas. We can offer that! This is how we grow. Listen, the local high schools produce a handful of graduates who want to go to college. We get spouses, a couple of dozen. Some foreigners. And that's it. In quantity, in quality, they are limited. Likeable, yes, as you say, but limited. Growth comes from Asia, China, Taiwan. There are thousands, tens of thousands, looking for a way into America. We can offer courses in language, business, law, medicine. Today's college will look like a kindergarten! We will get bigger and better . . . and richer. A college, a university, with an international yet American reputation. That is how we grow."

"I see," I said. I studied the puddles, the peeling paint, the shuttered Tony Roma's restaurant. I couldn't help wondering what it felt like in there, the air, the water, the smell that came out of dead refrigerators and freezers.

"You've given me a lot to think about." What a banality. Had Balboa said such a thing, when he climbed that mountain and first saw the Pacific? I hated myself. "May I have some time? I mean . . ." Now I was vaporing. "The building can wait a couple of weeks. It looks like it's been on its own for a while."

"The building can wait," Rosales conceded.

"Is it the owner?"

"The owner is anxious."

"Well then, if he's anxious we get a better price," I said. Now I knew why administrators were detested. It was because they were—I was—detestable. "The longer we wait, the better. Though I grant, it's pretty depreciated already."

"It's the college that can't wait. The legislature is looking for a new home, on our campus. They may just shut us down, if it comes to that."

"Then a week is all I need."

"Fine. It's all that I can give."

Mel Brodie

❦

"I knew it! I knew you'd come up with something out there!" Maximum Lou was shouting as soon as I described my Saipan retirement village. "The people . . . the islanders, I mean . . . are great guys, Americans all the way, but when it comes to economic development, the Japanese and Koreans eat their lunch. And—oh my God—the Chinese. They cook it and eat it! What you've come up with is a project by Americans and for Americans. Amen to that!"

"I guess you like it." I sounded like a kid, at least to myself. Maybe that was because of all the things I'd ever done, and never done, this one mattered. A dangerous attachment. And after Florida, I was looking to get into the win column.

"I . . . love . . . it," Lou said, underscoring all three words. "And let me anticipate your next question, which is—unless you've jumped out of your skin—about money. It won't be a problem. I have access to lots of Americans who'll go for the idea of establishing a presence on that battleground island. That's one angle. And then there's some Native American tribes I work for. The idea of connecting with Pacific Islanders . . . another kind of tribe, when you come down to it . . . and making money in the process, that'll appeal. They've got to get beyond casinos. Though, come to think of it, there might be something we can do in that direction on Saipan. I'll set up an operating expense account tomorrow. A million to get you started."

"You'll be wanting me to come back for presentations? To investors?"

"Don't worry. I'll take care of that. You've got a mission on Saipan. And hey, Mel, how are those two little cuddle bunnies you put on your payroll?"

We talked a bit longer about the ups and downs of various sites I'd looked at, that I kept changing my mind about every time I drove out to them. That was new for me; I used to be the guy who made up his mind and never looked back, fast handshake, light feet, honeyed tongue. Now I was going on about sunrise side of the island versus sunset side, a sandy coastline—safe for swimming—versus crashing rocky shore, and mountaintop versus just beyond the water's edge. Walks along the beach appealed but there was something godlike about being up high, the island spread out below. Somebody would have to decide these things and it would probably be me, because I sensed Lou's interest subsiding, once I got to the nitty-gritty. I pictured him checking his appointments calendar, gesturing to his secretary while we talked.

"Okay," I said. "I talked too much. Just one thing before you go. I need your guidance."

"Sure, shoot." He was in his finishing kick now; he could afford to relax, knowing we were almost done. So I told him that there were at least three hotels on the island that I was sure I could buy, places that were shut down or limping along, and if I looked harder I could find more. The shorter list, come to think of it, might be the hotels that weren't for sale. It might make sense for us to purchase one of those: we'd get out the gate a lot faster, and it was a buyer's market. The problem was, these places had a lot of rooms, even if you renovated them into suites, which might cost a lot more than starting from scratch.

Silence at the other end. I felt stupid, the way you do when you realize a connection's been broken and you can't tell how long you've been talking to yourself.

"You there, Lou?" I asked.

More quiet. "Yeah, I'm here," he finally answered. "Listen, Uncle Mel. When it comes to rocks versus sand, beach versus mountaintop I can't tell you. Your move."

◊

About Cori and Lourdes: something was changing. It started one way, customer and lady—ladies—and the customer is always right. But it became something else. On Sundays we drove to some of the sites I was interested in. They liked to cook for me, Filipino food that tasted better than it looked. Saturdays me and my girls went to the farmers' market down on the beach in Susupe, a mostly Filipino operation, Lourdes and

Cori picking out bananas, greens, eggplants, empanadas and tapioca cakes, haggling and giggling, first price, last price, best price, fried chicken, grilled fish, stews of okra and greens and pork, and we were like family, those two and the old duffer carrying the bags and pulling out his wallet when one of them said, "Need money, Uncle Mel." They worked as my aides, which isn't as silly as it sounds, because Lourdes had okay English and Cori crunched numbers. And if this story lands somewhere between senile and sentimental, you'll get no argument from me. Call it empowering, call it exploitative, it's up to you. We hadn't done a thing, honest, but sex was still in the neighborhood. I didn't have to ask; I guess they felt I ought to have it, the way a nurse feels it's time for your meds. It was Lourdes who came to me and she came unasked. Maybe they talked about me, flipped a coin, who knows? Maybe Lourdes was the one who liked it more. Or liked me more.

I needed to go to Manila and I offered to take them with me, as my associates; round-trip tickets for both of them. They were my first hires. And J. Lo was counsel to my firm. At first we kept things tentative, preliminary, conditional, words like that. He pressed for details, where did I want to put the retirement community? I put him off, which probably marked me as an amateur, a dabbler, but I'd worry about that later. Manila came first: builders, developers, managers, manpower agencies.

Manila was kind of a joke, on Saipan. Whatever mission brought you there, whoever you got to pay ticket and per diem, there was heavy sexual innuendo about the trip. Hint, hint, nudge, nudge, you didn't go there without having your ashes hauled. For me it was business, pure and simple, and the sooner I got back to this beat-up, half-beautiful island of Saipan, the better. I'd never had more fun than when I was looking at sites; maybe I'd never have such fun again. I knew that I needed a pristine place, isolated, lonely, beautiful. Fair enough. But I also had a yen for the Saipan that was trashy, crowded, all screwed up, naked by day, neon by night. On busy nights, I loved the buzz; on quiet nights— desperation and failure in the air—I felt sorry for everybody, the salesgirls at duty-free shops looking like statues at Madam Tussaud's, the bar girls and masseuses.

From the Saipanese point of view, I knew that outsiders were old news. That thrill of discovery, Captain Cook sailing into Tahiti, was gone forever. Everybody had gotten laid by now, everybody had a history. It was like dating women in your sixties: no such thing as first kiss, first love, first anything. Last and next to last is more like it. The world was older and smaller, all right. Still it felt fine on Saipan, sitting out at night, drinking beer, eating barbecue, listening to people bullshit and sing old songs. That island thing still had something going for it.

Young enough to be my daughters, young enough to be my grand-daughters, Cori and Lourdes sat beside me on the Manila flight. We were three across, an older Jewish guy flanked by two girls with glittery T-shirts. I had five days in Manila and, it went without saying, I wasn't the kind of guy they'd bring home to their families. The same taxi that dropped me off at the hotel took them to the bus station that connected them to the deeply loved, piss-poor provinces they called home. A ton of relatives awaited them, awaited money from Saipan. Working at Magic Fingers, they'd expected to send home a couple of hundred dollars a month. After deducting for food, lodging, uniforms, they'd managed fifty dollars. Thanks to their new jobs with me, they carried five hundred dollars. So there I stood, outside the Manila Hotel, my luggage waiting for me at the check-in desk, watching them disappear into the smoggy, crowded, noisy world they came from, headed for a family reunion I would never be a part of. And suddenly, nothing had changed since high school, nothing had changed in fifty damn years. I stood there wondering what they *really* thought of me.

To do anything on Saipan, you needed three main things. You needed land, obviously. That was what the island contributed and that was about all. Money, which came from outside, in this case from Maximum Lou's stable of clients. And talent—chefs, waiters, dishwashers, garden-ers, electricians, plumbers—coming from Manila. And, oh my god, musicians. Did I want Elvis Presley? How many Filipino Elvises did I want? And Tina Turner? I could have one of those, or six, I could have a choir full of Tina Turners. Why buy a single banana when you could pick up a bunch? When did I want them? Next month? Next week? Why not try one or two tonight? A private audition? Didn't a wise business-man always sample the goods?

It pleased me to get back to the hotel as soon as I could, escaping into that imperial lobby, all polished marble and dark tropical hardwood, past the Champagne Room, with its Guiness World Records chandeliers, past the nightclub lounge where some Filipina invited folks to "Hit Me with Your Best Shot" and then, out into the Manila air, out past the swimming pool, out to a chair that faced Manila Bay, where a rust-bucket armada was anchored and, late one afternoon, I saw a small boat-load of hookers get ferried out to service the crew. Beyond the ships, I could see an island they told me was Corregidor.

The fun times were over. Before long, I'd have to choose the site and get moving on the land. I'd bring one of the architects I'd been talking to over to look at the site. I'd be arranging financing through Lou. My last night in Manila I sat there thinking about Lou, about myself. But that's the wrong way to put it. I didn't sit down, check out the lights from the ships at anchor and *decide* to think about Lou. It was the other way around: thoughts came to me, uninvited, answers to questions I'd never bothered to ask. Sure, I'd be lost without him. But with him I might be lost, too. I'd come to Saipan because our Florida project bottomed up and lots of people were very unhappy. I was the president but that was just a front. I was a figurehead, a hood ornament on a car that Lou owned, fueled and steered. And that was all right with me. Well, he'd gotten me to Saipan. Go ahead, Uncle Mel, he said. Honor your unlucky dad and build a resort that's both patriotic and profitable, that's the name of the game these days, love of money and love of country perfectly in tune.

❦

I waited down in the lobby, a great lobby, a place that made me feel important, but now I was leaving, my limo was waiting and the girls weren't there. I got nervous; after a while the driver got nervous, too. Anxiety compounded. Where were they? What had happened? I stepped out in front and let the bellhop page my driver. They weren't coming; I could have waited all day and it wouldn't have made any difference. But still I watched out for them as we went out the driveway, as we turned on to Roxas Boulevard, traveled along the edge of the bay, moved inland, way beyond the point where they had any chance of being. I'd been planning our return to Saipan, a meal at a fancy Italian restaurant in the Hyatt and, over the weekend, a boat ride over to Tinian, where their idea of a good time was a go-for-broke attack on the slot machines. They always got ahead before they fell behind, not knowing when to quit. They packed so much up and down emotion, more melodrama into that hour at the slot machine, the sudden jackpot and the draining losses that followed, I wished I had a camera. All it took was a couple of rolls of quarters and they were happy. So where were my girls? A dad and his kids, a boss and his staff, a sugar daddy and a pair of gold diggers, call it what you like, call it anything, never mind. Call me lonely, on my way home. They couldn't have written a note? Phoned? Said thanks, sorry, good-bye? Said something?

Khan

The three of us sat in a waiting room at a government office, a place that handled abandoned workers who'd come to Saipan with contracts from companies that didn't exist or died after they arrived. And the island was full of dead businesses, you saw the remains everywhere, shops with shutters down forever. The laws of trade were changing, I learned. Quotas on foreign clothing coming into the U.S. would be lifted and then there would be no point in bringing Chinese women to sew under the American flag on Saipan. I saw cars for sale up and down the roads, and when you went into stores in the morning, the cold drinks were warm because refrigerators were shut off at night.

I was afraid. I had passports and papers, everything that I ought to have for the three of us. If we were to get properly started on Saipan, we had to begin here. But how I worried! We might end up in a camp, waiting to be sent home, for I'd heard that the Saipanese were hostile to Islamic workers. I'd learned this from the Azis brothers.

They were the ones who had found the mosque, which was not like any I'd seen; a sad green shack, once a small store, on the outskirts of Garapan, around the corner from a Chinese brothel. On my first visit, I saw a car pull in front, the driver, an American, roll down his window and signal to a woman on the second floor. He pointed to his watch, extended one finger. That was when he'd be back, after lunch. Then he raised three fingers. "Okay?" he shouted, laughing. "Okay," the answer came. Three girls at one in the afternoon.

Inside the mosque there were carpets, Korans, a mihrab and five men sitting against the walls. They were our people, Bangaldeshis, and suddenly the brothers—mute and intimidated by Saipan—turned talkative, even playful.

"You're still here, you boys," said one of the men.

"Were we supposed to leave?" Abdul countered.

"Were you supposed to come?" the older man countered. I knew him now. He was the guard who'd watched us from the gates of the garment factory, the first time X and I went out to explore the island. The factory had closed, the man said, and now he was jobless. He had eight years, he said, good years, though the company owed him three months of pay he was trying to collect, and a ticket home. That was all that kept him here, he said. That was the only thing.

"What kind of place is this?" I asked. "What are our chances?"

"Not so good, for us. Some Filipinos have been here many, many years. The Chinese stick together. The Koreans have money. But we are the lowest. We might be terrorists. I'm surprised you got in. Our numbers dwindle. You might be the last. Where is the other boy?"

"Who?"

"The one who was with you."

"He went off on his own."

"He's doomed then. Does he have a trade?"

"No, he's not a worker."

"It doesn't matter. There's no work here."

"He thought he was going to America," I say.

"Hah! I know the story. They tell us and we believe it. A short ride to California from Saipan! You can drive it! No problem! Then they come . . . and . . . you can't get there from here." He shook his head, smiling a sad smile, as though he were remembering when he'd had the same hopes. "This is the beginning and the end. This is as far as we get."

◆

"Do you speak English?" asked the clerk.

"Yes."

"Speak it," she said. She'd been dealing with a long line of Chinese in front of me.

"I am from Bangladesh, and I have come here because my friends and I arrived and our supposed employer is not to be found . . ."

"'Supposed employer'. . ." The clerk's distaste for three very dark men was overcome by her relief at not having to deal with an interpreter. "You have passports? Contracts?"

"Of course," I said, handing them over. She checked and photographed the passports.

"You arrived a while ago. Three months. Where have you been?"

"On a pig farm . . . waiting . . . for nothing."

She glanced at our contract, noted the name of our employer, checked the computer. For BVD Enterprises.

"It doesn't exist."

"What about the company owners? The ones who signed? Do you know their names?"

She looked at the contract but did not answer. "I noticed there are four names on this contract."

"One left us after we arrived."

She shrugged. So much for X. He was out there somewhere and until something happened, good or bad, he didn't matter. How many others were out there? Nobody counted people who did not count.

The clerk explained the rules: abandoned workers had forty-five days to secure new employment. If they failed, they'd be deported.

"How many abandoned workers are there now?" I asked. It seemed like this was something she should know. Take the sum of admitted workers. Subtract the employees of failed companies.

"Next," she said, looking beyond me.

❦

We went to work in Garapan, Oleai, Susupe, Chalan Kanoa, San Antonio, the villages on the busy side of the island. We knocked on doors of automobile repair shops, warehouses, restaurants, grocery stores, supermarkets. Every time, we encountered foreigners, Chinese, Koreans, Filipinos. Sometimes it felt as though we were the first people to come through the door that day. There was a bit of excitement, shock, that someone had come, which gave way to alarm, when they saw three dark men. I had a speech, something polite; we were seeking any kind of work, nothing we would not do, no matter how dirty or hard or temporary. My English was better than the storekeepers' but it didn't matter. Not once did I get to finish. It was, No, no, nothing, get out, please get out. As if we were scaring away customers.

After three days without even a smile, we tried places where foreigners lived. We waited until mid-morning, when the men had driven off and the women, or their maids, answered the door. They were frightened, too, but they listened and perhaps felt ashamed of the fear they'd felt on seeing us.

❧

Mrs. Jenkins was our first employer. She was young and pretty and seemed glad to have visitors. She asked us into her house and made tea. She had no work for us, of course, nothing she could think of, yet she didn't want us to leave. We'd made her morning, she said. After a while, the brothers walked outside. They spoke no English, preferred to walk around the property. I remained and listened to the woman. She was very lonely. Why else would she have spoken to me? There'd been tension in the house, a strain in her marriage even before she arrived, she said. The idea of an island, a simple life in a small place, had appealed to both of them: a place to escape from relatives, to recover what they had lost "somewhere along the way." She needed me to know about her husband's Filipina secretary. She needed to tell someone. Anyone. At last, she snapped her fingers in delight. An idea had come to her, a surprise, a garden, "a tropical island garden." While the brothers stayed behind, pulling rocks out of the ground, moving soil, Mrs. Jenkins drove me to a place where plants were sold. She asked advice. I was her consultant, her adviser. We talked like old friends, equals, almost. We whispered. She was happy with me. How desperate she must be! I thought.

We planted hibiscus and bougainvillea at the side of the house, and after that she wanted a wooden trellis that vines could grow on, which would make an "accent point" in the backyard, and then we needed benches at the edge of the property where she and her husband could watch the sunset and make plans.

"She talks so much," Qazi said to me. "What does she talk about?"

"Herself," I said.

"So much about herself?" he asked.

"She is far from home," I said. "Just like us."

"She is far from home," he said. "But not like us."

Abdul went back to work setting rocks in the ground for a fireplace. Mrs. Jenkins liked the idea of what she called "cookouts." We should have worked slowly, that was in our best interest. But after a week of idleness the Qazi brothers attacked each project as if it were a meal: they were starving for work. There was no slowing down. And whenever I glanced at the house, Mrs. Jenkins was at the window, watching us make magic, planning one project after another. It could go on for months.

It lasted until the fourth morning. We had left the palace at dawn, walked for an hour to get to work. Usually Mrs. Jenkins met us with tea, toast, fruit, so the day began with food and twenty minutes of talk about new ideas. This morning the house was quiet; no one stepped out to greet us. We moved around the back and resumed work on the fireplace, setting a metal grill between the rocks. We'd been promised a chance to cook there; Mrs. Jenkins was interested in our "native curry."

"So you're the guys," someone said from the back of the house, an American in shorts and T-shirt, walking towards us with a cup of coffee in his hands.

"Sir?"

"You're my wife's dream team."

"Thank you. She has been very good to us."

"I guess. But that'll be all for now. My wife isn't having such a good day today." He nodded back at the house. Mrs. Jenkins was standing at the window, watching, as if confined within.

"We can come back tomorrow, when she is well."

"Well, actually we won't be needing you too soon." He drank the coffee, enjoying the taste. "I don't suppose she paid you."

"No, sir."

"Did you talk money?"

"We say twenty-five dollars a day for each of us. So seventy-five dollars."

"And how many days? My wife wasn't sure."

I guessed this was a trap. "This is our fourth day, sir."

"All right," he said, nodding. "So I gather." He took three hundred dollars out of his pocket. "Today's on me."

"You want us to . . ."

"Just clear out." We walked off, like badly behaved students sent home from school. And Mrs. Jenkins was no longer at the kitchen window. I wondered what would happen to her, though not as much as I wondered what would happen to us.

❦

The money would feed us for a while. But then what? If not for the husband, Mrs. Jenkins would have kept us for weeks and she might have recommended us to her friends. Now we were no better than before, walking from house to house. Two days later we connected with an American schoolteacher married to an island lady from Palau. They lived in a square cement house with a flat roof that had been built as government housing. It was meant to keep out the rain and endure the wind and that was all. The screens were rusted, the windows were loose and some of the floor tiles were missing. You could not catch rain off the roof, you could not open the house for a breeze. The schoolteacher was learning a lesson local people knew all along: you do not live in such a place. Your life happens outside, under a roof that is thatch or metal, usually rusted, and is supported by unpainted wood beams with many nails on which to hang things. Huts, lean-tos, cook-houses, sleeping platforms: every island house had such a place. This is where what mattered in life—cooking, talking, sleeping—happened. Such a shelter was what the schoolteacher wanted. We could have done it in a few hours, but this time the brothers knew better than to hurry. It lasted four days, and then we were back home with no idea what would come next.

So far we had not sent a dollar home, to repay the villagers who sent us to a job that did not exist in a place that was not real America. We talked of sending a letter, to explain. We pictured the people we knew waiting for a letter and reading it. They didn't want to hear of our troubles. Their troubles were greater, every day.

"We can keep looking," Abdul said.

"Three days here, four days there . . ." I had my doubts.

"We can keep looking."

"Not for long," I said. "We have less than a month." I was glad of this. Then the search would be over and we would be in someone else's hands. They would do with us what they wanted, send us where they wished. I hated the idea of knocking on doors another day. It was easy for the brothers, who stood by smiling while I went through my speech, my humble introduction, my heartfelt plea.

The night after we finished work at the schoolteacher's house, I stretched out on a picnic table, praying for sleep. The brothers slept on mats they placed on the tennis court. The nights were the best part of our day. Dawn wasn't something I welcomed, for it brought heat and worry, it forced me to think and, as much as I thought, nothing new came to me. What can one think about a dead end? Saipan was that, it was what it was, and it wasn't going to change for our benefit. A new day was an old day, all over again. But at night—how I looked forward to it—the winds came in off the sea, and when I opened my eyes, the stars were brighter than ever, and so many of them. I wondered about the distance to them and the distance between them. What mattered during the day, the fate of three unwanted alien workers on a medium-sized half-American island in the Pacific, meant much less at night. Meant nothing. Sometimes that was comforting. So I slept on the picnic table and when I woke up, now and then, it was to confirm that dawn was not yet visible. Stay, darkness, I pleaded, let me sleep. And then, from up the road, near the gate, we heard a car, its engine racing. A moment later we heard the horn, loud, insistent, angry.

We looked at each other. Should we run to the cliffs, hide out somewhere along the coast? Would they follow us there, with flashlights in one hand, a pistol in the other? It was another one of those moments that I was supposed to make a choice for the three of us.

I headed up the old driveway, carefully, along the side, staying in the shadows, and the brothers followed. Behind the gates was a car. The headlights were off but a radio was playing music, popular music that I did not know but I heard the words again and again: "Knock, knock, knocking on heaven's door."

Just then, the car's headlights came on. They caught us, blinded us. We stood there waiting for whatever was meant for us. Then the car started backing away and we walked forward, wondering what happened, what it meant. The car turned and drove off.

At the front of the gate, we found a bag of rice, a box of cooking oil, crackers, even chocolates. A case of some sort of sodas. Some shirts and pants, soap and towels. And a brown envelope with a thousand dollars inside. And a box of Winchell's donuts.

"X," I said.

"Why didn't he stay?" Qazi asked.

"He did not stay because he didn't want to talk. Answer questions. Only help us."

"He's doing well here," Abdul offered.

There was no denying that, I thought.

"But he scared us."

"I think he must be scaring other people, too," I said. The brothers waited for more but I left it at that. "At least," I said, "we can send a letter home now."

V

The Master Blaster

Enough! Slavery, human trafficking, prostitution, gambling from cock-fights to poker to casinos, drugs from pot to ice to crack, corruption, nepotism, swindling, crimes against tourists, sanctuary for Japanese and Chinese gangsters, disbarred lawyers, tax evaders and trust fund fiddlers. Was there no end to the flow of bad news about Saipan? Once it started, it never stopped. Old stories never went away, reforms and improvements were slighted. It was time for the people who lived on this island and loved it to defend it, to write letters, cultivate friends, make themselves available to visiting journalists and develop a web site, iluvsaipan.com, to counter Saipan's oldest and most durable enemy, The Master Blaster.

The first speaker was a businessman (car rentals, dive boats) who adopted the angry, Latin-style rhetoric Saipan politicians favored. He wouldn't have been out of place in Manila. What happened in Manila was supposed to stay in Manila, but the story of his belated discovery that an ardent, willowy hooker he'd taken to his room was a male was locally famous. Tonight, though, he rolled along, righteously. To have one's island insulted was like having one's mother defamed: it was even worse than that, for the island was our common mother.

The crowd applauded his performance. The Master Blaster was among the last to stop clapping. He felt completely comfortable. His long residence on the island, his love and loyalty to the place he called home were well known. He donated most of the books he read to the library, gamely participated in clean-up campaigns, harvesting the paper plates and beer cans that got left behind on island beaches, plastic sandals, empty bottles, used diapers. He'd sponsored local youths at U.S. colleges, and to this day he received Christmas letters from them in Seattle, Stockton, Phoenix. He'd hoped they'd return, that was the point.

They chose not to, all but one. Hey, it was a free country, right? The Master Blaster, it turned out, was the one who stayed on Saipan, sitting here tonight in one of the picnic shelters that the government built along Beach Road. It began at dusk, with the remnants of a colossal sunset floating above the horizon, out beyond the pre-positioned military cargo ships, their lights brightening as the western sky went from orange to purple to black. Behind where The Master Blaster sat, cars and trucks sped up and down the road. Unlike most islands, Saipan had good roads, had them since the end of the war, thanks to the U.S. military. In Palau and Yap and Ponape (now Pohnpei) and Truk (now Chuuk) there were cars that had never known the taste of third gear.

"Let us be honest," said the next speaker, "mistakes were made." An older fellow, in and out of the Department of Education, now in the legislature, he cast himself as a calm and easygoing moderate, the kind of man who kept his head. To confirm this, he smoked a pipe, favored cherry blend tobacco. Tonight, as usual, he made concessions, chuckled at his own people's folly. It was all foreplay, though, building to the moment when, tested beyond endurance, the man of reason finally exploded. He was getting there now.

"After years of colonialism, the Spanish, the Germans, the Japanese, we chose to join America. We suffered when they came, lost homes and lives in the war. Yet when they needed our islands for military purposes, we told them yes, we are your partners. Now our young men and women serve in the Middle East and when they die, we mourn and honor them. We are good people, we are loyal Americans. Generously we welcome to our island thousands of people from around the world. Has an island anywhere, ever, been more open? More accommodating? Yes, mistakes were made. But does the long-ago mistreatment of a handful of workers outweigh the thousands who have worked here and returned home wealthy? After an occasional purse-snatching or unfortunate death by misadventure, might it not be recalled that hundreds of thousands of visitors have shared our beaches, our climate, our air and water and return home happy from our beautiful island? Or that no less than Congressman Tom DeLay pronounced Saipan a 'Petri dish of capitalism'? And yet a certain Master Blaster and his ilk . . ."

The Master Blaster knew the end was coming, well before he heard his name. When Saipanese politicians pumped things up a little, Filipino phrasings crept in: "It will be recalled," "No less than," and "A certain person."

"This is a good place, kind and generous," the orator-educator concluded. "Is there anyone here who has not invited a stranger to their table? Yet we are maligned. Magellan called us an Island of Thieves. And nothing has changed since then. Until . . . I hope and pray . . . tonight."

The crowd rose to applaud, The Master Blaster among them. He was asked to follow the two main speakers to a buffet table: barbecued fish, chicken, pork, yellow rice, salads. How many hundreds of tables had been set for him like this, over the years, that he had never reciprocated? The island had its generous side, the speakers weren't wrong about that, and once they sat down to eat and drink, their anger drained away. Maybe it shouldn't have, but it did, replaced by random, wandering conversations that he completely loved. They talked about fishing, local baseball teams, overboard drinking on payday Fridays, American officials past and present, long-dead High Commissioners, their foibles and flirtations, carpetbaggers and treasure hunters, hustlers and missionaries who'd washed up here. Amelia Earhart lived. Among scholars, doubt prevailed, but there were people on Saipan who claimed to have seen a white woman in an aviator jacket in the local jail. She'd died of dysentery, the story went, and her navigator, Fred Noonan, had been beheaded. War stories were still around, desperate Japanese preparations, endless shelling, colonial cities reduced to rubble, flight inland, hiding in caves, last sight of Japanese, first glimpse of Americans, all these were war stories were like the last flickering of a fire that would soon be ashes, so The Master Blaster listened closely. They faced out towards the sea, where the day's last joggers passed along the running path. He liked it, that they turned their backs on getting and spending, success and failure, and confronted the sea. It was what he liked about them, about all islanders. They were always in touch with something larger.

At nine p.m., he was the first to leave, wondering what people would say about him after he was gone. Speculate about his age and health no doubt, look for a wobble in his walk. With reason. He wasn't in good shape, he knew. Death wasn't exactly knocking at his door but it was in the neighborhood, like a salesman who slipped a note under the door, Sorry I missed you, I'll call again at a more convenient time. As soon as he arose, they pressed food upon him, enough meat and rice to feed him for days, and thick slabs of chocolate cake with electric blue icing he'd avoid at all costs. Again and again, The Master Blaster was reminded of Saipan's kindness towards him. It was a pattern that had begun in the old days, quasi-colonial times when any state-sider was part of a privileged community on an island that respected rank. But it had carried over into the Commonwealth days, it survived his retirement. All those former students, children and grandchildren, knowing and honoring their old teacher. They were the ones who'd be hurt if they knew he was The Master Blaster. He had to spare them that. But he couldn't spare himself.

He drove slowly down the road to San Antonio where the guard he'd seen before stood at the gates of a garment factory. A few hours before, The Master Blaster had a puzzled mechanic put on a nearly-flat spare tire in place of a healthy one. He'd driven slowly to the meeting on the beach, slowly to the factory. When The Master Blaster feigned a car problem right at the gate, the guard came over to see if he could help. He had the flat tire off, the healthy one on in five minutes.

"No problem, sir," the guard said.

"Hold on. Where are you from?"

"Bangladesh, sir."

"Your name?"

"They call me X, sir."

"As in X marks the spot?" His cleverness escaped the guard. "Well, then, you've been nice." He passed the man a five-dollar bill.

"Not necessary, sir, but thank you."

"Have you been here long?"

"Not so long."

"What goes on, behind those gates? These days?"

"The factory is dead."

"So you guard an empty factory."

The guard shrugged at this.

"No one in there tonight?"

"No sir . . ." he said. "Not tonight, not tomorrow."

"Can I take a look?" The Master Blaster pointed inside, mimed a walk, pointed at his eyes.

"No, sir. Cannot."

"Just a look?"

"No, sir . . ."

"I'm just wondering. How much do you make in an hour, standing around here? No, let me guess. Minimum wage, $3.05." More of a charade: three fingers, a zero with his thumb and his forefinger, then five fingers in the air. The guard nodded. "I'll give you three dollars . . . *per minute.*"

The guard got it instantly, The Master Blaster was sure. But he thought it over a while.

"Three dollar and five cent," the guard said, "per minute."

"Yes."

The Bangladeshi glanced up and down the highway. Farther south, a night market was set up outside another factory that hadn't closed yet. "Okay," he said. "You come in."

The Master Blaster had never visited any of the three dozen garment factories that had sprung up on Saipan. He'd driven by them, he'd glanced fences, he'd braked for workers crossing the road at night. Inside, the size of the place impressed him, a complex of buildings on one vast floor of concrete. The island was buried beneath it somewhere, with no room to breathe, as sealed off as a body in a casket.

"Those buildings are locked?" The Master Blaster asked.

"Yes."

"You have keys?"

"Yes."

"I want to go inside the buildings."

"Costs more." The Bangladeshi didn't even have to think it over; it's as if the rates for a peek from outside, a view from inside had been established long before The Master Blaster came along, faking a flat tire. "One hundred."

"For everything, right?"

"No. One hundred plus three-oh-five per minute."

"Okay. I'll make it fast."

"Take your time," X said. Then, with an unexpected flash of humor, he added, "Time is money."

❧

The Master Blaster heard that when garment factory owners, Chinese, mostly, gave up the ghost, they slipped away quickly on a flight to Japan or Taiwan, in order to avoid final payments to their workers:

one month's wages, medical bills and the cost of tickets home. What he didn't realize is that this left the factory very much as it had been on the last day of work. In the offices, there were telephones and computers, charts and blackboards with production and shipping schedules, desks and lamps and, in one corner, a small library of pornographic videos. In the factory, he found long lines of machines that cut and sewed, fabric and buttons, piles of scraps. And orderly stacks of labels that said "Made in U.S.A.". He walked from one building to another, Administration, Manufacturing, Shipping, taking pictures as he went. The barracks were the emptiest of all. Bare cots and clothes hangers and dying potted plants were all that the workers left behind. Some were still on the island, probably, God knows where, scuffling for work. Filipinos came and went; Manila was an easy plane ride away. Chinese held on longer. This is the way the world ends, this is the way the world ends, The Master Blaster told himself. This is where America ends. And it ends here first.

When he came back out, he took out a pen and a piece of paper. Forty-three minutes times $3.05 came to $131.15. Plus another hundred for entering the buildings: $231.15. Calculations done, he walked to where the fellow who called himself X stood watching traffic. A bright fellow, no doubt about it, just the kind of immigrant who did what it took to get ahead in America, but Saipan wasn't America. Too bad. Before long, he'd speak better English than some of the locals.

"It's amazing," he said, after he'd handed over payment, rounding it up to $240. "Have you ever been inside?"

"Yes," said the guard. Then his eyes met The Master Blaster's and suddenly—this can happen with a tour guide or a waiter, but not often—they were on equal terms. "But when I go in there," the guard continued, "it is with no camera." Now the Master Blaster felt outwitted. Had the guard noticed the flash? Suspected what he'd carried in a bag, the same bag he was pointing at right now? His eyes drilled The Master Blaster. Those photographs he hadn't mentioned could get the guard in trouble. He hadn't thought about it, The Master Blaster admitted, and if he had, it wouldn't have stopped him.

"I'm sorry," he said.

The guard didn't respond, didn't even nod.

"What I don't understand," he said, trying to recover "is that all over the island people are stealing copper wire out of lamps in the park, out of buildings, off job sites. But in there . . . computers, TVs, window air conditioners . . . You know what I mean?

"I know," said the guard.

Now, thought the Master Blaster, we are at the point of no return. We can go further if he wants. I'm game. I owe him a favor. But it's up to him.

"I need a truck," the guard said.

The Master Blaster could hardly hear him. As if whispering something made it less dangerous, less criminal.

"Do you have a truck?"

"Yes." The Master Blaster answered, nonchalantly, as though someone had asked him for a match. His everyday ride was the yellow jeep that was parked a few feet away. But he'd never sold the truck he used, when he was terracing his hillside, putting in the garden, carrying his seedlings, soil, cement and Filipino workers uphill.

"I need your truck," the guard said. "One night. Tomorrow?"

The Master Blaster waited before answering. If the guard got caught, The Master Blaster could always claim the truck had been stolen. He was at no risk here.

"Joe Ten Shopping Center in Susupe," The Master Blaster replied. "Tomorrow night. Keys will be on the floor under a newspaper. An orange Ford pickup. Return to same place when done."

"Okay."

The Master Blaster waited for something, a good-bye, maybe a thank-you. He'd helped the man out, they were, in a way, partners now. But, though he stood there, nothing came back at him.

"Thanks for the help with the tire," he said.

The Bangladeshi walked back to his post, a molded plastic chair at the side of the gate, and sat down. The Master Blaster drove off, knowing it was pointless looking back, for the guard would not be attending to his departure. He drove along Middle Beach Road, watching for garment workers, then turned uphill towards home. He drove carefully; there were dogs along the road at night, scavengers called boonie dogs, some tame, some feral, some close to wild.

Something was wrong. A car on the grass, where he always parked outside his house. But the lights in his house were dark. Had it come? The moment he'd feared forever? Payback? As often as he pictured this, he'd never decided how to handle it. Right now he could lock the car doors from the inside, back around and go safely back up the driveway. But that felt wrong. An evasion, at best a postponement. So he stepped out of the car, looked around, headed for his house and noticed something, someone, sitting in the chair where he took his nightly cigar and cognac.

"Mosquitoes bothering you yet?" he asked, walking over. He still couldn't make out the person sitting in his chair.

"My name is George Griffin," the visitor said. "I just want to meet The Master Blaster."

George Griffin

As proprietor of *Faraway Places, Backyard Adventures* I visited most of the world's beautiful places. Take any scenic calendar, the kind your insurance agent sends you over the holidays, with a knockout picture for every month, Matterhorn, Manhattan, Milford Sound, Angkor Wat, Farewell, Portofino, I'll nail at least eleven out of every twelve. So here's the question: why is it so hard for me to leave, even to plan to leave? On a scale of worldwide attention getters, ten points being the highest, I give Saipan four points, tops. And still, I'm hurting.

When Stephanie Warner convinced me to write as Amelia Bligh, what had been an open-ended stay evaporated fast. I put together a list of stories that Amelia would write, and e-mailed my editor via an account I'd set up in Amelia's name. I started thinking through her stories, trying to move beyond travel-column clichés: the can-do entrepreneur, the ironic curmudgeon, the gnarly native, the wise patriarch, the local expatriate, the usual cast of characters. This was Amelia, not George Griffin, dealing with the continental smoothie, the Latin Lover, the strength-through-joy German, the Eastern European thugs, all the world's Dodi Fayeds. Bottom line, I had lots of material already. But not enough. I'd been around three months. One more and I'd have to leave.

I wasn't happy about leaving Stephanie Warner. We worked and played well together, but I wondered whether our hitting it off on Saipan was only a slightly enlarged version of a shipboard romance. I hoped not. I liked my life here, at the hotel, the college, the bars, the wise guys. And the old Japanese gent that I saw every day, at dawn and dusk. As the days were numbered, I enjoyed them more. I was missing the place before I left it.

"Mr. Griffin!" Saito was standing in front of the hotel when I came home from a morning run in Marpi. "Come." Without waiting for me, he headed through the hotel and out towards his garden, and my first guess was that one of his exotic plants, something that bloomed once a year or maybe once in a lifetime, was waiting for me.

He opened the gate and gestured for me to step inside and behold what some kids had done. I remembered there being a power outage the night before and it turned out that Saito's electric fence had gone down just when some kids showed up. They left behind beer cans, that wasn't so bad. And spray-paint cans in several different colors; they'd used those to attack the trees, so there was subway graffiti on them, swirling curlicues, sometimes obscenities. The flowers, the orchids especially, were now gobs of purple and black where blossoms used to be.

"I'm so sorry," I said, though it wasn't my fault. But maybe it was, because I was part of all the things that came to this island from outside, the hodge-podge of what passed for progress. Then again, it wasn't Chinese garment workers or American tourists who got into Saito's garden. It was local kids.

Then, Saito's staff, his skeleton crew of six or seven, emerged. I saw the Chuukese maid who made it up to my fifth-floor room once a week, and the Filipino desk clerk I'd bargained with the day I arrived, and the kitchen crew who accommodated the trickle of tourists who still came from Japan. We all stood, as though at a burial.

"Never mind," Saito said. "I'll fix." He turned to me and signaled I should follow him back to the hotel.

"What are you going to do?"

"Work," he said. "Fix." He was one tough old man; bent, bow-legged, but now broken. Yet he had to know, from what he lived through, that there were some things that work couldn't fix. The thing was, though, that didn't stop him from working.

"Sit," Saito said. We were in a place I'd never been, a little office separated by a beaded curtain from the reception desk. Saito went to the shelves against the inside wall, took down a scrapbook, pulled his chair next to mine—it felt intimate—and started turning pages.

It was the landscape of his youth, the Saipan of the late thirties and early forties, portraits of a stern-looking father in shorts, kneesocks, leather shoes, short-sleeved shirt, sun helmet. Not a handsome man by any means, closer to those geeky, bucktoothed Japanese you saw in the old war comics, but there was a calmness in his eyes, a steadiness as he addressed the camera that said: here I am. Saito's mother was a local—a flowered dress, dark hair pulled up into a bun, brown skin, high cheekbones and eyes that regarded the photographer as an enemy. An island beauty, well on her way to becoming a matron. Saito pointed to himself, a shaved-head kid, maybe three years old. His finger moved to older kids, a boy and girl. Then he pointed upward: they were dead. There were half a dozen kids, neighbors, maybe relatives, and they were in a garden, the parents on lawn furniture, a dog at their feet, and the garden had crushed coral paths, a stone border, and coconut husks with orchids growing out of them were wired to the tree trunks. Saito used the same technique out back. He studied the photo for a while, the way you check out a gravestone, making sure the dates haven't changed since the last time you visited. Chances were, I guessed, that old Saito was the last one in the photo who was alive.

He flipped the pages. There were street scenes in Garapan, the main Japanese settlement, now a collection of hotels, restaurants, souvenir shops, massage parlors. Then it was a tidy colonial town, graceful low-rise buildings, shops and prewar automobiles, women on sidewalks, carrying umbrellas against the sun. There were outings to sugar plantations, where they sat on porches in wicker chairs, trips to the beach and picnics to the tiny offshore island of Managaha, and what got me was that though the photos were more than half a century old, the island was there. You couldn't miss it, you couldn't mistake it for someplace else, the curve of the lagoon, the mountain rising up in the middle, Tinian across the straits, the cliffs on the north end. People came and went, taking pictures, but the island stayed.

"You know my belief?" Saito asked me. "Saipan people see them come and go, the Spanish, the Germans, the Japanese. They are thinking okay, that is right. This is our island, belonging to us."

"What about the Americans? Come and go? The Chinese, the Koreans, all the rest . . ."

He shrugged. "Don't know. But my belief? My belief is, a place belong to people who love it. What do you think?"

"I wish."

❧

At the back of Saito's garden, there were two trees, ordinary trees that you saw everywhere along the Saipan shoreline, but I saw these two every day, I studied them. The tall one, the one with long, lacy needles, was called ironwood. Nearby, with no need of an introduction, was a coconut palm, just half the height of the ironwood. Its palm fronds glistened in the sunlight and about a dozen green coconuts nested up where the fronds joined the trunk. Many mornings I'd sat there, trying to nail what was happening between the squat, nut-bulging palm tree and that fine, lanky ironwood. Like a violin and a cello, maybe, or a sailboat and a tugboat. No good. I'd been away from the column for a while and it showed. Sluggish similes. I sat watching those two trees. The ironwood was an elegant courtesan, veiled and swaying from side to side, and that stubby palm, with a cargo of coconuts loaded with milk, and a sap that islanders tapped for coconut wine, that palm tree strained forwards, touching but not quite connecting. A squat man with a laundry bag of testicles straining for a statuesque woman who was, and was going to remain, out of his league. That wasn't bad. Which tree was America? Which was Saipan? It wouldn't stand a chance of getting into my column. But, I realized, it suited Amelia Bligh just fine.

❦

The Master Blaster had a beer at Hamilton's at five and drove his yellow jeep to a meeting that had been announced in the newspapers, an organization for people who objected to the bad press that Saipan kept getting. Love for Saipan was their slogan. I saw him pull onto the grass along Beach Road and walk, in his gimpy way, to where the other plaintiffs were sitting. The Master Blaster was a spindly, elderly fellow, the sort of nerd who might have collected butterflies in his younger days, and now, I guessed, had fun with an aquarium of tropical fish. Someone younger popped out of his seat as soon as he neared the table and The Master Blaster got a place of honor at the table. It was like they couldn't get started until he showed up. His name was Willard Huntoon and he had been on the island since Trust Territory days, a teacher, a principal, and a poet. I'd read his stuff at the College of the Islands library, expecting rhyming, user-friendly stuff, just barely above the level of a greeting card. But what he came up with was dense and sharp, often like a haiku, meditations on war and weather, the drumming of rain, the explosion of bombs. A cycle of short poems was set at the ruined Japanese hospital that sat in the boonies, near the airport. Haunting stuff. But I couldn't help wondering, who read it? Odd fellow, The Master Blaster. His web site was anonymous. His poetry obscure. No name on the stuff that people read. No audience for the poems he signed. Despite that, maybe because of that, he wrote.

After the meeting he drove south to San Antonio, through an alley of shops, hotels, bars, that gave the place a border-town look, a Chinese Tijuana. I followed, wondering what the iluvsaipan.com folks made of this garment factory world. If you loved the island that God gave you, why lease it out to the foreigners? Why raffle off God's gift?

Whoops. The Master Blaster was up to something. He pulled up in front of a garment factory. I drove on, pulled a U-turn, came back and parked across the street, in front of a Thai restaurant, got out and studied the menu in their window, turning in time to see my man go into a pretty theatrical I'm-a-senior-citizen-with-a-flat routine. The factory guard came trotting over; he had an act of his own. In no time, the tire was changed and the guard got slipped a couple of bucks, but that wasn't the end of it. Deep conference between two new friends. A moment later, The Master Blaster disappeared into the factory, an empty factory, and the guard resumed sentry duty. It was time to drive home. To The Master Blaster's home, that is.

❧

Most Saipanese live along the coastline, just inland from the beaches. Outsiders—big shots—go for the heights. That view of the sea must inspire a lord-of-the-domain feeling; way better than barefooting it on the sand. So, in a more modest way, did The Master Blaster, with a view of the sea, but from further down, a low ridge on the back side of the island. He lived alone. At Hamilton's I'd heard that his wife had died a few years ago, leaving a son in Hawaii and a daughter in Florida. Later on, he'd hooked up with a Chinese woman. She was gone now, too. There was a night they still talked about when he arrived drunk and disheveled, reeling to a seat at the bar. "Get this," he'd said, pulling a note out of his shirt pocket. "I found this on my bed, on my pillow." It turned out to be a one-line note that he read aloud. "I have left with your best friend." Now that they thought about it, some of the regulars could have seen it coming. An upscale Chinese girl and that bookish old goat. It was no surprise. What startled people was the old guy's behavior, after he read that one poisonous line. He read it again, hell, he didn't have to read it, he had it memorized: "I have left with your best friend." He looked up and down at the four or five regulars, pointed at each of them in turn. "You're here," he said to one, "You're here," to another, down the line. "So," he said, and it was sad and also so funny you almost laughed, "I'm just asking. Who the hell is my best friend?"

❦

I parked in full view of the house and the driveway. I came in peace, and, let's face it, as an admirer who was hooked on the idea of a writer who lived in the place he wrote about, took chances, told secrets, put his ass on the line, got no byline and didn't make a cent. My time on Saipan was running low. I needed to know why he'd come, and stayed, how his gentle lyrics could be reconciled with his scattershot web site. What was it about him? What was it about Saipan? He was an anonymous hero in an obscure place, art for art's sake, that's what it was, and I really wanted to see him. And now—the flash of lights on tree trunks and rock wall, he comes, he slows down when he spots my car but he nonetheless steps out—he hasn't seen me yet and heads towards his house. Then he senses me, sitting in a chair, the whole south of Saipan and Tinian over my shoulder. He walks over.

"Mosquitoes bothering you yet?"

"My name is George Griffin," I say. "I just want to meet The Master Blaster."

"Do I know you?" he asks.

"No. But at the Hyatt . . ."

"You asked a question. I guessed you were a travel agent."

"Not quite. Travel writer. I sent you an e-mail."

"Oh really." He doesn't take the bait. If he said he'd gotten my e-mail, he'd be admitting who he was.

"Have you been waiting long?"

"Twenty minutes, tops. I was out there, along the beach, while you signed up to protect the reputation of the island. I followed you down to the garment factory and saw you touch up a guard to let you in. A full evening, I'd say. I'm thinking that factory'll be another Saipan Monument on your web site."

"I could call the police."

"Please don't."

He goes into the house. Is he calling the cops? If so, I can't stop him. But he comes out with two cans of beer, two glasses and a bottle of cognac. He signals a question, Do I want some? Yes, I nod, but I pass on a cigar.

"What is it then?" he asks.

"Could you just say it? Aloud? I'd be honored."

"What?"

"You know. Say it."

"Very well, then. I'm The Master Blaster."

"Am I the first one you've ever said that to?"

"No. There are three or four people who know . . . sources of mine. But . . ."

He takes a sip of cognac, draws on his cigar, as if this were the last moment of a part of his life that the next second would change forever. "But you're the first one I've told . . . whom I had no reason to trust."

That brings me up short. I can't think of anything to say. I just do what he does, sip some cognac and let the moment pass.

"You lead a double life," I offer.

"One life," he counter. "But it divides into pieces. Add them up, maybe it comes to a whole life. A little more. Or a little less. I'm not sure."

"What's your game?" I'm blowing it, I feel like a sports guy on TV, shoving a microphone into a quarterback's face after the game.

"No game." He drinks again, enjoying his cigar. "Listen . . . Griffin. You can come here, lots of people have, and do well, live well. Put a castle on a mountain. And there are the short timers, two-year contracts. the merchant marine, the teachers, lawyers. You fish, you dive, you explore, you cruise bars, pick up girls, avoid U.S. taxes, until the day comes that you realize you need to do something else with your life and you look back on Saipan with complete sincerity . . . and say it was the happiest time of all. But if you stay it's different. Very."

"You stayed."

"And it got complicated, yes. It was always complicated . . . small islands dealing with big places. Leads to odd behavior on both sides. It got more complicated when, presto. they became American overnight. That's what got me going. That's when it began. It was never just about

Saipan. Or even mainly about Saipan. It was about America, too. Seeing
America from here. Seeing America come here. Like Blake. 'All of nature
in a blade of grass.' I had to say something. You don't intend to betray
me, do you?"

"Of course not. I'm your biggest fan."

"Is that so? Well, listen, listen to The Master Blaster. This is from
me to you. What I'm doing now, that scrapbook of ruinous projects—an
inventory of serial crimes perpetrated upon this island—that's the last of
it. After that it's time for poetry, in private. I'm shutting down. Understand?"

I have nothing to say. The whole search seems meaningless and petty.
Long run for a short slide. Then something comes to me.

"It's my turn to take a chance," I say. And tell him about that night
at the Hyatt, about Congressman Tex Von Schmidt. And Larissa.
Moscow Nights. And how I couldn't keep from wondering about it all.
About Saipan.

He hears me out, waiting a while to respond. "This is a little out of
your normal line of work, isn't it?"

"For sure," I say. Larissa's phrase. "I don't know if I'm cut out
for it."

"I don't know what to tell you. Whatever just happened to that girl
has already happened. If anything. It might be business as usual, after
they keep her out of sight for a while. Or maybe a night flight out of
Saipan . . ." His voice trailed off. There were other items on his list, I
could tell, but this was as far as he went.

"Will the police get anywhere?" I ask. "It's a murder case. An
execution."

"Well, they identified the victim and retrieved the body."

"That's it?"

"What more do you expect? Really, Griffin. A local police force up
against the Russians? The Chinese? The Koreans? They're out of their
league. Remember that movie, Jack Nicholson wearing stitches in his
nose?"

"*Chinatown?*"

"This is more of a *Chinatown* all the time. Take my advice. Stay
out of it. There's no role for you to play. Or only one, the fool. Stay out
of it."

"It's the grown-up thing, I guess." We're done now, I suppose. "I do admire you. Okay? That's all. The search for the Russian girl, the search for The Master Blaster. Over. So the site is history?"

"Any day now."

"No one to pass it on to?"

"No one." He finishes the cognac, studies his cigar, which has a few puffs left in it. "Usually, the drink and the smoke finish at the same time. Took years of practice. Suppose I've been talking too much. So I'll talk a little more. A few puffs' worth. I'll ask you a question. You say you admire what I do. And you're obviously into this island. It's yours if you want. The web site."

I sat there, not knowing what to say. That this has happened so fast! That it happened at all! An abrupt offer. It reminds me of what happened to Stephanie Warner. All-of-a-sudden college president. Now it's my turn. I'd gotten what I'd wondered about, what had impressed me, what I'd spent hours envying. And it scared me. Be careful what you wish for.

"At the end," says The Master Blaster, "I think what happens in this place is important. Hardly anyone cares, of course. But that doesn't mean it doesn't matter."

I don't respond right away, but then I said, "I'll think it over," hating myself. "I'll think hard." Hating myself more.

"Sure," The Master Blaster says. "You do that."

The Stephanie Warner

The Pink Elephant is a mess, it stinks of failure and miscalculation. It's a birthday cake left out in the rain, a party no one came to, prey to mice and rats, boonie dogs and bats and monitor lizards. Worse, it's been vandalized. People have camped, slept, gotten drunk, built fires, left toilet paper and condoms in corners, and when I visit, I picture that other campus on a hill, those barely serviceable buildings, those scraps of lawn. Grow or die, I keep saying to myself, grow or die.

I'm president of the College of the Islands. Acting president. My colleague left abruptly. I don't know why. He stole money, he insisted that his wife be hired, he was having an affair, he had liver cancer, he turned out not to have the PhD he said he had, he hadn't held the jobs he claimed, back in the States. There's no end to gossip. I've called his home, heard a message that he and his wife were traveling, which might date from before his departure for Saipan or from after his return.

The problem is, well, there are two problems. The first is to decide what I think of the Pink Elephant. To have the College of the Islands purchase the place, renovate it and move in seems absurd for an institution where the roofs leak and you're required to account for every page that you feed into a copying machine. Then again, it's because the roofs leak that a new home makes sense! Sense for the college and sense for me. At the old college I'm an administrator, at the new campus I'm a pioneer.

The building is a dump but the location is great, right where the island gets beautiful, and right across the street from a luxury hotel. And I like the idea of bringing American education to China's doorstep. Of course we'll have to serve the locals, but doing that will get us only so far. Henry Rosales is right. Those long lines of geeky, brilliant Chinese could be the making of us.

So it goes back and forth. I'm bothered about how little I know. I don't know the politics of the island or the college, and if this is like any other place, it's not the idea that matters, it's the person who proposes it, the person who benefits. Who is that person? I wonder. Is it me?

◊

"So what do you think?" I ask George Griffin. We've been running in Marpi up the road to Suicide Cliff and back down. At the end of our run, a line from Tennyson comes to me: *sunset and evening star and one clear call for me.* I drive to the Pink Elephant and stop in front.

"Do not curb appraise," I say. "A previously owned property. A challenge for the handyman. Needs TLC. Consider the possibilities," I rattle off realtor phrases while we sit in the car, windows down, still sweating.

"I wouldn't set foot in that place without a tetanus shot," says Griffin.

"All right, just listen." I lay it all out. My perplexity about the Big Pink, my first problem.

"So what's the second problem?"

"It'll sound selfish," I admit. "It's about what's best for me. I want to make it here, George, and if I do something remarkable, if I can take something small, local, ordinary and grow it into something large, international, unique . . ."

"I get it."

"There's no telling where it might lead. I could stay here forever. Or write my ticket out. Because the phone will ring, I guarantee you, feelers from headhunters. Not just colleges. Universities. Foundations."

"Wow. Look at you." He was the one who was looking. He was seeing a side of me I hadn't hidden from him yet it nonetheless gave him pause: ambition. He wasn't without ambition himself, but what he aspired to was writing. I wanted rank and power. "You say Rosales gave you a week to think about it, right?"

"Yes," I said.

And then George Griffin said something that startled me. "Give me an hour."

◊

Back at George's hotel, I showered and changed clothes—I had a closet to myself there. We were a couple now. One day we weren't and the next day we were and neither one of us could have said what had happened. We were easy around each other, around the island, in our apartments, in bed. We gave each other pleasure. The first time George was worried. He'd been down on himself, the sense of compromise and failure all over him, so the sex began with coddling and nursing, which is what I did, in an X-rated way, and it worked splendidly. He grew confident; we were well matched. He finds me in the shower, water spraying, soap suds all over, and after a moment there, he leads me onto the bed, dripping, and how nice it is, the way we lie there with the door to the verandah open and the breeze drying us off, and there's something in the way he holds me, something that I can feel in his touch, which is his dread of leaving this island and leaving me. What makes it worse is that by now we've begun to learn how islands work. When you're here, you're here. Marked present. Observed. Acknowledged. Tolerated. When you're gone, you're forgotten. You'll never get a letter, never hear a phone ring from across the sea. Never.

George rolls out of bed, signaling for me to stay put, and heads for the little kitchen. What we've come up with—well, George is the one—is a war against menu drift. We re-create recipes that, thanks to shortcuts, substitutions, changing tastes, have lost contact with what they were supposed to be. Corned beef hash. Creamed spinach. Eggs Benedict. Caesar salad. And tonight George makes German potato salad, with oil, chives, onions, bacon and no mayonnaise. There was a place in hell, he said, for the man who invented mayonnaise. This is the sort of thing that people do on islands. The sort of improvisation that they miss when they are gone.

We sat down to potato salad and crisp French bread with some gorgonzola that he'd gotten from one of the hotels. And wine. And, after that, Irish coffee. Another victim of menu drift. He did it right, with flaming brandy and crusted sugar, with lemon, with black coffee, Irish whiskey, real whipped cream. It was perfect; one of those times when everything clicked. We sat there, totally companionable, no other place we wanted to be, no other company desired, two people on a hotel verandah that might as well have been deck chairs on some slow boat to God knows where.

"Okay," he said. "The hour's up. Just one question and I'll tell you what I think. I know about Henry Rosales. But what about the other trustees?"

"Regents."

"Whatever. Anybody you've met you can sound out? The chairman . . . chair whatever?"

"An ancient American gent. I hardly know him. So the answer to your question is no." A few weeks before, they'd given a lovely reception at the Hyatt. The food was fine, the wine generous, the conversation polite and miscellaneous, with lots of assurance, at the end of the evening, that we'd be seeing a lot of each other. But not a scrap of urgency. For all I knew, the next such party would be when I departed and there would be little difference between this party and that party, no more difference than between a sunrise and a sunset, indistinguishable except in that one the sun is coming up and in the other it is going down.

"I thought about consulting someone," I continued. "It wouldn't work. The moment Rosales found out I was calling around, asking questions . . ."

"Okay." He leaned forward, his feet slipping off the hassock, and took my hands. "Go with the Pink Elephant. It's not a choice. There is no choice. If you criticize, you're gone. You haven't been here long enough to take a stand. And besides, the idea is interesting—that international education thing—no stranger than Russian hookers or Chinese garment workers. Taking a dump and turning it into a dynamo . . . you could be a miracle worker."

"It could be a fiasco," I said. "There's no way of knowing."

"If there's no way of knowing something, then you can't be expected to know it. Listen, you're not supposed to be an expert on this place. The place is lousy with experts."

"Where . . . where on earth will they get the money?"

"Not your problem. It's his idea."

"I don't know," I said. "Maybe it's supposed to be my idea." What George had said made sense but I still was uneasy. I'm a careful woman. I didn't choose fights I couldn't win. But on this island I couldn't tell where the fight was, or what it was about or who was in it.

"You have to put your doubts away, Stephanie. You have to get behind this one hundred percent. They don't need skepticism or irony from you. They won't appreciate it. Okay?"

"Okay," I said, but I sounded like a woman—a *young* woman— in doubt. Question marks were hanging in the air. "You're so sure of yourself."

"Myself is exactly what I'm not sure of. Other people . . . no prob-lem." It was dark now and there were fires down on the beach and sounds of music and a moon rising, a full moon, which was much more of an occasion around here than it was in other places. It was something you didn't want to waste.

"So the Pink Elephant it is," I said.

"Yes."

"And when you come back, you'll be at work on Amelia Bligh's book."

"My book. Yes. Here. Not a bad place to be, for a ghost writer. It'll go fast. You'll see."

"And after that?"

"There's another project, could be fun. No money in it, at least no direct money, but you never know." He hadn't answered my question, so I waited. He put his hands over his ears, his eyes, his lips: hear no evil, see no evil, speak no evil. "Mum's the word. Promise? Cross your heart and hope to die."

"Yes." Our feet were back on the hassock and, with the moonlight, something was stirring in me, lazily at first, now insistently. With my toe, I touched the sole of his foot. Do you believe in reflexology? He looked at me, we were on the same page. But he had one thing to say.

"I found The Master Blaster."

"Who?"

"You know him," he said.

"I do? Who is it?" I asked.

"Can't say," he said. "I gave my word."

"Not even me?"

"Not even you. Anyway, I think you'll figure it out on your own."

Mel Brodie

❧

"Mr. Brodie," said attorney Jaime Lopez, "I cannot count the projects that have come to me for advice. Garment factories, hotels, colleges, clinics, golf courses, those things you would expect. Amusement parks, cattle ranches, you have no idea. Treasure hunters in search of Amelia Earhart's body, George W. Bush's airplane, Spanish galleons. Gangsters too, I admit it, Yakuza for sure, and Chinese tongs and some Russians I have my doubts about . . . or, should I say, hopes for. But I am so happy to see you! Coffee?"

J. Lo's coffee, when it came, was delivered by a well turned out Filipina who operated a serious espresso machine in an office that announced, everywhere you looked, that you were in the presence of a local boy who'd made good. There were pictures of Jaime shaking hands with Don Shula, Willie Nelson, George W. Bush, Tom DeLay, Jaime smiling next to a dead marlin, Jaime on a golf course with Lee Trevino. Driving around in Gregorio's taxi, he'd been down-home, folksy, eager to please. I wondered about my new friend, who he was and what was his game. Not until our third joyride with Gregorio did he mention he was a lawyer. It was as though premature disclosure would frighten me off. Once a sidekick, now a lawyer. And I was his client. So I sat back and let him take me to school for a whole, billable, hour.

Lesson one was about land on Saipan and it was from him I learned—how could I have missed it?—that outsiders couldn't buy land. It was reserved for people of Northern Marianas descent.

"Hold it," I said. "Let me get this straight. *You* can buy land in the U.S. . . ."

"And do . . ." he interrupted. "Puget Sound, in my case."

"But here . . . I'm a foreigner?"

"For these purposes, yes. This was to protect our people from losing land. This small island is all we have. You can lease the land though."

"Lease with an option to buy? Like a car." This was something I'd only heard of, in TV ads. It was nothing I knew about, really.

"No. Lease. Period. For private land, fifty-five years. For public land, forty years."

I didn't like what I was hearing. It's like the old joke about one hundred years is a long time to live. Until you talk to a man who's ninety-nine. And as the lease aged, the value of the houses on the land, which was supposed to appreciate, went flat or down.

"It's a wonder anyone comes here."

"But they do . . . as you know."

"Yeah," I said. A lease like that encouraged quick-buck artists. But I was in Patriot's Rest for the long run. I wanted it to be around, when I wasn't.

"It's not as bad as it sounds," Lopez continued. He said chances were that the law favoring locals would be repealed before the lease ended, long before, and for two reasons. The first was that there were locals who wanted top dollar for their land and they weren't getting it from other locals. The other was that with intermarriage, bloodlines were thinning and fewer and fewer locals qualified. So it looked like the problem might solve itself. I nodded, I understood what he was saying, but I couldn't picture myself explaining all this to people who were moving halfway around the world to make an investment that depended on a Saipanese decision somewhere down the road.

"Think about it," Lopez advised me. "I can walk you through this, every step of the way. But the first step, you have to take it." He sounded like the old man in the room and I was a kid, just off the boat. That's what happens when you show up in a place you've never been. You're a kid all over again, not just a kid, a toddler. Eating safe food, warned about dangerous places, guided and guarded everywhere.

"I'll be in touch," I said, getting up. I was cold. The office was air-conditioned and the secretary was wearing a sweater, like some tootsie hanging around a chalet, après-ski.

"Before you go . . . I'll be off the island the next two weeks. Vancouver. New York and Maine. Bar Harbor. Have you been to Bar Harbor?"

"Not so far north," I said. "Went to L.L. Bean's in Freeport." He wasn't impressed.

"While I'm away, if you have a site, I could ask my staff to do some preliminary work. Ownership, title search, those things. Formalities. And all in confidence, of course."

"I see," I said, and I asked myself whether this was a moment I'd remember and how I'd remember it. "Yes," I said. "There's a place I like."

"Which is . . ."

"Let me just check it out again."

❦

The place I liked or, to put it more accurately, loved, was on a ridge off Capitol Hill, a narrow spine of grassy land that looked north towards Marpi, at the Philippine Sea to the west, the Pacific to the east. There was always a breeze up there and it was one of the only places where you could see the sunrise and the sunset.

I drove there right after leaving Jaime's office. I had no idea who owned this land, where property lines began and ended. I only knew it was empty, except for a little house, island style, one room with a tin roof, a porch and lean-to, a weekend hangout that no one had been using lately. I could see Tinian from there, and the patch of ocean that had claimed my old man. We had something in common. We'd both wound up near the end of our lives in a place we didn't have a clue about.

Whose land was it? Was I trespassing? Was there water around? Power, sewer, no way. Was the ground stable? Fertile? Did the earth shift and slide in heavy rain? I'd need to find out real soon. So this afternoon was the end of the beginning, the simple happy time, that I wanted to enjoy a little longer, even if it made my lawyer wait. God, what a place, what a view, the birds so far below were more like fish, going with the current. It wasn't beautiful, in that Caribbean way; it was rough along the shore, rough inland. You couldn't think of it all the time but you had to think of it now and then, how this island felt for the men who fought here, the ones who had made Saipan and Tinian safe for my father's plane to land on though not, in his case, to take off from. And, yeah, there were peace monuments all over Saipan, plaques, pillars, crosses and markers. Still there was a menace in the air. You couldn't count on the island to be nice, any more than you could count on niceness from the sea surrounding it.

❦

With Cori and Lourdes AWOL, I spent a lot of nights at Hamilton's, where my fifteen seconds of being a feminist hero made me a colorful character. My retirement idea was no secret and, at Hamilton's, I learned it was nothing new. The Japanese had talked it up a few times—"silver hair" communities—but the absence of world-class medical care was a problem. I had that covered: a helicopter to Guam, a flight to the Philippines, and a nurse on Saipan. I had to do it, but I did it grudgingly, because if you came to Saipan to die, I figured you should live as well as you could until the day came and not make such a fuss, copping an additional, highly-medicated month or two. But not everybody bought my bright idea.

"They won't come," one of the guys along the bar said. A retired schoolteacher, I think. "A handful of veterans visit for a week. But live here? I have my doubts. Ten, fifteen years ago ago maybe, but now . . . I'm afraid the ship has left the dock." I'd have to shift from veterans to younger retirees, he said, and maybe he was right, but I'd go out of my way. I'd accommodate for *free*—that was it—the first veteran who committed to the place! When I told the teacher that, he backed off, changed the subject. Someone challenged him to recite the name of the presidents, they bet he couldn't do it, and I heard names I didn't recognize: Arroyo, Estrada, Ramos, Aquino, Marcos, Macapagal, Magsaysay, Quirino, Roxes, Osmena, Laurel, Quezon, Aguinaldo. It's the names of presidents of the Philippines. Backward, latest to first. I wished my girls could have been there. Lots of laughs. Then something happened. Remember that scene in old Westerns where a stranger walks into a noisy saloon and, all of a sudden, the place goes quiet? Could be Jack Palance or Clint Eastwood. Well here, the newcomer was Big Ben.

"Son of a bitch!" someone exclaimed. Half annoyed, half pleased.

"We're in trouble now," Davey said. "The Wizard of Oz. The *capo di tutto cappi*. The secret sharer."

"Pour these gentlemen another drink," Big Ben said. "I've checked. No police checkpoints to vex you on the way home."

"It's been a while," Big Herb said.

"Busy times," Ben answered, shrugging. He waved at his stomach. "And I have to watch it."

"Takes more than watching."

"I suppose. But I wonder about you fellows," Big Ben said. "Are they still here? I ask myself. Still talking, conjecturing. Should my ears be burning? I miss you, a little bit. May I say that, across the gap of war?"

"We're not fighting," Davey said. "Just watching. Harmless old farts. We're too old to fight you. And not close enough."

"We're on the same island," Ben said. "That's close."

"So . . ." Herb said, trailing off.

"So . . ." Ben acknowledged. Awkward. As if some people who'd known each other well a long time ago met by chance, years later, and couldn't quite connect. I guessed there were all sorts of things they couldn't talk about, that would ruin things, so they rummaged around to find something they could settle on. It was baseball. They talked about Japanese and Korean team who were spring training on Saipan. And after that, they went back to—would you believe it?—Micronesian Olympic game in 1969! When an unbeatable Palauan team confronted a Trukese team led by a fortyish pitcher who'd played in Japan and, so they said, faced Joe DiMaggio in an exhibition game. They went inning by inning, the Palauans ahead and the Trukese threatening, when a devastating pick-off play snuffed out the potential tying run. It pleased them, all of them, to remember that game. Silence followed but it was relaxed silence, as though they'd accomplished something together. Davey offered another round but Ben excused himself.

"One's my limit," he said. "None's my limit, actually. I just wanted to come and pay my respects."

We watched him walk out and I saw the guys up and down exchange shrugs.

"Pay his respects?" Davey asked. "Has someone died?"

After Big Ben left, talk resumed, slow at first and then, a flood. It was hard to follow, all out of order, stories from thirty years ago, from yesterday, stories about things that hadn't happened yet. Not only out of order but mixed, so mixed that it seemed impossible it was all about the same guy. He was a lawyer who never appeared in court, a politician who never tried to get elected, a government big shot without an office, and, hell, they weren't even sure where he lived, which was an odd thing not to know on an island this small. On any night, it seemed, there were any number of apartments, hotel rooms, houses where he might be staying. He was brilliant, he was corrupt, he had deep feelings and he just didn't give a shit. He hated Americans, or didn't. Ditto Japanese, Koreans, Chinese, Filipinos. Double ditto, someone said for his own people. He had all sorts of friends, high and low. But real friends? No one knew. It went back and forth. They didn't know him, that's what I decided, and it drove them crazy because if they didn't know Big Ben, how could they—these long-term island guys, these expat experts—claim to know Saipan?

"I'll say this and that's all I'll say." This came from the old-timer who'd told me that World War II vets were way too old to move to Saipan, and then went on to rattle off a list of Filipino chief executives. The campus poet, they called him. Mr. Huntoon. "He was the best student I ever had. There were plenty bright ones. But of them all, he was the only one I'd consider a serious reader. Not romance and thrillers. Serious stuff. Every year he'd read something by whoever won the Nobel Prize."

"So?" Davey asked. "What difference does that make?"

"I can't say," Huntoon replied, turning away from the others to finish his drink. That was the theme of the evening. They couldn't say.

⟡

I drove home from Hamilton's feeling blue. When people doubted my project, I doubted it myself. Yet I pictured it, clear as day, old timers getting up each morning, like another day was a great gift, stepping out for a morning walk—"the dawn patrol," they'd call themselves—and returning for a long, bullshitty breakfast, all of it seemed so clear. But it was getting complicated. So I pulled into the apartment hotel I'd moved into after I left the Hyatt, down in Chalan Kanoa, and stepped into the lobby, where a bunch of Chinese kids in T-shirts and bathing suits were tracking sand onto the carpet.

"Mr. Brodie," says the clerk, a kid from Nepal, "you have a guest."

"A guest . . ."

"The guest asks you to meet on the beach."

"Who is it?"

"Sir, please, I can say no more."

So I headed across the lawn, onto the sand. On Saipan, the beach belongs to everyone, a hundred feet in from the high water line, parents and kids, picnickers, crack smokers, watercolor painters, fishermen casting nets. But there was no one here, no one parked in a car listening to a radio, or sitting at a table eating and drinking, hours on end.

It happened fast. Someone came from behind, put their hands over my eyes, perfect, and tight enough I couldn't turn. But the hands were soft and the voice, when it came, was familiar.

"Hi, Uncle Mel. I came back." It was Lourdes and we were hugging like I don't know what and I lost it a little bit, more than she did. Maybe it meant more to me than it did to her, but I was all right with that.

"Where were you?" I asked when I got it back together. "No message, no phone call, no nothing. I waited for you, looked for you all the way to the airport."

I sounded like a parent, scolding a kid past curfew. All these things got tangled together now, cash and carry, age and youth, sex and friendship, randy old timer and kindly uncle.

"What happened?"

"Uncle Mel, my mum is getting very sick, she is not eating, only a little, and we have her to hospital and the doctors are examining her and they think she has a blockages in tummy and we are praying."

"And?" I knew this was important stuff but the emotion of the moment didn't stop me from wanting to cut to the bottom line, and one thing about Lourdes, when she told a story, it was like reading one of those columns that summarized a weeks' twists and turns in a soap opera.

"Better now," Lourdes said. "Our prayers . . . We find this wonderful woman, she is a faith healer and she is knowing how . . ."

"And Cori . . . Her mother got sick, too?"

"She send big kiss and she is very sorry. Big, big hug but her boyfriend comes back from Saudi Arabia and is wanting to marry her."

"Nice guy?"

"Okay." That was enough on Cori, I saw her decide. Cori was history. "You are glad to see me, Uncle Mel?"

"Yes, I'm glad you came back. It's been a little bit down."

"We can fix," she said. Her English could be comical, easily mimicked. She sounded like someone who couldn't be taken seriously. But she was a sly one. She read people the way I did, studied the angles, found the weak spots and the soft ones. Found mine, all right.

Back at the desk, the guy at reception was beaming. They liked her. Could be, they liked me, too.

"Nice surprise, Mr. Mel?"

"She'll do." I guess. Lourdes leans against me, vamping, singing, "Together again . . ." Then she looks at me.

"You will bring up my luggages?" she asks.

Khan

There was a gas station with jobs for us and the owner was crazy. That was what the brothers said. Once again they surprised me. They had found chickens and vegetables, they had found the rich man's place and now they found work on Saipan, not by knocking on doors, but at the mosque, where we now were waiting for someone who was interested in hiring Muslims. I wondered what cruelty was in store for us.

Then the worst-looking truck on the island pulled up. It missed a fender in front and the tailgate was gone. The man who stepped out was different, darker than most Saipanese, and not fat. He nodded at the security guard, who pointed at us.

"You come," the newcomer said.

"But, sir . . . Our contracts? Our terms?"

"You don't like it, I'll bring you back here."

"But, sir. Your name?"

"Arnaldo." As soon as we climbed in, he asked, "Where you stay?"

The brothers were in back. Most of the truck bed was gone. They had a good view of the road below. I was next to the driver. I gave him the name of the village. When we got to the village, I pointed him down the road. When we approached the palace gate, I saw him start to smile; when we stopped, he laughed out loud, couldn't stop laughing, kept laughing as we walked through the gate and down to the shelter by the swimming pool and tennis court.

"Smart boys," he said when we returned. It hadn't taken long to pack. "You live like kings."

"I am Khan," I said. I introduced the brothers. "The king is dead a long time," I said. "We borrowed the place. We are not sorry to leave it."

The gas station was on the road that ran around the back of the island, a brand-new building where I saw that the per-gallon price of gas was almost a dollar more than we would make an hour, which was $3.05. Every tank of gas filled would match our daily wages.

Arnaldo took us inside where his wife, Regina, ran a little store that sold beer and other drinks, canned goods, snacks. There was also local food, bread and donuts, onions, greens, bananas, papayas, watermelons. Also, this pleased me, there were newspapers.

"The vegetables are from the farm," Arnaldo said. "I'll show you later. But first . . ." He gestured for us to sit down at a little table near the food. We seated ourselves and waited while he went to pour himself some coffee. That was when his wife cornered him. It was an argument, I was sure of it: three black men did not please her. He listened to her for a minute then ended it with one sentence and returned to us.

"Coffee?" he asked. No, we said. "Coffee you can have, anytime. No need to ask. And tea. Tea bags over there. The local food . . . you take when you're hungry, okay? But nothing from the cooler. You do not touch. You people do not drink beer. Yes?"

"No beer."

"You pray plenty. Five times a day, is it?"

"They do. I can skip sometimes."

"That's good. You always have to cover the pumps. And more. People are lazy here. You wash the windshields. You check the tires. You wipe the rearview mirror. You say good morning and thank you. You and your friends. They speak English?"

"They will learn."

"You—is it Khan?—are the one who handles the cash register. Now I ask you a question. Think carefully before you answer. Are you an honest man?"

"Yes, sir."

"Sir, is for customer. You call me Arnaldo. Or you call me boss."

"I am an honest fellow, boss. My friends are honest. Very honest."

"You steal, this is serious crime. Felony. You steal, I report, they deport. Two misdemeanors or one felony, they deport. Understand? All right, I train you this afternoon. Pumps, oil, credit card, cash register. But first . . ."

He got up and looked outside. Across the street was an air-conditioning repair place and market and a beauty salon, English names with Chinese, maybe Korean, writing underneath. To the left, on our side, was an apartment building, two stories, with rusted metal rods sticking out of the roof, but the first and second floor were boarded up. There were two colors of paint, purple and white, like something you might see on a car, but the paint was fading. There were many such buildings on Saipan. You couldn't tell if they were going up or coming down. They resembled each other, the way an infant, newborn, curled up and crying, resembled an old man on a deathbed. Helpless, both of them.

Just then a truck pulled in to the pumps. The Qazis jumped up, ready and willing, but Arnaldo shouted to his wife. She went to a window and called at someone else and after a while a local boy came out yawning, shuffling toward the truck where the driver was already filling his tank. The young man stood and watched, waving at a passing car.

"Look at him," Arnaldo said. "He thinks he works here. Not anymore. Never hire your relatives." Now Arnaldo started out on his own people. Others might never talk to strangers about their own people. But Arnaldo welcomed the chance to talk, and I guessed he'd been needing someone to listen. What a fine island Saipan had been, he said, always able—able to this day—to give food and shelter to its people. Four foreign rulers came, he raised four fingers, and people suffered. War came and people suffered. Three foreign powers—three fingers for Spain, Germany, Japan—left, and in 1975 three quarters of the people here voted to join America, to become American citizens on an island which would become part of America forever. This was a speech he had given before, I knew, and he was only beginning. At $3.05 an hour, I was ready to listen. Now look at the island, full of hotels, factories, tourists, strangers. Look at his own people, in love with steaks, air-conditioning, television. Unskilled, overweight, outworked and overmatched, any place but here, where they lived off government jobs. He could not, he would not, hire his own people, even if they were relatives, *especially* if they were relatives. His people did bad things to foreigners sometimes. He waited for me to agree but I gave a nod that only signaled understanding and he resumed. Worse was what his people did to themselves, they lost their skill, their drive, their sense of purpose, their identity. On an island that belonged to anybody, they were nobody. Americans who had never been to America! What was that? A joke? It made him laugh, it made him weep. That boy out there, his wife's sister's son, leaning against a truck. If he felt like hopping in for a ride, he would do it. He had done it many times. And, please, there was no end to his holidays, his sick days, the weddings, baptisms, funerals he attended.

"So I hire you," Arnaldo concluded. "You understand?"

"Yes, boss."

"Good," he said. He got up, went over to the cooler and reached inside for a can of beer, which he snapped open and drank from, sitting across from me. Half the can went down in one swallow.

"Okay if I drink beer in front of you, Khan?"

"Yes."

"Do you think less of me, drinking beer?"

I saw a trap. If I said I did not, he would guess I was lying. If I said I did think less, he would admire my honesty. Or let me go.

"Do you think less of me?" he repeated.

"Not yet," I said.

"Good answer, Khan. I like you."

◊

In T-shirts that said "Arnaldo's Shell," we began our new life. From six in the morning until ten at night, we worked. When the station closed, one of us was to sleep in the station, on a cot in back of the cash register. That was going to be me. I could read newspapers, Arnaldo said, if I folded them up and put them back. There was a bathroom with a sink in back, and a restroom around the side of the station and, best of all, a lamp I could read by, out of sight, behind the counter. I looked forward to my first night.

At closing time, Arnaldo came down a road that led to his farm. He carried some chicken and rice for me.

"Ready for bed?" he asked the brothers. They nodded. "Well, come . . ."

"Where is he taking us?" Qazi asked.

I saw he was scared.

"What's he saying?" Arnaldo asked.

"He says they would both be happy to sleep here, on the floor, boss. No problem." That tile floor, that I'd just swept and mopped, must have looked like heaven to the two brothers. And it was cool, if you rolled over near the beer cooler.

"No, no," said Arnaldo, "I have a place for them on the farm."

As they walked off, the Qazi brothers turned towards me, as if they might never see me again, and I remembered our first night on Saipan, the ruined building, the rusted fence, the pigs. What they saw then, they feared now. For myself, though, I was content. I lay on a couch, a lamp on the chair beside me, feasting on newspapers, the two from Saipan and one from Guam. And that first night I saw a story that, when I read it, felt like a letter written just to me.

Two Korean tourists visited the northern part of the island, which I had not yet seen. The tourists went to a place called Suicide Cliff, where they enjoyed a view from a high place. They had it to themselves and everything was fine. And then another car came up the road, stopped and parked where the Koreans had left their rental car. Two young men got out and walked towards them. They were wearing masks. They told the Korean woman to give them their purse. She refused. They touched her with a kind of electric gun—the newspaper called it a taser—which knocked the woman to the ground, in shock and pain. The husband offered his wallet without a fight. The robbers went back across the parking lot. One of them took something, something sharp, a knife or screwdriver, and cut the rental car tires, took a can of spray paint, pointed it at the windshield and painted "X".

❧

I worried about the farm Arnaldo had taken the Azis brothers to, but they came back with him the next morning smiling, carrying stalks of bananas, baskets of lemons and papaya. Back and forth they went, three round-trips before they were done with the vegetables. Then Regina brought out lumpia, empanada, donuts, sandwiches, cookies, and something we could never touch, that was a favorite of the store: a pile of cold rice, wrapped in a black, papery leaf, with a slice of pink meat on top.

"Spam sushi," Arnaldo said. "For sure, you do not touch that, Khan." He had his arm around me, he liked me. On an island where workers were tools that washed, sewed, carried dishes, cleaned and danced and performed sex acts, I was Khan. Arnaldo was a good man. His wife had doubts and the boy who left when we arrived comes and goes with a stone face. To be fired and replaced by a Bangladeshi is an insult. But Arnaldo was a good man.

Just then, the Qazis came in carrying plastic bottles filled with a cloudy, milky liquid. They put the bottles in the cooler, carefully, quickly. Everything Arnaldo asked, they did at double speed, smiling all the way. This was America at last, and they wanted to do well here. To them, California was just out of sight, beyond the reef. Not Guam, California.

"Is that touch or not touch?" I asked, pointing at the bottles. "For us."

"I'm not sure," Arnaldo said. "You want to see? Come on, we go to the farm. You can decide."

The old road we took to the farm began just in back of the gas station, crossed some burned-off grass, curved into thickets of brush and struggled uphill through a canyon that was almost a tunnel, dark and wet.

"The Japanese made this," Arnaldo said, "for their railroad. For sugar." Then the road opened onto a clearing, a grassy place with plants all over and trees and vegetable patches. Arnaldo's place was on one side of the field, its back against the mountain. Beyond, was a smaller place where the brothers' clothing was hanging from a clothesline.

The place was green and quiet, hidden away and protected. Things grew here. There were dogs and chickens and some cattle.

"Those other two, the brothers, are asking if they can have goats here," Arnaldo said.

"They did?" It surprised me that the brothers had an idea and that they had managed to ask permission.

"Okay with me."

"Do you have pigs?"

"Over there," he said, pointing to a place behind his house, a fence enclosing a patch of mud. "Okay with you?"

"Yes," I said.

"That's the way we get along, Khan," he said, slapping me on the shoulder. Life was hard, he told me, as though he were talking to a son he didn't have. That was why his wife was bitter. The world was full of children and none for her. Only relatives. Living without children was hard, he said, but living with in-laws was harder. He preferred friends, people he chose, people who chose him. By now he'd walked me to a grove of coconut trees, right where the mountain at the center of the island came down to the edge of his farm.

"What you saw in the store, in the plastic bottles, came from here."
He pointed up into the branches, to where the flower of the coconut
emerged at the end of a long stalk. Next, he picked up a ladder that was
on the ground and sat it against one of the palm trees. He climbed up the
ladder and pulled a knife out of the pocket.

"Watch me, Khan, then I have a question for you." He held the
knife. "It has to be sharp. You need a clean cut." He made a quick slash
across the stalk that had flowers at the end of it. "You don't want to cut
it off. You only want it to lean forward. You do this for five or six days.
Sometimes twice a day. After a while the juice comes. So far, okay?"

"Yes. But what is the question?"

"Not yet, look over here." He walked to another palm, pointed
upwards where a plastic bottle was attached to a drooping stalk. "Take
the ladder, Khan. Bring down the bottle."

I did as he said, handed him the bottle.

"This is what we sell at the store. Tuba, we call it. Some people add
lime or pineapple or chili. You want a taste?"

"Is it all right? For me?" It was strange, asking him to decide such a
question. It surprised him, too, and he thought it over for a while.

"Now is fine, I think," he said. It was sweeter than I expected but not
too sweet, and it was cool. I liked it.

"It starts one way, innocent, and it becomes something else that is
alcoholic," Arnaldo said. "You can look after those trees if you like. I'll
show you how to cut. Twice a day, sometimes."

"Why so often?"

"You cannot let the plant heal," he said. "Otherwise . . . nothing to
drink."

As we walked down to the gas station, I asked myself what Arnaldo
had intended, whether there was some kind of lesson he meant for me.
Was it that time turned what was fresh into something that was forbidden? Was that his message? Things started one way and became something else? That some cuts didn't need to heal? Or was it just that he
needed someone to talk to, it didn't matter who?

VI

The Master Blaster

❦

God had a sense of humor. And some of God's jokes were funnier than others, outright hoots, you rolled on the floor laughing. But there was also gentle humor that elicited nods and knowing chuckles, and dark humor that caused doubt and pain. The Almighty performed in a variety of venues, large arenas like the Middle East, where thousands of people converged and searchlights swept the audience. But there were intimate little venues where God addressed an audience directly, contended with hecklers, called customers up on stage. Saipan was God in a small club, riffing, goofing off, trying new material. Sometimes God yielded the mike to the audience, an unmoved mover, and let things happen. But never for long. Eventually God asserted himself, aiming lightning bolts at, say, a retired American who limited himself to a nightly cigar, lived for years in the world's cleanest, if heaviest, air, hundreds of miles away from traffic jams and smokestacks, and who would, it turned out, die of lung cancer. Now, right now, he felt all right, but he supposed that was what they said, all the condemned, after they got the news, like the man who jumped out of a skyscraper, passed the thirtieth floor on the way down and shouted "Okay so far!" At seventy-five, it was too late to call foul. But the manner of death, lungs filling with fluid, a kind of inner drowning, he wasn't so sure he could handle that, the terminal, gurgling, choking struggle. Or the doped-up coma. He wasn't sure about that at all.

He worked harder than usual on his web site. Memorials of Saipan generated quite a stir. People never knew where his camera would point, whether at big, bankrupt deals or pathetic little failures. Last week it had been a big deal, a U.S.-financed Star Wars installation up in Marpi, a Reagan-era radar station designed to detect incoming missiles, half Peenemünde V-2 launcher, half Mt. Palomar observatory. When he photographed it the other day, the sentry house was decrepit, graffiti-covered, the gate was down, the buildings within had been thoroughly vandalized. God, the locals were not good, they were *great*, when it came to eviscerating an empty building, not only stripping it of fixtures, lights, wire, but desecrating it with garbage, graffiti, shit. Still pointed heavenward, the radar tower was covered by robustly peeling paint, brown stains from rust and rain, a ladder that had lost its steps. Cause of death: peace.

Cognac and cigar. Would he have time to finish this bottle, and another, before his time came? And what about the cigars he ordered last month? He took a sip, took a puff. If this was what killed him, so be it. Meanwhile, faithfully, his Saipan twinkled down below. Maybe Saipan was his cause of death, that kept its hold on him for so long. The deaths that came, weren't they people connected to the lives they lived and, if that were true, weren't deaths, all deaths, a kind of suicide?

How, he asked himself, was a man to prepare himself for imminent death? He wondered about staying on Saipan. What was the point? Stoic resolve? He guessed he might travel a bit. Go back to places that had mattered, visit some he'd never seen. He shrugged it off. Saipan would do. But one change occurred, almost by itself, in his reading. It had been substantial, favoring history and serious fiction, along with an unapologetic yen for mysteries and thrillers. A book a week, all through the years. But after his last visit to the doctor, he turned to poetry, and the poetry that spoke to him was what poets had written in the face of their own mortality, running out of time to write, or live. Matthew Arnold's "On Growing Old," Chidiock Tichborne on the eve of his execution in the Tower of London—"The day is past, and yet I saw no sun / And now I live and now my day is done"—Tennyson's "Crossing the Bar," and, best of all, D. H. Lawrence's "Ship of Death," which pictured a voyage into darkness and nonbeing, with just a glimmer of hope, a purpling of the sky, on the far horizon.

George Griffin

❡

The College of the Islands' much publicized grow-or-die campaign has taken over Stephanie's life. But she's a willing victim. She's on television, in front of the legislature, in newspapers. She travels to China to talk to feeder schools, recruiters, to Hong Kong and the Philippines to interview prospective faculty and administrators. Her office is full of those "artist's conception" sketches, with billowing clouds, happy birds, fountains, benches, mature trees and busy book-carrying students walking to class. She's been interviewed, at length, in *The Chronicle of Higher Education*. She's a woman to watch, she's a woman on her way.

We haven't run in weeks. That time of exploring the island together, the wild parts of it, are over now. When she shows up, usually with no notice at all, she's tired, harassed and, not to dance around it, horny. Cars have driven in and out of Jiffy Lube more ceremoniously than Acting President Stephanie Warner, when in need of immediate servicing. There's something punitive that's crept into our sex, hit me with your best shot. She comes on like a schoolteacher in a porn movie, suggesting that she's been a bad little girl in need of punishment.

When I suggest that we go running, it sounds quaint, like something we did before we found more grown-up ways of exercising. But she checks her busy schedule and grants my wish, a late afternoon run on Lau Lau Beach. We run downhill, past the ruined restaurant where I'd spotted the yellow jeep that turned out to be The Master Blaster's. We reach the beach. What a place to be in the late afternoon, all golden and mellow! We go further than usual, up a rocky road, then down to a turning point, a beach where Japanese skin divers are calling it a day, rinsing themselves between an outdoor shower, piling tanks, masks and fins into tour company vans. They seem pleased with themselves, a day well spent, and are in no rush to end it. Neither are we. We turn back, grateful for the chance to pass that perfect beach again. They're still fishing out near the reef, even as shadows lengthened, night declaring itself. No gaudy sunsets on this side of the island, just a subtle minute-by-minute shift of tone and mood.

That's when we smell it: another discovery. God knows how we missed it on the way out. Was it the mood we were in? The direction of the wind? Hard to know, hard to miss because what's rotting off the road has been there for a while. If one of us, either one, would say it is probably a dead boonie dog, we'd be gone. But we keep our mouths shut and step into the boonies. I remember that bodies turn up in odd places on Saipan, tourists and garment workers. The smell gets stronger and I know it is no dog. It's a woman, lying on her stomach, skirt up past her knees, blonde hair and the muscular legs you'd find on a ballerina. No ballerina here, though. Pole dancer, more likely. Her face is on the ground, turned a little to one side, so we can see the bruise above and below a yard of clothesline that no one had bothered to remove off Larissa's neck.

"They got her," I say, kneeling beside her. "For sure. Shit."

"You know her?"

"A little bit."

"Who is she?"

"A Russian girl," I say. "Larissa."

I can tell Stephanie's stunned. Odd as it sounds, she maybe felt a twinge of jealousy. Not that there was anything on the ground to be jealous of.

"Listen," I said. "You have a cell phone in the car, don't you? So go up there and call the cops, meet them and come back down. I'll be here . . . out on the road anyway."

She looks annoyed, marches away with the kind of step that says I'll pay for this and soon. Just after she leaves, a vanload of Japanese divers comes by, the same ones we saw before, enjoying the end of a beautiful day. They're still in a good mood. I tell them to give Stephanie a lift.

The police come in twenty minutes and Stephanie is with them. The two cops follow us to the body.

"We smelled her," I say. "Too much for a dog."

"Okay," one of the cops replies.

"She was murdered," I said, pointing to the cord. "Strangled"

"Can we go now?" Stephanie asks.

"Okay," says one of the cops. "We wait for the truck. We cannot put her in our car."

❧

The time for running has passed and our mood has changed. It's still beautiful, falling into evening. But now Saipan feels sinister, dangerous, a bad place to be, its whole history a series of accidents and mistakes. Stephanie walks quietly beside me—a walk that seems endless—and says nothing. Not hostile, just distant. Someplace else, entirely.

"I'll call you," I say, after we drive back to where my car is parked, at the college. "There's something I want to share with you, but I don't want to get you in trouble. The less you know, the better."

"Well, right now I have something to share with you," she announces. "I fired eleven people today." She's just checked her watch. We're back on the clock here.

"What did they do?"

"It's what they didn't do, can't do, will never be able to do," she says, "which is teach competently, every day at the college level. Some of them couldn't pass a course in the subjects they teach. Are you shocked?"

"Forget me. Were *they* shocked?"

"Indignant. Hurt. Crying. And, it goes without saying, threatening to sue. Thank God, they don't have tenure here. Listen, George, there's hardly a college in America, certainly not a junior college, that couldn't fire ten percent of their faculty every year, hire new people, and be better for it and at less cost."

"Maybe. But you just came on board."

"Now's the time for me to make my mark."

"Make enemies."

"Not everybody on the list, I hope," she says. "You were on the fired list, George. I'm sorry. I know you liked popping up there on short notice, taking someone's class. And you were good, better than good. But . . ."

"But what?"

"I can't afford it, having you there after firing all those others. You know what they say. She's fucking this substitute teacher. Do you see? I'm the one who has to make, and be seen making, the tough decisions. Anyway, you'll be leaving, so what's it matter?"

Tough decision? My ass! I couldn't imagine her agonizing about it much. And it was one of the greatest paradoxes of language that the f-word she just used—and used with increasing frequency in bed—referred to an act of love that brought people together and made them one for a while. It also referred to harming someone, demolishing them. And she, on the same afternoon, had demonstrated both meanings.

◊

After Stephanie left, I drove home along the beach in time to catch one of those huge evening skies that, if I never came back, *especially* if I never came back, would remind me of Saipan forever. And that brought me up short. I was thinking of Saipan in the past tense. A goner, already. I saw Saito puttering in the back garden and, as usual, he gave me a wave. He never failed to sense my eyes upon him. Would he be here when I came back? If I came back? What about Stephanie? Would she be here? For me? What then? A couple of weeks ago, I'd been sitting at my laptop at a coffee place near the American Memorial Park and a woman sitting at a laptop nearby asked if I knew the difference between farther and further. "I *walked* farther than usual to talk *further* to the woman I loved," I said. I looked her over, this Filipina woman. Filipinas, like most of the other outside women on the island, come in two varieties, worker bees and queen bees: docile workers, saving money for the folks back home, and then gorgeous, amiable predators with something about them that says "for export." This was one of the latter. In tennis shorts and top, like Ali MacGraw in *Goodbye, Columbus*, sexy and youthful, just testing her looks. And I was an American, middle-aged, presentable, serviceable words like that, and in this part of the world, that gave you bonus points, the way frequent flier miles get you upgraded to the front of the airplane. We talked awhile and we exchanged e-mail addresses and I left it at that. Stephanie and I were locked in, I'd thought, but that didn't keep me from wanting to know this girl's name and whereabouts. I put her card in my pocket—she managed a boutique at Duty Free—and left it there, not planning to do anything, just happy to have it. I felt the twinge of letdown, no doubt about it, when she wasn't there the next time I came to the café. But when I opened my e-mail later that day, there was a note from her, titled "hello, it's me." Photos attached. They weren't X-rated, they weren't even what we used to call cheesecake. One was a portrait, the other was on a beach. The beach shot was okay, but the head shot was a winner, because she had a bit of a pout, as if all the men she'd met hadn't impressed her much, but she was still open to offers. The accompanying text: "Just thought I'd jump start our relationship."

So it was there for me, whether or not I deserved it, the same long and winding road my buddies at Hamilton's had traveled, waiting for me if I wanted it, not a bad life, and I'd regret not taking it, if I didn't come back at all. The Master Blaster's offer was going to nag at me forever. It would follow me wherever I traveled, everywhere, anywhere, working the Amelia Bligh franchise for all it was worth and knowing that, on this small island, I'd missed a chance to be a better writer and a happier man.

Stephanie Warner

*

"There she is!" exclaimed Henry Rosales, sounding as if the balance of the sentence were, "Miss America." My meeting with the board of regents was about to start and I hoped that, whatever else happened, I'd walk out knowing somewhat more about the college I was endeavoring to turn from remedial and local to cutting edge and international.

"Shall we go?" I asked. The meeting was in one of the newer class-rooms in a neighboring building, though I had noticed there were only a couple of cars in the parking lot when I pulled in.

"President Warner . . . Stephanie," said Rosales. "Relax. Sit. We have things to settle ourselves."

"Well, then . . ." I took a seat at my desk, behind the unfortunate nameplate that I'd been presented with a few weeks before, a carved block of wood that, in addition to presenting my name in thick, blocky letters, was framed by a background of fish, outrigger canoes, palm trees and thatched houses. I hated it a lot.

"This board is mostly advisory," Rosales said. "Unlike U.S. institu-tions. The regents don't run the place. Or fund it. I will not say they're figureheads . . . not quite. They do have ultimate responsibility. So, we have to be a little careful . . ."

"About what?"

"The idea, the plan, that you have developed for the college. It came from me to you, yes, but it's important that the idea—'grow or die'— must not be credited to me. Or any local. It comes from you, only you. That will give it a certain cachet . . . and fuller consideration. Do you understand?"

I understood, all right. By this time I'd been living with the grow-or-die idea so long, it felt like my own. I'd researched it, elaborated it, defended it. All right then, if I acknowledged him, it would be the way people give a nod to the Vikings for bumping into America a few centuries before Columbus.

"Okay," I said. "Is it time yet?"

"No, not yet." He sat there, our eyes met and locked and I could feel a connection. To him, it wasn't a question of when, and where. "Island time," he said after a while, still measuring me.

I wanted to break out of a staring game I didn't want to win or lose right now, didn't want to be alone with him any longer. "I hear about island time," I said. "All over the place. The rest of the world is ruled by schedules. The watch, the clock, the calendar. Island people are wiser. Tomorrow is as good as today. But . . ."

"Yes?"

"Except I notice at the college," I responded, "when the paychecks are cut, every other Friday, there's a line at the window. No island time, when it comes to money. Receiving it, that is, not paying."

"Touché," he said. "No island time when it comes to money."

I smiled, content to have scored a point.

"Then again," Rosales said, "some people would say you Americans made us this way. Shall we go?"

❦

I'd met the regents at a reception but the chairman was new to me—a retired American and, so I was told the minute we shook hands, a wonderful poet, a lifelong educator who "lives and breathes Saipan." When we were seated, he asked all the others to reintroduce themselves and so they did. The report . . . the proposal, that is . . . they'd received from me sat in front of them. I wondered if they'd done the homework. Those reports, fifty pages in all, had the look of unopened textbooks. The chairman then asked me to describe the "challenging" future I foresaw for the College of the Islands.

Automatic pilot. I honored past pioneers, current heroes and limned a future that compelled the college to make a quantum leap. Before I got to my closing point, that this was a "concept only" meeting, the chairman had fallen asleep. I watched it happen, we all did. He battled it, leaning forward, straightening up in alarm, eyes open, and then sagging again.

"He's an ill man," Henry Rosales told me.

"I hope it's not serious," I said.

There followed a discussion in Chamorro, the local language. At first I bristled at being left out. They all knew English. And it also bothered me that they didn't turn off their cell phones; periodically a few notes of "What the World Needs Now" and "Happy Trails to You" announced an incoming call. Then again, I realized, local language was one of the few defenses they had left. Their tastes were American, their houses, passports and money, their religion Catholic, their last names Spanish. And if, as I sometimes suspected, they were talking about me, I'd might as well let them.

"Very sick," someone eventually said. "On medication."

"I'm sorry," I said, returning to my proposal. This was only about the idea, which I asked them to approve in principle.

I asked for questions. Nothing came. At this crossing-the-Rubicon moment, only the ringing of another cell phone. "Doo-wah-diddy-diddy-dum-diddy-dum," one of my ex-husband's favorites.

"Questions, comments, criticisms, observations?" The chair awakened. Did he have some internal timer that sniffed closure while he slept? "Do you approve? Do you object?" More silence, but this time the chairman joined me in scanning the table, looking from face to face.

"I suppose we have an approval . . . in principle," he said. "Was there anything else, Dr. Warner?"

"A committee, I suppose. Three or four people to carry things along."

"Mr. Rosales," the chairman said. "May I oblige you to chair the committee?"

Rosales nodded.

"Not a good meeting," the chairman then pronounced. "Not good at all."

I was dumbfounded.

"Everyone agreed? Not good."

People nodded, shook their heads. What kind of terrible mistake had I made?

"Not a good meeting," the chairman repeated, sadly. "A *very* good one."

I sighed, the board chuckled and I gathered this was a joke they played on all newcomers, probably including my unseated predecessor. They arose and left. Rosales was last. "I'll be in touch," he said. At the end, I was left with the chairman, walking him to the edge of the parking lot.

"The night air here," he said, breathing deep. "Nothing like it."

"I love it, too," I said.

"Honolulu used to be the same way. Whoosh! You felt it the minute you stepped off the plane. The smell of flowers . . . and the smell of green things . . . the color green itself, almost . . ."

He was a poet, I recalled. I'd pictured someone writing jolly rhymes to kick off a baptismal feast or ratchet up a graduation. Maybe he was better than that.

"Land in Honolulu now, it's like you've landed in a piece of California," he added. "It's nice enough. But I can't feel that greenhouse whoosh, that mix of leaves and flowers and sea. Not like before." He paused and found the keys to his jeep. "I'm glad I came here when I did. Not sure I'd fall for it the same way, if I came now."

"May I ask you something?" It had just occurred to me, to take a chance. If it didn't work out, no loss. He was harmless. And sick. "Was that okay, what happened in there? I couldn't tell."

"Oh, it was fine, just fine," he responded, the way people say they're fine when you ask how they are. Then he surprised me. "Want more?" he asked.

"Yes."

"You asked for the endorsement of a concept. An agreement in principle. And you got it. The bad news is that an agreement in principle doesn't mean much. Something comes along, you don't say no to it, not at the start. Maybe later. But look around, the island's sinking under the weight of things they didn't say no to."

"So it doesn't mean anything?"

"Of course it does. It means . . . game on." He turned away, wincing. "I'm on a schedule that involves certain medicines at certain hours. I've got to go."

"Can I just say . . . thank you?"

"You're welcome." I watched the chairman of the board of regents open his car door and get behind the wheel and sit there, exhausted, before he turned the key in the ignition. Then it came to me. I remembered where I'd seen this yellow jeep before, on the way to Lau Lau Beach, outside a dead restaurant. I remembered how this had led another writer to search for, and find, The Master Blaster. George had told me I'd make a connection. And he told me that I knew him. So I did.

Mel Brodie

❦

"Look around you, folks," I say. "Take your time, a full turn, check out the ocean, reefs and mountain and ask yourself if you've ever seen anything like it. Take a minute. We're in no rush here."

Thanks to Jaime Lopez, I got the land all squared away, a long-term lease, plus incorporation as a condominium. I got lucky on the land. The owners were his relatives, it turned out. Small world, small island. They trusted him and that made it a lot easier to do business. Not bad for six months. Maximum Lou came up with investors and a few of them are in the crowd in front of me, about a hundred people, politicians, my lawyer and his clan, the girls I rescued from Magic Fingers, and Big Ben Romero, from the governor's office. Lourdes is over by the house, keeping the flies off the food.

"Okay," I say. "It's breezy and it's beautiful. It was beautiful the first day I saw it and it's been beautiful every day since then and it's going to stay that way, even during construction. Especially during construction. I hate those drawings that developers hand out, they're supposed to show what a place will look like when it's built. Lies. Fantasies. But this place is different. Talk about a Garden of Eden! We got mango, breadfruit, orange and lemon trees, we got mountain apples and no snakes. So walk around. This is how it's staying. One other thing. Look over there, behind the food and drinks.

"That's the model house. More coming, I hope. That's where I live. Makes me the model man, I guess. It's not American housing and it's not island style. Some of both, just like Saipan. At the core, there's solid concrete, with bedrooms and living room, air-conditioned, typhoon- and termite-proof, watertight and solid as a rock. But what's around the house is wood and screen, a porch in front, a cooking area in back, and that's where you'll talk and eat and read and nap and maybe sleep, because you'll love the wind up here and the sound of rain on the roof, and hey, if there's any storm damage, I have a crew that can put on a new porch, at no cost to you, in three working days. It's in your contract."

I pause, take a breath. "I'm your new neighbor," I tell them. And then, I can't help myself, I invite them to look at Tinian and the waters between here and there where my father went down and I tell them this is all a labor of love for me, my first and last. It's corny but it's true.

❦

What with the eating and drinking, people leave later than expected. No kidding, it was the kind of place that made you want to stick around. And sure, you could love a place and not have to own it. But who wouldn't be happy with a home here? A thousand miles from the nearest smoke stack? I say good-bye, shake hands and I'm feeling good. I've been a good host. I'm a good guy, offering hospitality to new friends and neighbors. I watch Lourdes and her pals wrap up what's left of the food. Not much. Saipan is the home of the plastic take-home container. The law is you never eat your own leftovers but you eat everybody else's. It works out. It's late afternoon and I'm enjoying the quiet. Rarest thing in the world. Quiet equals peace. Then I see two stragglers walking up towards the house in neatly creased slacks and white shirts, like a pair of Mormon missionaries.

"Hi, guys," I say when they get in range. "Like what you see?" Had they been part of the bunch I spoke to, I wondered, or drifted in later on?

"That we do," one of them said.

"Top of the world, Ma," said the other one, imitating Jimmy Cagney.

"There's food left. And beer."

"No thanks."

"Soda? Bottled water?" That missionary thing stuck to them. They didn't look like drinkers. They shook their heads again.

"We're not in the market for a house," said the other one. Call him Jack Webb, from *Dragnet,* expressionless and factual. "We came for you."

While they let that sink in, they introduce themselves, flash some ID. They're both with the government, one with the U.S. Attorney General's office, one with the Department of Treasury, Washington, D.C.

"You came all this way for me?" I sound more unbelieving than I feel. What I feel is this sickness in my stomach and tremble in my legs. They've come for me. "You sure you don't want a beer?" No, again. "Okay. You want some wrists?"

"What?"

"My wrists." I held them out. "For handcuffs."

"No," says Jack Webb.

"Not yet," says Jimmy Cagney.

"Does this have anything to do with my friend Lou?"

"Bingo," says Cagney. "Sharp cookie," he says to Webb. "We've come to offer you a choice, Mr. Brodie." Within a week, Maximum Lou was to be indicted on a list of charges as long as your arm, he tells me. Ninety percent were things I'd never heard of and that I didn't understand. Maybe I'm smart, maybe not, but I'm not that kind of smart and what they say washes over me, like I'm listening to J. Lo speak Chamorro. Sure, I catch a phrase, a name and I can guess about where they are headed. But I couldn't pass a quiz. That, I'd flunk. It's trusts, foundations, profits and nonprofits, it's Indian tribes and offshore banks, PR firms, political action committees, campaign contributions, deferred payments, public offerings, voting and non-voting stocks and—this one I understand—expense accounts.

❦

"What we got from Lou Maxim—this is early skirmishing with his lawyers—is that he was just a silent partner down in Florida," Jack Webb says. "It was your project, top to bottom, beginning to end. Something he did to set you up in life. You took in the cash, you invested it. You pissed it away. Or hid it."

"He said that?" It amazed me. Ass backwards. I was the salesman. He owned the dealership. "No way."

"He set you up out here on Saipan, it seems."

"Definitely. Put me on a plane, gave me travel money, a list of people he said I should call. Once we got going, Lou found some seed money for this project. Anything wrong with that?"

"Not that we know of," Jack Webb says.

"Listen, Mel," Cagney says. "About this project, we don't give a shit. Understand? This is so far beneath our radar. It's a popcorn fart on a carnival midway. Okay? Go make a million. What interests us is that while your buddy was setting you up here, he was setting you up in Washington. In front of a grand jury. So this is where you get to say it can't be true, he's practically family, you knew him before his piss started to stink and he'd never do anything to harm you."

"Skip it," I said.

"What?"

"That part."

"Are we getting touchy?" Cagney asks.

"Listen, Mr. Brodie," says Jack Webb. "I know this is hard for you to hear. And hard for you to choose. You can let Lou Maxim's account, which you indicate is false, stand unchallenged. That'll get you in trouble. Not so fast, not tomorrow . . . we've got bigger fish than you to fry. But eventually you'll be in court. Or you can talk to us now. And tell the truth."

"We'll know if you're lying," Cagney adds.

"I'm sure you can tell," I say. Then I turn to Webb. "What do you want from me? I can't leave here."

"Don't have to. A deposition. We ask questions about Florida, you answer."

"When?"

"Couple of days."

"Why not now? Here?"

"Hey, slow down, Mel," Cagney said. "We're here for four days. Break us off a piece. Tomorrow we're over to Tinian, spending a night at the casino, playing a little golf. Touring the A-bomb pits. Good guys like to have fun, too."

"Okay. Your time, your place."

◊

After they were gone, I thought it over. I wondered, though, if I were such a small fry, like they said, why'd they come so far? Maybe they needed me more than they said. Cagney and Webb. Funny how they behaved when they came to Saipan. They took the same kind of tour, minus a visit to a garment factory, that Maximum Lou's congressmen and aides, neocon columnists and talk-show hosts took when we sent them on junkets here. Golf and gambling. Girls, too, I heard. Maybe that's why they came looking for me. It wasn't whether I mattered a lot or a little. They just wanted to get out of the office. Everybody loved a junket. Maybe it was that simple.

Khan

❦

Two months after Arnaldo hired us, the brothers had goats and I was a competent harvester of tuba. We spent more time at the farm, though one of us always had to be at the pumps. And the place kept getting busier—I could see it happen and it was all about the brothers. With gas up to four dollars per gallon, people wanted something extra for their money, and the brothers provided it, washing windshields, wiping mirrors, polishing tires. The way the brothers raced from chore to chore, customers felt like race car drivers at a pit stop. They laughed, they applauded, sometimes they even tipped. And in the next few weeks, there was another surprise. The brothers started doing small repairs, installing windshield wipers, replacing headlights and soon—in alliance with the body shop across the street, one business helping another—they were poking underneath the hoods. They consulted the Koreans, who sometimes came across the street to offer a second opinion. And I sat behind the cash register watching two non-English-speaking races communicate, laugh, slap hands. At night, the Koreans shared food with the brothers. I was invited as well, but it was only a courtesy and I begged off. The brothers were the stars here.

Day after day, week after week, Arnaldo talked. He wondered about my country. What did I miss about it, what would I do when I returned? He asked about Islam. He wondered about life after death and how long it had been since I'd had a woman and I told him: since I was born. He talked about fishing, the way an old man might talk about his past, when he could stay out longer, dive deeper. I wondered why he talked to me. Was it because I was a person of no importance? Was I the son he never had?

"It's not so much around here anymore," he told me. "Inside the reef . . . forget it. And outside, all the places I used to go . . ."

He paused and I could not think of what to say. Fishing was not something I worried about.

"Would you like to go out sometime, Khan?"

"Fishing?"

"Yes."

"In a boat?"

"Yes."

"What about the gas station?"

He shrugged. He'd get his wife to cover for me. It didn't matter. The gas station, everything that happened on and off the road was business. What mattered was the farm where we sat talking late at night, easy conversations and easy silences, and when I saw his wife's face when she had finished cooking and sat quietly at the end of the table, it told me that she was happy I had come here. And it was all right if I went fishing with her husband.

No matter how late I sat up with Arnaldo, I read the newspapers when I returned to the station, to my cot behind the counter. How it pleased me to be there, how happy I felt, reading newspapers. But one night, when I was about to turn off the reading lamp, there was a tapping on the door. The pumps outside were dark, so was the sign that lit up our prices. No one could think we were still open. Still, people sometimes tapped on the door. They could not see me, though, so I stayed where I was. But this time the tapping continued, it got louder, it came from someone who knew where I was. I arose and saw that it came from X, standing outside the door. The last time we'd met he'd killed a man.

"Want one?" he said, gesturing to a pair of Chinese women in his car. "Or both?" The Chinese dressed like schoolgirls during the day. By night they dressed in short skirts. I studied those women, I really did, their hostility, desirability, availability, and I was closer than X knew to accepting his offer. What would it matter? But I took too long to say yes. "Never mind, Khan," X said, waving the idea away. Later, I wished he'd given me more time to consider. "I need a favor from you," X said. "I need you to attend my wedding."

"Which one are you marrying?" I asked. The women stared back at me, as if daring me to say something.

❧

"Listen, Khan," X said, when he arrived the next morning. "This . . . today . . . is a local woman. You marry a local woman, you are I.R., Immediate Relative. You can stay. Work. Maybe get a green card. No more worry. Lots of Bangladeshi marry this way, local women."

"How did you meet her?" I asked. "Is she nice?"

X laughed and said I would see for myself. Soon enough. We pulled into a parking lot at a government building, with the flags of America and the Commonwealth of the Northern Marianas. X knew where he was going, a courtroom that was already crowded, though the judge wasn't there. There were secretaries, officials, spectators, some eating lunch, others laughing and chatting, enjoying the air-conditioning. This was a Saipan that had clean hallways, polished chairs, computers, water fountains.

Now the judge appeared and began working his way through cases about parole violation, traffic, vandalism, unpaid child support. An American who enjoyed performing: he laughed, made faces, shrugged and gestured, playing to the audience. "Truth is power," he told his audience. "So people lie a lot."

"Where is your bride?" I whispered to X.

"She's here," he said. But he did not point her out. I glanced around the room. Secretaries. It would not be one of them. Some cleaning women sat in the courtroom, taking a break. These people came for the fun of it. The funny judge had a following.

"And now," he announced, "it's love in bloom." He asked X to come forward and then he read another name which I did not know.

People laughed, elbowed each other, covered their faces as X's bride shuffled forward, her rubber sandals slapping against the marble floor, her progress towards X and the judge drawing giggles. When she arrived, she stood behind X, as if he were ahead of her in line.

"Actually," the judge said, "the bride stands opposite the groom." She didn't understand. X nudged her, maneuvered her into position, facing him, though their eyes did not meet. I studied her. I am not someone who makes fun of people's appearance. That is unkind. I was taught that for everyone there is a partner. I believed it, for my own sake. But this woman! She was heavy, she was old, she missed teeth, her face was covered with warts out of which long hairs depended, curling down below her neck. Her face had no expression, her eyes were clouded; one was almost all white.

"Well, kids," the judge said. "I can't help wondering how you two met."

"Through friends," X quietly said.

Behind him, people were laughing. This was the show they had come for.

"Love at first sight?"

Neither replied. The judge sighed. "I'm just wondering . . ." He turned towards the woman. "Not that the law requires it . . . What is your husband's first name?"

She was ready for that. X had coached her. The island was discouraging sham marriages. They asked questions, they watched to see if the couple arrived together, if they chatted and sat next to each other while waiting to be wed.

"This man is X ," the woman said.

"X," said the judge, making an X in the air, as if slashing with a sword. "One more taxi driver coming right up."

I knew about this: the right to drive a legal cab was reserved for local people. But many taxi drivers were Bangladeshi. And some of them had married local women. They paid as much as a thousand dollars. Or as little as a cell phone. Saipan had many such businesses. Arnaldo told me of Chinese women, eight months pregnant, entering on tourist visas, delivering their children and flying out with a U.S. citizen in their arms, umbilical cord not yet dry.

The judge invited the couple to hold hands. They both hesitated. Everybody could see. Only two of X's fingers touched the woman's hand.

"There now," said the judge. "That wasn't so hard." He walked them through the vows, not more than a minute, but it felt longer, knowing that these were lies.

"I now pronounce you man and wife," the judge said. And, even as they started to walk away, he added, for the benefit of the audience: "You may kiss the bride."

It was a joke that everyone, except the married couple, was waiting for. The whole audience watched, giggling, as X and his woman faced each other.

"You may kiss the bride," the judge repeated, making it sound like an order. I turned away and studied the audience. I suppose it was funny. But just then I hated this not quite America for the things it put us through. "You may kiss the bride," I heard it for a third time. X leaned forward, only to have the woman back away, waving him off, and they walked out, the woman first, X trailing behind.

❧

He drove her home. I was in front, she sat in back. I could smell sweat and coconut oil. No one said a word. We turned into a village, stopped at a shack that had dead cars and barking dogs. The woman got out and walked away without looking back. X backed out, turned onto the road and drove off.

"Why did you want me there?" I asked. I had played no part in the ceremony, signed nothing, said nothing.

"I wanted a witness, Khan,"

"Of what?"

"Of what I did. What was done to me. Knowing that you were there, that you remember it, means that I will remember, too. Okay? You won't forget?"

"No."

"Neither will I. I will hate you for having seen this. And I will hate myself. But not as much as I hate . . . them."

"Who?"

"The ones who laughed at me."

VII

The Master Blaster

❦

Sluggishness, loss of appetite, a cough that wouldn't go away: he could feel it now, the end that was coming. These were all things he had felt before—who hadn't had off days?—but he wasn't going to get better this time. He felt fear, not as in, I'm afraid I'll be a little late, I'm afraid I have to disagree, which were situations that involved no fear at all. This was the beginning of a fatal final conversation between The Master Blaster and his body. The only thing that had not been decided was whether he should take leave of life before life left him. Like two people coming to a doorway at the same time. "You go first." "No, please, you first."

If he were in a nursing home somewhere, he'd be clinging to stage one, independent living, shuffling around, preparing simple meals, clinging to a towel rack while standing in the shower. Assisted living would be just around the corner, then intensive care and then hospice. But he wanted to go no further. This was it. He slept badly at night and napped in the late morning and mid-afternoon. Mostly, he thought about the island. He'd walked around it at the water's edge, dived below the waterline, climbed heights, descended into caves and grottos on rope ladders. Lived so well. He pictured all the places he'd lived and worked. What pleased him most was to picture the brightness of the morning, the vast sunsets, the stars at night and, best of all, the full moon, bright enough to read by, that turned every banana leaf and palm frond, every breaking wave all silver. Enough, he said. More than enough.

The web site would not survive him. Griffin hadn't been heard from. No surprise there. But a few issues were left. One of the satisfactions of an underground web site on a small island was the daily contact he had with the people he wrote about. It sounded petty, even cruel, and sometimes it was. But not always. There was a fellow named Mel Brodie who'd been on the island a while, a Jewish fellow, a comedian and a bit of a huckster. He'd been promoting a retirement scheme for Americans, all this in alleged tribute to his father, who died near Tinian. He had to be added to the long list of rogues who'd washed up on Saipan, but the man was likeable, good-humored and lively, even as he climbed in bed with a network of island operators. He wouldn't get far, The Master Blaster suspected.

Out of curiosity, he did some research. A land scandal in Florida, an alliance with a soon-to-be-indicted lobbyist who had done business in Saipan, the celebrated Lou Maxim. Once Maxim fell, Brodie would lose whatever protection he had. A meatball in a piranha tank. As he read on, The Master Blaster couldn't help be impressed at how Brodie managed to walk around with a smile on his face. In the old days, The Master Blaster would have blown the whistle on such a man. Now, maybe his disease was talking, he realized it didn't matter much what he did on Saipan or what Saipan did to him. Besides, in the little time he had left, healthy time, there was another candidate for exposure, much closer to home. A dangerous story. Did the fact that he was going to die soon make him braver? If so, then death was his collaborator.

George Griffin

❦

So it comes after six months, my last day on Saipan. I hate to leave but the old rule still holds true: when you're so close to going, you're anxious to be gone. My flight isn't until four a.m., which means, since I wake up at six a.m., when my last day rolls around, it's got twenty-two hours in it. Talk about a long good-bye and no one in particular to say it to. I lose the airport bet. I'm the first to go. I say I'll be back but no one believes me. I see it in their faces, the conviction that I'm gone for good.

Stephanie is off the island, "unavoidably." Whether that was by design, I can't say. Things haven't been the same since she fired me. We've had scraps of conversation and an occasional meal but nothing more than that. And, to be fair, she's been busy lately and felt the need to go to Guam to confer with people at the university there about some kind of partnership. It sounded urgent. There's a shit storm building about the Pink Elephant. A few days ago she was blindsided by a newspaper account of a meeting she didn't even know had been held, the faculty voting against the move to a place which, they suggested, ought instead to be turned into a red-light "adult entertainment zone." Take the girly lounges and massage parlors out of the tourist district and leave the college where it is. On TV, in newspaper interviews, Stephanie sounded angrier than I've ever seen her; words like "betrayal" and "disloyalty" came out.

Something lay below her indignation though. She was avoiding that last conversation about what we had, where we stood. No time for that. College business to the rescue. She proposed intercepting me at the Guam airport if she could find a hole in her schedule, but then I pointed out that I'd be passing through at four in the morning and, besides, the Guam airport has, post 9/11, more Mickey Mouse than Disneyland. So that was that.

On my last morning, I drove out to Banzai Cliff, ran longer than usual. At the hotel, I found Saito in the garden, not especially communicative. Then, I'd planned on this, a late-morning weariness crept over me. My last nap, air-con on, windows open. A couple of beers guaranteed it would be longer than usual and it was. It felt like I'd fallen into the bottom of a well. Eventually I showered, laid out the clothes I'd wear on the plane. That got me, knowing that I was wearing the same clothes that I'd have on when I stopped off in Guam, in Honolulu, in Los Angeles. I felt like a man condemned, last meal, shave my head, dead man walking. I'd allowed two hours for packing. It took ten minutes. Nothing I'd purchased here was going home with me. Heaviness not in my luggage, heaviness in my heart. Christ, I could hear Amelia Bligh laughing at me.

So, with my room empty, I hopped into my car and drove around the island for a couple of hours, all the roads I'd come to know, and gassed up for the last time at a gas station where I saw the same dark guys who'd arrived with me. I'm pretty sure they were the same. The cashier gave me a kind of nod. Recognition. I told him I was just topping off the tank before I turned in my car at the airport.

"Leaving?" he asked.

I told him yes.

"Then you lose the bet," he said. "Does it feel like you are losing?"

Our eyes met. "Actually it does," I said.

After my last sunset subsided, I went to Hamilton's and the regulars were there. Tonight they were talking about something that was off my radar screen, that was waiting for me to learn about it on my last night: the islands north of Saipan, a half dozen volcanic cones and rock clusters, two with a handful of people, the others uninhabited. They were hard to get to: as soon as I heard that, I longed for them. You had to hitch a ride on a fishing boat or hire a helicopter from a hotel. Some of the regulars had been there and as they spoke, proposing one last trip, I wanted to be with them! This was a torture devised for me on my way out the door. They talked of volcanic eruptions on a place called Pagan, Japanese stragglers on Anatahan, perfect black sand beaches on Agrihan. Wild goats and easy fishing and hot springs and villages half-buried in lava. It went on for hours and now we were drinking tequila chased by beers and that was fine with me, because something was coming alive, listening to this talk, this wonderment, this half-assed planning for a voyage north. They were caught up in it, feeding off each other, fueled by alcohol and memory. They were out of shape, dicky hearts and beer tumors and cranky knees, but I made them promise they would e-mail me as soon as they had something solid. "Pagan or bust," I said as I hugged them and went out the door, drunk. That was when Mel Brodie offered to drive me to the airport. It made sense, he said. We'd arrived together. He was a semi-regular at Hamilton's, on the edge of things, waiting to be asked in. We transferred my luggage to his car. I gave him the keys, which he'd get back to the rental place tomorrow.

"Feel like home now?" he asked as we made our way down the wee-hour streets.

"Yes and no."

"Yeah, I know what you mean. It's a yes-and-no kind of place. Maybe that's why I like it. It's not all one way. It's a small place but not like a small place in . . . I don't know . . . Ohio? You got the island thing, the American connection, Asia knocking on the door . . . all this *stuff*."

"Stuff is right."

"Plus the land and the sea. You get that every day. Hits most of my buttons, this place."

"How's your project? Patriot's Rest, was it?"

"Good days it feels I'm making progress. Some other days, it's the kind of progress a fish makes, when they're reeling him in towards a boat. But I'm in no rush. Know what they say, about people who come to islands who are running away from something. Or running to something."

"I remember. I've thought about that."

"Well . . . both apply to me. They're not exclusive, you know."

❦

So I am back at the Guam airport. Somewhere on this island Stephanie Warner sleeps tonight, sleeps through my leaving. I was drunk when I arrived, I recall, and I had too much tonight. As I contemplate my face in a restroom mirror, I walk past empty gates, browse and make no purchases in duty-free shops and tell myself, try to tell myself, that if what comes next is good, I will need to come back to this place. And if it is bad, I will need it even more. That is what I try to tell myself.

Stephanie Warner

❧

I thought the distance between my secretary and me was about rank and nationality. American versus islander, boss versus employee. And those things surely figured in my anger and her indifference. But there was more to Bernadette's late arrivals, her lame excuses, her dawdling personal phone calls, the food that she ate and sometimes prepared at her desk, so there were more food scraps—papaya pits, mango peels, coffee grounds—and paper plates than waste paper in the basket outside of my office. There was something more, something personal, woman to woman. The way she sat at her desk with a While You Were Out memo pad at her hand, checking off every call I'd missed. My former husband came to mind: his pad, very similar, was entitled, While You Were Fucking Off. Appropriate enough in his case. And recently in mine.

On the night that George Griffin departed from Guam, I walked to the balcony of the Guam Hilton room I was sharing with Henry Rosales and wondered if the plane I glimpsed overhead, lifting off, had George Griffin on it. Would my just-consummated affair with Henry Rosales have happened, if sad, loyal George had not been outward bound? Probably so. Henry and I would have found our way to each other, it was only a question of when, not if. He tells me he felt certain of it the first time we met, in Hawaii. I sensed it when he drove me out for our first look at the Pink Elephant.

Henry tells me that he is always ready to make love and, so far, this is no empty boast. He is never not game. Takes a licking and keeps on ticking, we joked before our final round at the Hilton. Eddie Covington made the same claim and that made me wary of Henry. It might get boring; these self-proclaimed sex machines have their uses, but in the end there is something shallow about their obsession. Not Henry. He is charming, knowledgeable, funny; also complicated in the way people who straddle cultures can sometimes be. At ease anywhere and with anyone, always at home yet always a visitor. Comfortable in his skin and easily the most skilled lover I've ever had.

So there I stood, watching what might be George Griffin's flight get smaller and smaller as it headed across the Pacific. What would become of him? Happiness and sadness both were in him. I'd shared the happiness but, in the end, would not bet against the sadness. From behind, just then, Henry called to me.

❧

How, how on earth, does one conduct an affair on a small island? On a place where home address, place of employment, make of car, shopping and restaurant preferences are well known? Where the mere sight of two cars parked side by side at the edge of a hotel parking lot tells people everything they need to know? Henry sought out hotels that were foreign staffed and, if possible, under-occupied. So I felt a twinge when he pulled into the very place George Griffin and I had shared. Not that anything showed on Mr. Saito's face when we entered. Still, I felt bad; it was as though I deleted the very memory of the travel writer, fouled the nest, destroyed any slim chance that he would ever be back here with me.

The first time, we had a ground-floor room, facing Saito's embattled garden. While Henry attended to his cell phone, I stared out at a stretch of beach I knew by heart. What I would want George Griffin to know, if he somehow saw me now, is that what drew me to Henry was his mind. His ideas, his vision, his ability to surprise and amuse and impress. He thought ahead, he was thinking ahead, from before we met. So many people, island people, put up with the world as it arrived. They accommodated, stalled, waited things out. Henry was the exception.

❧

As to Bernadette, a few days after my return from Guam: there she sat, with a half-finished sandwich from Subway, a slab of cake with blue and white icing, and a Diet Coke.

"President Warner?"

"Yes . . ."

"For your trip to Guam, I have your airfare and meals." She ges-

tured at a pile of receipts, stubs, boarding passes, right next to a stock-
pile of catsup, mustard, mayonnaise and soya packets she collected.
"But not hotel . . ."

"Oh, I see." Something in me froze.

"It was the Hilton . . . yes?"

"Yes."

"No problem. I will call and get a copy."

In an instant I saw it all. I could picture it: the phone calls, the faxes,
the check of invoices, the matching room numbers. I saw my undoing,
courtesy of a cheerful, fussy, lazy, hostile local secretary who took comfort, profound inner comfort, in knowing that just as she had seen me
come, she would see me go. She couldn't stop this parade of foreigners
landing on Saipan and maybe she wouldn't want to. But, in individual
cases, she could speed things up substantially.

"Don't bother," I said. "Now I remember. The meeting was at the
Hilton, but I stayed with a friend. Elsewhere."

"A friend?" She pronounced it "fren." And like that, I recalled a lex-
icon of names for mistresses that the travel writer and I had compiled:
"local wife," "spare part," "u-drive" or—in reference to a moonlighting
garment worker—"Chinese takeout." Now: "fren."

"A friend at the hotel?" she asked.

"I really don't think that's any of your affair," I said, wincing at the
word affair. "There was no money involved. No charge. No reimburse-
ment. All right?"

I stalked off towards my office. From behind me, Bernadette announced that "some woman" was waiting for me.

The woman was Galina, the Russian bar girl who was, hands down,
my best student. Bernadette, I guessed, saw this as two whores meeting
in the college president's office.

"You are ready?" Galina asked. "I have wheels."

"Oh my God," I said. This was the day for our much delayed shopping trip. My makeover. And from the way Galina eyed me, it was high
time. On a basically drip-dry island, I was attired in dark blue polyester
pants. But static between knee hose and polyester distorted the pants line
and, as a byproduct, generated little balls of stray fiber, up and down
my leg. Not classy. My blouse was white with cotton buttons, my shoes
were black flats, and black coral dangled from my ears.

"You are looking," said Galina, "like the before picture in a before-and-after ad. You dressed this way on purpose?"

I had a dozen reasons for begging off. Problems I knew about, others I could only guess at. Bad things closing in on me. But that was all the more reason to escape. Out we marched, arm in arm without a word to Bernadette. By Galina's car, two other Russian girls awaited us, Tanya and Sofia, whom Galina introduced as "fashion consultants."

"Today," she said, "we are professor and you are student. Okay?"

❧

What followed was funny and expensive. And something more, something that was rare on this island, rare anywhere perhaps: a disinterested act of kindness. I'd worried that the girls would tart me up, squeeze me into flimsy getups inappropriate for my age and position. But as we passed from duty-free mall to obscure shops to seamstresses working at home, I saw they had a shrewd sense of what was right for me, dark gray knee-length dresses, gray slacks, jackets that flowed, some brightly colored. There were scarves and shawls galore, silver jewelry, black shoes with two-inch heels. Cotton and linen ruled. I was flattered that the Russian girls had taken me along with them. At the end, Tania and Sofia departed with promises to meet again. I wondered where and when. They were returning to a bar called Moscow Nights. I was bound for the College of the Islands. I'd have changed places with them. After we dropped Tania and Sofia off in the Ginza, Galina offered me "coffee or something" and we drove to a place halfway up Capitol Hill, took a table with a view of the shoreline, the lagoon, the ocean beyond. I wondered aloud about what Saipan would feel like if it were an inland place, with roads leading off in all directions. I liked the surrounding sea, that sense of small and distance. Galina nodded. We had a lot in common. She was un-neurotic, unapologetic and smart, with nothing of the victim about her. And then I thought of the victim we'd found on the road to Lau Lau Beach, a necklace of rope around her neck. A true choker.

"Was . . ." The name took a minute to come to me. "Was Larissa one of you?"

"You read in newspaper?" The local papers had published a short piece: Russian bar girl found dead off Lau Lau road, identified as Larissa Andreyev, employee of Moscow Nights. That was all: not a gesture towards investigation. A body had been found, retrieved, and named. Case closed.

"I found her when I was out jogging. I saw her."

"She was nice," Galina said. "Best of all of us." And there it stopped. I didn't press, I waited, as in class, for more. "Things happen here. Is a strange place. Not our place."

"Whose place is it?" I asked. "Not mine."

"America, they are saying." She made it sound like a piece of gossip, a rumor that couldn't be counted on.

❧

Later that week, I drove out to meet Henry Rosales for our midday appointment. I was first at the hotel, where a key was waiting for me. I recognized the number. George's old room, fifth floor. Was this a message from Saito? A reproach? The elevator still wasn't running. Would it ever? Five flights of steps. My memory lane. Sometimes the travel writer raced me up, sometimes we supported each other after a late night at Hamilton's, and other times we embraced—and undressed—as we ascended. Fun times, I thought. Well, I was looking forward to some time with Henry and wasn't going to let a stray memory get in the way. But the emptiness of this particular room got to me. There was nothing to indicate that the travel writer had ever been here. Not a trace, in a place he loved. Maybe we're all transients, no matter where we live and how long we stay there. This thought occurs to everyone. But it came to me on Saipan.

Henry was late. It had happened before and a delayed arrival challenged us. We had twenty minutes for sex and food and phone calls, the three missions combining comically. I listened for the door closing down the hall, I studied the beach, the garden and I waited, and then I knew he wasn't coming. Our first broken appointment, I told myself, wondering whether this marked the beginning of a downhill trajectory, hits and misses contending, misses winning out, the way they always do.

❧

"I have a message for you," Bernadette announced when I got back. "There will be an emergency meeting of the board tonight."

"Oh," I said. "Who told you?"

"It came from the governor's office."

"Really." I hadn't met the Commonwealth governor. He was often off the island, in Washington, Tokyo, New York, Manila, Taipei. In the same way that U.S. university presidents spend much of their time off campus prospecting for money and employment, the governor traveled around.

"Was the call from the governor?"

"No. His office."

"Offices don't send notes, Bernadette. Offices don't make phone calls. People do."

She mumbled a name, Vicente somebody, I didn't know. Romero? And I couldn't bear to ask that irritating woman anything. I headed for my office but Bernadette wasn't done. She called me back.

"This came for you," she said, handing me an envelope. "He dropped it off." She waited for me to ask who. When I didn't, she added: "Your friend. Special friend."

I opened it up as soon as I got to my desk. "Go to The Master Blaster," Henry had written.

This week's Saipan Monument was the Pink Elephant, the proposed future home of the College of the Islands, with a photo at the top: puddles, trash, peeling paint, rusted metal, all of which I knew well. The place's very decrepitude had been turned, by me, into a selling point: the trashier the place, the better, for the transformation I proposed. Sad beginning, happy ending. Magic! When I read the opening, I hoped that The Master Blaster had endorsed the idea, that he'd applauded it! In a landscape of failure, something would grow better, larger, more profitable. And at the start, The Master Blaster merely paraphrased the case I'd been making far and wide. Had Saipan's bitterest critic became my ally? Then my heart sank.

It will never happen. And it shouldn't. Many of Saipan's troubles, and troublemakers, come from outside; disbarred lawyers, unscrupulous businessmen and bankers, tax dodgers and treasure hunters who treat Saipan as the last American frontier. We have seen them come and go and maybe we have learned something in the process: the art of the rip off. And in this case the con game is home grown. Local handicraft, indeed.

Abruptly named President of the College of the Islands, Stephanie Warner has been promoting the College's relocation to a decrepit shopping mall. Having been here a matter of months, she is convinced she knows what the College needs, what Saipan itself requires. Her faculty is in unanimous rebellion, the hard-driving, hard-flying and heavy-partying President is controversial. But let's not blame the outsider. Forget Acting President Warner: she doesn't matter. Consider, instead, Henry Rosales, the savior and it turns out, part owner of the Pink Elephant. Is he saving the College? Saving the Pink Elephant? Or saving himself . . . ?

Gossip, insult, innuendo, this from the chairman of the board, the sick, kindly poet-doctor in the yellow jeep! The Master Blaster! It wasn't fair. I was set to fight. Until I read the paragraphs that followed and, like that, the fight was over. The Pink Elephant was linked, in its water and power systems, to the hotel across the street. The shopping center had failed and left behind a pile of utility bills that the new owner—the college—would inherit, even before it began to renovate. And now it turned out that Rosales, through his wife, owned the land on which the Pink Elephant reposed. And there were lawsuits from tenants, suppliers, maintenance crews related to inferior materials, sub-code workmanship, sand mixed with salt water, long delays, inflated costs, materials diverted by the truck load to other jobs, by a construction company Rosales was linked to. "Rarely have incompetence and cynicism been so richly commingled," The Master Blaster concluded. "And never before by a local rip-off artist, by a native of Saipan. The laissez faire, local-friendly ethical climate of the island is well known but if any integrity remains, the College of the Islands relocation will be stopped and its sponsors dismissed and prosecuted."

❧

I left my office and stayed away the rest of the day. Was my office already locked? Was my computer blocked? Was Bernadette at her desk, inhaling empanadas and doughnuts? Or celebrating elsewhere? I had a dinner at one of the resorts, a place with a non-local staff, including a full complement of young and not-so-young hunks catering to Chinese and Russian tourists. The College of the Islands wouldn't follow me there. I lingered over a second espresso and a third. I saw hefty Russian men and hideously dressed wives, happy to be here, paying cash and tipping generously. Just a few of them ventured down to the beach and they didn't linger: they liked having an ocean in the area but they had no personal plans for it. I heard laughter and splashing and, after a while, music, for this is a world that abhors silence. Had I come to Saipan as a tourist, these pleasures would be mine, a carefree couple of weeks, lazy mornings, sleepy afternoons, sunset happy hours, international buffets, carnal evenings if I wanted them, side trips and shopping optional, what was there not to like? It was possible to have nice memories of this place. But if you came to work and if you took work seriously, if you wanted to accomplish something, then you were asking for it. You got caught up in your mission and you forgot yourself. So maybe they had it right, the tourists and the people who catered to them, the ones who offered native dancers, fresh coconuts, spotless restaurants, guided tours to safe locations. An artifice, a tourist, bubble, a pretend world, but so what? The problem came when you tried to really get to know a place. And when you succeeded.

Though the governor was in Beijing, the board meeting was in a conference room adjoining his office, in a two-story building on Capitol Hill, left behind like so many other places by the CIA. When I arrived, about half the regents were sitting at a long table. They greeted me; someone pulled out a chair for me, then they resumed talking among themselves. They spoke quietly: none of the kidding I was used to. Maybe the place intimidated them, a gallery of people who'd run the island since the war, old black-and-whites of naval admirals and, after them, a convoy of Department of Interior–appointed high commissioners. Then, coinciding with the advent of color photography, half a dozen elected local governors on the wall, shaking hands with congressmen and vice presidents. On the table, a newspaper proclaimed: "College in Turmoil." I guessed I should have read today's paper. Then again, maybe not. What difference would it make?

"Good evening, everyone." Someone came into the room from behind me. I was at one end of the table; the newcomer at the other. The trustees called him Big Ben. No last name or offer. A competent president would know, a loyal secretary would have briefed me. So: Big Ben.

"We can begin now," he said. "Mr. Huntoon, our chairman, is ill tonight and Mr. Rosales has been called away . . . to Manila on personal business matters." Big Ben rested, to let Henry's absence sink in. I don't know how the others took it. Something between playing hooky and a plea of nolo contendere. They wouldn't have to deal with him this evening and that came as a relief. They had only to deal with me. Alone.

"We all know why we are here," Big Ben said. "And this meeting will not end until we have decided what to do."

What an approach! None of the congeniality, the automatic politeness I was accustomed to. Nothing island style. Big Ben looked like an islander, more a glowering Samoan bouncer than a Saipanese, but he spoke like an American. And, when the regents kept their mouths shut, it was him I spoke to.

"I'm sorry," I said.

"Yes?"

"I'd been led to believe I'd met all the regents. Are you a member of this group?"

"I'm a friend. Here by invitation."

"I might be the only one . . . the last one to know . . . but I was called to this emergency meeting without being told what it was about. And, sorry to say, I still don't know."

"I think you do," he countered, a rebuff that hung in the air. "But all right then. It's one way of starting. The island web site operated by a certain Master Blaster has issued a report on the College of the Islands' proposed move." He turned and nodded at me, giving credit where it was due. "*Your* proposed move to an abandoned mall. Your campaign is well-known. Quite a program, for an acting president. You propose to uproot the college. This was followed by faculty firing . . . subtractions from a group which, nonetheless, voted unanimously . . . bravely . . . to oppose what you proposed. All this was well known. But now, before we go further, do you have a comment at this point?"

"Yes," I said. "Definitely. I am convinced that the move is warranted, that the conversion of what you consider a ruin into an institution with strong local roots and thriving international connections is a good way for a college to grow, a college that has to grow or die. And I stand by that position."

"Fine," Big Ben said. He glanced at the regents, all of whom had endorsed the proposed move at least in principle. "Any questions?" he asked the others. They had no questions, none when they backed me, none when they listened to Big Ben. They were spectators and bystanders on their own island. They watched, they waited, said hello and good-bye.

"Well then," Big Ben resumed. "We come now to the so-called Master Blaster. We do not accept his say-so. His hate for the Commonwealth, especially its elected leaders, is well known. Yet we do not—we cannot afford to—disregard him. So we have looked into what was said. To protect ourselves, we had to investigate. Do you understand? President Warner?"

"Yes."

"Unfortunately, what we found . . ." he was at a loss for words, so it seemed. He sighed heavily, backed up and started again. "The Master Blaster claims that the move was Henry Rosales' idea, not yours. That the Rosales family owns the property on which the mall sits, that it owns an interest in the hotel across the street, that there are unpaid utility bills and pending litigation and that, even without these undisclosed encumbrances, the cost of renovating the facility would bankrupt the college. It could not function, it could not meet its payroll if it went ahead with the move . . ."

"Excuse me," I said. "Shouldn't you ask Mr. Rosales about this? Shouldn't he be here?"

"He's in Manila," Big Ben said. "For his health."

"You just said it was personal and business matters," I reminded him.

"The same thing," he snapped back. And I found myself wishing that we all had a Manila in our lives, a sanctuary in which sex, medicine, dentistry and karaoke were all on sale, for a little money, when things got uncomfortable at home.

"Well, I don't see how you can proceed in his absence," I said. "I was hired by Mr. Rosales, mainly, to join the faculty of the college. After Mr. Simpson's departure, I agreed to serve as acting president. I don't know what there is to add. Except my conviction that this meeting is illegitimate."

"Was the idea to move the college yours?"

"I made it mine. I worked night and day to implement it."

"Night and day . . ." He seemed amused and he gave the others time to appreciate his smirk.

"The idea came to me from Henry Rosales. All right? But it was a good idea. An idea that good, the source doesn't matter. The idea was the thing." Even as I spoke, I knew I had it wrong. On this island, the source mattered more. Where it came from, and who it would profit, outweighed larger benefits. Still, I tried. "Let me add that the details of ownership, acquisition, budget were to be his concern. And the board's. Really, Mr. Rosales should be here. I don't think you can accomplish much in his absence. To be frank, I don't think you can accomplish anything."

"Perhaps not. Let's see." He pulled a little notebook out of his shirt pocket, a tablet you might use to keep tabs on miles per gallon. "It's hinted at . . . it's between the lines, that your relationship with Rosales went well beyond business."

"I can't believe this!"

"Neither can I. It is unbelievable. That you traveled to Guam and shared a room with Mr. Rosales for two nights."

I had just heard my death sentence. I was a goner. Saipan was where I used to live.

"We checked at the hotel. Two people in the room. Phone records. You called the college from the room. And . . . yes, Mr. Rosales is in Manila. But he was here this morning. I found him at the airport, sought his comments. He sends his greetings to you. And his regrets."

"My private life is no business of yours."

"It is. We could have managed to suppress this self-interested proposal . . ."

"Mr. Rosales was the interested one. I owned nothing."

"And an affair, that too. But not both. Especially in the public domain. We have to put them behind us. Do you understand?"

"What do you want?"

"I thought you understood. Your resignation."

"When?"

"Now. Tonight. At this table."

"Effective when?"

"Now." His manner took my breath away. I didn't want to ask these people for anything, I thought, not even the formality of a vote, but at the very edge and end of things, I couldn't help but picture what it had been like at the start.

"I could return to teaching," I offered. It was too late to add, my students are my children.

"No, you could not," Big Ben replied. "Not here. We'll pay you for the rest of the year, though we're not required to, and we'll pay your airfare home. All of this on the condition that the terms and conditions of your leaving be kept confidential."

"You mean I can't defend myself?"

"Do you want to? Really?"

"About Henry Rosales. Does he even need to defend himself? He hired me. He promoted me. He promoted a scheme that he, not I, stood to profit from. So what do you propose for him, in the way of justice? Punishment? What kind of proceeding? A meeting like this? An interrogation like this? I have my doubts. I picture a clubby occasion, beer and sashimi in the neighborhood, a few jokes about Manila, a few jokes about me. Island style, island rules. Am I right? Does anybody want to tell me I'm wrong?"

Big Ben raised his hands, shrugged. An extraordinary fellow. What had made him the way he was? Where had he learned that prosecutorial tone? The islanders I'd met were polite, to a fault sometimes, eager to please, good-humored and, on important points, evasive. Get along, go along. Here was someone who was focused, formal, laser locked on a target, which was me. Impressive, I had to admit. Chalk one up for the home team. But I couldn't help defending myself, after all, on my way out.

"Fine. I'll leave. But I'll leave wondering if you have any idea of how amateurish you are . . ."

"And you were professional?" Big Ben interjected.

"How sexist, how xenophobic. You're betrayed by one of your own, you blow him a kiss as he hops on a flight to Manila, and then you call me in for punishment. And you take your cue from a renegade web site. You let The Master Blaster spoil the future of the college. Again, you are betrayed by one of your own."

Now! Now, for the first time I had them. Before, they reminded me of my first class at college, of students who slouched, covered their mouths when they laughed, spoke in whispers, wondered what they were doing, which made me wonder what I was doing. I had gotten to that audience. Now I had this one, too.

"Betrayed by someone who lives among you, sits among you." Stop! An inner voice insisted. It was a matter of life and death, it really was, a secret. It scared me, what I was about to do. But I told myself, knowing that I'd be repeating it later on, what was my duplicity, compared to The Master Blaster's? Compared to Rosales? Compared to almost everyone's? "The Master Blaster presides over this very board," I announced.

"Oh, please," Big Ben said. "That will do."

"Do what?"

"People have been guessing about The Master Blaster forever. It's a game. It doesn't matter. And this meeting is over. Leave your letter of resignation with your secretary tomorrow and she will obtain a ticket. Is the day after tomorrow too soon?"

"Not soon enough," I said. "How about tomorrow?"

"It comes to the same thing. The day after tomorrow. The four a.m. flight."

◊

After Big Ben marched out, all the regents arose, shook my hand and said farewell. They were relaxed, once it was over and Big Ben was gone. And small courtesies died hard. They wished me well and in a few surprising cases, thanked me for what I had done or, as a few of them put it, what I had tried to do. So there were some people with minds of their own and I was wrong not to have gotten to know them, one at a time.

That night, I drove away from my house on Capitol Hill, wondering whether the next president would live here, whether anyone would live here, how long the house itself would last, before a Korean golf course or a Chinese condominium claimed the old CIA hill. Of course I arrived at the airport early. Two a.m.! I parked and opened the doors on either side and let the air blow through. The idea of being confined to an air-conditioned terminal, browsing in a duty-free shop, getting sealed in a plane, appalled me. And this night air, this warm, wet soft air, was something I was bound to miss. After I checked in, got my boarding pass, I took a seat outside a shut-down snack bar. That night air, I wanted more of it. I took out my appointment book. How busy days here had been! The days ahead were also full, but all that was canceled now. No date in my book, no keys in my pocket. Jobless and homeless, that was me. It didn't bother me as much as I thought it would.

"Professor Warner?"

I jumped. Who would find me here, now? Except a woman who got off work late from a place called Moscow Nights.

"Galina? What are you doing here?"

"I am coming to say good-bye," she said, sitting beside me. "I heard you were going away. Soon. The secretaries were making laughs."

"Are you alone?"

"My boyfriend drives me," she said, gesturing to a car parked near the rental places. "He will wait, no problem. Professor, I am sorry you are going. What they say, it is sounding like Mickey Mouse."

"Is Mickey Mouse, Galina."

"I'm sorry."

"I made some mistakes. Big ones. I realize that."

"Everybody is making mistakes," she agreed. "I make mistakes all over the world. Many nights in a row I make mistakes." She laughed at that. "Mickey Mouse." What a wonderful phrase. It captured the nonsense that we got tangled in as we moved around the world, what we did to others, what they did to us, what we did to ourselves. And yet there were those who, though doing things beneath them, managed somehow to stay above them. Through humor, mainly. Galina was like that. I hoped that I was, too. But I was surer about her than about myself. What bothered me most was The Master Blaster. I prayed nothing would come of that and, if it did, that George Griffin would never know. What happens on Saipan stays on Saipan, I hoped. As in Las Vegas, the normal American rules did not apply.

"There is something else," Galina said. "Something I want you to know."

"Yes."

"You ask about Larissa."

I nodded. That would be a Saipan memory, for sure. That girl, twenty feet off the road. And George Griffin crouching down beside her. "They got her," he said. Whoever *they* were.

"She was our star," Galina said. "Not for looks or sex because she is seeming so innocent. So nice. Driving men crazy. They send her to hotel room for visitor. Politician comes to famous battle island.

War hero, they say. And he is given chance to conquer Russian girl, Larissa says. But he cannot perform. Larissa trying to assist and she can make tiny gecko into mighty dragon. But he walks out onto what you call . . ."

"Balcony. And jumps."

"Larissa comes back in morning. We worry. She did nothing. But in hotel room with politician. Not good. She stays in apartment. We wait and nothing happens. We feel good. Then someone comes. This is your friend, Mr. Griffin. He teaches at college, sometimes. He is a reporter he says. He asks about Larissa. I call our boss. Later on he is saying Larissa must go home. He has orders from above. From someone important. Get rid of Larissa. Or they shut us down for punish. He says he takes her to the airport, so sad, he says. But there are people watching at the airport. The airport is the first choice. The second choice is Lau Lau Beach. And so . . . if your friend does not come making question . . . she is not dead. Everybody likes Larissa . . ."

"That's sad . . ." The things we get into on this island, we Americans, meaning no harm.

"So now you know."

"Now I know," I said. And wished I didn't.

"I bring you something," Galina says, brightening. "No good, I know . . . but still." She hands me an envelope which turns out to be an invitation to her wedding to one Enzo Rossi. Reception to follow at the Hyatt.

"Is this Mickey Mouse?" I ask. It wouldn't be so bad, her hooking up with an affable, aging foreigner.

"Not Mickey Mouse!" she says, excited, clapping her hands together, then leaning forward. Girlish excitement: she still had it in her. "Is hotel chef. Very good in the kitchen. Okay in bedroom. Nice guy. Tall, not too fat. And . . . shiny head."

"Bald. Can't have everything."

"I'm liking him very much. He plays piano also . . ." Her voice trailed off. "Are you ever coming back?"

"Will you be here?"

"Maybe not. Enzo likes see world while he works. He's been worker in Switzerland, Fiji. Maybe, next stop, Dubai. So . . . "

"Yes."

She takes the wedding invitation back and scribbles an e-mail address. "I would like to know where you are going."

"So would I," I reply.

◊

Now I'm in the terminal, eating a wee-hour bowl of ramen, watching my flight come in, whiz down a runway that is far too long for a propeller driven puddle jumper. A member of the ground crew pushes a stairway up to the side of the plane, the doors open and I recognize the first passenger. Perfect! It's my ex, Eddie Covington. I watch him walk across the tarmac and I can't help smiling. There is a God! Play it one way, he could be arriving in the nick of time. Play it another way, I am leaving in the nick of time. Eddie will be disappointed to find me gone and he'll listen with interest to accounts of my downfall. But this is a nice island to recover from a bad marriage. He'll sing, he'll dance, he'll clown. He will not lecture, judge, plan or advise, and he's not rich enough to fleece, not talented enough to threaten. People will like him more than they liked me. For him, the place is perfect. I watch him cross the tarmac, disappear into the terminal. I study my boarding pass. I wonder about making the same mistake twice. About making two of them.

Mel Brodie

❦

It's a morning kind of place. Six a.m. or so the night starts breaking up and I arise without the need of an alarm clock, and Lourdes is always up before me and I smell bacon and coffee, except on the mornings when she slips back into bed with this old man and makes some magic. Funny, she reads me so well, mind and body, she knows when I'm ready. So give or take a half an hour, I'm up with the sun. Sunsets get all the postcards but the early morning is fine. We have the place for ourselves except for a night watchman, a Bangladeshi guy J. Lo made me hire because there's guys on the island would cut through a jungle to rip off a few yards of copper wire. I'm guessing the Bangladeshi might have been one of the guys who came on the same plane with us but he doesn't talk much. And then there's this one morning, I'm drinking coffee, it's the time of day I miss the sports pages, he comes running, to tell me that trouble was in the neighborhood.

"A woman is bothering the boys," he says. "And she is screaming."

"She screamed? What about?"

"Cannot say. And she has a knife. She runs after the workers."

"Christ!" I get out of my chair. "Where'd she come from?"

"Not from the road. I sit in my truck all night. She must come from . . ."

"The boonies?" As soon as I said it, I saw it was a new word for him.

"Please, sir."

I shout to Lourdes, inside the house, to call Jaime Lopez. I swallow what was left of my first cup of coffee and I follow the guard down to the construction. With Maximum Lou out of the picture, I decided on starting small. My guys were pouring slabs for eight tidy cottages.

❦

There she was, an outright hag in a raggedy flower-print dress that covered her like a tent, badly pitched, and yes, she had a machete in her hands that she swung angrily, all the time shouting things that no one could understand and other times it was just howling, like a funeral. She was crazy for sure, and dangerous, but the guys were taunting her, running towards her, ducking, dodging away, laughing and dancing, one after the other, like bullfighting or bear-baiting, and there was nothing I could do. I couldn't talk to her, couldn't calm her down, not with that machete in her hands. So the joking and jiving kept on, until I almost wanted the hag to get lucky, but that would be terrible, what a machete could do.

At last, a Lexus came down the driveway, my attorney on a house call, slamming the door and walking forward, and instantly things calmed down, the workers backed off and the woman stood by herself, quiet, machete at her side, as if on a dance floor with no partners. J. Lo crooked a finger, motioned her towards him and she obeyed, like an actor in front of cameras, after the director shouted "Cut." At his car, they talked a while. The workers were back to toting pipes and unreeling spools of copper wire. Then I saw the hag get in my attorney's car. He walked over to me, frowning.

"Sorry about this," he said.

"What the hell's going on here?"

"We have a little problem. She claims that this is her land, her family land. And"—he gave a deep, on-cue sigh—"she may be right."

"Wait a minute, counselor. This can't be happening. We made a kind of in-house title search. 'A mere formality,' you called it, since they were your kinfolks, the property owners. No need to contact a title search firm."

"Yes, that was my advice."

"I remember. I was there. I paid for it. Fifty-year lease so long as I run a legal operation, maintain the property, et cetera. So where does she get off . . ."

"You're naïve," Jaime said.

"Because I took your professional advice on a title search?"

He held up his hand. "No more, please. I'll talk to her now. And to you tomorrow." With that, he moved around to the driver's side of the car, opened the door, and slid behind the wheel. In back, the woman was sleeping, and I don't mean nodding off a little, I mean head back, eyes closed, mouth open.

"Hey, just one more question," I said. A little lightbulb started blinking in my head, the sort of thought that usually arrives when it's too late. "The landowners are your family. Yes or no?"

He gripped the steering wheel, flexing his fingers in a way that signaled a battle for self-control. Lawyers asked yes-or-no questions, they didn't answer them.

"Yes or no?" I repeated.

"Calm down," he said. Then he said it again. "You're naïve. You're forgetting where you are."

✦

Remember those TV documentaries that tell you how the whole human race, kit and caboodle, came out of a river gorge someplace in Africa? And how, what with DNA, everybody can eventually be connected to everyone else? Out in the big world, you shrug. Africa isn't my homeland and whether I'm forty degrees of separation from Einstein or Hannibal doesn't matter to me. A lot of time has passed and the world is wide. But Saipan isn't. It's a gorge-sized place and everybody's related and if you try to do business, that's not good news.

"That woman," a guy named Davey told me at Hamilton's, "is an archetype." It sounded like a tribe.

"What?"

"A recurrent cultural figure," he said. "Something like a myth or legend. The hitchhiker that you whiz past on the highway who pops up, again and again, down the road. That kind of thing: the woman who comes out of the boonies . . . and onto a construction site, with a machete in her hand, claiming ownership. Not at the start, ribbon cutting or ground breaking, but later on, after you've put your money into things. You're just pouring slabs right? I'm surprised she didn't wait until the houses were up. Anyway, that was where she grew up, she says, where she hid in a cave during the war, where her ancestors were buried. This was her place and her family's. How dare you?!"

My attorney had kept me waiting and I declined coffee and just sat there, making his model secretary nervous: coffee is supposed to pacify these situations. You're supposed to believe you're doing something, having a coffee, while sitting on your ass waiting for a lawyer who's late. While I sat I had dangerous thoughts. Lately J. Lo had been less of a glad hand and hail-fellow-well-met. More lawyer-like, formal, distant. Something had changed, and I guessed I knew what it was. J. Lo had always known, and liked the idea, that I was sent out by Maximum Lou. Lou was my patron the minute I stepped off the plane. But now his clout here was history.

After half an hour, J. Lo rushed through the office, asking if I'd been offered coffee, and said he needed ten minutes with his secretary. A few months before, he'd have sent her out for lunch, barbecued ribs and chicken, beer for me, soft drink for himself. Now he opened the door and let his secretary precede him into the inner sanctum. Ten minutes later, he opened his door for me. Inside, Miss Philippines was nowhere to be seen.

"Where'd Rita go?" I asked. I knew her name since she and Lourdes were friendly.

"She went home to rest," J. Lo said. "She works hard you know, gets in all kinds of positions."

"I see. So what do you have for me?"

"A complication," he said. He leaned back in his chair, pulled out a lower desk drawer to rest his feet on, tented his fingers, like he was about to give an interview. Thanks to the guys at Hamilton's, I was ready for what came next. This was an island where lives were tightly woven, large families intermarrying, divorcing, breeding, adopting, you name it. You would need a genealogist, a DNA expert, a local historian, you'd need a subpoena and a syringe of sodium pentothal to be absolutely sure about a title search. And the land, the land itself came with problems of its own, what with old customs yielding to Spanish, German, Japanese and American practices and a war rolling through, destroying records and complicating life. Did I understand?

"Aren't there . . . I think you mentioned . . . title insurance outfits?" I asked.

"I mentioned them . . . to you. I told you I didn't think it was necessary. You agreed. At least you didn't disagree."

He had me there. I was a sucker for shortcuts. "So who is this woman? A relative of yours? A long-lost aunt?"

"She is . . . a sad case. But it's her brother. He lives in the States, in

Bakersfield, California. He has not been here in, I don't know, twenty years? He put her up to this."

There was something wrong in what he was saying, but I couldn't quite get the handle on it. It would come to me later, added to a long list of things I might have said. I cut to the chase.

"So what does she want?"

"She says she wants her land back."

"That's all? I can accommodate her. Know where I can get some kerosene? Matches, I've got plenty . . ."

"Don't be that way, Mel," J. Lo said. "She'll take money. And sign a release. As will her brother."

"Yeah, but will that be the end of it? No distant relatives, phoning home, reaching out to touch someone. Namely, me?"

"I'll take care of that. A legal advertisement in the newspapers. Small type. Advising any claimants to notify us . . . me . . . by a fixed date. A month from now we'll be safe."

"And the woman? How much?"

"She wanted fifty thousand. I talked her down to twenty-five."

"Twenty five? That's a reward for what? For being Saipanese? Or being American?"

"You don't want to contest this. There are some judges here who . . ."

"Play for the home team? I get it." I took a deep breath and admitted to myself, it was less than I feared. But only if it didn't happen again. "Okay," I said.

"Good move," he congratulated me, clapping his hands, getting up out of his chair to shake hands, ending another billable hour. On the way home it came to me, just like in the funnies, when a lightbulb goes on in someone's head. This was what was stirring, when I sat in J. Lo's office. That loco aunt of his couldn't lick a stamp or place a phone call. So who contacted the Bakersfield brother and invited him to take a shot at me? My bet was J. Lo. It was all in the family.

❧

That night, after the workers leave, after dinner, Lourdes and I walk the property. The concrete slabs are poured, pipes and wires in the ground, bungalows ready to pop up like mushrooms after a rain. I haven't made any sales yet: I'd learned that lesson in Florida. But we have a waiting list of expats and a few locals on Saipan and, thanks to advertising in veterans' magazines, two dozen expressions of interest from Maine to Guam. Some of those will melt away—old-timers like getting mail—but it pleases me that they're still remembering Saipan and maybe picturing themselves here, at the end of their life. They're in for a discount if they come. I picture them as they are now, living with their kids, living in a downtown hotel somewhere, a past-its-prime place converted to senior living. Or maybe they're in a so-called convalescent home, hoping to get better and maybe they really do get better, when they think of coming back to a place where they, and the frigging country, once were young and golden.

Lourdes and I walk like a couple, holding hands, and we've got a couple of boonie dogs following us, marking the territory. I tell Lourdes about the twenty-five thousand for Jaime's aunt. It's supposed to be good news but I'm not so sure another Grandma Moses might not come out of the woods. I've been looking forward, like I can taste it, to the time when people are living here. I hear conversations, I smell barbecue. Folks will be busy in the morning, sleep and read during the day, step out at night, card games and bullshit until the wee hours. Who cares how late an old man stays up? We're on our way, I keep telling myself, but we're not there yet. Lourdes tells me, anything that happens, we can handle it. I'm not so sure.

❦

Sunday nights, I take Lourdes along to Hamilton's. Some of her friends sit outside, expat women and Filipinas playing Scrabble. I leave her outside and go into the bar and there's Davey, the lip, and Big Herb and Rudy the lawyer and Tom the Priest who, the story goes, donned a clerical cassock to get a discounted ticket to Saipan twenty years ago. A mellow group, as a rule. Not tonight, not for me.

"Give this man whatever he wants," Davey tells the bartender. "And keep them coming."

"Us Jews don't drink much," I say. It's a joke line. I've used it before. Over drinks.

"You will tonight. You might be needing a ride home."

"Father Tom," Herb says. Father Tom drinks tequila, works as a freelance speech writer up at the legislature, turns shit into Shinola.

"Your place is a condominium, right?" he asks. I nod. "Okay. Do you happen to know if there are any other condos here."

"Nope. I might be the first."

"Or the second. There's this big Korean golf course operation on Marpi. Almost two hundred units. You know it?"

"I've driven past," I said. "Little houses, right? Mini chalets? Didn't know it was a condo. Looks like Pinocchio might live there. So you're saying it's a condo?"

"Well, Mel . . ." He looked over at Davey. "Give our friend a refill." Then he's back at me and he comes off as a priest, confessional and confidential. "It's not about you. But you might be in for trouble, anyway."

"What are you saying? We lease the land and we own the units. What's the problem?"

"Well, the island's law on condos is . . . What's the word I want? *Evolving* . . . They're roughing out some legislation, with the Koreans in mind, on condos. They tossed in a little wrinkle. A unit that sits on land, that has a *footprint* on the land, is a no-no. What kind of buildings you putting up, Mel?"

"Concrete slabs. Eight of them is all."

"Have another drink . . . It's not about you, Mel, really. You're small change."

"You know, I keep hearing that. Small change, small fry, little guy, small potatoes. Not worth bothering. But that doesn't stop them."

"I'll tell you what they'd say," Father Tom answered. "I've written this stuff a hundred times. This is a small island, we are a minority, our land is precious, our culture is unique, our language also, and if we lose our land we lose everything. We give a warm welcome to visitors from across the sea, our island hospitality is well known. But our land must be ours forever."

"So they're screwing the Koreans."

"Yup."

"What'd the Koreans do to them?"

"It's what they didn't do . . . make friends . . . the right ones . . . the right way. They're tough. Mule stubborn. Again, it's got nothing to do with you."

"Yeah. I feel better already."

"One thing, Mel." At this point the bartender slides a tray in front of me, about five shots of tequila in little glasses. "Your lawyer, J. Lo. His brother's in the legislature. A cosponsor of this condo legislation. So . . . did your lawyer tell you?"

"No," I said. "I wonder what he was waiting for."

◊

Nine months after I arrived on Saipan, believe it or not, my customers started arriving: a retired schoolteacher from Hawaii, an ex-marine who thought Guam had gotten crowded, a Long Beach, California, painter who was drawn to tropical settings, an Italian chef with a Russian wife, a lonely pharmacist from Oklahoma who'd lost his wife and sold his business. He was the only World War II veteran who'd signed up. Then there were the Arroyos, Filipino-Americans dying to escape Manila air. There were more coming, already booked, and I could go on to a second-phase development. Never happen, though. This suited me fine. The Filipino construction crews were gone, replaced by a handyman, a gardener and a couple of guys, recommended by J. Lo, who handled plumbing and electricity out of a utility building on the edge of the property. A great place for naps.

Everyone was happy, it seemed to me, maybe because I was happy, too. My place was a winner. Tourists came to take a gander, snap some photos, reporters wrote me up: I was on the cover of AARP magazine. A Japanese TV crew had been through and I wondered whether Japanese and American war veterans could live side by side.

This much was for sure: I had a winner. Was it brains? Was it luck? I mulled it over in the wee hours. One thing my customers had in common was a feeling that the place where they'd lived and worked didn't suit them in their old age; if it had been good it turned bad, if bad, worse. So, at retirement, they looked for a new start. And that's when the old dream of islands got to them. They weren't going to Tahiti or the Caribbean but to an island under the American flag, a safe bet. The island felt safe and so did my place, up a hill, off the highway, through a gate, that was guarded at night by a Bangladeshi watchman. They were able to be choosy about Saipan, a beach here, a golf course there, a drive out to Marpi at sunset, dinner at a hole-in-the-wall Thai place. They engaged with Saipan on their terms. I wished that I could do the same.

❧

"I hear you're an architect," Jaime said. We were in a parking lot outside a supermarket. We met by chance, after weeks of silence. I had been keeping my distance, so had he, and so far it was working fine. Only it wasn't over. He'd moved from friend and sidekick to by-appointment lawyer to a guy I didn't trust. Would he become my enemy? Was he my enemy already?

"Me? An architect? Not hardly. What did I ever design?"

"You put high heels under your houses."

"Well, I heard about the condo law. Just in the nick of time. Put stone posts under all four corners of a new wood floor. Took some work."

"Very good."

"Wish I'd known that law was coming . . ."

"Those rascals in the legislature . . . hard to keep up with them. One day they want to legalize marijuana, the next day it's casinos. How's business?"

"Pretty soon we'll have to put up a No Vacancy sign." I wondered if I'd said the wrong thing, because on Saipan success wasn't an accomplishment. It was a target. The more I drove around the island, the more failures I saw. Thanks to The Master Blaster, I saw a lot of bright ideas that had come to grief, stillborn or smothered in the cradle. A dream, and dream buster, of an island.

"It should be clear sailing from here on out," I said. I didn't believe it but I wanted to see how he'd respond.

"I hope so," he said. "You've earned it."

"I might not need a lawyer," I said, half-joking.

"That'll be the day, Mel," he replied.

❧

The water was out one morning, just about the time people were taking showers, watering gardens, filling up their coffee pots. No way was this a first, and people preferred the rainwater they collected off their roof, the idea of it and the taste of it. So we'd gotten used to water outages, joking about living in paradise, sounding smart. But that same night, the power went. Gone was the light to read by, the turning of the fans, the stereo, the coffee pot, the bedroom air-conditioner, all subtracted. People walked out on the street and confirmed that it was happening to all of us. They felt for their flashlights and walked up to my place, which was dark, too. I called Hamilton's: no problem there, a cold beer waiting for us all. My people followed me down to the utilities shack. Our electrician-plumber, Manuelito, had the keys. The place was locked as usual, but now it had a chain around it, too, secured by a padlock, so it looked like they were about to drag the shack off someplace. And the flashlights found a sign: PRIVATE PROPERTY/CLOSED BY OWNER.

"Aren't we the owner?" asked white-haired Mrs. Heilbrunn, a librarian married to a schoolteacher. She did the talking for both of them.

"Of the houses, yes," I said. "Not the ground." I was ahead of Mrs. Heilbrunn. I pointed to the utility shed, a square, windowless cube with a door at the front. It sat in the ground, below the ground. It had to. This is where the pipes and wires entered.

"Then who owns it?"

"The landowners."

"But . . . surely . . . they are obliged to act in good faith." She had a point. How long would it take, though, to get a court judgment? To find a lawyer for that matter, because I figured that Jaime was playing for the other team now. We're in for it, I thought. If you build it they will come . . . after you. Again and again. And they only have to win once.

"Give me a minute," I said, sounding like I needed to think and not fooling anybody: I was like a salesman pretending he had to agonize about a last, best price. I knew what I was going to say. If I held up a minute, it was only because I hated what was coming.

"I can't do anything about this tonight," I said. "Tomorrow, I'll make some calls. Try and find out what the problem is. Meanwhile, there's a hotel I know that always has a room. Nice place, too. Anybody wants to stay there tonight, I'll set it up. At no charge to you . . . This time tomorrow, I'll know more than I do now."

I led half of them—a nine-car convoy—to the hotel where the travel writer used to live and told Saito my problem. He gave me a price that was right out of the 1950s, thirty bucks a night as long as I wanted, same price he gave me for the girls from Happy Fingers. And no haggling. Thirty bucks, right off the bat. Why so accommodating? A Japanese guy taking in some American refugees from Patriot's Rest.

"Could I ask you a couple of questions?"

"You can ask," Saito said.

"Why the bargain rate?"

"And the second question?"

"Why do you stay here?"

"Two questions. One answer. A place does not belong only to the people born there. It belongs to the people who love it. You are one of them I think. And I am."

"Sure. We're buddies. Shake on that." It didn't come easily to him, but he gamely offered his hand, which I didn't let go. "Why do you love it?"

"That," he said, wiggling free, "is another question."

❧

I spent the morning buying generators, finding guys who agreed to install them, paying top price for equipment and labor. They'd be in, sitting on pallets off the ground, in a couple of days. At night, when my neighbors fired up their generators, it would sound like the Indianapolis 500, but what else could I do? Yet it wasn't much of a fix. What they'd come for was peace and quiet. So I was feeling down. What did I do to deserve this? I asked. Why did they have it in for me? This was the cleanest project I'd ever touched. Labor of love. But why get all Jewish? It wasn't about me. Did that first Spanish galleon crack up on the reef only to have the captain say, What did I do to deserve this?

❧

Never let them see you sweat. I walked right into the Hyatt for the monthly luncheon of the Saipan Chamber of Commerce, shaking hands and slapping backs, wisecracking every step of the way, pulling weeds, cutting grass and watching generators go in. All the folks who'd spent the night in the hotel were back and they all pitched in. The lease specified that the place had to be kept in good order. That was why someone pulled the workers. Count on it, they thought, the place would be a jungle in a week. So I worked, and my people worked, wondering what next. When it got hot, I went home, poured a couple of buckets of water over myself, put on an aloha shirt and waved a cheerful good-bye. Soon as I left, it later turned out, they formed a condo association!

You couldn't dislike the businessmen of Saipan, not one of them you couldn't drink and talk story with. We whispered and chuckled while somebody from China discussed the benefits of sister city status with a brand-new metropolis none of us had ever heard of. I'd be happy to go on a road trip with any of these guys, visit wineries or monasteries, throw horseshoes, bet on elections, compete in spitting contests, shake hands outside a courtroom in which any one of them might have attempted to screw me. Including J. Lo.

"Mr. Mel," he asked, as if seeing me made his day. "How are you?"

"Never better," I said. "Work hard, play hard. That's the ticket."

"And our project?"

"Great, just great. An idea whose time had come."

"Oh really?" My response surprised him. "I'm glad to hear it." Now I knew he was lying. "Anything you need me to do for you?"

"Stay tuned," I said.

We sat across from each other during lunch. I remembered how I'd thought I was to have connected with him, because there was no way an outsider could make it on his own. Now, I guessed, he'd targeted me from day one. But we'd had some fun along the way. And he was fun today, making sure my iced tea got topped off, asking did I want seconds of anything, signaling for the waiter to clear the dishes when we were done. Afterwards he walked me out to the parking lot.

"I was sorry to hear about your . . . family member . . . Mr. Lou Maxim."

"What about him?"

"He was sentenced to six years in prison."

"Well," I said. "Happens in the best of families."

"He was a great friend of Saipan," J. Lo said. "He protected our control of immigration and of minimum wage. Anybody who asks, that is what I will tell them."

"That's fine."

"This must be a sad time for you, losing your sponsor. Rest assured, if there is anything you need . . ."

"You've done enough."

I opened the doors on both sides of my car and allowed a couple of minutes for the heat to escape. Midday turns the car into a death chamber. And, with no air-con at home lately, it reminded me of how vulnerable we are, no power, no water. Like the island itself was just biding its time, waiting to slough off all the stuff that comes in off the sea, get back to basics. They talked about it at Hamilton's, sometimes, whether it was possible to go back to fish and farming, grass and thatch. Now that they drove cars, lived in houses built of cement blocks, worked in air-conditioned offices, could they go back? Could they go back to what they were? It was hard to picture a return to island ways. Rich or poor, they were Americans now. For better and for worse.

"Mr. Brodie?" I'd just slipped behind a steering wheel that still felt like a radiator pipe. A kid was standing right outside and I kind of remembered him. I knew that we'd met, I knew at least that much. My mind did that funny reconnaissance, rummaging around. Then I had it.

"Hello, Erwin." It was the reporter who'd made me the Simón Bolivar of Saipan's massage parlors. A long time ago, it seemed. "How are you doing?"

"Very well, Mr. Brodie."

"Lots of good stories on this island, I'd bet."

"Plenty of stories, yes. Almost too many. I'd like to talk to you about one of them."

"What might that be?" It's in my nature, somebody shows an interest, asks a question, I don't blow them off. I answer.

"What happened to your real estate development?"

I didn't act surprised or ask him who his sources were. The world was full of people who made their day saying "No comment." Not me. Turned out he knew I'd raised the houses after I heard about the condo law. He knew about the power and water shut off, the locked utility building, the disappearing workers. "They were shifted to a new golf course connected with Mr. Lopez," Erwin told me. "They send their best."

"Sounds like you have it, Erwin."

"Only one question, Mr. Brodie. I could ask many questions but it comes to only one."

"What's that?"

"What does it feel like to be you?"

◊

An hour later, we were done. I talked, he listened. Talking to him was like chicken soup to a dying man: it couldn't hurt, it might help. I headed toward Saito's to see what the tenants were up to. I passed the American War Memorial, passed the right turn up to Capitol Hill.

It felt, all of a sudden, like someone was jumping on my chest. It hurt a lot. I just managed to turn onto the shoulder of the road, tangan-tangan branches swiping at my windows, the car at an angle, in a ditch, I guessed. I'd seen people acting like they were having heart attacks. "I can feel it, it's the big one, coming now." Take it from me, when you have a heart attack, you know it, and it doesn't leave room for a line like that.

❧

I wonder if everybody who shows up on Saipan doesn't have a date with the airport waiting for them. A kind of death, in its way. Lourdes is with me, waiting for the four a.m. flight to Guam and, after that, to Manila, for tests and treatment at Makati Medical Center. The heart attack brought out the Catholic in her, prayers and rosary and all. Okay with me. It also brought out the Filipina. We might stay down there, after I get better, and we could find a beautiful place in the provinces, a place with clean air, fresh vegetables and lots and lots of her family in the vicinity.

I expect to be shipped off anonymously, only one degree of separation from flying freight, but I see a bunch of people and they're not checking luggage. They've come out, it seems, for me. There's the girls I took out of Happy Fingers, saying they'll pray a lot for Uncle Mel. And the condo owners. They're making phone calls to people in Washington, to veterans' groups. And Erwin's article, that I haven't even read yet, has been picked up by lots of papers. Half dead and three quarters broke, I'm touched, teary eyed. Is this what happens, you go soft when you die? Everyone's talking, praying, wisecracking—"You don't look any worse than usual"—and then there's a moment of silence. No kidding. It's happy-hour babble one minute and quiet the next, except someone muttering "What the hell?" Standing over me, holding a flower lei, I see J. Lo. I look at him, he looks at me and there's a sense that we're both playing a scene we haven't written. He doesn't risk putting the lei around my neck so he places it on my chest.

"Like flowers on a coffin," I say.

"I hope not." Maybe he means it. It's not like he wanted to kill me,

I guess. "I always liked you." Now he's kneeling next to me, as if capturing a memory of what I looked like, the last time he saw me. A camera catches us in the act of reconciliation. "You started a wonderful project for our island and for America and when you return, I will work tirelessly on its behalf . . . and yours." He spoke loud enough for everyone to hear, made a V for Victory sign when he was done, and backed away. But it wasn't over yet, because a big, dark blob hovered overhead and hunkered down beside me. Nobody wanted to talk down to me today, not even the man known as Big Ben. For a big man, he had a shy, soft voice, and what he said wasn't meant for others, though I saw people straining to hear him.

"You should have come to me, Mel," he said.

"Thanks," I said. I'm thinking he ordered J. Lo to pay his respects. The newspaper article, the tenants' phone calls got his attention, too, I reckoned.

"You are welcome." And he repeated it, so it wasn't just a thank-you, it was saying he liked having me here on the island.

"But what did you do, exactly?"

"Solved a few problems for you," he said, waving aside the details. "Trust me."

"You mean . . . in the end . . . on this island . . . there are rules?"

"Oh no," he said, laughing a little. "Not rules, not exactly." He went quiet. Maybe another time, another place, there'd be a lot more he could say. He settled for just a little more.

"Not rules," he said. "If we play by the rules, we lose. But there are exceptions. Always exceptions." Then, with an effort, he hoisted himself up. I wondered how long he would last if they got him on a treadmill in Manila. He stood above me, catching his breath, then walked through the crowd.

◆

I'm stretched out over three seats and all I can see is the top of a plane that's not much larger than an iron lung. I'm flying—let's face it, being flown—over the same patch of ocean I crossed a little less than a year ago. That night we had a moon that lit up the clouds and the ocean and the islands, islands lit up like ships, stars all over the sky. I can't see them now, but I remember them all right. It was something.

Khan

❦

I won the bet. The travel writer is gone: he topped off his rental on the way to the airport. Professor Warner has quit the College of the Islands. And Mr. Mel Brodie left the island, very sick. I read about it in the papers, which were full of his business and health troubles and how the governor intervened to rescue him, to correct wrongs done to a stranger, to show that the island welcomes investors. We were asked to pray for him but he died in Los Banos, outside Manila.

I'll miss him. He was a regular customer at the station, for gas, for lube, for wash and wax and he was always happy, making jokes. "You still here?" he'd ask me. "As you can see," I would answer. "No plans to leave?" "No sir." "Me neither. This is quite a duel we got going. But I wonder, what's the winner get? If everyone who loses leaves, how do you collect?" I didn't know. "To stay," he suggested. "That must be it." That was the last I saw him. But a few days after he left the island, someone brought me an envelope to the gas station. It was for me, from Mel Brodie, with two hundred dollars. And a note: "The winner stays."

I stay. I wonder about that. So do the brothers. They miss their families, but homesickness is something we cannot afford. The brothers make money night and day and to trade this for the sight of their parents is impossible. The village would grieve at their return. And it is not clear whether they could come back to Saipan, if they left. Our numbers here only go down. So they work, night and day, they sell gas, they sell goats, they repair cars. Sometimes they find a car and drive down to the garment factories to find Chinese women. They do this once a week, sometimes twice. It's their way. They were the ones who found chicken to eat, discovered a palace for us to hide in, visited a mosque and heard about a crazy man who wanted to hire Bangladeshis. When it comes to Saipan, they discover things first.

I also stay. I have learned some of the local languages, Chamorro and Carolinian. Arnaldo taught me. And when he found me browsing through a course catalog for the College of the Islands he told me to go. He would pay for it, on one condition: I could take any course I wanted. But I had to take a course on the history of Saipan and report, in detail, back to him, what the professor said. That was why he sent me, he said. He wanted to know what the so-called experts said about the island. He'd never go himself. It meant sitting among students and he couldn't bear that. Still, he was curious about how wrong they were, so he sent me to school. And, he added, he guessed I might not want to work in a gas station forever.

I worried that I would not be welcome, that I would not fit. Before the end of my first class I knew otherwise. The place was full of strangers, Chinese, Russian, Filipino, American. Sitting in the back, I heard a professor tell the class she was an American, had served in the Peace Corps in the Philippines and had been living on Saipan for two years. Then she gave her name and, looking up, I knew her: the woman who'd hired us for yard work, the one with the bad husband. This evening, she was nervous, happy, full of energy. She looked forward, she said, to our learning things together, talking freely, asking questions. We had a wonderful mix of backgrounds and perspectives, she said.

At the end, I followed others to the front desk to enter my name on a sign-up sheet. She had promised to learn our names quickly and to pass out a copy of this sheet so we could know each other also. There she was, greeting students as they signed in. I was the last. I signed my name. She picked up the paper.

"Khan?" she said. "*That* Khan?"

"Hello, Mrs. Jenkins."

❧

"God, I looked all over for you," she said. "I slowed down whenever I saw someone who might be you . . ."

A black man, she meant to say. We were in a coffee shop closer to the gas station than to the college and she had purchased an iced coffee for me that cost three dollars. I would not spend such money. But it appealed to me, sitting in an air-conditioned place, taking my time, talking to a

teacher. It reminded me that I was better at being a student than at anything else.

"I wondered where you'd gone. You were special. Our talks. I
needed them, more than you know. You listened. Maybe you were just
being polite."

"How is your husband?"

"Gone," she said. "Gone from me. And from Saipan. He's in the
Philippines. That last morning . . . me looking out at you from the
kitchen, while he paid you off and asked you to leave . . . you must have
known."

"Yes. Something was wrong."

"It's over. But . . ."

"But you stayed."

"This job came along and I didn't want to go home, like a loser. Another one of those mopey, embittered housewives who got traded in a for
a new model as soon as her husband stepped onto the car lot. Where
have you been?"

"We worked where we could. Stayed in . . .various places."

"All four of you?"

"Now there are three. One of us has gone on his own way."

"On the island?"

"Yes."

"Don't tell me. That would be X." It surprised me, she remembered
X, that she had studied us that much. "There was something in him. I
watched you fellows. It was something to focus on. And I said, X won't
last so long in day jobs. Where is he?"

"Still here, somewhere. Working mostly at night, I think."

"And the brothers?"

"Just down the road," I said. "At the gas station."

"That place? Those two black boys scampering around? That's
them? Oh my God! I was on the line there and I saw the show they were
putting on. Such clowning. Racist stereotypes. Demeaning."

"I see," I said. "Well, those clowning black boys send money home
to poor people who are always on the edge of starvation. Starving villagers . . . is that another stereotype?"

She flinched at that. She wanted our reunion to go well.

"Then again," I added, "you can buy your gasoline anywhere . . .

there are stations all over Saipan. The price is the same all over the island. Not so much as a tenth of a penny difference. I work there, too. I work inside."

"All right. I take it back. I'm sorry."

"Please," I said. "I'm your student."

◊

Mrs. Jenkins drove me back to the gas station. She said it was her lucky day, meeting me again. When we arrived, the brothers rushed over to her, gave the car the usual treatment and declined a tip. Inside, Arnaldo was like a parent watching for his son's return from the first day of school.

"How was it, Khan?" he asked. "Tell me everything." The teacher was an American woman, I told him. That surprised him. The students were outsiders. That was sad to him, but no surprise. I handed him the reading list, Spanish chronicles, German and Japanese materials, anthropologists on ancient Saipan, collections of songs and folk stories, political analyses of the U.N. Trusteeship and the coming of the U.S. Commonwealth. Sometimes he nodded, sometimes he shook his head in dismay.

"You know the problem? Our history belongs to outsiders."

"What would you say to them?"

"To them . . . nothing, It's no use."

"My professor is a good person. She would like to meet you. You could come to class."

"I won't talk to her," he said. " 'A local informant,' she would call me. Raw material, for notes, for tape recorders, for cameras. As if we should be honored they have come so far to talk to us. Then they leave and they say what they want. I'll talk to you, Khan."

Arnaldo wasn't arrogant, though he could sound that way. It wasn't even anger I saw in him. It was pain, that the things he loved were dying and that what he knew would die with him. So he could pass it on to me. Why me?

Once a week, at least, Arnaldo and I walked through history. On Saipan there were cliffs where ancient islanders had fought, won, lost, committed mass suicide, rather than be tamed, renamed, converted. He knew Spanish and German places, Japanese buildings in the boondocks, the landing strips the CIA used, the caves at the center of the islands where Japanese stragglers lingered until 1951. He brushed past shopping centers, poker parlors, subdivisions, gave nothing more than a nod to the people we met.

"Are the brothers happy here?" he asked one day. We were sitting on the chairs in front of the gas station. It was not quite closing time. "I wonder, sometimes."

"Happy? Hard to say. They cannot go home, yet they cannot stay forever. I don't know about happy." That was all I could think of. Besides, I was feeling lazy, tired, ready to sleep, but Arnaldo wanted to talk.

"I've never been anywhere," he said. "Saipan and three or four other islands. Strange, no? A whole world out there and I see so little of it. Stay here, live and die here."

"You could have left," I said. "These days you can travel to the U.S., no problem."

"Yes. But the world comes to us. That's what I told myself. No need to go out. The world comes in. I had chances, you know. A job on a ship. And my uncle in California, American citizen, wanted me for his business. Roofing business in Anaheim. Watching you, I wonder how I would have made out . . . Compared to you I'm an old man, Khan, and I say what I want to say. I see you come here and take a chance. The whole world comes here and we go nowhere. We stay and work for the government. And I wonder what those other people have that we don't."

A plane passed overhead, not very high, turning towards the airport. A big plane, not from Guam. Chinese, Koreans, or Russians, I guessed. What did they have that Arnaldo's people did not? I could have told him in a word: hunger.

"What I told myself is that it was important to stay. To be what I was, where I was—an islander on Saipan. Only one Saipan. Stupid, no? I had not been anywhere. So how do I look to you? Sad case?"

"Never."

"Crazy guy? Old man who talks too much and nobody wants to listen?"

"I listen," I said. "I learn. I think you are a man who loves this place."

"It's worse than that, Khan," he said. He turned towards me and our eyes met and I had never had anyone talk like this to me, at least not here. "It's . . . used to love."

❧

"A *what*? What did he call it?" Mrs. Jenkins asked.

"Last voyage."

"His or yours?"

"He didn't say. He said he wanted to take me fishing."

"Where to?"

"A place called Pagan."

"Oh my God, it's a last voyage for both of you, all right."

"Not just us. He's taking a few friends. A few days up, a few days on the island, a few days back."

"It's insane. You can't go. You'll have to tell him no, Khan." She looked at me and turned away, glanced outside. Not much of a view there: the parking lot. And when you looked out of an air-conditioned café into noonday Saipan, you realized how fragile your comfort was. The idea of living and working in the heat was for other people.

"All right," Mrs. Jenkins said. "I'm ready now. First thing, Khan, is I care about you. I won't want to talk about it, but you were there when I was at my worst and you were sitting in the back row in my first class and . . . you're special. Let's not worry about that now. I may not have to worry about it at all, if you go on this trip."

"Why?"

"Just listen. I studied this place before I came. I love research. I studied it more after my husband wandered off. So let me just ask you, before I read you the riot act, what did your friend Arnaldo say about Pagan?"

"He said going there was the last thing he would ever ask of me."

"I can believe that," she snapped.

"You were not there, Mrs. Jenkins. You did not see the look on his face."

"He can't go without you?"

"I don't think so," I answered. "He really wants me there."

"Who are the others?"

"Old friends," I said, "of his." I almost added: I didn't know Arnaldo had old friends. And I wondered about them as much as I wondered about the unknown island. Who did he call friends?

"All right," she said. "Here goes. The island of Pagan is about 180 miles north of here, across open sea. You pass some other islands. After eighteen hours at sea—that's if you're lucky—you come to Pagan. It's a double scoop of lava, two volcanoes on one island. The whole thing sits above an ocean floor that's at war: the Pacific plate colliding with and going under the Philippine Sea plate. The bigger volcano, Mount Pagan, had a huge eruption in 1981. Lava covered the village, covered half of a little fighter airstrip from Japanese times. There've been eruptions of smoke and ashes since then. Sound fun? An unstable, uninhabited, hopelessly isolated island in the middle of a typhoon-prone sea that could swallow any mountain, all above an ocean floor that spawns earthquakes. I rest my case."

Now she sat back, pleased with herself. Her best lecture yet. And, behind it, her caring for me. We both sensed it. I reached out my hand and put it over hers and kept it there, black on white. We looked down at the same time. We both had wondered what it might look like, how it might feel.

"Arnaldo told me it was the last island," I said. "Not just the last for him. The last for everyone. The last of something, the end of something. And he told me it was beautiful and dangerous and angry. He said we would climb up the crater . . ."

"That's a must," she said, sarcastically.

"There are black sand beaches. A half-buried church. Wild goats and cattle. Hot springs that the Japanese bathed in . . ."

"Ideal." She was still joking but I stayed serious.

"There is something else. This island called Pagan. It's in danger."

"You bet it is."

"Not the way you think. The danger is people. People here. They want to make money. Lava on Pagan has something called pozzolan that might be valuable. It improves concrete when it is added. So people talk of mining the island."

"It hasn't happened."

"Not yet. But there is also the U.S. military. They know the government is poor. Cannot pay bills. Fuel, salary, retirement, hospital, insurance. Arnaldo says the U.S. will help. If they can use Pagan for training."

"Shit," said Mrs. Jenkins. I'd never heard her talk like that.

"It scares Arnaldo. He wants to see the island one more time. So do his friends. And want to see it too. And now I have a question for you. Two questions and I hope the answer to both of them is yes. I will be happy with one yes. But I hope for two."

"A pop quiz, Khan?"

"In the hope that—as you say in class—we are on the same page."

"All right then," she said. She was smiling, amused, a little bit play-ful, and I knew then that there was something between us, that we found ourselves in a new place and were appraising it, how it would be to live there.

"First question. Will you drive me to the boat, when we leave? It will be quite early, I'm afraid."

"And the second question?"

"Will you come with me, with Arnaldo and his friends, in the boat to Pagan?"

"Yes."

"To which question?"

Now she paused, perhaps already beginning to doubt herself. Or re-peating the name of the island to herself, an obscure place which con-tained a piece of her life, her near future at least. Pagan, Pagan, Pagan. With another name would it have been so intimidating? So attractive?

"Yes to both," she said. "I must be crazy."

❧

"You want to bring your teacher along?" Arnaldo asked. He acted shocked. But I could tell he liked the idea.

"She wants to learn more about the islands. And I think this is the only way you'll talk to her. Talk history."

He nodded at that. "She knows nothing about boats."

"I didn't ask."

"It's okay," he said. "None of the others know anything. I'm the only one."

❧

The Saipan Marina, like everything else on Saipan, was once military, lined with metal walls, filled with navy vessels. Now it was filled with pleasure boats, white and shapely and with silly names: "Heartbreaker," "Surf and Turf," "Nasty Buoy." Arnaldo was on board one of them, ar-ranging ice chests, gasoline tanks, bags of ice, cases of beer while three men looked on, offering to help and getting waved off. Me, he sum-moned on board. His old friends, three of them, were Americans, and that surprised me. He must have known them years ago; I hadn't seen them before and they were old. One was short and bald and old, another was heavy and bearded and old, and the third a little bit younger, busy loading a rucksack with bottles of tequila and a bag of lemons. That was all he brought, all he needed, maybe.

Arnaldo put me to work. "The guy from the gas station," the tequila man said. I heard the others chatting with Mrs. Jenkins. One of them greeted her by name, Nora, and asked what she was doing here. She didn't answer. She wanted first to know what they were doing.

"It's like this," the short man—his name turned out to be Davey—said. "We all were up there years ago, when they still made copra and the government sent up a field trip vessel three or four times a year to collect the stuff. That's how Herb got there, me too. Father Tom over there flew up on a small plane. Scouting locations for a pornographic movie, he says . . ."

"So you've all been there."

"Once. Seems like we all need to go back."

"Our age, you don't give a shit," Herb said. "Or maybe, for the first time in your life, you do."

"All right, shipmates," Arnaldo said. "Just seventy-five miles to Anatahan." For some reason, the old men cheered. "Ninety miles to Sarigan, 130 miles to Guguan, 146 miles to Alamagan." More cheers. "And 178 miles to Pagan." They cheered, they slapped hands, as if they'd already finished the trip. They were like boys on a day off from school. "Come aboard," Arnaldo said. "The lady professor first."

The Americans backed away, surprised to see Mrs. Jenkins take Arnaldo's hand and hop on board. They followed, sitting where Arnaldo told them. It wasn't a large boat, twenty-five feet, maybe, with a shaded cabin in front, where steps led to a tiny place below. Shade would be precious before long, but who worried about sun? They were excited, like children up to something dangerous. I wondered if anyone ever grew up here. In my country people were born old. Here, the child remained inside, waiting to reveal himself, break out from behind white hair, yellow teeth, weariness.

Arnaldo backed the boat away from the dock, then pointed into the channel that led out to the lagoon. Before long, we found a break in the reef and were at sea. For a little while, Saipan grew larger as we sailed away from it. We could see down the coast, across to Tinian and we could take in Mount Tapochau at the middle of the island. We followed the island north, past the last hotel, and then it was Saipan's turn to dwindle and vanish. The Americans talked of Anatahan, of Japanese holdouts on the island, men and women, a story of violence and murder that someone had made into a film. They were good fellows, the old timers, interested in me, intrigued by Mrs. Jenkins. They included us in their talk: all their old stories were new to us. We would know each other well, when this was over. They would help me, they had connections, might know of jobs, training, scholarships, all because I shared this trip with them. This last, great trip. To them, this late in their lives, islands were an addiction: they always wanted one more. Another place, another chance.

Passing Anatahan that afternoon, we sailed close to a rocky, unfriendly shoreline. We did not land. I was pleased to see the place but what I felt was nothing, compared to what Arnaldo and his friends were feeling. Every island to them, was another chance, a new discovery, a possible life. How excited they were!

"The way I see it," Big Herb said. "These little islands . . . how tall are they at the most? Arnaldo . . . Pagan. How high?"

"A little more than Saipan," Arnaldo answered. "Eighteen hundred feet."

"So," Herb went on. "A quarter mile out of the water is all. But how far off the bottom of the sea? The bottom of the Trench? Four miles? Five? These are mountaintops. Himalayas. We're going from Everest to K-2 to Annapurna, to Kanchenjunga. No ropes, no forest, no crevasses, we waltz ashore on black sand beaches carrying tequila and Spam. And good company!"

"And good company," Davey and Father Tom repeated and so did Mrs. Jenkins.

"And good company," Arnaldo said, his eyes on me.

So we pointed further north, into the Northern Islands, towards Pagan. I was the one who won the bet about staying on Saipan and I would not have predicted that. And, when I left Saipan, I'd thought it would be back to Bangladesh or . . . east, to U.S.A. Not headed north in a small boat to a place called Pagan. But as I stood up, scanning the horizon, I liked the direction I was headed in. And the people who were going with me.

Epilogue

The Master Buiider

♦

If you wanted to take control of your death, you couldn't wait for the very last day or week. You'd be like a mouse at the mercy of a cat, a sadistic, dawdling cat that, though it might toy with you now and then, showed no mercy. You had to be able to think clearly, to walk, to drive, and to accept that even though the next day might be bearable, it was time to go.

So this, The Master Blaster thinks, is his last night. He sits at the edge of his property, as usual, looking out across the island, the towns, the beach, the straits to Tinian, taking it in for the last time. Enough of that, enough of attaching "last" to everything. Last cigar, last cognac. Enough.

"Depend on it, sir, when a man knows he is to be hanged in a fortnight, it concentrates his mind wonderfully." A line of Samuel Johnson's. But so far, his own musings were disappointing. And what concentrated his mind was something he would never have expected, that very morning.

♦

"Hello? Knock, knock? Anyone in there?"

"Barely," he responded. "Wait." He was on his knees in front of a toilet, vomiting a breakfast of corned beef that he shouldn't have risked. He arose and steadied himself on the sink, noticing how rusted everything was—dappled rust on the toilet and bathtub. The refrigerator and freezer and stove top were still worse. They wouldn't survive him for long.

There, in the doorway was his protégé, his best student, his scholarship boy, his project, his disappointment. Big Ben. And, despite years of disappointment, despite the cancer that was conquering him now—as far along in him as the Americans were when they sighted the high cliffs at the north end of the island, the places that would be called Suicide and Banzai—the sight of Big Ben pleased him. Grow old and part of you yearned for final conversations, poignant closures with long-lost friends, first loves, unforgotten enemies. You assumed it would come along, it would have to happen. And then, much later, you realized it didn't. But now it did.

"I thought I'd drop by," his visitor said. "I was in the neighborhood."

"Hello, Big Ben. It's a small island. You're always in the neighborhood."

"May I come in?"

"Sure." He followed him out to the back porch, took a chair that he checked first. He was too big to sit in just any chair.

"Hot today," Big Ben said.

"This is true."

"You remember . . . I think of it often . . . when you asked me if natives, I think you said 'locals' . . . felt the heat as much as Americans. And I said, how could I know how hot an American felt?"

"Clever answer," The Master Blaster said. "Now that you're an American citizen?"

"I feel the heat," he admitted.

I'll bet he does, The Master Blaster thought. Not just Saipan heat, Washington heat, too. The IRS, the FBI, congressmen, bureaucrats, they'd get to him sooner or later. That wasn't what he'd hoped for. Of the five students The Master Blaster sent to U.S. colleges, he alone had returned. Odd: he heard from all the others, Christmas cards, family photos, picnics and hotel buffets when they visited, gratitude to him mixed with a bit of an apology. They meant to return but there were so many opportunities on the mainland. You could do anything you wanted. Of course, Saipan was always in their heart. Big Ben returned— and kept his distance and made his way. The man you needed to know. And yes, it would cost you to know him. But it would cost more if you didn't. How old was he now? In his forties? With the pleasure that the old take in noticing the advance of age in the generations behind them, he noticed that his student's heft, once robust, now weighed him down, slowed him up, punished his stride, his breathing. The infectious urge for friendship that he'd carried off to college and in school had turned inward. And angry.

"I heard you're under the weather."

"Under the weather? I'm finished, Ben. The termites are in me."

"I am sorry," he said, slowly, softly. A whisper really.

"Why'd you come? I'm happy to see you but it's been so long and it's too late to talk about how things turned out. Besides, we've been playing on different teams around here, haven't we? That wasn't what I hoped for . . .Then again, it's a free country."

He sat there, mulling over what to say, nodding his head in agreement with himself. "I've known you were The Master Blaster. I heard your voice . . . your way of thinking."

"You never came after me."

"No. I screamed, I protested, I cried foul . . . and when they mentioned your name, I laughed and waved them off."

"Well thanks, I guess," The Master Blaster said. Then he relented. "Make it . . . just plain thanks."

"You're welcome." A nice moment passed. "There is a problem. The college president who left, Warner, gave up your name. She did it in anger. Maybe she regretted it."

"I'm not surprised. Her boyfriend, that *Faraway Places* guy, found me. Had a fantasy about taking over the web site. He probably told her."

"I hear that someone is very angry. Someone has to do something about . . . you, he says."

"I'm dying, Ben."

"All the more reason to get after you. They want you to be punished. That last business with the college was especially unpopular. A lot of people were set to benefit."

"Benefit? Do thieves *benefit* when they rob someone?" The Master Blaster asked. "So it's Rosales. He's the one who's after me? Rosales?"

"Never mind," Big Ben answered. "It could be lots of people. It could be me. You've taken a bite out of me, more than once."

"You deserved it."

"How about a guard, parked at the end of your driveway? You might not care. But I'd feel better. Do it for me."

"All right," he said. "If it'll make you feel better."

"That's all the business I have. But I want to ask for one more thing."

"Yes?"

"A drink with you, my friend. And a cigar."

❦

"Sunset and evening star and one clear call for me." The Master Blaster didn't know if people read Tennyson much anymore. But if they did, they remembered him. Crossing the bar. A few more hours in this house, on this island, in this life. It was good that Big Ben dropped by. His warning convinced The Master Blaster that it was time to go. But it did more than that. They'd talked—"talked story," as they said—about legendary typhoons and drunkards, congressional delegations and U.N. missions, spies, bars and baseball games, the kind of things people talked about, slowly, thoughtfully, back in the days when everyone knew, or sort of knew each other. They didn't talk about what the place had become, what they'd become. They were past that. "No one rules guilt-lessly," Big Ben said, a quote from Saint-Just that The Master Blaster had given him. "Maybe," Big Ben suggested, "we all get what we deserve." At the end, he hoisted himself up and stood in the doorway a moment. "I know I disappointed you. But there was no stopping America. And no stopping our people from joining America. No way of saying no. I know that. But I learned a lesson from the Japanese."

"What did they have to teach?"

"Until Saipan, the Japanese tried to stop the Americans on the beaches. They exposed themselves to naval gunfire and ground attack from over-whelming forces and were slaughtered. On Saipan they yielded the beaches, the fought inland, in the mountains, the caves, the jungle . . ."

"So . . . who won?"

"Of course they were doomed. But they weren't wrong. It's the way it is on the islands. Let them land, settle in, raise their flag . . ."

"Invest . . ."

"Yes. You cannot prevent their coming. There's no way. But you can affect—how to put it?—the quality of their stay."

"Oh. You mean cut a deal, enrich yourself, rip them off, entangle them in land cases, lawsuits. Pick up what they leave behind at a dime on a dollar. And you're the agent, the consulter, the go-to player. Well, that's a strategy, I guess. Self-interested and short term."

"Self-interested and short term," Big Ben repeated, looking at The Master Blaster, wondering whether to say something or let the moment go. Talking to a man about to die might encourage you to say something meaningful. But if what mattered hurt, if it led to an argument, why bother? The Master Blaster was running out of time. What difference if Big Ben just walked away with a nod?

"Come have a seat," Big Ben said, motioning towards the chair which The Master Blaster had enjoyed his cigar and cognac for years. Too early for them now. Also, too late. "Well, self-interested, yes, so we are. Small island, small time, small town, I suppose. Outsiders advise us to be transparent, open, logical, evenhanded, that's the way investors want it, that's what progress requires. And we do not always oblige. Because if we play by outside rules, we lose. Chinese rules, Korean rules, Japanese and Filipino. And American rules. We lose."

"But you chose America. Three quarters of the people voted for Commonwealth. U.S. citizens overnight."

"America chose us. We recognized the fact. But listen, old friend. Here's the long view. We are islanders. We cannot control what comes here. We cannot make our own history. Not with the Spanish, the Germans, the Japanese or the Americans."

"Did you vote yes on the Americans?" The Master Blaster asked. "Not my business. Just wondering. And, let's face it, who am I going to tell?"

"I voted no," Big Ben said. "And it didn't matter. That's the point. That's the long view. We didn't control the past. We don't control the present. Or the future. You've read it, I'm sure, these islands are the next Pearl Harbor, if there's trouble with China. So, call me self-interested and short term. But in the time we have, we get what we can."

"For yourselves," The Master Blaster protested. "But look what you're doing to the island. What about the island, Ben?"

That got him. The Master Blaster could see it. He was back in the classroom, just for a second. "I saw you, all those years ago, I said to myself, This is a leader. I look at you now, I don't see a leader. I see a dealer. Same six letters. Different word. Different meaning."

"I'll miss you," Big Ben said, after a while. "No lie."

"Thanks. I'll miss all this. That is, if there's a way of missing things after you're gone."

"Do you believe there is?"

"No . . . I wish. But I can hope." And he saw Big Ben nod. They agreed.

"Well then," he said. "Let's hope." But there was no hope in the way he said it.

"I never hated anybody here, Ben. You know that. But the way things turned out, I had to say something. I was disappointed, all right. But I didn't leave, did I? Maybe there's some magic left. But I'm glad I came when I did. I'll say that."

"I understand," Ben said. "I had to come. I couldn't let you . . . just go. Are we okay? You and I?"

"We are."

❧

The Master Blaster got into his car and, avoiding a last look, turned up the driveway, through a corridor of hibiscus, croton, bougainvillea, past a neglected grove of lemon and orange and papaya trees. A tricky driveway for visitors but he knew every pothole by heart. Where his driveway met the road, a car sat at the edge of the road. The driver was talking into a cell phone. Big Ben's guard, he guessed. He'd be waiting a long time for The Master Blaster's return. Now he was in the zone of last things. He'd never go back down that driveway. But he had a choice: go downhill to Beach Road, through the tourist zone, or take the back road through farmland and boonies. He took the road downhill—more sunset that way—and took his time passing the hotels. Before long he was in Marpi.

Sea: Banzai Cliff was first choice. That turbulent water, that mix of waves and foam, those gnashing rocks and the colors . . . deep, fatal blue, aquamarine and turquoise, and the way the setting sun poured golden light over everything. The chance of sharks bothered him but he guessed his life would be over before they found him. But Banzai, it turned out, was impossible: a busload of tourists were posing in front of peace monuments, joggers and cyclists came down the road and, worse yet, some fishermen at the cliff's edge. They could be there for hours. It was a scene he'd stepped into many times. He should have known better than to expect that he would have it to himself. He didn't want to be seen jumping, didn't want tourists—with cameras—recording his final ups and downs. So he sat in his car, knowing he would have to leave, and that this was a place he would miss, wincing at the illogic, to think that he would be missing anything. Then again, maybe he was missing it already.

He was tired—hadn't been out of the house for a week—and it took a special effort to turn the key, shift gears and head away from the coastline, up the winding road that lead up to Suicide Cliff. That place attracted fewer visitors this time of day and, besides, there'd been some muggings. Tourists came and went by the busload earlier in the day, but now it would be empty. Almost empty, it turned out, a couple of Japanese were taking their chances. Alarmed when they saw his car, they relaxed when they saw a harmless, unhealthy old man get out. The American nodded politely, walked over to the railing at the edge of the cliff. His jumping off point. His second choice: land. He was hurting—nauseous, light-headed—but nonetheless Suicide Cliff still got to him. The memory of the hundreds of Japanese, Okinawans, Koreans, soldiers, sailors and civilians, men, women and children who chose death over surrender, even as Japanese-speaking American soldiers begged them not to go. There was more: the height, the breeze, the tip of the island, the sea, he was above them all. The Japanese couple nodded, as if to thank him for something, walked to their car and drove away.

He put his hands on the railing, deciding whether to climb over the top railing, waist high, but lifting himself up that way was beyond him. He'd have to crawl under the lower rail. He took a deep breath. The last great effort of his life. In the distance he heard the Japanese car drive away. And then, damn it, the sound of a vehicle coming uphill. He looked back, waiting for it to show itself; he stood like a man at a urinal, interrupted when he wanted to be alone. He recognized what came, his old truck, the one that—to no surprise—the Bangladeshi had never returned. The Master Blaster was pretty sure he had not come to return it now.

The Bangladeshi stepped out of the truck, checked the empty downhill behind him and walked towards The Master Blaster. He was sizing up the situation, checked left and right, the railing, the edge. Only when he finished that did he meet The Master Blaster's eyes.

"X," The Master Blaster said. "Isn't that what they call you?"

"X." Dressed in black denim jeans and a black polo shirt. He moved closer. Any minute he might spring. And push. The Master Blaster did-n't want that to happen. He wanted to do this himself.

"You've come . . . for me? To kill me?"

X nodded.

"Who sent you? Was it Rosales?"

"I do not know that name," X responded.

"What name do you know?" He sensed an opening. After a life in the classroom, he knew when a student could be persuaded to speak. "What's the difference? We're done in a minute here."

"Big Ben."

"I see," The Master Blaster said. And he did. Enough to be grateful for that final talk. For small courtesies.

"Think you can do this?" The Master Blaster asked. No expression. A yes answer. The Master Blaster fell onto his knees. X, he saw, guessed a plea for mercy was coming. Contempt crossed his face. But then the old man rolled under the railing, pulling himself to his feet on the other side, steadying himself. Now he stood at the very edge. X could attack him there. But there was no room for error. He saw a flicker of something . . . not doubt . . . but a late, small intimation of complexity. Nothing that would stop a murder. "Your lucky day, X. No need to kill me. I'll do it myself, I think. And . . . a one-time-only special . . ." The Master Blaster tossed his car keys on the gravel parking lot. His wallet followed. "You can tell the people who sent you, mission accomplished."

Then The Master Blaster did what he'd planned, something learned from the Japanese he'd seen in war footage. He took one backward step, not looking at what was or wasn't there. His foot hit the ground. The next backward step would surely be his last. A second or two in the air, a likely loss of consciousness and a landing that was beyond imagining. He stepped back, and on X's face he saw a decision—too late—to stop him. His foot, when it came down, met air. He fell backward and down; below, his island awaited him.

Acknowledgments

I first saw Saipan in 1967. I was a Peace Corps Volunteer. When I left in 1969, I promised myself that I'd keep coming back and so I have, a dozen times. I couldn't—still cannot—bear to admit that the future might not hold another trip to Saipan. Though *The Master Blaster* is a work of fiction, it draws on forty years of visits. My thanks to friends on Saipan. They enrich my life, and this book. Thanks as well to someone I haven't met, the proprietor of a controversial website, Saipansucks.com, who permitted me to use some of his site's slogans, which appear in the novel's first pages.